DR. MITCHELL

Billionaires' Club Book 1

RAYLIN MARKS

Raylin Marks

Chapter One

Ash

I'd zoned out so hard on my term paper that I hardly heard the barista calling out my name. I popped up from my seat and weaved through the crowd of people that had swarmed the coffee shop.

"Annie Position..." the barista announced again. I was feeling pretty amused with myself for my fake-name choice—until all of the city showed up and heard it. "Matcha Frappuccino," she said as I stepped up to get my drink.

"Right here," I said, cheeks hot with the attention my lame-ass idea caused.

"Cute," she said with a wink.

"Ha," was all I could manage.

I turned to get the hell out of the mob and the next thing I knew, my stupid alias was no longer the attention grabber.

"Shit!" I said as my Frappuccino crashed directly into the center of a white button-down shirt.

"Fuck," the guy growled, his arms out and eyes roaming over the green stain, slowly oozing in a frozen blob down his shirt.

"Damn it. I'm so sorry!" I said, not knowing the first way to redeem myself for spinning around too fast to pay attention to the couple standing behind me.

His eyes met mine after I made some super effort to throw the offensive drink in the trash and grab napkins. I instinctively threw a pile on the ground and took the other handful to wipe what was left on his shirt.

His hand covered mine, and his blue eyes sparkled as the sun would over a tropical sea. *Holy fuck!* I thought, trying to keep at bay the rapidly approaching, third embarrassing thing that could happen in five seconds. This guy was the sexiest man I'd ever laid eyes on—Hollywood hunks included.

"I've got it," he said, his lips turning up into an irresistible grin.

"Good God," a female's voice screeched with annoyance. "Go!" she waved me off, reminding me I'd caused enough damage already.

I eyed her. "Let me at least do something," I said, her green eyes narrowing while her mauve lips pursed in annoyance.

She folded her arms. "Do something?" she questioned me with an arch of her perfectly shaped eyebrow. "Maybe you would like to lick your silly drink off his chest?"

"Go order her another one," the guy I'd assaulted with my drink said in a half-humored, half-demanding tone to the woman.

"You don't have to boss your girl around over my dumbass mistake."

"She's not my girl," he said, glaring at the woman before he leveled me with a darker stare. "What's the choice of beverage that I have the luxury of adding to my wardrobe colors today?"

What the fuck?

"What's the drink?" the bitch seethed.

Who the hell were these two, the power-suit couple? They were dressed and *looked* the part of two wealthy people who came to San Francisco to take over the place.

"Matcha Frap," I said, trying to let this shit show move forward so we could stop the back and forth, and I could hide behind my computer, waiting for them to call my *real name* this time.

"Name?" she asked, folding her arms and rightfully annoyed.

"Um, right, it's—"

"Any Position," the man said in the same demanding tone he'd used for his gal pal. "Isn't that what they called before you painted my suit green?"

"Annie," I smiled, cheeks flushed, knowing my face was beet red.

"Nice name," he answered, blotting the stained shirt.

"Are you naturally nice to strangers who ruin your wardrobe and an asshole to your friends?" I asked, thumb pointing to where the blonde with mauve lips stood in line with eyes of fire directed toward me.

"I'm feeling rather compassionate for someone who appears to be having a rough day." I felt my breath hitch, and my heart reacted to his turquoise blue eyes.

"Nice of you to assume that." I half-smiled. "And the reason your friend is stuck with *my problem?*"

"Long story." He smiled. "She'll get over it. Trust me."

"Wow. Well, I am sorry about this." I sighed. "I'll just go wait over there." I pointed toward my laptop. "I have five minutes at most to turn in my essay now."

"All the more reason that my *friend*," his eyes shifted toward the woman and back to me, "is ordering for you."

"Yeah," I said. "Thanks again."

The guy was too gorgeous for words, and there was no way in hell I was looking back at him or up from my computer to catch another angle of the black-haired god who'd given a facelift of beauty to the coffee shop when he walked through the door.

I hit send on my essay with one minute to spare and waited to hear the *swoosh* sound on my email before I could collapse back into the booth seat and let my nerves crash after everything that had happened.

By the time I gathered myself, my dumbass attempt to be funny name was called again, and the couple was nowhere in sight. *Thank God.* The coffee shop was still busy, but I was on my way out anyway. I needed to get back to my hotel room and wind down.

I was supposed to go out with some old high school friends who lived in the area tonight, and at this point, I could use a drink, or ten, or twenty. Or not. Tomorrow was my cousin's wedding day, and I probably shouldn't be hungover while having to sit through the superficial ceremony I'd been forced to attend on mine and dad's behalf. Dad owed me for this. Big time.

I PULLED UP THE BACK STRAP OF MY HEELS ON MY LEFT FOOT, hobbling on the right foot in the new stilettos I knew I'd hate by the end of this weekend. I'd bought them to match the burgundy dress I was to wear to the wedding, and I'd decided to break them in tonight. Something told me comfort wasn't part of the expensive shoes that I shouldn't have let the sales associate talk me into purchasing.

One last glance at my strapless bandage dress, and I was good to go. I tried pulling my natural waves up, but it wasn't working.

"Screw it. It's not like I'm out to meet guys tonight." I laughed at the idea. Let's get *part one* of my trip to Frisco out of the way...hanging at a rooftop club with friends I hadn't seen since high school.

The Uber dropped me off at a super fancy hotel that was well lit and immediately oozed wealth and power out of the front doors. Flags from across the world hung over the entrance while the luxury cars that lined up made my compact Uber selection appear to be dropping me off at the wrong place.

"What the hell?" I whispered.

"You might meet a famous person," the Uber driver informed me.

"Good Lord," I answered as I exited the car.

I weaved my way through the cars and people entering at the same time as me. I was surrounded by luxury and needed to find my friends *fast!*

"Ashley Taylor," I said to the concierge as Beth had instructed me to do when I got here.

"Miss Taylor." He sifted through papers. "Will you be staying with us tonight?"

"I'm here to meet friends at a rooftop lounge," I said softly.

He reached for a pen to scroll along a screen installed in front of him. "I see," he answered. "Richard," he waved someone over to him, "please escort Miss Taylor to her party on the top."

By the time the doors admitted me through secret elevators, and I'd arrived at the rooftop bar, I was somewhat grateful I had on expensive heels at the very least.

The atmosphere was euphoric, but it was definitely for the wealthier patrons. I followed Richard to the outdoor area where I heard my name called and finally let out the breath I seemed to have held since following Richard to the elevator.

"Hey," I said, eying the three friends I hadn't seen since graduation night.

"Ashley Taylor." Gabby laughed and hugged me. "You look awesome."

"Thanks; you all look great too." I smiled at my girlfriends and the men with them. "It's been too long."

"Six years," Beth said. "Here, let's get the introductions out of the way." She pointed to the tall, prematurely balding man next to her, "This is my husband, Max." She smiled with pride before looking on. "Go, Gab."

Gabby threw her blonde ponytail back. "This is Jon." She smiled at the blond man who was standing stiffly and uncomfortably at her side. "He and I hooked up about a month ago." She ran her hand down his polo shirt. "He's not into the night scenes." She giggled.

"I'm with you on that." I tried to smile to help the poor guy loosen up some. "I think I'm going to need a drink to process this *venue*."

"That's on me," Liz said. "It's been so damn long, babe." She hugged me and kissed both of my cheeks.

What the hell happened to shy, sweet, Valedictorian Liz?

"That's quite a greeting." I laughed as I ordered a cosmopolitan. "Where's your guy?" I teased.

The girls laughed while Max and Jon fell into a conversation, leaving the girls to chat while they returned to their drinks.

"Divorced." She shrugged. "Being a doctor sucks."

"Well, obviously it's good money." I waved my hand around the stunning lights of the city and the vast view of luxury from the rooftop.

"Well, it is." She sipped her martini. "But truth be told, I'm still paying off student loans and probably will be until I die."

I sipped the drink that was placed in front of me at the high table where we stood. "Why in the hell would you reserve a place like this if you're paying off debt?"

"It was one of the perks of the medical conference I had to attend today," she said with a strange grin, then her face straightened. "I heard about your mom. I'm so sorry."

These were not the same girls I remembered from high school. Maybe this is why I've heard so many stories about ten-year reunions sucking. Everyone is different but trying to be not to be. My friends from school were giggly, awkward, and—well, not what I expected. Maybe I was the weird one.

"Yes," I answered her, gulping down half of my cosmo. "We thought her remission would last a lot longer than it did, but we lost her two years ago."

"Dang," Beth said uncomfortably. "Is your dad okay? Are you okay? You don't have a man with you, so are you single? Why are you up in Frisco?"

Okay, I started drinking too late. I smiled. "Cousin's wedding. Dad made me show up here on his behalf. They helped us out financially while mom was sick, and the bills were burying my parents. I have no idea who these people are, but I guess the wedding is a big ordeal, and they insisted we come."

"Ugh. Annoying," Gabby sighed and reached out to me. "Not what they did, but having to be around people you don't know like that. Right?"

Nothing compared to what I'm experiencing at the moment. Either they'd started drinking too early, or I was standing around three strangers who I probably would've never been friends with if I didn't grow up with them.

"It's fine." I motioned for another drink, noticing I'd absently gulped down the first.

"Well, what have you been up to?" Liz asked. "I'm ready to fuck our keynote speaker from the conference today," she said, my eyes widening at her abrupt words.

"Well, I had to drop out of city college, and put it all on hold," I answered. "I needed to take care of my mom, and ever since she died, I've been sort of getting by while deciding my next move."

"Girl, you have to *do you!*" Gabby stated, pointing at me.

"I am." I sipped my drink.

I'd apparently lost the interest of my friends after informing them about my boring life plans. The conversation shifted—not to what we'd all really been up to, but to orgasms, broken relationships, and any male specimen who passed our table—as if Max and whatever the other guy's name was weren't there with us.

Thank God for the shift in our environment. The music grew louder and changed as the sun started to set, and now my obviously drunk friends were flinging themselves onto the dance floor. Stuck with their significant others, I bowed out as nicely as I could, but I wasn't leaving these views just yet.

I walked away from the crowd and found a slice of heaven on the rooftop that gave me the most stunning view. I stared at the millions of twinkling lights that illuminated the city and tried to burn this image into my mind. I'd seen cityscapes painted and photographed, but feeling it while experiencing the sight itself was something I'd never captured no matter how many canvasses I'd painted. I had to find a way to breathe life into a painting that would help people sense what I was sensing by looking at this magic.

"So," a smooth voice said to my right, "I feel we might have met before?"

I looked over, and my drink sloshed in my hand when my left ankle weakened, and I almost fell off to the side after seeing the dream guy I spilled my drink on at the coffee shop earlier. "Yeah," I said as he caught my fall by reaching for my arm.

He glanced down at the cosmopolitan I held. "I can safely say that if you spill *that* particular drink on me that I'm not one who looks good in pink."

I smirked. *Um. You would look good in anything...or nothing!*

"No?" His eyes roamed over my face.

"Yes," I answered, stunned and too buzzed to hold a conversation with Mr. Gorgeous.

His lips twisted. "What brings you here tonight?"

I looked at him in confusion. "Friends, and you?"

"Work." He smiled. "Did you handle your assignment from earlier?"

Why the hell is this guy even talking to me?

"I did. Thanks for asking and actually remembering."

"How could I forget? The moment I saw you tonight, all I could think was that this is the girl known as *Any Position*."

"You here on business, Mr.—?" I narrowed my eyes at him.

His turquoise ones glistened. "I am."

"And I'm guessing you're most likely here *with me*—bringing up that stupid name—because you're looking to have a little *fun* on your trip?"

"Perhaps."

My body went into electric spasms at the thought, his fucking hot looks, and that I would even suggest this to him. Hell no. I wasn't going to be some home wrecker because I came out to meet friends—which was a total fail—at a damn bar. I wasn't that drunk, or maybe I was? The hell if I knew.

"Yeah." I smiled. "Sorry; I can't help with that."

"A shame." His voice was low, and I was starting to become hypnotically charmed by this man. "I was looking for the only person *not* drunk to enjoy this amazing view with."

I smiled at him to hold my exterior confidence. Good Lord, he was gorgeous. The dark shadow on his jaw worked to carve out the faultlessness of his chiseled face. His coal-black hair, a tousled mess of perfection, set off his eyes that seemed to bore straight into my soul as he stared into mine.

A glance at the man who was leaning against the ledge, body twisted to face me, gave me all I needed to know about how I sort of wished he was asking me to spend the night with him. His dark ribbed sweater hugged his chest and muscular arms, waking up all the dormant female parts of my body.

"Yes." I sighed, gathering my thoughts and wishing I had some water to hydrate and shake this alcohol out of my head.

"The views are stunning," he said, bringing his attention out to the city. "May I ask why you're over here and not enjoying the company of the women I saw you with earlier?"

"Spying on me, eh?" I teased.

He licked his lips, and then they parted into a sexy smile that revealed perfect white teeth. "If you call taking notice of a beautiful woman in this toxic atmosphere of *after-hours fun* spying, then I guess I'm a spy."

"Toxic atmosphere?" I laughed. "Who the hell are you anyway?"

He sipped what I assumed was his glass of scotch. "A man who positively does not want to be here this weekend." He glanced around the ritzy rooftop. "And not even the slightest bit tempted to appreciate the bullshit conference I was forced to attend today—even with the *perks* that come with it."

I leaned up against the ledge, letting the crisp air continue to clear my thoughts with my mystery dream guy. "I guess that means you had to go to the medical conference or whatever in the hell my friend Liz called it, too? Too bad you're not a chick because all I've heard about tonight was how the keynote speaker made a week's worth of conferences manageable."

He chuckled. "Is that so? I found the jackass to be dull and ridiculously boring."

"So, you're a doctor then, eh?"

He eyed me, his brows pulling in as those damn snake-charming eyes roamed over my face. "I'm reconsidering my love for that particular profession after today."

"What the hell?"

"I'm fucking with you." He laughed and motioned for a waiter, "Can we get..." He looked at me. "What are you having? It's on the medical group that's hosting this shin-dig."

"Water," I stated. "Shin-dig?"

"Water?" The corners of his eyes crinkled in humor. "Trust me, the group that put this ordeal on can afford it."

"I'm not being modest." I smiled at the waiter. "I'll have water, please."

"Water for the lovely lady, and I'll have another scotch."

The waiter bowed out and left Mr. Gorgeous and me back to what-ever in the hell we were talking about.

"So, am I going to get a name other than *Annie?*"

"Why don't we just keep it at Annie," I said with a smile. "Let's face it; we're complete strangers, and I don't think this is going any further than us both complaining about being up here."

"All right, no names then," he said, studying me. "But what if it went further than us complaining about this pretentious party that we're at?"

Okay. He's not here for the chit-chat. Why the hell would I think he was? He was gorgeous and an asshole doctor who was most likely doing what my friends were doing—sizing up the place for someone to screw. I was clearheaded enough now to know this was all superficial on my part too—wanting a piece of this guy because of his looks alone.

"Yeah, going to have to pass on that." I smiled and gulped my water.

"And she shatters my self-esteem." He mockingly covered his heart.

"I'm sure you can get plenty of girls up here who would take you up on that offer."

"I'm not interested in any of the women up here. As I mentioned, I am merely out here and have *spied* on you earlier tonight because you are the most attractive woman in the club."

"While I appreciate the compliment," I patted his arm—Shit! Bad idea, this guy worked out at least three times a day, "I have to get my ass out of here."

He laughed and stood. "Let me call for your ride."

"I have an Uber," I said, pulling out my phone and using the app to seal the deal and get me out of here before I did make a *real* fuck up with this guy other than spilling a drink on him earlier.

"Then I guess you are leaving me to the wolves." His lips frowned in some irresistibly handsome way.

I hadn't been laid in over a year, so one night with a stranger, no strings attached, surely that wouldn't send me straight to hell, right?

He leaned in, and his fingers traced down my arms, "It's been nice seeing you. I only wish it could have been more than small talk."

His lips grazed my ear as he whispered, and I couldn't respond. I was paralyzed by the smell of his cologne, his warm breath caressing my neck, and the devilish grin he gave me before the man left me standing on the balcony cursing myself for always playing it safe and being too damn proper all of the time. I wanted to chase him down and tell him I was down for whatever he was looking for. We were both strangers from out of town—we would never see each other again, and well, a few more drinks, and I wouldn't give two shits about whatever the man wanted to do.

I never was one to be approached by guys...never. Yet, here I was literally at the top of the city with the most handsome man I'd ever seen in my life, and I just fucking turned him down? I went to follow my dark side and find where he disappeared into the crowds, but then the text from my dad came through.

Dad: *Hey, kiddo. You never called. I hope everything is well and you had a good visit with your friends today. Don't go too wild.*

I SMILED AT MY DAD'S MESSAGE, PULLING ME BACK INTO A reasonable mindset. Here I was about to go fuck some guy because he was hot and because my meetup with friends was an epic fail. I had no idea where the hell the girls or their men were at this point, and I had to go to this stupid wedding tomorrow. This reunion was a complete waste of time, and I almost threw the entire reason I was up here to the wind all because some hot guy wanted to be more than *friends* tonight.

Ash: *Yep. Heading back to my room now. I'll text you tomorrow after the wedding. See you on Sunday night. :)*

Dad: *Love you, kid.*

Chapter Two

Ash

After a restless night of analyzing the conversation with Mr. Gorgeous, I woke up in a more *rational* mindset. San Francisco brought out a side of me I never knew existed, a daring side that actually believed I missed out on a one-night stand with some random hot guy.

It was never even close to that. I was thinking clearly now and still slightly annoyed I was headed to a wedding with strangers as a *thank you* for my dad, who wasn't feeling well enough to make the trip.

So many things associated with this trip were going through my mind. Number one, Dad was going back to his doctor when I got home. Being this tired all of the time couldn't be a good sign for the sixty-five-year-old heartbreaker, and sneaking a fast-food breakfast with his classic car buddies every chance he got lately could be another issue affecting his health. He wasn't a healthy eater, no matter how hard I tried, and my *so-called friends* bringing up Mom losing her battle with cancer had me thinking about the fact that I wasn't going to lose my dad too. The fact that I was here without him was a good enough reason for me to force him to see a doctor for an overdue check-up.

The stubborn man owed me, and now I knew how to make him pay up.

Number two, I thought it was funny how I met up with friends and ended up leaving early after not being able to find them—and after checking my phone this morning, there was still no word from any of them.

Ping.

I looked at my phone that displayed Liz's name as if I'd summoned the text.

"A million hours later," I said, putting down my mascara and opening the message.

> **Liz: Hey. I couldn't find you last night. I'm so sorry we ditched you. I was so wasted and woke up in bed with a stranger! Did you see who I was with? Plz god, tell me WTF I did last night.**

I looked at the phone and covered my smile. Maybe I had been out of the real world for too long. Now, I go out of town for a random wedding, and it is turning into the *Twilight Zone.*

> **Ash: Hey. No, I couldn't find you guys after you hit the dance floor. Are you okay?**

> **Liz: I need to get tested. Fuck. I was so messed up last night.**

I ran my fingernail over my bottom teeth. How the hell was I supposed to respond to this? I felt horrible for her, but if I was honest, my brain was all twisted up after meeting the same attractive guy twice in a day and then him hinting at me to get my ass into the same position as Liz. I wasn't going to dare judge her.

> **Ash: You'll be fine. Get tested, though. Did the others see you go off with him? Do you think someone put something in your drink?**
> **Liz: No. This was all on me. Everyone said that I was so shit-faced that I just grabbed some guy off the dance floor and told**

everyone I was going to fuck him. I feel like such an idiot. He's in the shower. I think I'm going to get out of here.

What the fuck am I supposed to say? They took off on the dance floor, and after my small talk with Mr. Gorgeous—Mr. G—I couldn't find them to say I was leaving. What a fucking weird night, and now this text?

Ash: *Sorry, I couldn't find you guys so I just took off. I have the wedding to go to today. Keep me updated if you can.*
Liz: *Sorry for ditching out on you. It was nice catching up. I'll get through this. Take it easy, Ashley.*
Ash: *You too. Thanks for the invite out. I hope everything works itself out.*
Liz: *Well, it's not the first time I slept with a random guy. It just sucks waking up hungover and not knowing how it all went down. See ya.*

I didn't have time for this. I was fake-texting a friend about her shitty morning hangover and guilt from screwing a guy she couldn't remember. This wasn't my game. I was trying to put that entire weird day behind me and move into this one.

I was determined to show up at this wedding and do my best to show my distant cousins—the Johnsons—the appreciation my dad and I had for their help when my mom was sick. I had no idea of the relationship my parents had with these people. Still, I was going to put my best foot forward and enjoy them celebrating the marriage of a cousin I used to *play Barbie* with when I was three.

I left my phone in the vanity area on the charger, music still playing, and danced my way over to my closet. I pulled out the short slip dress I got for the wedding. It was more costly than the heels, but after slipping it on I felt refreshed and beautiful.

I ran my hand over my stomach, thankful I wasn't bloated, and the dress hugged my frame perfectly. The burgundy color held a soft shimmer under the light of my hotel room and made my skin look like I'd just laid out and enjoyed the sun's rays.

Nice one, Clay! I internally thanked my best guy friend who had fashion down to a science. He and his boyfriend, Joe, were the best guys I knew. Joe wouldn't let me head up to San Francisco unless I received his *favorable* touch to my hair. Thank God for that, too—the soft red highlights and layers he added to my chestnut hair were perfect.

I covered my chest when my Uber pulled up to the same hotel I was just at the previous night. *What the fuck?* I laughed at the fact that I was probably going to be on that rooftop again for the reception. It made sense, though. This was the hot spot for the wealthy people, and the Johnsons were definitely that.

After tipping the driver, I stepped out. I instinctively covered the deep V in the front of the dress after seeing a few guys taking notice of my cleavage. I walked through the hotel entrance and followed the crowd through the vast and luxurious hotel lobby. The intoxicating fragrances of lilies alerted me to the massively decorated and immaculately designed wedding ballroom.

God-dang! This had the touch of an artist to create an atmosphere of love and make a single fool like myself wish I were on the arm of my *one true love* to enjoy such splendor. I loved every ounce of this décor. It was more than décor; it was art. It was all fashioned with candles, flowers arched along the walls, along with some diamond-like vases holding greenery that glistened under lights placed above them. It was flawless, and a smile spread across my face; I was feeling the serenity of true love wrapping itself around me.

"Third time is a charm."

A familiar voice snapped me out of my daze as I stood at the entrance, waiting to be ushered to my seat. *Holy fuck!* Am I still asleep and dreaming this man into being at the wedding with me?

I looked at Mr. Gorgeous, sucked in a breath, and placed my hand in his arm when he reached out to me. He had been transformed into a model from a wedding magazine. The silver vest under his black tuxedo and his smile completed the atmosphere of intoxicating love this place was exuding.

He leaned into me. "You don't have to say anything. I was quite speechless after noticing you in the doorway. You look..."

He paused, and the sexiest smile lit his ocean-blue eyes. "Yeah," I swallowed hard. "What are the odds we meet here?" I laughed.

"Perhaps it's fate," he said, standing tall and resuming his walk down the aisle where the ushers were seating guests. "Maybe you and I will find out later."

I smiled at him, lost in his beautiful face, but resuming my walk, or he'd be pulling me from falling on my face in these heels. "Um, I'm with the bride's guests," I informed him when he led me to a seat to the right.

"That's all fine and good," he answered. "However, I will have the best view of you during the wedding if you are seated with the groom's guests."

"Nice one," I flirted back. It had to be the wedding flowers making me drunk on happiness. "I'm with the bride."

"I disagree," he said with a smile. "You're officially with me, and now that makes you a part of the groom's family."

"Who the hell are you?" I whispered with a laugh.

He glanced around with that same devilish grin he left me with last night. "The man you're desperately grateful you ran into again. Now, Miss Annie." He arched a knowing brow at me. "You are causing a scene, and this is the bride's day. I'll kindly ask you again to please be seated in this row, four chairs in."

I felt some bizarre sense of familiarity with this handsome guy. His sexy smooth voice and those eyes that spoke to my soul somehow. What in the hell did I do to capture his attention? How in the world am I meeting him randomly for the *third* time? Good God, stuff like this never happened, and it sure as heck didn't happen to me.

"Fine," I said, my heart hammering in my chest, now caught in his seductive gaze. "You can explain your *screw up* to the bride later," I said, trying to hold my own against him.

"She'll never know." He winked as I walked to the seat that he'd ushered me to. "I look forward to seeing you at the reception," he said and then turned to resume his wedding duties along with the men dressed in matching million-dollar wedding tuxedos.

How wealthy was this family? I spotted Mr. Johnson. That's all I knew him as—Mr. Johnson, the father of the bride. Was I on some kind of strange high from seeing Mr. G. again? Yes. Absolutely, and I couldn't wait for this to be over to meet him on the dance floor. I was drawn to the guy. It could just be the fact that it was his superficial fucking hot looks and the fact that he brought my female parts back to life—but I also had my own duties to attend to with this wedding.

I had to somehow weasel my way through all of these fashionable people to find Mr. Johnson and sincerely hope he gave half a damn I was even here. I glanced around at the romantic atmosphere—Clay and Joe would've died just seeing this place. This was beyond even my artistic mind's dream. I took notice of the ballroom, filling fast with guests as they quickly took their seats. I leaned over and tried my best to conceal my phone to text Clay.

> **Ash:** *This place looks like I'm at some royal ceremony. I love you for helping me with my outfit.*
>
> **Clay:** *I told you. Now, own it like the gorgeous babe you are. Xoxo! We want pics and details when you get home, girl.*

I could feel Clay's smile through his message. I owed him and Joe dinner for this. If it were up to me, I would've been hiding in a corner, wearing some cotton casual dress, but my guys weren't having any of that once they learned I was coming to the Fairmont for the wedding.

The music changed, and I relaxed confidently into my seat and prepared to watch the ceremony begin. The groom and his groomsmen were the first to enter from a front side door and stand on a stage of flowers and sparkles.

There he was, outshining everyone on stage...the man without a name who seemed to fall out of a dream and play into the real-life situation I was forced to go through alone. He stood taller than the rest, and his eyes went directly to mine. What the hell did he think about all of this? I was still stuck on how I grabbed his attention after doing the most annoying thing that could happen to anyone—spilling an ice-cold drink on him.

His eyes left mine, and an odd expression fell over his face when he looked to the back of the room. Then a challenging smile fell on his lips, prompting me to turn back and see the bitchy chick who was with him at the coffee shop. The one he said *owed him*. Her blonde hair was pulled up elaborately in a fashionable bun, and her eyes were on Mr. G. Her cheeks flushed red, her green eyes sparkling along with her silver gown. She seemed as captivated by him as I was.

Who wouldn't be? Who'd ever heard of a groomsman stealing the beauty from the bride? I glanced around and smiled at the realization that all the young women my age had eyes continually drifting to the Greek god who was standing, sharply dressed in a tuxedo.

I sucked in a breath of excited nerves while the bridal march started, and we all stood to turn to acknowledge the bride.

Damn it, I was always too short, and I wasn't going to catch a hint of my cousin walking down the aisle. I turned to look over my shoulder...obviously more interested in my dream guy. My breath caught when I noticed his smile and eyes on me, not the back of the room where my cousin was heading down the aisle.

He bit back a smile, my heart trying to jump out of my chest and up to where he stood regally and sexy as hell. I was some crazed fool who was captivated by this mystery man, and now I needed to stop gawking at him. I was going to figure out who he was exactly, and I was going to follow through with whatever happened. Third time meeting him? It was definitely a charm.

Chapter Three

Ash

The wedding ceremony was sweet in an old-fashioned way, all the way down to the scripted vows. Regardless of vows and songs played and prayers said over the couple, the ceremony was beautiful, and love was in the air.

I slid into the crowd of people being guided by the organizers to another area of the grand hotel for the reception. My trepidation of going to the wedding reception alone was replaced with the excitement of engaging with Mr. G again.

I had to remain focused on priority one, though. No matter how many times my focus shifted from the beautiful bride and her groom toward the sexy man who stood with the groomsmen, I kept my mind keenly aware of why I was here. The rest could sort itself out later.

The reception hall was not the rooftop experience from the night before. It was a more elegant atmosphere—of course—with silver and black décor enhanced by the lavish florals and greenery arranged with floating iridescent lighting, spotlighting everything to add a taste of romance.

I followed the attendant, who was speaking to someone in his earpiece, to one of the many tables blanketed with a shimmering silver cloth and arranged candles in a unique rectangular glass.

Table twenty-one was written in beautiful calligraphy against a foiled paper. The flowers in crystal vases smelled delicious, and after a cursory glance, it was easy to see that each arrangement probably cost over a hundred bucks.

My lips twisted to see if I'd be the only one at what now seemed to be the leftover guest table, and I felt a twinge of nervousness wash over me.

No. I would not let myself be guided by the insecure Ashely Taylor, who previously did everything she could to get out of coming here. That Ashley would have me rudely running up to the Johnsons, tripping over words to thank them for what they did for my family, thoroughly embarrassing myself because I genuinely did not know these people from Adam. I was three the last time I saw any of them, and I had a shitty memory to start with—why would they think I could remember a cousin from twenty-five years ago?

"I was seated here," a young man's voice snapped me out of my daze as I absently sipped the glass of wine poured for me once I was settled at the table alone. "I hope I'm not taking anyone's place."

I smiled over at a younger man, gorgeous hazel eyes to match his smoothed-back, blond hair. He had to have just past legal drinking age, and his smile was quite contagious too. *Might be a good conversation buddy,* I thought, swallowing my wine.

"Not that I'm aware." I smiled back at him.

"I get so jealous..." a young woman's voice sounded humored but honest when she and four other young women sat with her at this wedding guest reject table.

"Calm down, Beck," a stunning redhead said, sitting properly at our table. Her eyes slid around the table, falling on me and the guy who'd sat before the girl-pack showed up in their super revealing, high dollar gowns. "Hey there," she said, eyes meeting mine.

"Hi." I lifted my chin with a smile. "I'm Ashley." I used my thumb to point to the guy sitting to my right. "I don't think you mentioned your name."

"I'm Dave," he said, seemingly enamored to be the only guy at a table of beautiful women. "I guess I'm the luckiest man in the room." He chuckled.

"You might second guess that after being with us single and very desperate ladies by the time they open the dance floor," a beautiful woman said. She had chestnut eyes and a chocolate skin tone I would give my right arm for.

"Yeah." He sipped his wine.

It didn't take long for their conversation to blow up in gossip. The girls started in with snarky remarks about my cousin's ceremony from the décor to this beautiful reception. I was appalled, uncomfortable, and at a loss for words. How anyone could go out of their way to be so nasty was beyond me.

By the time we finished the five-star meal, I was ready to get out of here, Mr. G or not. So, what; we'd met randomly three times now. There was no relationship, it was surface fun, and I wasn't tempted in the slightest to stick around any longer than to find the family who'd helped mine, giving them my best wishes, and leave. Strange how such a beautiful environment could become toxic with jealous women who had nothing better to do than degrade a bride on her special day to make themselves feel better about being single.

I went to stand up and head toward the Johnsons, who were seated in front, but the lights flickered, and instantly, the room was transformed. It was now dark, spotlights pointing toward the empty space on the dance floor. The bride was seated in a chair on the stage, and the music changed to some hip tune.

A spotlight blinded me when it turned to beam at the back doors that opened into the vast room. Blinking a few times to get the stars out of my eyes, I noticed the groom leading a choreographed dance—his groomsmen following in step behind him.

The men had tossed their jackets to the side to reveal white shirts and suspenders. I covered my mouth when I saw Mr. G had some sexy dance moves among the others. His smile was devious as his body moved in step to entertain the bride.

This guy was ripped to perfection. His muscles were pressing against his button-down shirt, and unlike the others, his sleeves were rolled up, exposing his chiseled forearms.

I pulled out my phone to video the dance that the guys must have worked on for weeks to make this impressive presentation for the bride. I was pretty sure the superficial haters at my table would have something shitty to say about it, but I loved it. It was romantic, corny, and cute all in one. I'd seen stuff like this on social media, but to see it in person was quite another thing.

I turned my focus from Mr. G to my cousin, who cheered as the men danced around her. She was a beautiful bride—a very pregnant beautiful bride, I might add. The white dress was cut perfectly to show the flattering swell of her belly. I could only dream of looking so radiant when I was pregnant. Her long black curls bounced, and the diamonds placed the pinned-up part of her veil twinkled as the spotlight followed the groom and his men up to her.

The hate talk resumed once the show was over, but thank God the wedding planner had moved the reception forward quickly. The next thing we knew, the cake was being cut, then my worst fear came into play—the traditional bouquet toss. I was lined up with countless young women and took residence next to a fun, gray-haired lady with bright red lips.

"You going to catch it for me, kid?" she asked in a salty voice.

I smirked at her, "I tend to repel these sorts of things."

"Watch those bridesmaids. I hear they're vicious." She nudged me.

Without warning and not even looking, the bouquet miraculously landed in my hands. Three women tried to rip it out of my grips before they were practically cuffed and dragged out by the wedding planner and his minions.

"Jesus," I said, running my fingers over the nail tracks on my arms from the claws of desperate women trying to take the flowers. I turned to the elderly woman, "Here." I smiled at her. "Caught it for ya."

I tried to bow out, but she stopped me with a solemn gaze. "It's yours." She arched an eyebrow at me. "You have the battle scars, honey."

I loud group of men's voices erupted from behind me, but I walked briskly back to my table where the gossip girls eyed the bouquet as if I'd ripped the jewels from the bride.

"You guys want this flower arrangement that badly?" I asked, pushing it toward them.

A blonde with glossy lips reached over and snatched it up. "Thanks," she said as I frowned at her immature, yet snobbish behavior.

"Here he comes, here he comes. Act fucking normal, Mellie," the redhead said.

Where the fuck is Mr. Johnson? I can't do this wanna-be Housewives of San Fran another second.

"I believe I'm confused." Mr. G's velvet voice sliced through my irritated thoughts, bringing my attention to his approach.

"Why?" the girls all nearly said in unison, faces flushed under his stare.

He looked at the blonde who stood with the bouquet in her hands. "I was never so thrilled to catch the garter so I could be in a photo with my future wife."

She exhaled confidently, walking over to his sexy smirk. "I guess that's what it means, right?"

He grinned. "That's exactly what it means. Allow me," he pulled the bouquet from her hands. "This doesn't particularly belong to you, whether it was handed down or not."

Oh, great! After being at the table with these girls since the beginning of the reception, I had a feeling they were capable of putting a hit on me if this guy did what I had a pretty good feeling he was about to do.

"Annie?" he arched a brow at me and held out the bouquet. "You and I are needed for pictures together."

"I'm good." I tightened my lips, feeling gazes of fire on me and wanting no part of any of this.

"I disagree." He pinned me with a stare that had me locked into a trance. "You can give it to one of these ladies after, but for now, you and I are the ones who are under the wedding folklore of the next ones to get hitched. I can't think of another stunning woman in the room I'd rather be with in this situation."

"Go," Dave said. "Sheesh, you're pissing off the entire table."

I looked at him with a stare of disbelief as I stood. "Sorry. Let's go take our pictures," I said, linking my arm in the guy's arm.

"How in the hell did you get seated with the bride's oldest enemies?" he asked while pulling me away from the group.

"My future husband," I played along, seeing his smile. "He's part of the wedding party and didn't ensure I was seated with the groom's guests."

"What an ass," Mr. G answered.

"Yeah, he apparently thought the whole thing would be funny after I wouldn't go to bed with him last night."

That one got Mr. G. He nearly missed a step but recovered smoothly and quickly. "Well, perhaps you should have slept with him, then?"

"We're saving ourselves for our wedding night."

I met the arch of his brow with one of my own. "Is that so?" he asked, taking my hand and placing the flowers in it. "If that's the case, maybe you'll make one small exception for him. You know, he did have to dress in this penguin suit and all."

Our eyes were locked on each other in this unscripted banter while the photographer took our photograph.

"He's the one who accepted the job—being a good friend and all."

He took my hand and led me off to the side while the bride and groom began their wedding dance. "You must have forgotten he was forced into this whole thing."

"Hmm." I smiled at the bride and groom, falling into a beautiful ballroom style of dancing. "I don't recall him telling me he was in the wedding."

"Wow," Mr. Gorgeous played along. "He really is a dick."

"Yep," I said. "Leaves me to fend for myself. It's why I probably will be leaving him alone to deal with the rest of this after I give my regards to the family I showed up for."

"You weren't impressed with his skill of dancing, then?"

"Not in the least."

"Well, I can't fault you. He only learned it a day ago."

"Talented," I said, looking around for the Johnsons while talking with this guy I'd somehow attracted like a moth to a flame.

"Well, save a dance for me," he said, and then he was gone.

Okay. I wasn't going back to my table, so I searched out the older woman I was determined to get the flowers to. Gorgeous guy or not, I was done with this whole wedding affair.

I found her, and she was sitting with the Johnsons. Two birds, one stone.

"Ashley Taylor?" Mr. Johnson's gray eyes met mine as he stood. "You look fantastic, dear."

"These are for that sweet woman over there," I said as I handed the flowers to him, and pointed toward the elderly woman in a conversation with who I presumed was his wife. "It is nice seeing you. My dad sends his best wishes but hasn't been feeling well these days."

"I'll give these to my mother," he said as he reached over and laid the bouquet on the table. "Is he still having difficulty after losing your mother?"

"He's just stubborn. Doing his own thing—it could be his way of grieving, but let's not bring that up." I smiled at the kind man. "We are so grateful for all you've done and so excited for today."

"Well, I'm honored you accepted, sweetheart," he said nicely. "I have a dance with my daughter. I'll catch up with Mark in the morning. Good to see you, kid."

I nodded and was left standing there, watching Mr. Johnson slide through the crowd and out to his daughter.

Fingers interlacing with mine caused me to jump. I looked over at Mr. G, standing at my side as if we were a serious couple, and all jokes were cast off to the side in the whole husband-wife thing.

"May I ask what you're doing?" I asked softly.

"Holding your hand, waiting for our dance, of course."

"You are quite bold," I said. "Listen, it was nice, but I seriously need to get out of here."

"You're not leaving me again. I lost you once—last night—after not being on top of my game. I'm not losing you again."

"Funny," I answered. "If you want to play this game, then who the hell are you?"

His eyes slid down to where I stood almost a foot shorter than him —in heels. "Most people call me Mitch," he said. "And you?"

"Most people call me Ash." I smiled. With each word this guy said, he slackened the imaginary ropes of tension tethered to each of my nerves. "But to the people I've just met, I'm Ashley."

"Well, since we both confirmed our husband-and-wife future back there, I believe I'll stick with Ash."

"You are presumptuous, aren't you?"

"I get what I want, yes." He grinned, not letting that comment naturally escalate into the douche bag category where it belonged.

"And if you don't?"

His eyes fixed mine onto them. "Trust me. I'll have you in my bed tonight."

I melted into a pile of God knows what with the sound of his sultry voice, his daring smile, his ocean-blue eyes I was now swimming in. I had no response to that, but the heat between my legs he'd conjured with that response told me I was about to be the one sending out the morning-after text like Liz had.

The difference was this was a guy I think I would hate myself for *not* fucking—not the other way around.

The music changed, the atmosphere changed, and the next thing I knew, I was in his arms being twirled out on the dance floor. *Thank you, Mom, for insisting I take the dance classes I swore I'd hate you for.* I fell into perfect step with each salsa and tango move this guy kept switching to.

Luckily, we didn't cause too much of a scene, but for the first time in too long, I felt wild and free. We both laughed, made silly trick dance moves together, and suddenly I was lost in some carefree world with this Mitch guy. I wasn't letting go of this gift of liberation I was experiencing.

The best part of this was that he had no idea who I was. I didn't have to see his brow crease with fake concern for Dad and me over losing my mom. That's what this trip seemed to have turned into. It was like having to relive her death everything someone asked how we were doing when in truth, I still had no answer for that. It only sent the emotion of rage to the surface, which was unfair to anyone who showed concern. It was a constant battle. Hell, I still hadn't gone to her grave. Part of me couldn't accept her losing the battle against the cancer she'd fought so hard against. Now, I knew why my dad wasn't jumping at the idea to come to this wedding. This whole trip was conjuring raw emotions.

As I twirled and was caught at the waist by Mitch's strong hands, he was somehow healing these freshly reopened wounds. Thank God I ran into him with my drink, and now, he might be able to enjoy the fact that he always *got what he wanted*. Except for this time, this was what I wanted. If I took him up on an offer to sleep with him, it would be for *me,* not him; and looking at how handsome he was, I highly doubted he would have hurt feelings if we used each other for one night and then went our separate ways.

Chapter Four

Ash

Quite a few drinks later, I was in my dream guy's arms as we fumbled through the door and into his hotel room. My body was practically ignited in flames from the exclusive elevator ride up, Mitch's hands all over me while we kissed as old lovers reunited would.

He tasted so good. His cologne was keeping me steadily under his trance of needing this more than I knew. His hands were soft yet firm in pulling my arms above my head while his lips pressed along my neck.

I was trying to keep my legs from buckling under the way he was making me feel against the wall, his hard cock pressed against my stomach. This was going to be the best damn night of my life.

"Fuck," he said, his teeth nipping at my hard nipples. "Your moans are going to make me fuck you before reinforcements arrive," he said in a husky voice.

I ran my hands through his soft, tousled hair while his desperate hands found the delicate side zipper of my dress. My eyes were closed and probably should have stayed that way, but in another gasp of air, as I tried to control myself from coming just by the guy virtually worshipping my body in the way he touched and kissed my flesh, they opened.

"Holy shit," I said, pausing in shock at the room we were in. "Are you the president or some prince from another country?" I asked, nearly killing the pursuit of the only reason I was in this extravagant— too big for one person—room.

He didn't let it stop him. His hands ran down my sides as my dress fell into a pile at my feet. He kissed down the center of my stomach to my legs, his fingertips gently caressing the sparks of electricity his lips created as they trailed down the inside of my thigh to my ankle.

Damn, he's good, I thought, leaning against the wall as he studiously took off each one of my heels. Then I was in his arms, his lips capturing mine again. His tongue aggressively found mine as we walked through this place that was larger than my dad's house.

I was involved in his tasteful kiss, but my eyes were actively noticing the baby grand piano he carried me past. The floor-to-ceiling glass doors that led out to a ridiculously large sized balcony and the other unnecessary items that added to the importance of the person who would stay in a room like this were too hard to look away from.

He placed my ass on a bar counter, spreading my legs while he stood in between them. The next thing I knew, my strapless bra was off while he nipped and sucked softly against the flesh of my neck, using his fingers to roll my hard nipples between them.

My head fell back, legs opening further as I allowed him to swallow me up, body and soul. The throbbing between my legs became painful. My body craved this man as he woke up every last cell of pleasure throughout my entire body.

"As much as I appreciate your sexy ass in this thong," he said, his fingers pulling against the sides of it, "I'm not a fan of it concealing the one part of your body I'm going to make sure is fucked until the sun rises."

His eyes were dark and his face sexier than ever before—I didn't think he could get any more handsome.

An enchanting tone serenaded through his hotel room. That's when I saw the devil in this man's eyes as he smiled. He teased my chin with a quick kiss, stepped back, and the hunger in his eyes as they roamed over my fully exposed body had me nearly climaxing by his expression alone.

"Give me a second," he said, and then took off in the direction of where the grand piano was positioned in the center of the living room.

With this second of reprieve, my brain began firing back up and started to work again. I looked over to find my thong torn and cast aside on the counter.

How did I miss that, I thought, wondering when he managed to tear the underwear from my body.

Now that my brain was taking back its control, I was feeling a bit vulnerable and quite fucking stupid, sitting on some bar counter completely undressed.

I slid off the counter, not knowing what the fuck to do. That's when I noticed him walking back in with a box of condoms. "What the hell?" I asked, laughing as he placed the box on the bar.

"Until tonight, that butler was just a fucking nuisance," he said, gripping my waist and hoisting me back up onto the counter. "Wine?" he asked, his eyes softer and more humorous now.

"Yeah," I answered, grabbing his silver bowtie and halting him from leaving my naked ass on the counter again. "But I'm not going to be the only one sipping wine naked."

He smirked. "I can't help it if I'm better at removing clothes than you are." He arched his brow at me. "Get to work," he said, stepping back, arms up, giving me full access to undressing him.

I needed that wine. I'd been out of commission in the sex department for far too long. Since before Mom died two years ago—at least. I had to absorb the confidence pouring off this man, and that's precisely what I did to keep a steady pace at undressing him...slowly.

Beneath his shirt were strong abs that highlighted his tanned and soft skin. His muscles were what artists created—what models worked hard to achieve to make the front page of a magazine. He was a god. There was no doubt about this.

He licked his lips, his white teeth gently covering his bottom lip as he watched me take in the beauty of his perfect body. He reached for the button of his pants—I was obviously going way too slow for his plans—but I batted them away, seeing the veins in his biceps popped and lining his arms in a way that carved out his unimaginably perfect-sized arms.

After his pants fell to the floor, I fought against his hard cock to free it from the boxer briefs he wore. *Fuck me now,* I thought, seeing the size of at least nine or more inches that my dripping wet entrance clenched in response to.

I instinctively dropped to my knees, running my hands down his muscular legs, and couldn't resist licking his perfectly groomed balls. Both of his hands reached forward as he groaned, and his dick bounced in reaction to the first time I found a man's testicles sexy and tasteful.

"Goddamn," he breathed out. "Suck my cock," he pleaded with me.

Enjoying the fact that he was at my mercy, I played further into what I knew he was struggling with. He was the one groaning in plea-sure now—and I was the one controlling whether or not he'd cum before he got a chance to use the condom box that he somehow managed to *send for*.

I had no idea who this man was, but to be in a place like this and from what I could gather, he was one important individual. The lack of knowledge both of us had of each other made this even more pleasur-able to me. I didn't want to know any more than I already knew, and he wasn't going to know anything other than possibly questioning whether or not I was virgin after not having sex in a few—very long —years.

I licked under his length, my tongue capturing the precum dripping from his tip. He pulled my hair into his fist, and I was only halfway down his length before I could swear he made a grunting sound of coming in my mouth. In that same moment, his cock was pulled from my throat, and in a swift motion, Mitch used all the glorious muscles I was previously worshipping to pick me up. I wrapped my legs around his waist, crossed my feet at my ankles, and graciously accepted his hard and desperate kiss.

He laid me back onto his bed, covering my body with his, and framed my face with his hands. "There's no fucking way I'm getting off before you, Ash," he said.

His mouth was on mine, both of us kissing aggressively while his hand slid down to my soaking wet entrance. "You're so wet," he said, pulling away and kissing along my breast.

I reflexively tightened beneath him after he slid his fingers inside me. His forehead fell to the center of my chest as he gently slid his fingers in and out of my pussy. He seemed to be breathing along with the motions that were working on loosening up the sadly-neglected-for-too-long slit between my legs.

"You," he breathed out huskily, "are so," exhale again, "tight," he managed while licking along the outside of my breast before bringing his eyes back to mine.

I went to answer his seductive eyes, but arched my back and bucked my hips against him when he turned his fingers and started massaging my G-spot.

"Oh my god," I said, coming all over his hand after only a few strokes to the spot my past two boyfriends could never find—nor did they consider looking for either.

"That's fucking right, Ash," he said breathlessly. "You're so tight and wet," he exhaled. "Please, tell me you're not a virgin." He chuckled.

"I think you can easily tell I haven't fucked a guy in a..." My breath hitched when his thumb began making swirls over my clit. "Oh my god, I'm going to fucking come again."

He smirked. "Like I said, all night." He sucked my bottom lip as my body went into another spasm of glorious pleasure. "And I'm taking you up, *Annie Position*, on what I wanted to do to you since hearing that fucking name at the coffee shop."

I closed my eyes, trying to ride the ecstasy of coming from this man's perfect touch, my flesh responding to him as if he were some kind of a sex god.

"Your turn," I said, grabbing the box of condoms that made it to the room with us.

I manipulated his body to lie on his back while I tore a condom out of the box. He pulled his hands up and clasped them behind his head. His confidence was about to be shaken.

"Roll it on." He lifted his chin with a sultry grin.

After putting the condom on, my pussy aching for this massive cock, I slid myself down onto him. Mr. Confidence practically choked, eyes rolling back, and his hands were instantly firm on my waist. When his eyes reopened, his hungry expression was almost dangerous.

"Holy hell. Fuck. God. Shit," he pretty much chanted out every cuss word in his vocabulary while I slid myself up and down his length.

His hands came up to mine, and he intertwined our fingers. "You like that?" I arched a brow at the sexy god who was at the mercy of my tight pussy.

He didn't answer with words. Instead, he used that strength to flip me onto my back, my palms still pinned under his while he pumped harder and faster into me. "Tell me you can come with me like this," he begged.

As soon as I reached for my clit, wanting to come with him, he pulled out of me. "No fucking way, that clit's mine tonight. Turn your ass over," he ordered. "You're coming while I ride that G-spot, angel."

He lined himself behind me and smoothed his hand over my lower back. "Arch that ass into me," he said, and I did.

"Yes," I screeched when the sensitive part inside me felt his thickness spreading me apart while it massaged along my G-spot. "Oh... my...." I breathed and bit into the pillow as he ran his fingers over my clit, fucked my G-spot, and used his other hand to rub my nipple.

He started pumping himself deeper and thrusting harder into me. His dick practically felt like it was in my throat with how hard and long he was fucking me. His groans were raspy and breathless until he made a loud grunt of pleasure before his hands caught himself on each side of me, his hands balling the sheets up into his fists. He slowly moved in and out of me while kissing the back of my neck and over my shoulders.

He eventually pulled out and flipped me over. He gently caressed my breasts, kissing my arm while I caught my breath, still horny as fuck. I hoped he meant what he said by fucking all night because we hadn't even begun to curb the pleasure that I hadn't realized I'd neglected myself of in far too long.

"That was a lovely introduction to what we'll be up doing for the rest of the night," he confirmed my internal wishes.

"Oh?" I smiled over at him, his knuckles coming up to massage along my jaw. "What's next on your agenda?"

"To fucking marry you so we can do this for the rest of my life." He smiled.

"I heard the nervousness in your voice, asking if I was a virgin," I teased.

He pursed his lips. "You didn't feel like you'd ever been fucked."

"That's because it's been too long." I sighed.

"Then I am about to take great pleasure in fucking that hot pussy back to life again."

"You think you can handle it?" I giggled.

"It's sort of what I do for a living." He brushed his finger over my nose.

"Oh?" I looked around the grand room. "I didn't realize a gigolo made this kind of money."

He rolled off the bed and walked into the bathroom. I heard the shower turn on, and then he walked in—literally with the fucking light of the moon peering into the room, spotlighting his perfect body and dick that I was still shocked I was able to take as easily as I did.

"Get your sweet ass in here, angel," he said, pulling me from the bed and throwing me over his shoulder. "Round two starts in the shower and I'm going to suck that dripping wet pussy dry."

I met his mouth with urgency and excitement when we entered the large shower. "And I'm going to drink every last ounce of cum out of your hard cock."

He pulled away with a glint of humor in his eyes. "Thank fucking God that you spilled that drink on me," he said, soaping my body up, "and that fate did see to it we ended up just like this."

I turned to him, more serious. "Don't get too attached." I smiled. "It's just one night. We're just strangers enjoying fucking and the fact that the universe made sure we wound up in this position," I said.

He rolled his bottom lip between his teeth. "If it's just one night," he said, "swear to me we don't stop fucking until the sun comes up."

"I'm down for that," I added.

That's when I spent the entire night in the arms of the man of my dreams, fucking all over that massive apartment hotel room, and wishing I had never snuck out when I heard him breathing deep in sleep by the time the sun peered through the curtains. As my Uber drove away from the luxurious hotel, I chewed on my nail, wondering if I should have left my number. I knew I was never going to have it *that* good ever again.

I glanced at the time. I was pressing my luck with the boarding time for my plane anyway. Shit. Well, fate did lead us together more than once, and I not only had the best sex in my life, but I strangely found myself being rescued by the man who seemed to keep popping up from out of nowhere on this crazy weekend in San Francisco.

Time to get my head straight again. I had to get home and get rejuvenated after this man worshipped my body all night long. For the first time in too long, I felt alive again; like anything was possible. I felt like pursuing my dreams of art more than ever before. I would go home and return to my paintings and sculpting as I did back when I was happy and wasn't stuck in the grief of my mom's death.

Sure, it was a one-night stand—but it was also more than that. Whether he meant the words he said or not, I felt beautiful again...like I was worth something again. There was something about this Mitch guy who called me his angel—or at least that was my fuck nickname for him throughout the night. There was something more than just getting fucked that woke me back up again. I'd been on autopilot this entire time since losing mom.

Until now, I hadn't realized I let myself die with her. I would never forget Mr. Gorgeous and how he oddly saved me with each interaction we had this entire crazy weekend. Part of me wanted to miss the flight and spend the whole day in bed with him like he'd begged me to before we both finally fell asleep in each other's arms as if we were the bride and groom from the day before.

No. I have to keep my head on straight. It was one night. The guy was obviously a player, and there was no way I was entering into some strange fantasy that anything more than sex with him could work. I didn't need a train-wreck relationship. I needed to get moving again now that I was jumpstarted back into a life that I'd closed myself off from.

There was a whole world out there I'd blocked, and doing something daring and sexy like I did last night was pretty much my swan dive back into life.

Chapter Five

Jake *Mitch*ell

One Year Later

I stood in the nurses' station, listening in on reports for my patients while flipping through their charts to ensure their recovery was moving along well after the two surgeries that I'd performed this week.

I tuned out the giggles and lack of professionalism coming out of Jackie's mouth—the one nurse who kicked ass in her job, yet grated on my nerves whenever there were newbies around. Unfortunately, I had interns standing on each side of me, so I couldn't tell Jackie to shut the fuck up.

Now certainly wasn't the time for messing around. The interns needed to take this part seriously. They could find out more about how I functioned as the chief of the cardiovascular unit of St. John's at a different date. Hell, most of them probably wouldn't last anyway.

"Dr. Mitchell, do you have anything to add? Or are you too busy for all of us this morning?" the RN questioned as my eyes roamed over Mr. Jackson's chart.

Did the woman seriously call me out like a first-grade student who wasn't paying attention to her class? Four other doctors were standing here doing the same shit as me—checking our patients' charts for shit's sake.

"You worked the graveyard shift as the charge nurse, did you not?" I eyed her, noticing the deadpan looks on the other nurses' faces standing around her.

"Yes," she said, placing her hand on the counter, her silver and short curled hair glistening under the fluorescent lighting of the nurses' station. "Is there a problem?"

"I gave the order for Ms. Davis to be brought to this CCU floor from the SICU before I left last evening. Why am I not seeing her charts here?" I asked the single-most-important question on my mind since arriving.

"Her charts aren't with us."

Are you fucking kidding me, I thought, gritting my teeth in anger, knowing this bitch dropped the goddamn ball and gave herself one less patient to care for. Well, I guess the interns were about to learn very quickly that I didn't put up with shit on my ward.

"*Nor* is she," I said, preventing myself from slamming my patient charts onto the desk before me. "Nurse O'Brien said she was calling down *to you* to have Ms. Davis transported to this floor for monitoring, and she was to be here so I could check in on her this morning when I arrived. Care to explain why you believed leaving my patient in the care of the SICU staff was okay?"

"Dr. Mitchell." Her eyes were wide under my glare. "I just—it wasn't like—we were full and understaffed last night."

I narrowed my eyes at her lie, then looked over at Glen and Rose, the two RNs, rolling their eyes at her answer. "Is this true? Were all of you understaffed, and room 394 couldn't accept a new patient?"

Glen gave me a look that told me I needed to figure out the charge nurse was not only lying, but she also refused my order so she could sit on her lazy ass all night long.

"She was Jackie's transfer. We were busy but not necessarily under-staffed, of course, Dr. Mitchell," Rose said while Glen looked as annoyed and pissed as I was. Must've been another shitty night with Jackie acting like she owned the place.

"We'll talk about this formally later," I said. "Report to my office after the shift change, and I'll have Sandy push back my first patient this morning." She went to talk but halted when I inhaled deeply. "It's negligence on your part to ignore any doctor's orders, and there are few people on earth who loathe insubordination more than I do," I said severely. "I will not tolerate it whether or not you've been with our medical group for over twenty-five years. If I order something, I want it done when I arrive the next morning unless there is a valid excuse as to why it can't be done. I will not have *my* patients' lives hanging in the balance because you think you know better than everyone else." Her cheeks were turning a shade of red that might've made me feel bad if it were any other circumstance. Unfortunately for Nurse Test-My-Patience, I was not in the mood. "While we're dealing with the topic of the best care for our patients, I would like you to transport Ms. Davis here *personally*, and then you can help prepare her room. And while you're finally doing as instructed, I'll be coming up with some bullshit excuse as to why I'm an hour behind with my office appointments today."

"Yes, Doctor." She straightened her scrubs and held her head high. She might've been a combative old bat, but she knew I was right. And she knew that shutting up was best, lest I decided to continue to humiliate her in front of the interns.

"The interns will accompany you," I stated flatly. "Explain to them that I do not tolerate laziness from my nurses while you apologize for being *late* in bringing Ms. Davis to her new room for care."

She stomped off, the young interns looking unsure of how to act after my tirade. Fuck this shit. I did not tolerate laziness or power nurse shit in the slightest. Now a charge nurse who acts like it's her family—not mine—who funded the entire cardiac wing of this hospital is calling me out, more than likely because three of the interns were cute and she wanted to act like she pulls strings? Fuck that noise.

Old-bat Nurse Jackie was convinced I'd fucked an intern once, and the money-hungry intern I turned down saw an opportunity to cash in on my family's money, so she didn't hesitate to play along with that narrative. My family lawyers backed my ass up on that fiasco—sadly, it didn't result in Jackie's termination too. Only Selene's.

Fuck. What a way to start my morning.

"Dr. Mitchell," the voice of Dr. King was humored when he called my name softly. "I know you're pissed, but you realize she doesn't work for *you*, a doctor, right?"

I smirked. "Of course, I know that. She didn't argue because she knows she fucked up and got caught. Perhaps there's more she doesn't want to be exposed about her practically taking the night off last night?" I arched my eyebrow at the cardiologist.

"Well, there are rumors."

"That shit is my brother's problem. He can uncover the HR issues she's getting herself tangled up in because she wants to mess around with Dr. Daniels in ER," I said as Dr. King and I walked farther down the hall, away from the nurses' station.

"Your brother sees her as an asset to this floor. She is a good nurse," King answered.

"Jim may see her that way, but I see her as an ass."

"Calling her out because she has no respect for a doctor in his late thirties?"

"Isn't that what it's all about?" I shook my head. "I need to call up to CICU. They might be a little shocked to see a CCU charge nurse doing a transport." I laughed at how stupid the woman was, yet she was so damn smart at the same time. King was right, though. The nurses didn't work for me, but I intentionally gave her an order to see how she would respond. Her response to following my request as if I were her boss only told me she was guilty of screwing the ER doc last night and didn't want any further questioning.

Dr. King left with the rest of the nurses who were starting their shifts, and I had to handle the BS of Jackie doing a transport now. I exhaled my frustration as I reached for the phone, sincerely concerned about my patient, who was left on the floor that I'd cleared her to leave.

"Yeah," I said when the nurse answered, "this is Dr. Mitchell. I have a charge nurse heading up to retrieve Ms. Davis. The patient has been cleared on my orders to be in CCU."

"A charge nurse?" she asked in confusion.

"Jackie?"

"Got it," the lady answered. "And, yes, we received your orders last night and expected transport hours ago. Jackie declined our transfer, but we'll sort it out now. I'll have Ms. Davis ready."

"There are four interns with Jackie. Please ensure that Ms. Davis is informed that I'll be sure to visit her after-hours today personally."

"Dr. Mitchell," the woman said, and I could hear the smile in her voice. "It's Jai," she chuckled. "You sound pretty upset."

Jai floated to the SICU?

"Hey, Jai." I relaxed some. The only woman to have ever tempted me in this place was this brunette with bright green eyes when she was floated to work my floor a couple of times. "Yeah, I'm a bit upset that my patient was left on that floor. I want her in CCU so she can at least see one family member. Jesus."

"Jackie was on one last night," Jai said. "As I said, she refused the transfer. Said it could wait until the next shift. She stated that CCU was full and understaffed last night."

Goddammit, you old fucking hag.

Jai laughed at my silence, probably well aware that I was internally cursing out the old bat.

My thoughts diverted to Jai's appearance that matched her contagious laugh. Why? Most likely because my brain was melting down at this point and short-circuiting because I couldn't throw something. The thought of Jai's hair color did a brain switch on me right then and there. And now I was thinking about Ash—again. *Fuck me, Ash, you will be the death of me,* I thought, pissed at the girl who haunted me and turned me into some desperate fool, wishing I'd never lost her. How could I not shake this chick after a solid year already? Goddammit! I had to stay focused and steer clear of thinking about the best sex I'd ever had over a year ago.

"You there?" Jai asked. "Oh, hey, Jackie's here—and pissed off." She laughed again. "I'll make sure we get your patient ready to be transported down. Jackie might have to help if she doesn't want to be here for an hour, though."

"The whole point I sent her up. And thank you," I managed and hung up.

I proceeded through the rooms, checking in on my patients, and ensuring they were recovering well or answering any post-op questions. I slid the curtain back and nodded to the respiratory therapist, who was fighting with Gilbert Jefferson. I smirked at the seventy-year-old whose last words as he was going under anesthesia were, *"You'd better not kill me, you son of a bitch!"* I looked at the veteran's Navy tattoo and had nothing but respect for this man. But he was as salty as hell, and I wasn't surprised he was giving Jenny a hard time over not wanting to do his breathing exercises.

"Doc," he said in his raspy voice, "tell her to get on out of here."

I smiled at Jenny, then looked at Gilbert. "If I tell her to leave you alone, then your last words before I put you to sleep might just come true."

He squinted and grumbled, mustering the most dangerous glare he could at me. "You're an asshole, Doc."

"I've been called worse," I countered. "You need to do the breathing exercises, or those strong lungs won't be able to cuss any of us out anymore. You and I discussed this."

He waved me off. "You can go."

"I'm not leaving until you take a few puffs off that machine." I arched a brow at him.

"Good grief," he said, looking at Jenny for help.

"Doctor's orders." She smiled at him.

"He's too young to be a doctor anyway," the old sailor started in with his insults on me.

"Tell that to your heart that's thanking me for the quadruple bypass." I looked at Jenny. "Jackie will be down with a new patient, Ms. Davis. I'll make sure she doesn't leave until she confirms that Gilbert here is properly doing his breathing work for you."

I finished with my rounds and called Jackie out and away from the patients and the interns. "If you ever speak to me or call me out in front of patients, nurses, interns, or even the fucking janitor again, you will be working another floor. Am I clear?" I should call her ass out on why exactly she refused the transfer after learning we were overstaffed, and Ms. Davis's room was left empty all night. I didn't have time for this petty shit. King was right. She was Jim's problem once I had my forty-eight off.

"That wasn't my intent, Jake," she stammered.

"Well, it most definitely made me look like an ass on the first day for these interns. You need to stay in your lane. Don't treat me like the piece of shit you believe me to be."

"I have nothing but respect for you, Dr. Mitchell."

"Yeah." I shook my head in disgust. "Right."

"You're the best—"

"Just stop." I held my hand up. "Consider yourself scolded. When I send a patient down to my floor or give orders to move them to another, do your goddamn job. I don't act like an egotistical dick of a doctor, but I can make sure you're sent to the floor where one is."

She sighed. "It won't happen again. I'm sorry."

"You have four or five interns to get introduced to the CCU, and it's probably going to hold you over until noon."

"Heather is on now as the charge nurse. She can take over." Her eyes grew severe.

"True," I said, eying the day-shift charge. "She can do rounds with them, and you can leave after you find a way to apologize to Ms. Davis for not bringing her down. I need to go. My patients are already in the office. I'm stacked in after two surgeries yesterday."

"Thank you, Jake," she said and then stormed off to make sure Ms. Davis's room was ready.

Shit. What a fucking good morning. I had to shake all of this off. Tomorrow I was on call all day, and if I was going to be dealing with any bullshit, the old bat was going to be on call with me. I needed to be in a good working mood with the woman, or I'd strangle her before the twenty-four-hour on-call was over.

THE NEXT DAY I WAS ABLE TO CATCH UP ON A SHITLOAD OF BACKED-up work. I sat in the nurses' station and sipped on my coffee while thumbing through the evening shift-change paperwork. The interns were annoying as hell, but shit, I was in their shoes once too. In truth, it was a slow day, so they were floating through the floor like disheveled messes, trying to find stuff to do.

I should have known that once I took a bite of the sandwich that it took Jackie an hour to bring me, the call that the interns had been praying for all day would come in.

I flipped through the man's chart who was being rushed into my OR, looking at everything in his medical history. CPR was being used to keep the sixty-five-year-old alive, and now it was my job to open him up and do what I did best.

With the stealth and the supreme skill of my staff, all hands were on deck as I went to work, saving the man from the heart attack that was desperately trying to steal him from the world.

I performed the bypass as effortlessly as most people would tie their shoes. Three of his arteries were blocked, but still allowing proper blood flow. The culprit was the plaque that blocked one of his arteries entirely. After bypassing that, his body and heart fell into a sound rhythm. Unfortunately, after three hours with this patient, I knew blocked arteries weren't the man's primary issue.

"Well done, Dr. Mitchell," my attending physician acknowledged while we worked to close up the wound in his chest. "I will take it from here."

I stepped back, knowing the patient was in good care with Dr. Chi. "I'll inform the family of his stability and what the future holds for the patient." I looked at the interns. "Two of you may join me. As you already know, his family is out in the waiting room, and they are in distress. They don't need the audience of too many interns."

I pulled off the glasses, mask, gloves, and the rest of my protective gear and tossed them in the hazmat can, and I walked out with two interns trailing me. I hated greeting patients in my scrubs and scrub hat like this—something about it was too sterile and intimidating for people who were waiting to hear if their loved one was alive or dead. I suppose there was no appropriate attire to receive such news, though.

I hit the auto-open button with my elbow that opened the doors to the visitors' waiting room of the ER-wing to the hospital. The family stood, and my eyes widened when I could have sworn the ghost of my Ash stood amongst the two older men and a woman in the family room. I had to blink a few times—nope, it was her, in the flesh.

"Good evening." I smiled, peeling my eyes from Ash and looking at the man who seemed to command the room. "I assume you're the family of Mark Taylor?"

"He's my dad, yes." Ash pried her way up between the two men who stood like bodyguards in front of her. "Please, God." She covered her mouth with her hands, and tears poured out of her puffy eyes.

If only I could bring her into my arms and tell her he's going to be okay...for now.

"The surgery went well. He's now in recovery." I pulled my brain out of Jake-Mitch mode and into supremely focused surgeon mode... the mode that I was in before I saw her stunning bronze eyes. "He's going to be fine. A nurse will be out shortly to go over the details with all of you. Can any of you tell me who his current cardiologist is? There was nothing filled in on his charts or paperwork," I said, thumbing through the papers I had and then looking up at the family again.

"He hasn't seen a doctor since before my mother—" Ash's voice cracked, and she turned into the embrace of the strong man she clung too.

I brought my attention to his red-rimmed eyes, eyes that were glassy and hardened from holding back tears of fear. "The nurse will set up an appointment with a cardiologist if he doesn't have one. She will go over the details as to why he must be seen soon after he's released and recovering from this surgery."

"What does that mean, Dr. Mitchell?" the man asked.

"He will need further evaluation. He is stable, but it is crucial that he be seen by a cardiologist much sooner than most of our patients after they're released to recover at home."

Shit. Ash needed to know her dad had a very critical situation with his enlarged heart, and the only way to fix it would be a transplant. I would need to inform Jackie that Mark Taylor must be my future patient. Being that Mark Taylor was my Ash's dad, I didn't trust him in anyone's care but mine.

After seeing Ash's reaction to almost losing her father, I internally prayed I could convince both of them of a heart transplant as soon as a donor was available. I had the best record in the nation on transplants —the media was interviewing me about that next week. Ash would lose her dad if we didn't get him a new heart. He had multiple issues, but the main problem from what I saw without the machines was that his tricuspid valve was not functioning correctly, otherwise known as Epstein's anomaly.

I'd learn more once he was my patient. Right now, I had to hope he'd accept me as his doctor, the idea of a transplant, and then, of course, the donor heart.

I left the room, Ash watching me through tear-stained eyes, and me not being able to do a damn thing about that. I was some fucking idiot flirt who'd fucked her all night in my room. How the fucking hell was she supposed to take me seriously a year later, walking into a room in scrubs, announcing her dad was fine, and doing my usual doctor routine of leaving the rest to the nurse to go over with the family?

I walked back to where Mr. Taylor was being transported out of the OR and up to the SICU wing of the hospital until he was recovered enough to be admitted to my floor.

I ran my hand over my scrub hat, pulling the navy-blue material from my head and ran the back of my hand over my forehead. I had to see Ash again. I had to help her and her dad. Call it doctor instincts— or just part of this crazy world of being stuck wishing I'd never let her walk out of the room that morning.

I'd forgotten how beautiful this woman was. How she mysteriously did what none other could do: capture my attention solely for her. Hell, we had to be meant for something. These crazy run-ins had to have meant more than I knew.

Chapter Six

Jake

"Last patient, and then you're gone until Monday, correct?" Sandy, the receptionist, asked at the end of my long-ass Friday.

"Correct," I said. "See you then. Enjoy the weekend."

"You too, Jake," she said with a beaming smile.

I walked through the empty waiting room floor, smiling at her boyfriend. "Are you two sure you're old enough to drink?" I teased the two.

Sandy laughed, pulling her purse up on her shoulder and shutting the receptionist's alcove lights off. "Asks the man-child chief surgeon," she joked back, coming through the door.

"How are you doing, Doc?" her boyfriend, Gabe, asked as he reached out to shake my hand.

"Oh, I'm sure Sandy can fill you in on the nonsense of the week." I smirked. "You two enjoy the beach this weekend," I said, knowing he was a great surfer, having surfed with him after Sandy begged me to hang out with him and give her my take on the kid.

These two practically lived at the beach and loved it when I offered up the beach house to them for weekend trips to Malibu when I saw her at wit's end with the others in my office staff. She was like a younger sister to me, and that was the only reason I trusted her with the house.

Surprisingly, I approved of Gabe. He wasn't an idiot or a player. She snagged herself an old soul who made me look like the immature guy no one should dare to enter a relationship with, lest they end up neglected or cheated on.

That was until Ash waltzed into my life, and all that playing, crazy-ass nightlife shit came to a screeching halt for me. I couldn't nail down the effects she had on my sorry ass, but until her dad was rushed to the ER that night, I could've sworn she was sent into my life that weekend in San Francisco as prayers answered for revenge from all the women I had screwed over with my fuck 'em and leave 'em lifestyle.

Speaking of taming my nightlife, I had rounds at the hospital tonight before I was free to catch up with the guys at Darcy's.

"Mr. Taylor," I said, smiling at Ash's dad, who looked a thousand times better since post-op checkups. "You about ready to get out of this place?" I asked, seeing his vibrant expression while flipping through his charts. "I see you're following all the rules." I smiled down at how well this patient was doing. "Except for one." I folded my arms, the curtain opening behind me, me catching a glance of two female interns kindly announcing their entrance to the room.

"Listen, Dr. Mitchell," he said, giving me an authoritative stare. "I've been walking, do the breathing..." He held his arm out for vitals to be checked.

"He's doing great!" Ash's voice was like a wave of energy that soothed me to my core.

Fuck. I smiled at her, sitting next to her father's bed. I had to hold my shit together. The last thing I needed was to find out she didn't remember who I was—don't think *that* thought hadn't entered my mind more than once since the night her dad was brought in. Now, I needed to keep my bedside manner the same. My God, if her dad wasn't here—*fucking stop this shit and focus.*

"He's our best patient," Nurse Rose said.

"Charming the ladies, eh?" I smiled at Rose, then Mr. Taylor.

Wrong fucking choice of words if Ash has put two and two together and realized the man she'd fucked all night was not Mitch but an alias I'd used. She'd screamed that name more than once, and my dick was going to start to betray me if I didn't knock this shit off. How the fuck can I think with this beauty in my presence? Her low-cut shirt and tight pants weren't helping my sorry ass at the moment, either.

"What can I say?" Mr. Taylor played along with all the young and beautiful women in the room.

Exercising the supreme skill of focus, my ability to think in chaotic environments, and having a meticulous physician's mindset while I was in the hospital—I switched over to *that* side of my brain so I could stay on track.

"Well, I keep getting reports, stating you will be missed greatly by all of my staff when you're discharged tomorrow morning," I said, eying his charts again. "Have you worked with a nurse to set up your cardiologist appointment?"

"I mentioned that I preferred seeing you, Dr. Mitchell, but you aren't accepting new patients." He sighed. "We'll find another if you can refer—"

Jackie, your old hag ass is mine! I thought, knowing that bitch would pull this shit behind my back. "Nonsense," I said, not looking over at Ash, who sat perfectly still in the corner of my eye. "I will have the discharge orders state that I will be taking you as a new patient," I said, writing that down in my charts. "You live close to St. John's?"

"We just moved here," Ash spoke up. "This part of LA County is a bit crazier than Santa Clarita."

With my feet planted firmly, I steadied myself and looked at her as my patient's daughter, and not the woman I desperately could not get out of my thoughts. "That it is," I managed, sounding like a jackass. "Listen," I said, bringing the seriousness that I knew was at hand to the surface of my mind. "I'm sure you were informed of what I found while bypassing the artery that failed."

"Yes," he said, eyes guiltily looking over to his daughter in shame and then looking back at me. "I just never gave a second thought to

the fact that my heart defect would come back and bite me in the ass."
He chuckled.

"Dad!" Ash rolled her eyes, and then she looked at me. "*Can* we lower his dosage on the pain meds?"

I smirked at Mr. Taylor. "I assume this is your daughter?" I asked, seeing Ash's face fall the second I said the words. *What the fuck did I say?*

"Yep." He shrugged. "Always keeping me in line."

"Well, she's about to keep you awake in pain all night if you don't stop swearing, it seems."

She leaned into him, all humor gone. "I lost Mom to something she couldn't prevent, and I'm sure as hell not losing you too."

He ran his hand over her cheek as a tear slipped out of the corner of his eye. "I know, sweetheart. That's why we're pretty lucky to have Dr. Mitchell take my sorry butt as a patient."

"The discharge nurse will go over the rest with both of you. I just left my office, and it looks like you're in luck, Mr. Taylor," I smiled at him. "I was informed my Monday afternoon appointment canceled. Hopefully, you'll be able to make that slot?"

"We'll take the first available," he said, his eyes apologizing to his daughter for reasons I could not tell.

I scribbled on the chart and flipped it over. "I'll have the information sent with your discharge papers to my office," I said. "Any other questions you have for me before meeting on Monday?"

"We're good, thanks," Ash said.

"All right. I'll see you on Monday, Mr. Taylor."

"Hey, Doc?" he called out.

I turned back.

"Thanks for saving my life."

I nodded. "Thank your daughter." I smiled at her. "She was extremely proactive, and after reading your charts and the events that led you to my OR, I can safely say she played the most critical role in keeping you alive, sir."

"That she did." He patted her hand on his cheek.

I couldn't stand here and gawk at this endearing moment. He was the father of the woman I couldn't get out of my head. A woman who, if she did remember me, I had no idea what the fuck she thought of me after our night together a year ago. God knows I wasn't acting like a goddamn chief surgeon in my room with her all night.

I turned to leave, keeping it my head that I was at least grateful she was in my life—if only by her dad becoming my patient.

"Dr. Mitchell?" Ash's voice called out softly from behind where I was walking toward the nurses' station.

I stopped and turned back to her. "Yes," I answered, entirely at the mercy of her long black lashes, highlighting her brown eyes as they peered up at me with uncertainty.

Her face scrunched up into some adorable yet confused expression. "I think we've met before, under different circumstances, of course."

"Of course," I was smiling inside only as I searched for the right words.

"Anyway," she seemed to shake off the words like a disease. "Thanks for everything you did to save my dad's life. I've been told more than once that he shouldn't have survived, but that Dr. Mitchell being on call is the reason he's still going to be with me."

Her voice cracked, and she brushed a tear from her cheek before I know I would've naturally wiped it away for her. "He's recovering well," I said, "but he must have an open mind when we meet on Monday."

"My dad finally admitted he's had that heart defect since birth." She exhaled in anger, "He makes me so angry sometimes. How could he never tell me about this?"

"Did he ever have a cardiologist before?" I asked. "Perhaps his medical doctor would have known this too?"

"I don't know," she said, slipping her hands into her pockets, my eyes following the gesture, yet getting stuck in her tan skin tone and those perfect breasts I'd worshipped along with the rest of her body that night.

One night, Jake! One night and now you're back with the one woman who brought you to your fucking knees.

"These are details we'll work out when I meet with him," I said, focusing on something other than wanting to take Ash back to my office, or in my car, or right here in front of everyone just to hear those moans coming from her again.

I had to get out of here before I did do something to screw my life up because of this woman.

"Then I guess we'll see you on Monday."

"It'll be difficult for him to travel. How far are you two from the hospital?"

"About an hour," she answered.

"I'll arrange for a more comfortable medical transport," I said. "I also have comfortable furniture in one of my office rooms. We'll meet there for his comfort."

She pinched her lips together. Did she even know what she was doing to me? Half of my brain was trying to restrict my dick from jumping out of this suit so I could fuck her tight pussy again. To feel—

"See you then."

While my mind was focused on keeping my shit together, she spun around, her perfect auburn hair swinging around in her ponytail. She looked exhausted and only wore leggings and a long-sleeved shirt, but she looked more beautiful than the supermodel look she'd sported at the wedding.

I WALKED INTO DARCY'S AND SAW COLLIN, JIM, AND ALEX AT OUR usual corner booth. This was the place where we tended to hide out when none of us were in the mood for the gold-digging chicks at regular clubs. It was also the place where my best friend, Collin—a neurosurgeon from St. John's—had fucked over a rich and extremely psychotic bitch. Ever since then, we'd been known inside and outside of our circle as the Billionaires' Club. The assholes who only fucked chicks with money so we could save our own.

"What the hell happened to you?" my older brother, Jim, asked as he sipped his bourbon. "I heard about your favorite RN this week." He smirked, and Collin and Alex laughed at whatever they knew outside of my company about what happened with the old bat.

"Oh?" I took the scotch that was waiting for me. "Did she come clean and admit that she's fucking that dumbass ER doctor?"

"No." Jim chuckled.

"Looks like you have an HR complaint slapped on your ass, brother," Alex, who was Jim's best friend and president of our family's empire, said.

"Oh, for fuck's sake." I rolled my eyes and took another drink. "I don't need this shit."

"The hospital buzz is this: don't work the cardiac recovery unit because Dr. Mitchell is a dick who thinks the nurses work for him." Collin laughed into his gin and tonic.

I eyed his disgusting drink of choice. I hated gin, but I hated this fucking nurse even more. "How do you drink that shit?" I snapped.

"Easily," Collin said and knocked back the entire contents of his glass. "Just like that, bitch!" he taunted me.

I ran my hands through my hair, regretting showing up here tonight. I couldn't get Ash off my mind since seeing her today. I couldn't stop reliving that night again. I was so fucked.

"Take it easy, Jake." My brother laughed. "Can he get another scotch?" he asked a passing waitress before she nodded and turned to the bar. "I handled it, Jake. I'm having Jackie transferred to another hospital." He sighed. "Was she that bad?"

"It's not her." I found myself biting my bottom lip, wishing I'd taken another drink before I responded to Jim.

"What the fuck is wrong, then?" Jim used his big-brother, asshole voice on me.

"Don't use your CEO-bullshit tone on me," I said. "You could have run all of this past me before making that decision, you know?"

"You weren't at the board meeting, prick," Jim said sternly, not backing down.

"On-call, fucker."

"Okay," Alex said, stopping Jim and me from turning this into a pissing match. "What the hell is wrong with you?"

"I'm fine. Long day." I wasn't telling them about Ash. No way in hell.

"Really?" Collin asked, concern in his voice. "You only act like this if you lose a patient. What the hell is going on? You're not acting right."

I went to speak, but Jim interrupted. "Don't you dare say you're tired. We've watched you go for days without sleep and still entertain us with your bullshit after coming off long weeks."

"It's a patient," I said, looking at Collin. "I didn't lose him, but he has more serious issues than what brought him into my OR. He's going to need a transplant, and it will kill me if I have to watch his daughter's response to him turning that idea down. She can't lose this man."

The table grew silent, and I knew exactly why.

"And the doctor has more concern over this young woman than his patient?" Jim pressed.

"I never said that," I said flatly.

"You didn't have to," Jim said. "Who is she? And how in the hell is my brother sitting there, lost in thought over her."

I held my hands up. "I can't fucking do this with you three."

"Why so defensive?" Collin smirked at Alex and Jim.

"Fine," I said, tipping back the last of my scotch. "Remember the woman from Frisco?"

"The one you hooked up with, and for the first time, you were being walked out on and not the other way around?" Alex asked.

"Yes." I took my new scotch and pointed to him. "That one."

"Oh shit, man." Collin shook his head while Jim looked at me deadpan.

"You know if you go down this road—" Jim's CEO voice started in.

"I've got this handled," I answered.

"Two scotches in, and it's handled?" Jim asked. "You're going to fuck yourself over bad if you take the man as a patient. I know you treat all of your patients like they're family, but this is playing too close —especially knowing the patient's daughter that you lived in hell over for a solid month after you got home."

Try a whole year. "It's different. She doesn't remember me. She knew me as Mitch, not Jacob Mitchell, her dad's cardiothoracic surgeon."

"Are you that fucking dumb?" Collin laughed, while the others sat back and eyed me in humor.

"Last I checked, no and yes." I rubbed my forehead. "I can't think."

"You can't think because you believe she forgot who you are?" Alex laughed. "And yet I can count a few women who took years to get over your just one night of fucking rule. No attachments—nothing."

"And now the tables are turned on him, and he can't handle it," Jim added.

"You three are ones to talk," I grumbled. "Even if she remembered who I was, can you imagine what the hell she could be thinking after I flirted like a reckless idiot and fucked her all over that goddamn hotel room?"

Jim choked on his bourbon. "Well, this is all news to us, Mr. *I'm not telling you assholes shit.* Care to give us her real name now?"

"Annie," I tried to confirm only to receive laughs from the three. "Fuck, I don't know. I told her my name was Mitch, and she gave me Ash. That's all I have, aside from the fact that her dad is Mark Taylor."

"Well, since you decided to take on the patient's daughter you screwed a year ago," Collin smirked, then arched an eyebrow at me. "So, I guess you'll be learning a lot more about the girl who made you feel like shit for sleeping with her," Collin finished with a laugh.

"This should be good," Alex said as he shook his head at me.

"This is going to be fantastic. You think you'll invite her up to the party?" Jim questioned.

"Party?"

"Um, the one we're having after your interview with the news stations about your flawless record of survival rate in transplants?" Jim answered. "It's being catered at your beach house. How did you forget that?"

"Fuck me," I answered. "I'm not up for it."

"Too bad," Jim answered. "It's excellent PR for the hospital, so do the interview, and if you like this woman, invite her to the house after all is done. We'd like to meet her."

"Yeah, not happening," I answered. "You assholes are going to have every single chick you want to take your pick of there."

"Afraid your eyes might wander while she's with you?" Collin asked. "Perhaps you might use this as your challenge if she's the one to tame the wild Jacob Mitchell."

It had to have been the third scotch because I took these douches up on their stupid challenge. I agreed to bring Ash up to the place, hang around snobs and celebrities—no doubt adding to the most uncomfortable night she and I would ever have together—and that's *if* she took me up on my offer.

Why the hell couldn't I think like a regular person right now? I needed to get laid. That was a definite fact. I hadn't been with anyone since Ash, and thank God my job kept me busy because it was certainly not like me to go an entire year without having sex. Maybe another scotch, and I'd cure myself of this woman—who most likely didn't return my sappy feelings—by getting laid tonight. My cock twitched at the thought, and now I was eying the women in the place, looking for a woman I knew I could fuck and not have to deal with the fallout after leaving in the morning.

"Vickie's here," I said, smiling at the guys.

"So, she's your ex, and you hate the woman," Jim answered.

"She's his friends with benefits partner," Collin said. "Whenever Jake needs to get a piece and doesn't want the hassle, it's Vick."

"Precisely," I said, the scotch fueling me into the decision further. "Besides, she owes me for throwing that stupid wedding on my shoulders last minute, all while I was trying to do the bullshit keynote speaker stuff that Jim mandated out of that trip."

"Why the hell are you going to fuck Vickie again?" Jim asked.

"To get the other girl out of my system. I can't take any risk in relationships," I honestly stated. "I would just end up screwed in the end. The hours I work are too much for any woman in my life to handle. I need to get a grip."

"No shit," Collin cheered to that truth. Being a doctor himself, he knew what I was up against.

"Well, reconsider that because we are having another board meeting, and we're changing hours on overworked doctors at St. John's. I'm not doing this without your input," Jim told me.

"Now, I need to get laid," I answered, getting up from the table. "I'm not in the mood to talk shop about hours and cutbacks tonight. I need to get myself under control before I see the woman who's fucked my mind over again."

"Dumb mistake, man," Alex said. "Fuck the one you like."

"That's the dumb mistake, my friend," I answered as I left the three staring at me as if I'd completely gone over the edge.

Seeing my gorgeous fuck-pal was enough to have me questioning what kind of reckless adventure I was on. Would I regret this or be glad I got this out of my system? Using Vick and—dare I even think the thought?—imagining Ash's face while I...

What the hell did this girl do to me? Voodoo shit? Was I under a spell or something with her? Hell if I knew.

Chapter Seven

Ash

By the time dad's Monday appointment rolled around, I was physically and mentally drained. We reached the hospital medical offices where we were to meet with the doctor. Yes, *the* doctor, and if the man only saw me as his patient's *daughter*, then that's the relationship we would move forward with.

I thought about changing dad's appointment to another cardiologist, but after I'd googled Dr. Jacob Mitchell, MD, Chief of Cardiology, cardiothoracic surgeon, I quickly changed my mind. He was a world-renowned heart surgeon who'd won multiple medical awards, he'd graduated at the top of his class at Harvard Medical School, he was known for innovative treatment for his patients, and his success rate was through the roof. My dad was in the hands of an angel—and I somehow met the devil in the guy a year ago.

I rubbed my clammy palms together, more nervous than Dad, sitting in this luxurious office that was nicer than the tiny two-bedroom home we'd closed on a month ago in Burbank. Dad demanded we purchase the place after I secured a job in the city at a fabulous art gallery. Then the heart attack hit, and now here we sat...in the office of a guy that I screwed like some crazy woman and thought I'd never see again.

Don't get me wrong, though. I never regretted a second of it. In fact, a tiny part of me wished I'd meet him in some crazy way again. I just didn't think it would take the grim reaper showing up to find the man I couldn't get off my mind since leaving that hotel in Frisco.

"Thanks. Push them out to four o'clock on Thursday, then." I heard his voice before he knocked twice and opened the door to his office.

"You're still set for your transplant tomorrow," a female's voice said firmly.

I glanced over at the long white sleeve that covered his beautiful hand as it rested on the door. He stepped back out of the office, and I heard his voice lower. "Is there some reason you're telling me this as I'm about to meet with a new patient? Can this not wait?"

"I just wanted you to be aware." Her voice sounded bitchy in response.

"Thank you," he said curtly, then entered the room. "Good afternoon, Mr. Taylor," he said to Dad before he eyed me with those stark blue eyes, and my heart raced in response to his serious expression. "I see you brought your daughter." He leaned up against his desk casually. "Has she threatened to take any pain meds from you lately?"

I watched the handsome man smirk at my dad, his dark green shirt and gray tie tucked into his sharply pressed slacks with his white over-coat—or doctor's smock—revealing his name and title that kept any thoughts of our previous wild night together far from my mind.

In this environment, he was definitely not Mitch from the wedding. Mitch from my dreams nearly every night since I left him, or Mitch, the man I continued to fantasize about every day since he turned my world upside down mentally and physically.

Dad gripped my shoulder, and I popped up on the couch, finding myself staring intently at the slate floor that his massive desk sat in the center of. I looked over at Dad's confused expression and smiled.

"Did I miss something?" I tried to recover. "Sorry, long week," I said, looking to see that Dr. Mitchell had seated himself in his chair behind the massive desk.

He cocked his head to the side, his eyes darker than ever, and expression seemed like he was disgusted that my head wasn't in the game.

Dad laughed. "Gotta love my Ashley. She's one to wander off whenever she sees beauty and art." Dad pointed to the stunning skyline of Los Angeles through the million-dollar-view windows behind the doctor's desk. "Anything to take your mind off the subject of your old man's neglected heart."

Dr. Mitchell smiled at me for the first time since seeing him again. "I believe any view of a skyline can keep one's mind healthy and sober," he said, glancing back at the view that mirrored the one on the rooftop where we chatted in San Francisco, and then back to the file he had on dad.

"Yeah," I sighed. "So, what's going on with my dad? Why did you take him on as a patient when you weren't accepting new ones? Is it that bad?"

"Ash." Dad patted my leg. "Don't put me in the grave just yet."

I rolled my eyes at Dad. His sense of humor was weird, but that's what I loved about him.

"I need both of you to have an open mind, as I know there will be many questions." He looked between dad and me. "Your enlarged heart suffered seventy-percent death due to the heart attack. I've also noticed the defect that you and I discussed is one you've had since birth. All of these can easily be corrected with surgery."

"What kind of surgery are we talking about, Dr. Mitchell?" my dad asked in the voice he always spoke to my mom's doctors in when they had that please have an open mind look on their faces.

His eyes shifted between my dad and me. *Shit, this isn't looking good.* I felt tears well up in my eyes. "Not again." I let the words slip out. I looked at Dad and held his hand. "I'm so sorry. I said I wouldn't pull this on you, but I can't help it."

"Do either of you want to know why I am asking for you to keep an open mind?" Dr. Mitchell's voice was slightly humored but calculated in its delivery. I could tell he'd done *t*his talk numerous times and most likely dealt with the same reaction I was having.

"Go on," I said stiffly, folding my arms and nervously bouncing my crossed leg.

"Unfortunately, Mr. Taylor, your heart is not likely to last another year, and so I would like to present you with a life-saving alternative."

Oh my God, I thought and swallowed the spontaneous cry that almost escaped my lips, pressing down every emotion I had so I wouldn't throw up.

"Very well, then," Dad said. "What's the plan?"

"Your blood type is very common, and a transplant—"

"Absolutely not." For the first time since falling in love with Dr. Mitchell's humor, wisdom, and wit, my dad snapped harshly at the man. "I won't take the heart of a grieving family's loved one."

I looked at Dr. Mitchell's calm expression as he nodded. "You'd be surprised at how many people share your sentiments," he responded. "However, after having done numerous transplants, I can assure you that we have an amazing program. I've witnessed families of organ donors who have met the recipients—such a thing is not required, of course—but it can be quite healing for the family of the departed. Some feel that it's a way of keeping their loved one alive." He rubbed his chin, and I could see his eyes must have been revisiting one of these situations he'd witnessed."

"I won't do it," Dad said, his voice shaking.

"Are there any other alternatives?" I asked numbly.

Dr. Mitchell seemed defeated in that instant, where I thought he'd press Dad harder. Then his eyes grew fierce and his cheeks flushed red as he sighed. "I can arrange for a Ventricular Assist Device, otherwise known as a VAD," he said mechanically. "This will be inconvenient, but you would have needed it while awaiting a new heart anyway. The implant surgery must be arranged immediately, and it will help the thirty-percent functioning part of your heart to continue to do its job. Please allow me to make it clear that this machine is an *assist* to the heart, and it may not last longer than two or three years. A new heart would rid you of the defect you were born with, however, and I would be able to correct a lot of the issues your body has dealt with since birth if you chose to do that."

"I just can't." Dad started tearing up, and that's when I grew more serious.

"When will he go in for his other surgery?" I asked, not remembering the doctor's jargon he was using.

"I have already opened my schedule up for the VAD implant a week from today at six in the morning," he said, eyes pleading with mine. "I understand this is a lot for both of you. I can see where you both have suffered a lot over the last few years, but I must insist that both of you consider it. Allow me to help you, Mr. Taylor."

Dad tried to stand, Dr. Mitchell and I rushing to help him. "Damn it," he said in frustration. "I will set the appointment for the implant," he grumbled through his tears. "The other isn't gonna happen."

I looked at Dr. Mitchell's saddened expression, feeling torn myself.

"Ashley," he said, my name rolling off his tongue like honey, "do you work, or are you available to remain at home to care for your dad after this surgery?"

"I work," I said meekly, "but I'll—"

"There is no need to call out of work," Dr. Mitchell practically read my thoughts. "I'll be sending an in-home healthcare nurse. The hospital provides nurses to be there as long as needed for patients in your father's condition."

"Thank you for that," I said.

"Lisa will see both of you out, and I'll be calling to discuss issues further should they arise," he said, knowing my dad was pretty much walking out on him.

"Yes, Lisa's been the one checking in with him, and she helped us when we got here," I said about his stupidly hot redhead nurse.

The doctor left us to load dad in the transport van with what seemed to be a pissed-off expression, and I couldn't get any of it out of my mind.

By the time we were home and settled, the nurse arrived, and we spent at least three hours going over Dad's new lifestyle plans together. She was a Mexican lady named Carmen, and for the first time since Mom was gone, Dad was flirting and enjoying the company of a woman his age who had an awesome personality. Nurse Carmen even took me up on my offer to sleep in my room since I'd pretty much gotten used to sleeping on the couch after Mom got sick, and Dad pulled his shit on me. I was always scared to be sound asleep in my room should anything happen.

DAD AND I SAT ALONE IN THE LIVING ROOM AFTER CARMEN LEFT TO pick up his prescriptions. It was the night before his implant surgery, and I was nervous as hell. I wanted him to get the damn heart transplant, but he wouldn't have it.

The stubborn man was convinced he was too old to take a donor heart from someone else who was younger and needed it more than he did. Carmen backed me up on the fact that being sixty-five wasn't a death sentence. He was young! He wasn't an old man who should let his life go because he felt he was too old to receive a transplant.

The computer seemed to be my best friend these days since work letting me off until Dad was settled and progressing well. In-home nurse or not, I wasn't leaving Dad—not at least until this implant to assist his dying heart was done.

"You're being selfish, Dad," I finally said, pissed-off that he could be on a donor list, but he was wasting time by sitting around and not having this discussion again.

"Now you sound like your mother." He smiled at me from his comfy chair, oxygen machine and all.

"Don't even go there to get out of this," I said, my legs curled under me on the sofa. "Why would you be okay to put me through all of this shit again?"

"Ashley," he said. Even with a weak heart, on oxygen, and hardly mobile, he still acted like stern, old Dad. "We're not having this discussion."

"Fine." I looked away from him. I didn't want to work up his blood pressure. Surgery was tomorrow, and the last thing I was going to do was fight with him when this could be the last time we spoke.

Carmen walked in at that point. She was a perfect shade of sexy, and I prayed to God that I looked as vibrant and sassy as the woman when I hit my sixties. She was a great confidant too, not just for Dad, but for me also. She kept both of us looking at the brighter side of all of this, and I was grateful for everything she was doing to help us.

"We need to try and get some sleep," I said. "We only get a couple of hours before you're in the hospital being prepped for surgery tomorrow morning."

Carmen backed me, and it wasn't long after that I laid on the couch, wide-eyed and unable to sleep. I knew it would go down this way too. Shit, I'd be a wreck tomorrow. No big deal, though. My dad was only going into surgery with the hottest man alive.

I SAT IN THE WAITING ROOM WITH ANOTHER FAMILY WHO SAT A corner, most likely waiting for those doors to open and someone walk through them to possibly change their lives forever with whatever came out of the messenger's mouth.

"Another coffee?" Carmen asked after the doors opened, startling all of us who were waiting for the words we all seemed to be scared to hear.

"If this girl has another coffee, she'll probably ruin the floors after pacing them," my Uncle Ken said with a laugh.

He and Aunt Carrie were the best, but since they were in their late seventies, it was hard to relate to most of their conversations. Everything was political with the two, and it was severely exhausting. Dad loved it, though—I think he just loved arguing with them over the news.

Fuck, I can't think. I rubbed my forehead and moved around the large waiting area of the surgical floor.

"Can't we get some kind of news?" I asked, wondering what the hell could be happening in Dr. Perfection's operating room.

Carmen looked at her watch. "It's only been four hours, *mija*. Dr. Mitchell said this implant could take up to twelve hours, given the condition of your dad's heart."

I tightened my lips. Dr. Mitchell may have had a flawless record, but that was my dad in there under his knife. My dad, who was going against his solid advice of getting on the donor list.

Carmen's phone rang after I sat, crossed my legs, and let the nervous leg bouncing commence.

"Carm?" I could have sworn I heard Dr. Mitchell's voice on the other end of her phone since the volume was turned up way too high. "How are we doing out there?"

"Is that Dr. Mitchell?" I asked.

She held a finger up, smiled, and nodded at me. "We have one nervous young lady out here," she answered in her enthusiastic voice.

"Understandable," he said. "Can you hand her your phone, please?"

She handed me the phone while I stared in disbelief at what the fuck was going on. "Yes?" I said softly.

"Ashley," he said, while I heard machines beeping, people speaking to each other—surgical talk. "I wanted to update you and let you know your dad is fine. It's just taking us a bit longer due to some unforeseen issues that were easily repaired."

"Are you in the middle of surgery?" I asked in shock.

"Yes," he answered. "You're on speakerphone."

"Thanks for the warning. I was about to cuss you out for talking on the phone while my dad's life was hanging in the balance."

He chuckled, and strangely enough, my heart reacted to the calmness in his voice, and the staff in the background that seemed to act like this is how these sorts of things went with Dr. Mitchell.

"Dr. Chi, please?" I heard him say, ignoring me. *Obviously, the guy is in the middle of surgery.* "Thank you, Doc," he said. "Still there, Ashley?"

"Yes."

"All right. Well, we are progressing extremely well. I wanted to ensure you were updated after it the current time in surgery was brought to my attention," he said. "I believe we'll be in here for another hour or ninety minutes."

"Thanks for the update. Please just keep him safe."

"My every intention, Miss Taylor," he said. "Can you please hand the phone back to Carmen?"

I handed her the phone and shrugged at the family in the corner who was staring at us oddly as Carmen ended the call. I couldn't blame them. Getting a call from a doctor performing surgery wasn't something I'd ever thought I'd experience. The doors opened, bringing my attention to the doctor walking through them. Naturally, my heart would be pounding in my chest, wondering if this doctor was here to deliver news to them or me.

"The doctor is still in surgery, but she sent me out to inform you all that everything looks great," the man said. "It'll be close to an hour before we'll be taking your son to recovery."

"Thank you, Nurse," they responded.

I looked over at Carmen who just hung up with the doctor. "Care to inform me what the hell our doctor was doing calling us while theirs sent a nurse?"

She patted my leg and leaned over to me. "The difference," she lowered her voice, "is your surgeon is Dr. Mitchell." She leaned back and smiled, smoothing her shiny, black hair over her shoulder. "He is known for calling out to the waiting room, or if a nurse is with his patient's family, he calls the nurse."

"He hasn't killed anyone by doing that? I mean, there is a reason phones are the cause of distraction and most accidents," I snapped, nervous and bewildered.

"No, no." She shook her head. "I've heard many stories about his OR and staff." She sat back in her chair. "The man is a genius with his skill, and he has a very level head. He's extremely focused while performing the surgeries. It's pretty much second nature to him."

"I've never heard of that."

"Even with all the googling you've done on Jacob?" She arched her flirty brow at me. "Well, he's known for not only treating his patients like family but also for making sure the ones in the waiting room aren't distraught."

"He's a damn fine doctor," a man my dad's age said from across the waiting room. "I hear they're doing some interview with him this week or next."

Carmen nodded. "They sure are. He deserves the recognition, but knowing Dr. Mitchell, he probably hates the circus around it." She folded her arms, totally chill, and had me intrigued with the man I'd ended up fucking all night in a hotel room.

There was no telling what the good doctor thought of me. He didn't act like our night together—where I knew him as Mitch—was as big of a deal as I thought it was. How in the hell was I so spun out on someone who seemed completely different than the man fixing my father's heart?

There was Mitch, the man who knew his way around my body like he'd created it himself, and then there was Dr. Jacob Mitchell, the man who blew everyone's fucking mind as a renowned surgeon. Both were an equal turn on, and now the pressing question was this: How fucking old was this guy? He'd looked my age, maybe a little older, when I met him. But to be a chief surgeon—and highly skilled one— with the media on his ass?

If I listened to the side of my head that loved fantasy novels, then he was an actual angel, hidden in a human's body, and I had the privilege of meeting both sides of this angel who held my dad's life in his hands. Call it instincts, his steady and humored voice during his in-surgery call, or just my total fascination with him—but I knew dad was in good hands.

Two hours later, the double doors automatically opened to reveal utter hotness in the dark blue scrubs and hat that concealed his probably messed-to-perfection hair. His eyes popped against the navy color he wore, and the light beard growth on his face made his razor-sharp jawline enticing.

"Miss Taylor?" he announced with three others trailing him.

I held back my gawking as I stood. I wasn't going to drool over this man who made scrubs look sexy. I needed answers. "Yes," I said on an inhale.

"Your dad is in recovery. He did extremely well." He smirked. "Though his heart is as stubborn as he seems to be."

"Yes," I answered. "Thank God." I wanted to collapse into his arms and thank this man for saving my dad.

"You'll be admitted to his room once he's moved into the CCU. Other than that, I'll see him in the morning during my rounds."

Carmen called after Dr. Mitchell, and I stood there, watching her walk alongside the tall man as the doors slowly closed to the waiting room after he left. I naturally envied the two blonde intern girls who came into the waiting room with him, and the young man seemed to look at Dr. Mitchell as if he were a god to be worshipped. They all carried looks of pride on their faces, and I could understand why. Working for a doctor like him must've been a dream come true in the medical field.

I slumped down into the waiting room chair and closed my eyes for what seemed to be the first time in the last twenty-four hours, finally relieved this was over, and now Dad had a machine helping his heart do its job.

Chapter Eight

Ash

I hadn't seen Dr. Mitchell since the afternoon of Dad's surgery, but I sincerely wanted to thank this man. The one night of passion I'd shared with him felt entirely in the past now. I was fortunate to have screwed the sexy doctor, but after seeing his non-doctor side, I could probably bet I wasn't the only chick he'd ever fucked without a relationship before. Hell, this entire hospital seemed to be staffed with gorgeous interns and nurses—men and women—and I wouldn't be surprised at all if that's the one thing the girls who worked here and I had in common—screwing Dr. D!

I sipped on my coffee, thinking about the whirlwind of a week this had been. Thank God for Carmen because we learned most patients would be in the hospital up to four days before surgery to prepare for everything. All of the x-rays, heart screening technology—all of it was able to be done with Dad comfortably being transported to the hospital and then sent home. I was still in shock when Dr. Mitchell allowed dad the comfort of home instead of just slapping his stubborn butt in the hospital.

All-in-all, it was done, and now dad had his handy-dandy VAD implant, and Nurse Carmen was paving the way to make it all-too-easy for him to go home after the doctor cleared him in three weeks instead of going to a rehab center. Her sass had better be up for this because dad would fight her, and I would be calling in to have him forced into the rehab center if he tried to slack off after rejecting the idea of a donor's heart.

It was the fifth day after Dad's surgery, and he had finally passed the test to be pulled off the ventilator. They pulled him off after Dr. Mitchell had come to do his rounds last night and saw Dad's lungs progressing well. I never seemed to be able to connect with the doctor since the surgery, though. If I weren't grabbing something from the cafeteria, I'd dozed off in the comfortable chair at Dad's bedside every time he came in.

I had already gone home today, showered and changed, and was back around six-thirty in the morning with the coffee I'd gotten for Carmen and me.

One of the noises coming from the nurses' station alerted me to more people on the floor, and Carmen left to go join in on whatever in the hell was happening outside of Dad's room. It was Friday morning, and this was the only loud noise of any party I was going to get.

"Ash," Dad's hoarse voice called my name.

I looked over at the man who'd been in and out of sleep since they'd pulled him off the breathing machine. "Well, good morning, handsome," I said. "You okay?"

"Throat's killing me, but you look like death." He lazily smiled.

"Thanks for the compliment." I laughed, my hair pulled into a tight bun and still wet from letting it air dry.

"Well, I guess I survived?"

"You're not talking to a ghost." I laughed, knowing Dad was talking to me heavily under the influence of his pain medication. "Dad, rest," I said, waiting for the nurses to come in and fill me in on whatever the doctor was planning with dad.

"Well," Dad said, ignoring me as the curtain opened, "I guess I got the implant."

"You got it, all right."

I went to look away, but then my dad laughed softly, and I looked at him, wondering if the meds were having some weird effect on him that I should be concerned about.

"Imagine that, Ash," he said as the room filled with hospital staff. "I got implant surgery before you!"

My eyes widened. "Dad!" I said with a laugh. "Good lord, go back to sleep—you're stoned."

"That was a good one, Ash," Carmen said.

I turned and smiled at her. "He's out of his mind, and I don't need you co-signing on his stoned, crazy commentary about implants."

That's when the other three in the room laughed. Two of them went straight to Dad's monitors and IVs, and the third was Dr. Mitchell. I smirked at his humored expression and ignored the handsome man standing in his suit with the white smock that pulled the whole sexy doctor ensemble together.

"Well, I see you're back with us and enjoying the good stuff," Dr. Mitchell teased, looking at Dad's monitors and then glancing back down at him.

"I feel incredible," Dad responded.

"That's fantastic. I see that all is working well, but the road to recovery will make you and Carmen best friends by the time this is over."

"She's a beauty, Doc," Dad said.

Dr. Mitchell grinned. "That she is."

"All right, he's loaded," I finally cut in. "Are there any new updates we should be aware of before Dad and you get going down a road that will most likely end up talking about implants and my lack of them?"

Dr. Mitchell's gaze was unreadable, but it seemed like my entire body picked up on what it meant—and in a good way. *Jesus Christ.* He can't stare at me like that—that's the Mitch, all night in the room, look.

"Very well." His face recovered from that devilish grin I saw more than once that night. "Your father will be transported down to our heart recovery floor this afternoon. His biventricular assist is performing well, and his body is accepting it just as I'd like. Have the nurses informed you on what to expect over the next three to four weeks of him being on our heart recovery floor?"

"Yes," I answered as professionally as he was now speaking, "and you will still be checking on him."

"Yes. He's under my care until we turn him over to my middle man," he winked at Carmen, "and my snitch of a nurse." He arched an eyebrow at Dad's embarrassing whistle at the mention of Carmen's name. "She will continue to work with him while he recovers and rehabilitates at home. Any other questions?"

"I'm sure Carmen will help us out with anything I'm forgetting," I said, mortified by Dad's behavior.

"He won't remember any of this," Dr. Mitchell said, my head turning to peer up at him. "Try not to give him too hard of a time when the heavy medication wears off."

"Thank you again for everything, Dr. Mitchell," I said in all sincerity.

"Thank you for trusting my staff and me with your father," he said, and then our eyes locked in a way that sent a shiver down my spine.

It had to have been his looks that were playing these games with my mind and body because it couldn't have been him flirting with me. My wet-hair bun, hoodie, and leggings made me look like a bum who'd taken up residence at St. John's.

"GIRL," CLAY SAID AS HE RUBBED MY BACK IN DAD'S LUXURIOUS suite of a heart recovery room, "you need to get out of here and get some vitamin D."

I looked over at my best guy and smiled as he messed with one of his long braids. The dude was stacked with muscle, mocha skin that made me drool, and a smile that beamed brighter than the sun. He was sharply dressed in his suit from showing some multi-million-dollar home today, and—dare I say it—he probably made the gorgeous doctor envious of him.

"You know I'm not leaving him." I looked over at Dad, who was in a giddy conversation with Carmen as they returned from his short walk out of the room.

"What I know is that you look like hell," he said, then he leaned in. "Although it doesn't seem to bother Dr. Sexy whenever he comes in."

"Please stop bringing that night up." I looked over at Dad from where Clay and I sat on the couch. "My dad cannot find out about it."

Clay rolled his eyes. "I'm going to tell him if you don't take a day off and get out of here."

"Fine." I lied to shut him up, knowing he most likely wouldn't be back with three open houses going on tomorrow. "I'll get out of here tomorrow." I covered a yawn.

"It sounds like I'm missing out on a party in here." Dr. Mitchell's smooth and doctor-ish voice alerted his entrance.

After two weeks in here, the doctor and I were on a communicate about dad's condition only basis—nothing more and nothing less. The worst part was that he was one of the best doctors in the world. Gorgeous or not, it was apparent he cared a lot about his patients, and it was also evident why I was in his hotel room that night.

The man's personal life couldn't exist with the way he seemed to be in a deeper relationship with this hospital, his job, and his patients. Getting laid was an easy thing for him to do—with anyone he picked—and that's probably how he got by. He was his own man, though, and I was just glad he was so attentive to my dad, ensuring he was healthy with his new implant. I couldn't ask for anything more from the man, and in truth, I knew the guy had nothing more to give in a relationship. That was simple to see after the past three weeks.

Their voices drifted off as they always did, Dad and the doctor bantering back and forth while I looked up the dates that I'd missed to enroll in the fall semester at the closest junior college. I still didn't understand how my new job was so understanding of this situation. I could've been made to come back to work, but they told me to take all the time I needed, and thank God. I just couldn't leave my dad. Not right now.

"I'm heading out." I looked over at dad and Carmen, who were watching TV after the doctor left.

"Why don't you rest at home tonight, sweetheart?" he asked.

"I'm not leaving you," I firmly stated.

"Dr. Mitchell said I'm doing fine, but he did mention my poor daughter might be admitted to the hospital soon enough if she didn't get the rest she needed."

"I'm sure he did." I smiled and pulled my purse on my shoulder. "You both tend to find good conversation with me being the butt of both your jokes."

"Go rest at home tonight, Ash," Carmen said with a sympathetic smile. "Take my advice as a nurse and a sixty-year-old woman with firm skin." She winked. "If your dad so much as misses a breath, I'll call you."

"I can't be an hour away, Carmen."

Carmen stood and walked over to me. "If Dr. Mitchell were the slightest concerned about Mark, he'd have him in critical care. Instead, he's recovering in a comfortable hospital bed and room. Are you concerned his heart will fail even after Dr. Mitchell just checked his echoes and new x-rays showing him how well the blood flow is?"

I sighed and looked over at Dad. "You will tell me if anything, I mean anything, happens."

"Yes, *mija*," she said.

"Come on, Ash," Clay insisted. "Let me walk you down."

AFTER SEEING HOW HEALTHY DAD HONESTLY LOOKED, I DECIDED TO go home and pretty much die on the sofa after this insane month. They all laughed when I said to call me in the morning because I knew I wouldn't be waking up if my mind let me rest. I felt myself hitting a wall, and it was happening faster than I could get to my car.

I was so fucking tired, and I should have just stayed and slept on that hospital sofa—that was nicer than ours at home, by the way. I blinked my eyes a few times before my car came into view. Once inside, I closed my eyes, praying for a second wind to help me get home. If not, I was sleeping in the car.

A couple of taps on my window, me wiping the drool from the corner of my mouth, and I jumped when I saw Dr. Mitchell leaning over and peering in at me.

I opened the door, instinctively thinking something was up with Dad. I jumped out of the car—pretty much half awake and paranoid—and ran directly into the man's hard chest.

The leather strap of his briefcase fell off his shoulder, and the case crashed to the ground as he worked to steady my impulsive reaction. I clung to him, feeling like I was a drunken fool.

"Damn," he said, oddly holding me against his chest. "Were you so determined to stay close that you chose to sleep in your car?" he asked as I got my bearings and stepped back from him.

I sighed. "I tried to take everyone's advice and sleep at home tonight." I waved at my yellow Accord. "It looks like I was more tired than I thought."

"I'll say." He smirked. "I heard you mention that you were an hour away; which direction? I can give you a ride. I'm sure you'll want to be back around the time I need to be here in the morning anyway. Six o'clock."

"Yeah, I'm not going that far. I took a nap in the car. I'll head back up to Dad. Thanks though; you've already been helpful enough."

He steadied my shoulders to face him. "Ashley," he said my name like the angel I believed him to be, "you're not driving home, and you're not going back into that hospital until you receive the proper amount of rest."

"You're not my doctor," I countered, tired as fuck.

"No, but I am a doctor, and I can tell you that if you don't allow me to help you, you can't help your dad either. Not in this condition," he said.

"I'm not going to my house. It's too far away." I started crying, and that's when I collapsed into the man's arms—sobbing all over his expensive suit. I was defeated, tired, and it had to have been the last few months of stressful events that led me to this embarrassing display.

I felt his hand massage along my back, and it was more soothing than the sleep I desperately needed. "You're coming with me," he said sternly. "I have a place that's twenty minutes from the hospital."

"You don't even know me," I cracked in response. "Why would you offer something like that to a stranger?"

"Fine, then. Where are the keys to your car?" he asked.

"Inside it."

He reached in the car, grabbed my purse and keys, locked it up, and pulled his bag back on his shoulder. He looked at me with some calculating look, and then I was in his arms.

"What the hell are you doing?" I nearly screeched.

"Handling this matter the easy way," he answered. "If you're not comfortable with staying at my place, then I will take you to a hotel just as nice."

"Goddammit," I said in frustration.

"Relax," he said. "Compliments of the medical group."

We were in a sleek, black sports car, the leather smelling just as luxurious as his cologne. I couldn't believe I was in the man's car, being shuttled to a hotel, and leaving my dad behind.

"Your dad is doing exceptionally well," he said, revving the engine, shifting gears, and switching lanes. "You, on the other hand, will join him if you don't allow your body better rest."

"Somehow, I feel like I'm keeping the same hours as you."

He looked over at me and smirked. "I'm a bit more conditioned for the job. I do, however, eat well, and sleep in my own bed—or at least a bed—and not a sofa."

"How do I get back in the morning? Does the hotel have a shuttle?"

"I'll pick you up," he stated.

"What if something happens to my dad while I'm gone? My car is at the hospital."

"Which is why you might want to take me up on my original offer to stay at my place. The house is large enough, and you wouldn't even know I was there."

"Again, why would you offer that to a stranger? Your patient's daughter?"

He pulled the car into a large parking area that led to a massive hotel. A valet came to his door, and one to open mine. The next thing I knew, I was sitting in a luxurious hotel lounge area, and he was at the alcove where the hotel attendant was helping him.

He turned back to me and motioned for me to stand. I did, but not without noticing that look again in his eye. He may have held a somber, pissed-off expression of determination, but he also had the sexy glint in his ocean-blue eyes.

We remained silent until a butler or some dressed-to-impress hotel personnel nodded as he opened the door to the room. I walked into another suite—one that was almost as impressive as the one in San Francisco—while he stayed back with the attendant.

"A hot meal is on its way up, and you will eat it," he ordered in a humorous tone. "I hope you approve of this room. I know it's not the splendor of the hospital room that you can't seem to shake, but it should work for the night."

"I don't know why you're doing this," I said, blown away by the gesture.

"You keep saying you're a stranger," he said, setting his keys, phone, and briefcase on the counter. "You might feel that way about me, but I certainly don't feel that way about you, Ash," he said, his eyes dark.

"Because I live at your hospital?"

He smiled. "Perhaps it's because a year ago, I met this woman I haven't been able to remove from my thoughts." He ran a hand through his hair. "I may be a stranger to you, only because I introduced myself to you that night as Mitch."

Everything woke up in me right then and there. "And do you remember all of that?" I cringed.

He laughed. "I can't imagine how you feel, knowing who I am after that night."

"Honestly?"

He rolled his bottom lip between his teeth. "Honestly," he finally said.

"I think you were amazing that night, and this," I waved my hand over at where he stood, hand planted on the bar area, "this person who saved my dad's life and blows my mind as a doctor?" I laughed. "You are quite the catch."

He arched his eyebrow at me. "Why did we not have the start of this conversation weeks ago?"

"My dad was dying?" I shrugged my shoulders, more relaxed now, knowing that if something serious did happen to Dad, I was with his guard dog.

"You should have come to my house," he stated.

"I have something crazy to ask you," I said, knowing I was off-topic again, thinking about dad.

"Crazy?"

"Not like that," I reassured him. "I know you spent the money to reserve this oversized room, I would probably go back to your place, but we're already here..."

What the hell, how did I ask him this?

"I would love to stay with you if it makes you more comfortable, and then you can eat and rest."

I decided to play with his gorgeous expression. "What if I wanted you to hold me in your arms all night?"

He grinned and stood up. "That would cost you," he said with a laugh, walking over to the phone, "and you don't have the energy for that." He winked as he picked up the phone and spoke into the receiver. "Yes, it's Jacob Mitchell in the presidential." He nodded, "Right, I'm going to need a driver to run by my office and pick up my wardrobe bag. I'll call security to help escort them in." He licked his lips, me watching everything as if I did fall asleep in the car and dreamt this all into reality. "Right, thanks." He turned to me. "Good to go. Now, do you need me to help you with the shower? Perhaps we relive our night in San Francisco?"

I smiled at him. "I will kick your ass if you make me do something as stupid as falling for my dad's doctor—or any doctor for that matter." I turned to get in the shower.

"You might want this robe," he offered as I headed down the hallway to the left. "I have clothes coming up from the boutique downstairs as well."

"I might want to eat chocolate-covered strawberries naked too."

"That's the sleep deprivation talking," he said with a laugh.

I stepped into the bathroom and let the state-of-the-art shower soothe me to my core.

Chapter Nine

Ash

I woke up having no idea where the hell I was or how I got into this bed. I shot up in a panic as last night came to me slowly. Dr. Mitchell found me drooling and asleep in my car and brought me here to be closer to Dad. *Right!*

With the energy that had returned after I'd passed out on this glorious bed, I stood up and remembered Dr. Mitchell had honored my request by staying in the mini-apartment hotel room with me.

I didn't recall us going into much detail, other than he remembered me from our all-night sex fest in his room in Frisco. That was it. I knew I should have been thrilled to know I made some kind of impression that lasted with the doctor, but I was too tired to care.

I ate alone while he took a phone call in the other room. I didn't care about that, though. The food was delicious, and the meal had helped add to the great night of sleep I'd had for the first time in a month.

I slept in silk pajamas that were sent up at the request of the doctor. The long-sleeved shirt and pants were made from the softest material I'd ever felt—and that's even after being dragged through the finest stores with Clay when he was shopping for himself.

So excited to feel refreshed and rejuvenated, I jumped in the shower to get my day going without a second thought. The more my mind woke up, a knot formed in my stomach. *Fuck, I didn't check my phone for missed calls or the time!*

I rushed through soaping up, shampooing my hair, rinsing, and getting the hell out of this mindset that freed me from the fear and responsibility of Dad.

I ran with a towel in my hair and one wrapped around my body, fumbling around the room looking for my phone. I found it on the nightstand being charged—I most definitely did not put it there. I flipped through the phone, no missed calls, and one new text from Carmen.

Carmen: *Your dad is doing great this morning. He already had his breakfast and did breathing and walked much better than yesterday. He said to take your time getting ready, and he'll show off for you when you get here—his words, not mine.*

I WENT TO TEXT BACK, BUT MY BLOOD WAS BOILING. IT WAS EIGHT o'clock in the goddamn morning. That asshole left me here! Fuck him.

I clicked on Carmen's name, my phone dialing out.

She'd better answer, I thought, chewing on my thumbnail.

"Hey, *mija*!" she answered in her peppy voice. "You sleep well?"

"Carmen," I nearly growled into the phone. "Why didn't anyone call me? And why did your text come through fifteen fucking minutes ago?"

"Hey, now! You'd better put a lid on that tone with me," she snapped back at my aggression before calmly continuing. "You needed the rest. After Dr. Mitchell saw your dad this morning, even *he* said you needed food and rest. He found you asleep in your car. You try explaining to me how this is healthy for you or your dad?"

I ignored the lecture. "Dr. Mitchell was already there this morning?"

"Yes," her voice was stern and solid against my furious tone, "and on his weekend off when he typically allows Dr. Chi to care for his patients in his absence."

"I don't—" The door latch clicked. He must be back. "I have to go. I'll catch an Uber and see you in a few."

"You need to relax, Ashley. Your dad is happy and relieved that you got some rest after Dr. Mitchell told him you'd been checked into a lovely hotel room. Don't work up his blood pressure because of this unnecessary guilt you are carrying around. Everyone has both of your best interests at heart. Remember that."

"Fine. And thank you," I said before ending the call.

"Dr. Mitchell?" I asked, storming into the living room area of the hotel suite.

"Right here..." Our eyes met, and his went directly to the towel wrapped around my body.

I crossed my arms around the towel. "Is there a reason you took off to the hospital without me?" I questioned, trying not to be entranced by his pristine suit and gorgeous face.

"Yes, I went to work. You were sound asleep. I also assumed you would appreciate the full rest you were able to receive after all you've been through," he stammered.

"That's lovely for you to assume," I said, not wavering. "I thought the entire reason for you putting me up here, you staying here with me —it was for your help to keep me close and get me back to Dad first thing this morning."

His face grew stern. "I understand that you desire to be with your father at every waking moment; however, if you didn't get as much rest as you did, trust me, you'd create more stress for the man when he learned you were admitted to one of our floor units."

"Don't pull that shit on me." I tried to counter his possible truth. "I can't leave him," I said, sorrow and guilt. "My God, you don't understand."

"Being in this line of work, I do understand that the family member of a patient can become ill with concern and guilt about not being with their family. It is why we advise other family members to help with that burden. In your case, Carmen has filled the gap of your family. Your uncle and aunt, I believe it was, informed me that their work and distance from the hospital would not make it possible for them to help your father and you. Carmen has volunteered to be there for as long as you and your father need while he recovers in the hospital."

I exhaled. "Fuck my uncle and aunt," I said in anger.

"Ashley," Dr. Mitchell said, walking toward me as I held out a hand out to stop him from closing the gap between us. "I'm no therapist, but I can easily see where concern over an issue that is no longer severe is not healthy."

"Who are you to judge how I handle my issues," I snapped.

"I'm not judging you. I'm genuinely concerned about your health, and now your stress concerning your father. As I said before, you are not helping him by slowly deteriorating in your health."

"My God." I covered my eyes. "I get it," I said, choking back tears, unsure why I was fighting with this man. "You see things on the surface. You have no idea what I've been through." I walked over and sat on the sofa, crying into my hands.

I was officially having a nervous breakdown in the company of a man I didn't even know. *Shit!* I couldn't pull it together, either. The burden of everything had been too much. My mother, the long-ass process of watching cancer eat her to nothing? I'd put my life on hold, unable to think about anything but helping and praying for a cure. That never happened. The funeral, the arrangements, the grief, Dad crying himself to sleep—all of it was slamming down on me right here and right now.

And now, my dad's life was on the line. I never want to relive the dread I felt as I watched him have his heart attack. The ambulance couldn't get to my gallery fast enough, and if another patron hadn't had aspirin on a fluke, Dad probably would've died. I was paralyzed as he received CPR, thinking I would lose him that fast, and now I was terrified it could happen again at any time.

"If I lose him..." I sobbed. "My mom was taken from me, what makes me think that seeing my dad's brush with death won't be his last?"

"I'm so desperately sorry for your grief," he said as he sat next to me and ran a warm hand over my back. "I will tell you with absolute certainty that your father is doing exceptionally well. I can safely say that if you're afraid for his life at this point, there is no need."

I looked at him in disbelief. "So, he magically doesn't need the transplant?"

"I didn't say that," he answered, eyes severe as they stared into mine. "The machine assisting his heart is helping him quite well."

I inhaled, my eyes not leaving his. "How long? How long until his enlarged and dying heart finally gives out, even with that machine?"

"I told you already," he answered. "He can live well for at least two years. Worst case, of which I will be monitoring, one year."

"Then I'm right back to where I was when my mom's cancer came back." I looked away from him, tears betraying me. "Fuck," I choked out. "I can't do this again."

"Is there a chance—"

"No," I stood and went to walk away. "He won't even have the conversation about the transplant." I sighed. "I need to get back to him."

"I'll drive you," he said.

I stopped and looked at his somber expression. "I'll call an Uber. Carmen already told me it's your weekend off. Please, enjoy it. You're a remarkable doctor, and trust me, I appreciate your help, but as you can tell, I'm in no position to appreciate anything fully right now."

Fifteen minutes after my meltdown, I walked out of the bathroom ready to leave for the hospital. I dressed in my clothes that Dr. Mitchell had laundered, my hair wrapped up in a tight, wet bun. Upon entering the living area of the hotel room, I heard Dr. Mitchell on the phone in the other room. The guy was a busy man. I didn't have time to apologize, and so I escaped from the room as quickly as I could.

I was in a jacked-up frame of mind, and Carmen sounded like she would chew my ass out if I showed up at the hospital ready to blame anyone because I slept too well. The Uber was at the hotel waiting, having sent for it right after leaving Dr. Mitchell in the room, staring at me like I was a crazy woman.

When I got to Dad's room, he was sleeping, and I sighed in relief that I was back. I looked over at Carmen as she walked over to where I sat on the sofa in the room.

She placed her hand over my shoulder. "You can't do this to yourself. The guilt, the worry, and the shame." She shook her head.

"How would you know that's what I'm doing?" I asked. "I can't lose him like I lost my mother."

"No, you can't, and you won't," she said. "But you also can't carry your mother's death around like this. It's not healthy. You will end up sick. It's not good for you or your father. It's not fair to either one of you."

I started tearing up, frustrated that I couldn't shake mom's death and just move forward. "I don't know what to do," I cried. "I thought I'd grieved her death, and then it all came back when I almost lost him."

"You are stuck in an unhealthy stage of grief," she said sadly. "You have yet to accept her death to heal from it."

"I can't just accept her death. I never will. She was stolen from me, and now I—" I waved my hand over at Dad, tears streaming down my face. "Now, I have to look at him like this and be reminded that he was almost stolen from me too?"

"He wasn't stolen, was he?" she said calmly. "He's still with you, *mija*. And it's not every day that the best surgeon in the world is the one who cares for him now. You are blessed in many ways with Dr. Mitchell and your dad's strong will to be with you. He's a survivor." She frowned and ran her hand over my hair. "Though you aren't acting like you are."

"I just want it to be over and everyone safe."

"In time." She smiled. "But if you don't start living your life for *you*, you will be in worse shape than your dad."

"I don't know how. I'm scared to lose him, to leave him."

"Because that is your only focus," she said. "You must find a distraction. We will work on it together. I will help you." She softly slapped my leg. "And I will help your dad."

"You don't have to take on our burdens, Carmen. You're doing so much already."

She smiled. "You have good souls, you and your dad. You are good people, and I like to help good people. It's why I do what I do." She stood, hearing shuffling outside of the room. "We will work to make you happy and healthy again." She looked at the curtain. "I'll be back. Your dad will be waking up soon."

I sat there, not knowing what to say to Carmen. She was a guardian angel, so much more than only an in-home health nurse. She and Dr. Mitchell were both God-sends to Dad and me. I just wished I could stop with these toxic feelings of worrying about dad.

I had to get my shit together, or all I'd be doing was reversing the work Dr. Mitchell did to save Dad, the work Carmen was doing to help him recover...all of it. I couldn't be the thorn in everyone's side.

Here I sat, knowing I'd walked out on Dr. Mitchell's ridiculous generosity like a crazy bitch. Jesus Christ, I could never face that man again. I couldn't imagine what the man thought of me now.

I didn't want to know. I wanted to find my happiness and free spirit again. I had to hope I could, or I was seriously fucked. The way Carmen spoke, I had a feeling she'd make sure I took care of myself. It didn't seem like she'd have it any other way.

Chapter Ten

Ash

After a month of being on edge, my nerves had calmed to a point where I wasn't in this obsessed and, as Carmen had noted, extremely unhealthy attachment to Dad's heart illness. I got my butt back to work. I needed it, and everyone around me needed it.

Dr. Mitchell's words haunted me, but I'd fucked everything up with him that day. After being insistent on not taking his help in getting back to Dad, and going off on him for what was just anger toward myself, I never wanted to face that man again. I was a total idiot, and still, the man was amazing toward Dad. Dad and Carmen saw him once a week, and there were times when Dr. Mitchell would even call to check in between his office patients. He truly was the best guy for Dad's condition, and I slapped him in the face for it.

I hadn't seen him since that day, letting Carmen accompany Dad to his doctor's appointments instead. Carmen and I'd had a lot of fun discussions about her childhood, growing up in Mexico, her family, and her life. She was a fascinating woman, and I started to take note of a more intimate bond she was sharing with Dad. I hadn't seen him this happy in far too long. She gave him his youth back—if not physically, mentally. I loved listening to them interact, and I truly loved her care for both of us. I swear to God that if Carmen wasn't in our lives, I'd need a therapist.

With her encouragement, I was able to return to work. It had been a month of impressive sales for the gallery, and I couldn't be more excited to return to my passion for painting and sculpting again. I'd been painting out in our garage, letting the brush strokes against the canvas fuel me into bringing any ocean inspiration to life. Lately, I found myself obsessed with the ocean—the waves, the surf, sand, all of it. The pastels were my favorite recently, and who knew, maybe one day, I'd finally have the guts to open my own gallery like the one I was working for and share my art with anyone who could appreciate it.

I walked around the floor and saw two men staring at a famous ocean print. This section was my absolute favorite, and mostly where I was inspired to find the serenity of painting the majesty and beauty of the vast sea realm.

"A million-and-a-half, and there aren't even any waves, not to mention turtles," I heard a man's voice scoff in humor.

The two tall men stood in the usual expensive suits that typically graced this fancy gallery. Both were dark-haired, and from standing behind them, facing the one portrait I loved most, I could tell they were easily attractive, but spoiled rich boys. Yes, we had plenty of those—those and the pretentious snobs who stared down their noses at everyone else.

"That's one of my favorite portraits," I said, not looking at their reaction. I waved my fingers over the brush strokes. "It's the craft and talent in the brushstroke that captures multiple colors against the canvas. It's abstract, yes; however, this artist has a way with his brush that brings the image he sees in his mind alive."

"And the reason brush strokes on canvas are worth over a million bucks?"

My heart leapt into my throat when I realized the voice belonged to Dr. Mitchell. *Holy fucking hell.*

I dared to look at the two men. One of them was smiling, and he could have been Dr. Mitchell's twin, except for the green eyes and cleft in his chin. His hair was longer, though, and in a wavy style of authority, and Dr. Mitchell's was the still the short and sexy messed-too-perfection style.

"It's not just the strokes," I said, shuffling for an answer after my mind went blank.

He came back with the Mitch I knew in San Francisco look. The smirk, glint in his eyes, and his hands sliding confidently into his pockets.

"I disagree." He arched his eyebrow at me. "I feel that if it's going to cost me a million bucks for some strokes, it'd better be something I want to see every day for the rest of my life."

His friend—twin—brother?—looked at him. "Can we please focus, Jake?" he asked in annoyance and looked at me. "Sorry about him."

Goddamn, there are two sexy gods in this room together?

"Don't worry." I smiled at the guy. "I'm Ashley," I said, seeing the man's eyes widen as if I had just spilled a drink on him.

He recovered the look of shock. "Ashley." He nodded. "Because my brother has insulted one of your favorite pieces, I'll buy this one for his home and continue to search for another for mine."

"James!" My lively boss clicked her heels as she scurried over to where we were. "James Mitchell, I thought I'd never see you come into my gallery."

"Excuse me." He nodded. "Nice to meet you, Ashley. Perhaps Lillian can point me in a direction with darker colors, fewer pastels?"

"Ashley can tend to your brother." She smiled at the doctor. "Dr. Mitchell." She nodded and said with a flirty voice, "Nice to see you again."

"Wish the feeling were mutual." He chuckled.

"Where are the more current pieces?" James asked my boss.

"Right through this hall. I have those I was texting you about..." their voices trailed off while I was left to stare in awe into his ocean-blue eyes.

"How are you and your father faring?" he asked.

"Listen," I said, taking his arm and pulling him to the side. "I don't even know where to begin to apologize for everything I did that morning in the hotel. To sincerely thank you for everything you did and continue to do for my father. I was horrible, and I'm so sorry."

"She begs my forgiveness?" He looked down into my eyes.

"I'm serious," I said.

"I am too," he responded.

"I just want to clear it up. I'm truly sorry. I don't know how else to tell you how apologetic I am."

"Date me," he said.

"What?"

"Let me take you out. I want to meet Ashley Taylor for real and have a normal interaction with her," he said and then reached his hand out to mine. "My name is Jacob. Most call me Jake."

I laughed, placing my hand in his firm, yet soft one. "I'm Ashley. Most call me Ash."

"Someone mentioned that it was Annie...something or other?" He arched an eyebrow at me.

"Someone mentioned your name was Mitch?" I lifted my chin.

"Mitch?" He chuckled. "That would be some douche bag who made the biggest mistake of his life."

"Oh?" I played along. "How so?"

"He let the most beautiful woman he'd ever met go—one who, he mentioned, was the best sex of his life."

"Wow," I said, my heart racing. "That sucks for him."

"Rumor has it, he hasn't gotten that night out of his mind in over a year, and trying to has fucked him over more than once."

"Damn." I covered my mouth.

"Yep." He sighed dramatically, then smiled. "That date, I will get on my knees here and now and beg you for it if you'd like."

I laughed at his silliness. "Shut up. I'd love to. Carmen will be happy to learn I've actually gone out with someone since being back to work."

"She's mentioned that to me."

"Breaking the doctor-patient relationship, eh?"

"You made it clear I wasn't your doctor," he countered. "What can I say? I was worried about you. I asked my favorite nurse how you were doing—it seems she and I both agreed that you needed to move forward." He smiled, and now my insides were going crazy for this man like they did in San Francisco. "You're doing a fantastic job of that. Now, I must ask, what has you working for the most ridiculous bitch in her art gallery?"

"I needed the money?" I laughed, knowing he was right, but Lillian also was more than understanding about Dad in the hospital too. "She also held my job for me while Dad was sick. Also, I love the artists who have work on display here."

"Interesting," he said. "And so, she loves art."

"It's my passion," I answered.

"Perhaps you'll be quite thrilled when you see your favorite portrait hanging on my wall, courtesy of my brother, of course."

"Is this another invitation to your home, Doctor?"

"Jake," he corrected me, "and yes. Actually, if you desire to see the print again, you'll have to be lying on my bed."

I laughed and rolled my eyes. "Lying on your bed?"

"Yeah, to ensure the million-dollar strokes are on display in an ideal fashion."

"You've lost it." I laughed, hearing my boss and his brother coming back.

He licked his lips. "I'll get your cell number from Carmen; are you okay with that?"

"That's fine."

"We'll arrange something then. What time are you out of here?"

"Tonight?"

"Indefinitely," he said with a sigh. "Of course, tonight."

"Five."

"You comfortable with me picking you up tonight?" he asked.

"Um, my—"

"I'll swing you by your house. We'll check on your father together, and then perhaps I can have the rest of the night with you."

"You think of everything, don't you?"

"I've had nothing else to think about other than trying to see you again." He went to step away. "I do hope you aren't working tomorrow either. I have the entire day off and would love to have you wake up in my arms—this time, I'm not letting you leave like before."

Chills covered my body, and I stood there in shock that this was happening again. Seriously, what the hell did I do to gain this man's attention? I watched as he and his brother walked out of the front atrium and disappeared outside. Both men commanded the area. It was like, together, they could run the country or something.

I had to thank Carmen for this freedom. Something also told me I had to thank Jake too. All I knew for sure was that if he kept looking at me tonight the way he did just now, I might just have to wake up in his arms and see just how my day off tomorrow would work out.

Chapter Eleven

Jake

I contemplated at least a million and a half different ways I could take Ashley on a date. I hadn't done the dating thing for years, and even when I did, I didn't feel this particular way about the woman I was taking out. I couldn't explain the draw I had toward her, but I wasn't going to fight it.

For more than a month, I'd watched her—a different side of the woman I'd met over a year ago—care for her father in a highly admirable way. From what I'd gathered on the few interactions I'd had with her since her father had his surgery, she was responsible, and it was apparent she'd put her life on hold for him.

Carmen was a saint for taking me up on caring for Mr. Taylor. I was thrilled to see Ashley, her dad, and Carmen connect on an entirely different level than I had anticipated when I offered to pay for Carmen to handle the in-home healthcare. Hell, I enjoyed Mark more than most of my patients. The man was direct and stubborn, yes, but he and I had built a unique relationship outside of what I expected. Perhaps it was my internal feelings of desiring more than just a one-night-stand with his daughter? Who knew? What I did know was that if he found out about that shit, he'd probably kick my ass, even with his heart condition.

Shit. I had to think. I had an hour until Ashley was off work, and I had made reservations close to my place in the Hollywood Hills in case she felt more comfortable there and closer to her dad. I didn't think she was still allowing her fear of losing him at any second to continue to rule what she did, but I hadn't talked to her since that morning I'd let her sleep in at the hotel. I would have preferred the retreat of my beach house in Malibu, which is also the place that her favorite portrait was delivered and received by my housemaid, but that place was more than an hour away, and I wasn't sure she'd be okay going that far. I hoped that she would be, though, so I had also made reservations at *The Penthouse* where seafood would be on the menu.

I strummed my fingers on the steering wheel of my car, stuck in traffic, and eying the clock to find I had about thirty minutes until she was off. My mind was all over the place, trying to make this a comfortable night out, and I knew I was overthinking all of it.

I'd called Mr. Taylor and was thrown onto speakerphone with Carmen's shrill of delight that I was taking Ashley out for the evening, and that settled my nerves more, but both were zero help in the dating department. They practically begged me to take Ashley off to a retreat to give her a break.

Thank God, Mr. Taylor thought well enough of me to say, *"Don't bring her home until Sunday!"* Having gotten to know Mr. Taylor on a more candid level, I knew that he was half-joking and half-serious.

Now to pick her up and hope I survived this date without making a jackass out of myself. I swear to God that I felt like I couldn't think around the woman.

"Shit, her car!" I said to myself, gripping the steering wheel and switching lanes where I found a hole in the traffic and accelerated to a piping-hot thirty miles an hour.

I used the car phone to dial out.

"What's up?" Collin said, answering with a laugh. "Wait," he laughed again, "you don't even have to say it. I know you're wondering whether or not I forgot to get Ashley's car."

"You finished?" I sighed. "And yes, I thought you'd have already picked it up and dropped it at my house by now."

"The pad, right?" he asked, using the term everyone referred to the Hollywood Hills house as.

"Yes," I said. "Have you dropped it off yet? Ashley said she was cool with you getting it when I texted her."

I heard him and a woman laugh. "I'm on my way there now."

"You're supposed to be at the thing with my brother in less than an hour," I mentioned in confusion.

"That I already know, brother," he answered. "It's why I'm in my car and not taking the Uber you suggested. I've got Katie with me, and she'll drive Ashley's car while she follows me to your place."

My lips twisted. *Who the fuck is Katie?*

"Katie can drive your piece of shit. You're driving Ashley's car," I said.

"I'm in the Lambo, man. Sorry, but no one drives this car," he answered.

"Collin," I said, not wanting a shit show to blow up over the damn car, but I told Ashley it would be Collin driving the vehicle, not some chick he picked up to wear as his arm candy at my brother's get together.

"No one drives this car," he said while I shuffled my thoughts.

"Katie, is it?" I questioned, jumping over Collin's commands about his car.

"Yes, here."

Good, I could tell I was on the car phone, and it was half the reason I wasn't calling my best friend out for throwing someone I didn't know in Ashley's car.

"You know how to drive a stick?" I asked, internally praying she did.

"Yes," she responded in a low, questioning voice.

"Do you think you can handle the horsepower of that car you're in?" I asked with a smile, knowing that Collin couldn't be a dick, and he'd put me in worse positions than the one I'd just thrown him into.

"Um, yeah." She sighed. "I'm just not sure—"

"Collin's cool with it," I answered for my silent and most assuredly pissed-off best friend. "Collin, take the side streets through the hills to the house."

"Jacob-fucking-Mitchell," his voice rang through my car in a pissed-but-humored tone. I could tell he was off the speaker, and I was talking to him alone. "You are an ass who owes me, number one. Number two, I'm in the parking lot to the gallery, staring at a Honda Accord that's oxidized so much the FBI couldn't figure out the factory color. What the fuck are you even asking of me?"

"To be my friend and take care of Ashley's car for her."

"You call my car a piece of shit, yet, I believe that's exactly what I'm looking at. Tell me again why I'm trusting a woman I met last night with my hundred-thousand-dollar car?"

"Because I'll buy you a new goddamn car if it gets a scratch," I answered, shifting gears and taking off after the traffic broke and the freeway opened up.

"You're willing to buy me a new Lamborghini if mine gets scratched, and the car you're asking me to take care of looks like it should be on the cover of *Rust-Bucket Weekly*." He laughed at his joke. "Shit, man, you *like* this chick, don't you?"

"Hey," I heard Ashley's voice through Collin's phone. "Are you Collin?"

"Yes, and you're Ashley?" he answered her. "Hey, Jake, talk to you later."

The line went dead, and I had a feeling Collin was using his smooth tactics with Ashley to let a complete stranger drive her car.

Goddammit. Please don't fuck this up, Collin.

I dialed Ashley, and it went to voicemail as I was getting off at the exit for the gallery. Instantly, she rang me back.

"Hey," I said.

"Hey there. So, your friend just took off in my car, and I guess he's taking it back to your place, eh?"

"Yeah, you cool with that? I should have asked."

"I don't care." She laughed, and the weird anxiety I let build up over this melted away.

I pulled into the parking lot, catching her just before she went back into the gallery. I rolled my window down after hitting *end* on the call.

"Hey, sexy," I said, prompting her to turn back to me in the car. "Can you save me the trouble of interacting with your annoying boss and text her that you're leaving ten minutes early?"

She laughed me off as I expected. "How about you wait for ten minutes, either out here or in the gallery?"

"Is the bitch still in there?"

Her face twisted up into the most adorable grin, her eyes sparkling radiantly. "May I ask why you have a problem with her? Your brother seemed to like her just fine," she stated.

I rolled my eyes. "One day, my brother will figure out why the woman is his friend."

She went to walk away. "Ah, interesting," she said, and then offered me a flirty wink that I wasn't expecting.

My breath hitched, and I felt like a teenager, not a fucking heart surgeon when my body reacted to a gesture that gave me hope that she was as excited as I was for this night.

After parking the car and pulling up my reservations, Ashley walked out. I stepped out of the car and walked over to her door, "So what shall it be?" I smiled at her as she slipped into my front seat, looking up at me, "Surf or turf for dinner?"

She smoothed the short red skirt over her thighs. "I love seafood."

"Then it's the beach for the woman I finally can have more than three minutes' worth of a conversation with."

"The beach it is," she said as she pulled the seatbelt across her.

Well, shit, I might pull this whole thing off after all. Ashley was smart, and if she lived in Burbank, the beach was about an hour away. If that idea bothered her, I know I would've seen that panicked look in her stunning chocolate eyes. Carmen was right when I inquired about Ashley yesterday at their appointment. The woman was putting herself in a healthier state and starting to live again outside of her father's situation. Carmen's smirk told me that she'd been hard at work and had seemed to have gotten through to Ashley. Now it was my turn to ensure Ashley had a fantastic night away, and the table I'd reserved on the patio overlooking the ocean was a superb start.

Chapter Twelve

Jake

I brushed my hand over Ashley's lower back, guiding her toward the table with the perfect view overlooking the ocean. I opted for the indoor corner seat next to the glass windows that gave us privacy from the other patrons in the restaurant to keep the distractions from the wind and other elements at bay.

The waiter led us to our table, which had the fine wine I'd requested already sitting in ice, while bread, cheeses, and other novelty delicacies were prepared for us on the table. After we sat, I nodded toward the waiter, thanking him for pouring the wine and leaving us with the menus.

"Oh, my God." Ashley's eyes and smile were wide as she glanced around the room. "Well, this is yet another new side of you I haven't met."

I draped my napkin over my left knee and took a sip of my wine. "I believe this is a side of me that *I* haven't even met." I winked at her playful expression.

"Really?" She arched a brow, and if she kept running her hands over her skirt, I was going to lose all self-control. "So, how is it that you and I have never met this man? Perhaps he has a name?"

"Very funny." I smirked, offering her a small dish for her to choose from pretty much every delicacy I had requested off the menu before we arrived. "Let's keep it at Jake, though." I raised my glass toward her. "I haven't been able to remove from my mind the glorious sound of the name Mitch coming from you either."

She sipped her wine, cheeks tinting red, and eyes diverting to the sparkling sea that the sun was slowly working its way to dip behind. Goddamn, this woman was beautiful, and I was lost as I watched her eyes change from what seemed to be embarrassed into a fascination with the water.

"Does the lovely lady approve?" I finally asked, knowing if I continued to stare any longer, I'd be transitioning from this man who was enjoying a moment with a woman he was interested in and into a hungry beast who wanted to relive every moment of that night in the hotel in San Francisco.

"The lady does approve," she flirted back, and I was about to down this glass of wine like a scotch if I wasn't careful. "This view." She leaned over to glance at the ocean. "I love views like this. I wish I could memorize them and paint them just as I'm experiencing them."

"Isn't that what cameras are for?" I teased.

Her radiant expression turned back toward me. "No. Well, yes, but no."

I chuckled. "Damn. If I thought like that while performing a surgery, I'm fairly confident my patients wouldn't trust me with their lives."

I went to pull the menu and start making suggestions of the finest seafood at this restaurant, but both Ashley and I were caught with a flash of light—practically in my face. I blinked a few times and then noticed it wasn't just an idiot with his cell phone taking one picture from over Ashley's shoulder, it was a goddamn mob.

"Can I help you?" I asked while Ashley recoiled to what seemed to be the entire restaurant pulling out phones to take our picture. What the fuck? Did I just summon the whole restaurant to take a picture of Ashley's view for her?

"What's happening?" Ashley asked with a nervous laugh, rightfully covering her face with her menu.

"We're getting the hell out of here. Jesus Christ!" I said, pulling her in close to me while she ducked behind her purse.

We looked like a ridiculous, unprepared couple who was getting blasted by the fucking paparazzi. I was trying not to trip over the feet of patrons who were interested in what the hell just broke out to ruin their fine-dining experience, and Ashley almost was shoved into a table twice. I couldn't do anything but get us both the hell out of here.

"Holy shit!" Ashley laughed after a waitress opened a side door for us to exit through.

"Follow me. I have no idea what is going on, but we will rectify this situation with you, Dr. Mitchell," she said.

"Your name?" I asked, making sure her efforts didn't go unnoticed after we got flash-mobbed by the cell phone camera crew.

"Jennifer, sir," she said, rushing us through the stairs and hallways. "Which car is yours?"

"The black Bugatti," I answered, looking for where the valet parked my car. "Over there in the corner."

"I'll get your keys and then use that side exit. I just started my shift and wondered what celebrity came in here without sending word ahead so we could ensure they weren't disrupted while eating."

"Hold up," I said, my tone annoyed. "First of all, I'm not a celebrity, and second of all, I am shocked that a restaurant such as this would require anyone to call ahead to ensure they had a private meal." She stared at me after getting the keys from the valet that ran out to meet us. "Forget it," I said, too pissed to talk. "You mentioned you believed a celebrity was here? Is that because there's a situation out front that I need to avoid?"

She nodded, and her blue eyes locked with mine. "Yeah." She exhaled. "I know this sounds horrible," she said to me as I stood there, holding Ashley's hand, instinctively keeping her close to me after our bizarre escape, "but can I get your girlfriend to take a picture of you and me before you leave?"

What the mother fuck? "You know what?" I forced a smile and loosened my suddenly tight grip around Ashley's hand. "Any other time would be great; however, I should like to leave and find a location where this chaos is not interrupting my meal."

"Maybe next time," she said, diverting her eyes. "Sorry."

"Thank you for helping us out," I said, taking my keys and marching with Ashley toward the car.

"Fucking unreal," I said. "I'll make this up to you. I just need to get us out of here first."

Jesus Christ. Did another fucking article come out that had more to do with my eligible bachelor status than my work at St. John's? Why was this happening again? I had to call Jim. I had no idea what happened to bring this on—tonight of all nights.

Ashley rushed to the passenger's side of the car as soon as we heard voices coming from outside the garage. I fired up the engine, and the low growl of my vehicle that loved top speeds was about to get exactly what it was asking for.

"Hang on," I said, navigating through the covered parking lot toward the side exit. *Shit. No-go.* The damn thing was blocked off as another entryway, and not the exit.

"Didn't she say this way was the way out?" Ashley said, glancing around.

"Looks like we get to go out front. I'm so sorry about this and everything I'm about to say until we get the hell out of here."

Ashley laughed. "Well, I've heard you growl out the word fuck before."

I looked over at her smiling face. "What?" I said with a laugh.

"Yeah, I haven't forgotten my favorite sounds coming out of your mouth that night, either. So, I guess I'm riding with Mitch now?"

Good God, the things this woman does to me, and she's not even trying. "Well, you're at least going to hear me say the word fuck like it's the only word in my vocabulary if I can't get us out of here without anyone trailing us."

"High speeds, eh?" she taunted in a sultry voice. "Let's do this."

Thank God she was living fearless and free because after pulling out of the parking structure, I was dumbfounded by what was happening. I ignored the crowds of people like we were on the red carpet in the car and maneuvered through them. Once we were on Highway One, I glanced up at my rearview, seeing two cars that seemed to be pursuing us. *What the fuck is going on,* I thought as I looked over my shoulder and downshifted to give the vehicle the gear it needed to lose the bastards.

"Shut up!" Ashley squealed, and I smiled in response to the more daring side I hadn't seen in her before. "This car is so—" she stopped and laughed while the G-forces of the car had her pinned into her seat.

"Thank God it's making up for you not eating dinner as planned," I said, focusing on the road, the assholes in my mirror, and debating on cutting up through the hills to my right to lose them. There was no way I was leading any of this madness back to my place.

"Definitely unexpected," she said, adjusting her dress.

Damn it—what I would give to rip the thing off of her and truly enjoy the experience of possibly getting my ass thrown in jail for blowing past a hundred miles an hour.

"Fucking finally," I said after rounding the Oceanside turn and the cars disappearing behind it. "I need to think," I said, knowing they weren't going to let up or possibly—for some crazy-ass reason—send others out to hunt me down.

"Did you lose them?" She laughed and rubbed my arm.

It was like electricity jolted through me. Her touch was something I had been craving. "So far." I kept glancing in the mirror.

"So, where to, Dr. Celebrity?" She chuckled.

"I swear I never saw this shit coming after that interview. I have no idea what the hell just happened," I said with a sigh. I looked over at her. "Do you mind if I call Jim? He might know a little more about why that happened to us."

She smiled at me. "It's your car, do what you want. Besides, watching the sunset while cruising up the coast is pretty great too. I'm not complaining."

"At the rate of speed that we're moving, if I don't get pulled over and thrown in jail for it, we'll be able to finish the sunset dinner at the house." I smiled, then called for the car to dial my brother.

"Jake," he said in an enthusiastic voice. "Did she ditch your sorry ass already?"

"She is Ashley, and Ashley is sitting here listen to your insults."

"What happened to dinner?" Jim's voice became more *CEO Jim* as soon as he recognized someone that he didn't know well was listening in on him.

"That's the only reason I'm wasting my time with Ashley and calling you. Either I'm being confused with some A-list celebrity, or another goddamn article came out on me."

"What are you talking about?"

"Let's just say I think Ashley and I are going to be on Twitter and hash-tagged or some bullshit like that. We were nearly mobbed at dinner, and I just ditched the red-carpet treatment we received leaving the restaurant."

"I'm not aware of anything, but I've been in meetings all day and now this event for board members. The restaurant didn't—"

"No, the restaurant didn't do shit but pretty much get our asses out of there so the rest of their patrons could dine in peace," I said, my blood boiling again.

"I'll look into it," he answered. "How's Ashley with everything?"

"Probably ready to ditch the douche bag with cameras following him everywhere." I looked over at her smile and grinned. "She likes the car, at least."

Jim laughed. "You like Chinese takeout, Ashley?"

"Love it," she answered. "And I'm fine. It was unexpected, but I'm enjoying the scenic drive."

"Chinese takeout?" I asked, shaking my head. "I think you can go better than that, buddy. I expect your sorry ass—who *begged* me to do this three-part interview documentary for the hospital PR—to handle the shit storm that it's turned out to be."

"Fine, I'll have a five-star meal sent to your place. When will you be at the beach house?"

"Turning down Ocean Drive," I said.

"Then enjoy a glass of wine, calm yourself down, and food will be delivered to my pissed-off brother in an hour. Good?"

"We'll be good when you figure out why I just had my personal life invaded from out of nowhere, and you fix whatever was written or picture posted that caused this."

"I'll have my staff look into it. Go enjoy the fact that Ashley's still in the car after listening to you complain to me like a little bitch."

I sighed while Ashley covered her smile. "Handle it," I said before I ended the call.

The car pulling up to the garage triggered the opener, and we drove down into the location where I could finally hide the vehicle and hopefully salvage the rest of the night.

We walked up the staircase to the first floor of the house. It had the best views of the ocean, the illusion of my pool seemingly spilling over into it. Ashley was instantly drawn to the opened glass doors that allowed the warm breeze to flow freely through the house.

My balcony was pretty much a party oasis. I commissioned a renovation of the thing, mentioning that I wanted some secluded island escape, but the designers went above and beyond. There were torches, a tiki bar, palms to give me privacy from any neighbors who'd care to look over at us. It was like walking out to an island retreat. It was the only way I could truly escape, and the main reason I loved coming to this home.

"This is beyond beautiful," Ashley said, walking around the lit pool. "I could live out here."

"I could fuck you out here," I teased, testing her mood.

She turned back and smiled. "I'm starved, though." She smiled at me. "And where's my glass of wine?" She arched her eyebrow sexily at me.

Fuck, I was spellbound by her charms once again, and I knew she wasn't even doing much. She was just friendly and polite, and my cock was enjoying every look, laugh, and smile she was offering me. I cleared my derailed thoughts to answer her. "I do suck as a host, I guess." I laughed. "I'll be right back."

Before I turned to leave, I watched in awe as her auburn locks blew in the wind, her red dress that hugged her body perfectly swayed against the breeze, all while she walked with dignity and grace toward the edge of the terrace.

I wasn't a fan of art—not in the way some people could look at paintings or pictures and get lost in their beauty—but this was a picture that I wanted to be recreated. I snapped a few photos as she looked out at the view, hoping she'd accept the challenge of the canvas I wanted to be painted for my other home.

Now it was time to try and salvage the night with the help of my most expensive bottle of wine from Napa Valley and enjoying the sunset, hoping to erase the bizarre intrusion on our dinner.

Chapter Thirteen

Jake

Before I could finish pouring the glasses of wine, the house alerted me to a food delivery service at the door. I glanced over at the screen the camera had on display to see a man holding two paper bags. I rushed down, and after I opened the door, the aroma of Chinese cuisine filled my senses. I kept a straight face, knowing I should've handled dinner myself. Jim was probably rolling with a strong buzz and trying to fuck with my night.

"Thanks, man." I gave him a hefty tip, mostly because I must've looked like a dick—annoyed that my brother would pull this shit on me. The kid took off, and I noticed the paper receipt in the bag, laying over the food containers with a personalized note attached.

Ashley sounded excited to have Chinese, and you wanted five-star. I believe I accommodated both by having Hai's delivered.
Enjoy the night,

7.

MY BROTHER COULD BE SUCH A DICK SOMETIMES, BUT HE PICKED UP on shit like this. I was still shocked the guy hadn't nailed down a stable relationship by now. He was like the chick whisperer or something. The fact that he did catch on to Ashley's excitement over this meal was why I hoped my second attempt at this date, or whatever you'd call this now, would redeem our last attempt at dinner. Hai's was hands-down the best Chinese cuisine in all of Southern California, in my opinion, and hopefully Ashley would agree.

"THIS WAS THE BEST MEAL I'VE EVER EATEN. I'M NOT EVEN JOKING," Ashley said, blotting the corners of her lips with her napkin.

I smiled over at her. Throughout dinner, we'd talked about her love and passion for art and the fact that she put it all on hold, and I watched her muscle through bringing up the death of her mother for a passing minute before ending the subject abruptly. With the small mention of her losing her mother to cancer, I began to understand her over-concern of losing her father more.

"I'm glad you enjoyed it." I looked over at the lobster tail on her plate. "I see that the noodles beat out the lobster?" I smirked, sipping my wine and pouring us more.

"I don't have a stomach big enough for all of this." Her smile was so sincere, and with every passing second, I became more fascinated by each of her mannerisms.

"I'm just glad you enjoyed it," I said, my mind lost in the flawless beauty of her sitting across from me, staring out at the ocean, the sun having set at least an hour ago.

"So." She snapped out of her daze, sipped her wine, and leaned back in her chair, "Tell me something about yourself."

"Well, I think you've pretty much been a part of what I'm most passionate about. Though I have to admit, I never believed in my right mind that I'd see you again, and," I shook my head, "that night was insane. Saving your father's life and then walking out to see the woman that I couldn't get off my mind for an entire year?"

"So that conference, the wedding, the coffee house?" She took another sip of wine.

"I was the keynote speaker at that conference. It was Jim's idea after knowing I got suckered into doing that stupid wedding to bail a friend out."

"Well." She arched an eyebrow. "Besides being the keynote speaker that I can now confirm my old friend from high school wanted to screw, I have to ask: what did you speak on?"

I licked the wine from my lips. "Heart transplants and the advances in medical science that have taken place so swiftly in the last few years." I shrugged. "It was everything I went over in that interview for the docuseries. Those people just got the privilege of being bored to tears, stuck in a room, and listening to me talk about it for eight hours."

She grinned. "You are definitely a man who's passionate about saving lives," she said, eying me. "I find that so attractive about you. Seeing the way that you treated Dad and everyone raving about Dr. Jacob Mitchell while living at the hospital for a month—wow. You have the looks and the brains," she teased.

"I could agree that you, Ashley, would be the one out of the two of us to be praised for both of those qualities."

"It's Ash," she said with an exhale. "I think by now you'd know that's what everyone calls me."

I chewed on my bottom lip—the alcohol was working on loosening up both of us. "Fine then, Ash. I must ask, though. After observing those who call you this—your friends—what if I entertained us being more than that?"

She smiled, looked away, and tucked a loose strand of hair that was blowing in the wind behind her ear. "What do you mean exactly about becoming more than friends?" She looked back at me with a daring look that my dick responded to first. "I didn't know we were friends, and yet here you want more?"

"If you keep looking at me like that," I rolled my bottom lip between my teeth, "I could physically show you how much more I want."

She chuckled and leaned forward on the table, my eyes lowering to her breasts hiding behind her dress. "Should I be afraid?"

I smirked. "Perhaps you should."

She inhaled. "I haven't been with anyone since you—since that night."

The wine is making my goddamn night. Fuck me. "I love that you just admitted that to me." I sat back and sipped my wine. I was determining how this went from wanting to learn more about this woman to being on the brink of reliving that night again.

She shrugged. "What about you?"

Fuck. "Unfortunately," I answered, "I tried to shake the fact that, with you, it was the best sex I'd had."

"How'd that work out for you?"

"I wished I knew there was a chance to have it again, or I wouldn't have wasted my time."

She giggled and stood. I followed and brought her into my arms. "Should we see if we still have it or if it was just the one-night-stand that made us both long for that night again?"

I ran my hand along her cheek. "I swore to myself that if I ever got another chance with you, I'd never fucking let you go." I pulled her into my body and tilted her chin up, eyes meeting mine. "I don't plan to fuck you all night and lose you again. I want more from you."

She ran her fingers over my lips and smiled. "Why don't we let *me* decide that." Her eyebrow arched in this sexy, seductive way, and after that, it was fucking over.

I was more than starved for this look, this acceptance, and whatever I did in this world to deserve this moment. Screw dinner, dates, and rude interruptions that threatened to ruin what I really wanted—her.

I restrained myself from the aggressive force that instantly built up in me as I took her face into my hands and brought my lips onto hers. God knows how I managed this as gently as I had, but I did. I tasted her bottom lip and her mouth opened with a sigh I thought I would never hear from her lips again. My tongue met with hers, smoothly pressing against it then searching her mouth for more of her tasteful kiss.

I felt her body melt against mine, and I held her tighter, kissing her with more power and letting a groan of my own confirm how desperately I needed this kiss and her hands pressing hard against my back.

Throughout the last month of torture in her presence, I'd memorized these lips. How they pouted when she slept in the hospital, unaware I was admiring her beauty even when she was wearing down each day, sleeping and spending every moment with her recovering father. These lips had put on many different displays of smiles that stole my breath from me; my favorite becoming the smile she held when she bantered with me for the few seconds that I'd caught her attention at the hospital. These lips had already captured my attention when they were wrapped around my cock the night we were together. I was lost in the taste of her, and I craved more.

It took her pulling away for air for me to cup her ass with my hand, pulling her belly against my hard cock while I kissed along her jaw and down the side of her neck. Ecstasy, fantasies of this moment for the last year, and alcohol had fueled me to carry her in my arms, and we barely made it inside the house before I had her slender frame against the wall, my mouth crashing down onto hers.

Her hands ran through my hair, gripping it tightly as I moved from her mouth to the center of her chest.

"God, yes." She exhaled, and now I was entirely at her mercy. "Tell me this is really happening."

I pulled away and rose, staring down into her dazed eyes. "It's happening, angel," I repeated the name I'd given her after she gained the title in becoming a gift from heaven to me that night.

She smiled. "Fuck me."

My heart was pounding in my chest as if I'd never been with a woman before. "I thought you'd never ask."

It was corny as hell, but I didn't give a damn. I reached down, feeling the smooth sides of her legs, gripping her dress, and pulling it up and off of her. Her black lace bra and panties were gone soon after, and I stopped for a moment to take in her full breasts, her shaved to perfection pussy—all of which I would ensure she knew I still trea-sured after all this time.

She leaned against the wall after my mouth covered one of her breasts, and my hand slid down her belly and between her legs. Feeling how wet, hot, and tight her perfect pussy was, I was lost in this woman, and there was no turning back.

"I have to be inside you," I growled, the hard tip of her nipple between my lips.

"Fuck, yes," she said after I rose, and she slid her hands into my slacks.

My eyes met hers in a wild state after her hands found my dripping wet cock. "Upstairs," I said, the need for this moment guiding me more than anything else.

I grabbed her smooth ass and pulled her up to straddle her wet opening against my stomach. Her hands caressed my face as her aggressive lips bit at mine, and we resumed another delicious kiss. I had the house memorized, and without thinking, I moved up the stairs and into my room.

My bed was positioned to gain the beauty of the ocean from where it sat in the corner and faced the glass doors and windows that made up an entire wall of the place. I could give a fuck about the ocean, but I knew she loved it and hoped that this night with her would be that much more with the view.

I laid her perfect body back on the bed, her legs falling open, and my mind shifting gears into needing to taste her delicious wet pussy again.

"I have to taste you," I said, climbing on the bed, reaching my hands into her tight opening again. I glided two fingers in, and with a slight twist of my wrist, I was on her G-spot and watching her eyes roll back.

"Right there," she confirmed what I already was seeing on her face. "Fuck, I forgot how you—"

She bucked into me as I pulled my fingers and ran my thumb over her clit, massaging all of her pleasure points in and on her pussy at once. I bit my bottom lip when her glossy eyes met with mine. She nodded and moaned with a smile of desire that could have made me come right then and there.

"Come on my hand, angel," I said softly. "You're so beautiful."

Her hands reached up into the pillows above her head, her mouth open, and hips rotating with the rhythm I found that was sending her into a cloud of passion.

"I'm...I'm..." She moaned as if she hadn't had this release since the last time I saw her.

"Come on me," I begged.

Her legs tightened as she groaned out loudly in pleasure, and that's when I had to feel and taste her cum on my mouth. I swallowed her warm pussy, my tongue probing in and out of her tight, pulsating opening that tasted like heaven.

The spontaneous woman I remembered returned while I was lost in the flavor of the only woman's pussy that I desired. I tended to be an asshole when I fucked a woman. It was my way, or I was over it. I was beyond spoiled with the woman I chose to fuck—and they pretty much allowed me to fuck them for my selfish pleasure, not giving a damn if they came or not.

I don't know what changed when I took Ash up to the room that night. I took her there to fuck her the way I wanted it, but she somehow charmed me into needing to see her reaction while she came.

Like she had done that night, she took control, and I was on my back—eating her pussy that she massaged on my mouth while her tits bounced with her soft mutters of pleasure.

After she slowed her movements, my dick was throbbing in pain to enter her. I rolled her onto her back while she fumbled with the buttons of my shirt. I kept my eyes locked on her bright ones and took the shirt off and reached for my belt.

"Goddamn, I need to be inside you."

"I'm still coming." She sighed with a drunken smile.

"Fuck yes, you are," I said, pulling off the last of my clothes and freeing my cock.

"I need to taste *you*," she said, licking her lips. "Now," she ordered.

"Jesus, I've dreamed of this," I let out as I straddled her.

"I forgot how fucking huge you are," she said, eying my cock and then running her tongue under the tip.

My head rocked back. She remembered the most sensitive spot of my cock, and this night was going to be a million times better than before. I closed my eyes and reached back for her pussy, finding her clit as she massaged my cock with the wetness that was dripping for her and licking and sucking like it was her very own. It was hers.

Before I came in her mouth, I was off the bed and going through my side drawers looking for where I kept my condoms. I glanced over to see her continue her orgasm. *Fuck me to hell. She's the sexiest woman I know,* I thought, watching her massage her clit and dig her heels into the bed.

"What the hell?" I said, my cock still dripping and waiting for the condom.

"What is it?" she breathlessly called out.

Her eyes met mine in the trance that held her, and it washed over me, possessing me to do something I'd never done with her or any woman. I was at the mercy of her in every way, and my negligence on making sure this box wouldn't be empty was fleeing my mind as I transitioned into a person who didn't give a fuck.

Thank God part of me still had reason running within me. "Baby," I sighed, climbing on the bed next to her. I moved her hand from helping herself, to mine helping her ecstasy stay right where it was. "I can't believe this, but I don't have any fucking condoms."

She licked her lips, and I could see her mind trying to replace this moment that snatched us both and held us hostage in need for more—condoms be damned.

Shit. Jake. Fuck.

"I'm on the pill," she said, pulling her hand to hold mine away from her pussy. To help me think? Nothing was going to help me think properly. She smiled. "I was also tested after that night with you." She nodded. "And like I said, it's only been you since that night. But you?"

"Fuck," I said, my head falling to her chest. "I have to be inside you."

She took my face in her hands and brought my eyes to meet hers. "I want you inside me, but we're at a point where you're risking knowing me well enough to tell you I'm clean and on the pill. And I have to ask if you are..." She chewed her bottom lip.

Goddamn, I'm such a fucking idiot to put us in this awkward situation.

"I've been with others after first seeing you again," I admitted like a fucking man-whore. "That bullshit ended as quick as it started. No one could replace what I'd had with you that night. That all said, I've always been tested after." I felt my dick want to grow limp at confessing this shit like I was a child in trouble with his parent. "I've never fucked anyone in my life without a condom."

She nodded and scooted away from me, pulling my cock into her hands—twisting and massaging up and down the shaft that grew hard in her delicate hands. "It's okay," she assured me. "we can find other ways to enjoy each other without sex." She smiled.

That was all it took...her smile, her voice that caressed my nerves, and her hand, bringing my cock back to life. I brought my lips to hers for a deep kiss while considering if I should fucking do this or not. Damn the ecstasy clouding my reason.

She's clean. I'm clean. She's on the pill—I know the odds of that, but the chances are fucking slim. Even if—fuck it.

I pulled away. "Are you comfortable with this? Do you trust me?"

She giggled as she maneuvered her body beneath mine. "I trusted you with the life of my dad. I think I can trust you." She leaned up and kissed my chin.

"Fuck me," I said, biting my bottom lip. "Since we're on the trust basis, I'm going to make sure you don't regret me fucking you without a condom tonight."

She grabbed my ass and bucked her hips up into mine. "Do it," she said with that arch of her eyebrow.

I lined my cock up to her opening, the warm tight entrance lured me in, and that's when any additional overthinking left, and we returned to the passionate state we were once in.

Her hands reached under my arms and pressed into my back as I slowly moved into her. "Holy fuck," I said. "Your pussy is so tight. It's so fucking warm," I gasped out, the bare flesh of my cock feeling the warmth of the inside of her body. "Fuck me," I started chanting as I slid deeper and deeper into her.

I fell into a rhythm while locked into a trance with her. She reached down for her clit, and my selfish passion was replaced by remembering what my girl liked. "That's my job, baby," I said, pulling out and rolling over. "I want you deep, but I know what gets you off," I said, probing the tip of my cock and thrusting it against her G-spot.

Her ass pulled back into mine, and I reached around to roll her clit with my fingers. "Oh my God, fuck, Jake, fuck," she said, climbing up to her climax like a fucking goddess.

Both of us cursed, groaned, and fell into a perfect pace of finding our orgasm together. "Tell me when you come, and squeeze my cock hard, angel," I breathlessly begged, holding back my cum with everything that I was.

"Harder," she growled, her hands in fists on my comforter. "You're fucking unbelievable." She buried her forehead into the bed and forced her ass back into mine. "Yes! Jake. God, yes!"

She called out my name when she climaxed, and her pussy clenched hard around the small portion of my cock that was rubbing against her spot. "That's it, fuck, yes. I'm going to come. I can't hold back," I called out in pain of needing the release.

"Deeper, baby, fuck me deep."

I flipped her over and gripped her wrists, all while managing it like a sex god, keeping my cock inside her. Her eyes were ablaze as my lips captured hers. I began thrusting deep into her tight pussy, feeling the most amazing sensation of my fucking life. To feel her pussy—My Ashley's tight entrance—with the flesh of my cock was the only reason I could bury myself in her. Any other fuck? Never. Ashley was different to me, and one day I'd like to know why I felt like she was mine—yet owned me herself—since the first day we met.

I gripped each side of her head, brought my lips to her neck, and with a loud growl, my cum filled the pussy I'd craved for too long. She moaned along with my pleasure and ran her hands along my back as my orgasm continued longer than it naturally would have.

Our bodies were moving slowly, my cock draining every ounce of me into her. Was I going to fucking regret the fact that I missed the one item that was always on hand at each of my homes? I wasn't going to think about that.

Fuck no, I wasn't going to regret this. For the love of God, I almost called out *I love you* to her at least ten times before I came inside her. I would ensure this—the night was just starting, and I knew this girl could fuck all night.

"Round one." She chuckled at one of the terms we used our first night together.

I thrust deep into her, causing her to suck in air. "At least ten more to go, angel."

Chapter Fourteen

Jake

I woke up with Ash curled up on her side, her back and perfect body pressed into mine, while she slept facing the ocean view from my windows. My bicep was her pillow, while my other arm wrapped tightly around her to keep this odd sensation of completeness I was experiencing going.

I was spellbound by the woman. There was no other explanation for any of this. The Jake Mitchell everyone knew all too well was a cocky bastard who wouldn't dare entertain the thought of a relationship. The Dr. Jacob Mitchell that everyone knew on top of my bachelor side, the man I truly was—this side of me understood very well that I couldn't think the way I was thinking. I had no idea what the fuck to do with any of this except go with what was driving me to keep this woman close and never let her go.

Was I selfish in all of this? That was a given, but I couldn't resist how being in her presence made me feel. There was no explanation for any of it. Period. I didn't fall for women—especially blindly fall for them as I had her. There was something in the way our eyes locked, her mannerisms of biting her nail while deep in thought over something, the way her face became lit with humor, her free spirit that I sensed every time I was around her. Most of all, she didn't react to me as most women had. There was a depth to her, and internally, I was drawn to it. I was mesmerized by her.

The sun was moving over the ocean, causing the calm sea that went on forever to roll in a shimmering fashion underneath its rays gently. The cool breeze of the morning filled the room with the salty air that complemented the vanilla and floral fragrance of Ash's hair I'd dipped my face to inhale.

"Wow," I heard her say, rousing awake.

I smiled when her hand came up, and she ran her fingertips along my forearm. "Finally, she's awake," I teased, pressing my lips into her hair.

"Sort of had a long evening," she said with a smile in her voice. "Some guy kept me up all night."

"What an asshole," I teased. "Surely he knew you needed your rest?"

"If I'm honest, I think he knew exactly what I needed. And now? I get to wake up to this majestic sight."

"I'm curious as to what your artistic mind sees."

"My artistic mind?" she said with a laugh, but never turned to face me. I wanted to see the wonder in her eyes as she stared out at the open sea.

"You made it perfectly clear you love to paint, and your ultimate dream is to create a painting of something that would pull someone to see through your eyes the emotion, passion, and beauty of what your mind absorbs in particular things. I would say that is an artistic mind."

"I'm curious as to what your artistic mind sees. Everyone has a creative side, so what do you see?"

"Look at you." I laughed. "You have a way of turning everything back toward me."

"Answer the question."

"I'm a scientist. You don't want my boring answer to this."

"Try me."

"Very well. I see a large body of water with the sun making it sparkle or shine or whatever."

"That's good. Now, dig deeper. What do you feel when you look out at your sparkly and shining sea?"

"Dig deeper?" I questioned with a laugh. "Okay. I imagine a large sailboat cruising through the water with two naked people fucking on the bow."

She laughed. "You do have a vivid imagination," she answered. "Why a sailboat, though? Why not a yacht or a little rowboat?"

I had no idea what the fuck we were talking about, but hell, I was enjoying it. "Well, the rowboat wouldn't work since it's the ocean and not a lake. And I believe the naked couple shouldn't have to worry about rowing when they should be enjoying fucking on the open sea. The yacht would be less intimate with a captain and his crew navigating it, and assholes somehow coming out of every crevice of the thing—drunk and obnoxious."

"So you pretty much visualize the glittery, sparkly, open sea as a sexual interpretation?"

I laughed. "What are you an art therapist?" I brushed my thumb across the bare skin of her breast. "I told you, the answer would be boring. Maybe it's just my interpretation of what I'm thinking of as I wake up with your sexy ass in my arms." I kissed her again. "The people trying to fuck in a rowboat, yacht, or on the sailboat...that's you and me."

"Well, you're quite the dreamer," she said, "because I'd probably get seasick and destroy the canvas you've just created by being the one barfing over the side of any of those three boats in your visualization."

I sat up, needing to stretch. She rolled onto her back, giving me the real portrait of what the artist in me needed: her full tits, nipples hard, and her taut waist. She pulled the sheets over her, probably seeing the want in my greedy eyes.

I used my elbow to prop myself up on my side. "You love the ocean?" I asked as she nodded in response. "You expressed your passion for bringing it alive on canvas." She nodded again with a smile. "Then why would you tell me you get seasick? How does that even work?"

She shrugged. "I can love and lose myself in the majesty and the beauty of the ocean without knowing whether or not I'd get seasick."

"Have you never experienced being out in the ocean in any form?" I asked.

She sighed. "Nope. Maybe it's a bit of fear from hearing how people get sick on boats, and I don't want to ruin my love for the ocean by it making me nauseous."

"That's absurd," I answered her.

"What are you going to do, big guy?" She ran her hand down the center of my chest. "Prove that I'll handle it just fine by renting a yacht or something?"

I smirked. "No, we'll start small." I brushed my finger over her nose. "With a fucking rowboat, then move up from there."

"You're insane. I'm not risking it."

"Suddenly, she's no longer into taking risks?"

"I'd say you and I both took the most insane risk two people could ever take—not knowing each other well enough like this—while having unprotected sex last night."

I wanted to collapse on the bed with the fear of allowing my sexual appetite to overrule my better judgment. The rational side of my brain was trying to bring this issue up all morning, but I ignored it. I didn't want this to haunt either one of us, and it was my fucking fault for not paying attention to the fact that I'd used the last condom out of that box over a year ago.

I sighed. "Now that we've thoroughly managed to have sex throughout the entire night, practically begging the birth control pill to fail us both, I have to know if you fucking hate me for not being prepared."

"I don't hate you for any of it." She smiled reassuringly at me. "I think we'll be just fine. Though, you seem to be the type to have those on hand."

"And she judges me harshly," I teased. "I deserve it. However, I haven't had a woman in this house in years. I stopped bringing that side of my life into the one home where I find my reprieve."

"But you brought me here?"

"I did," I said, our eyes locking, mine more serious. "Because you're not just any other woman to me. I wanted you here with me. I wanted to wake up with you in my arms at the one house where I'm most relaxed. I wanted to enjoy every second of being with you—and you would have imagined I would have expected us to move into a sexual situation and prepared for that shit. Instead, the other place has the condoms fully stocked for you."

"For me?" she arched an eyebrow.

I ran my fingers over her forehead. "As I said, I only want *you*, no one else. I made the mistake of trying to replace the memory of our first night together—believing it was just sex and any other woman could fill what I wanted again after you left that morning. It wasn't the same. Until you, I didn't give a shit, but now? Well." I ran my hands to pull the sheets down to expose her heavenly body to me. "You're stuck with me lusting over this angelic body until I die."

"Until you die?" She laughed and sat up. "Now you're trying to pull off some portion of wedding vows with your sexual lusting about me?" She ran her hands through my hair. "While I adore it," she turned to get out of bed, "I need a hot shower."

"You're a fucking tease," I said, watching her perfect ass walking around my room and laughing when she managed to find the concealed door, opening it to reveal my closet.

She turned back to me. "Don't tell me the bathroom is in some crazy nook—"

"Nook? Yeah, not in this place. Get your sexy ass over here," I said, opening the door that was fashioned to blend in with the walls, keeping everything in this room's focus on the open wall displaying the sea. "I'll get the water running, and if you're in the mood, I'll join you in ensuring you can find the shampoo too."

She smiled. "I'm sure you'll help me find more than that," she said, walking into the massive bathroom I loved more than any of the state-of-the-art bathrooms in either of my houses.

"You're damn right I will," I said, then worked to bring the large shower to life, setting the water to an ideal temperature. Might as well get the morning started right and work up our appetites for the breakfast I'd planned to make before I asked her to spend the day out with me.

. . .

THE MORE I HAD SEX WITH ASHLEY, THE MORE I CRAVED FROM HER. The more I wanted her. The sounds the woman made were enough to make me act like some sex addict who had to have her again—this time out by the pool...or in the pool. Both?

I left her to lounge by the pool and enjoy the ocean coming to life with sailboats and people headed out to sea. We'd just eaten what I now know was her favorite breakfast—French toast with powdered sugar and strawberries. I had every breakfast food I could think of delivered to the house. While finishing up the last of the dishes, I threw a dry towel over my shoulder and turned back to find my phone vibrating, alerting me to Jim ringing in. I closed my eyes and exhaled.

Dammit. I forgot about the shit storm from last night, I thought while I considered if I should ruin a blissful morning and answer the damn thing, or ignore it and wait until after I brought Ash home to deal with what Jim had learned. Fuck it. I'd text him. He said he'd handle whatever came out of it—I was going with that.

JAKE: BUSY. DID YOU HANDLE EVERYTHING FROM LAST NIGHT?

JIM: WE NEED TO TALK.

JAKE: I'M NOT DOING THIS SHIT RIGHT NOW.

INCOMING CALL: JIM

"GODDAMMIT," I SAID, SLIDING TO ANSWER THE PHONE. "I TOLD you to handle this shit," I said in a low voice so Ashley wouldn't be disturbed with me wanting to kill my brother at the moment.

"There's more to handle than just you in this situation," he said. "It appears that someone leaked photos of you and me at that club last week. You and I are now the world's most eligible bachelors, taking care of hearts and money."

"What the fuck are you talking about?"

"I'm still working on *why* you and I are capturing the attention of the press, but we are."

"I hate this fucking town," I fumed. "This docuseries is fucking us over. It was supposed to be about helping people trust the medical industry and how far science has come in helping people live longer lives—not this bullshit. It was *never* supposed to be about us. I made sure of that with every word that came out of my mouth in the interview."

"I understand that; however, someone must have a friend in the press or at a magazine, I don't fucking know. All I know is both of us have gained the interest of people, and from what I've learned, a high price was paid for the leaked photo."

"That's the thing, Jimbo. Leaked photos? Why the fuck would anyone pay for them? This is incomprehensible."

"We walked out of the club with those chicks. That interested them."

"So what? We aren't movie stars!" I answered. "I didn't take anyone home. I'm out. Fix this shit now."

"I am fixing it, Jake," he growled into the phone. "I'm also calling to let you know to lay low for now. If Ashley's still with you, stay out of the public eye. They seem to be after the more personal side of both of us. You because of the series, and me because of the company."

"Fuck me, man. I was going to take her on a drive up the coast today. I'm not playing this game. I can't live my life now?"

"If they're as aggressive as our lawyers believe them to be in wanting the inside details of our personal lives, then you might want to consider if they'll dig into Ashley's if they see her with you and want to know more about who you're with."

I rubbed my forehead. "If I remember correctly, which I do, we had a mob of phones taking our pictures last night. Are you telling me that whatever in the hell these people are doing will result in her being on the front page of magazines or something?"

"I handled that entire situation last night. Trust me, it wasn't cheap, but I handled it, and pictures taken of you with Ashley won't be released. The lawyers are involved to ensure her privacy after being seen with you."

"I don't do social media, and you know that, so is that handled as well? I'm pretty sure some might have slipped under your magic fix radar and posted something. Isn't that what everyone uses that bullshit for?"

"Any photos uploaded were deleted. It's handled. I'm calling you to tell you to lay low, or if you go anywhere, go somewhere that doesn't give a shit about following these headlines and stories, so you're not noticed. If you *have* to go out, then be smart about it until I get this settled down."

"Fine. We'll talk more about this tomorrow or after I drop Ashley off."

"Let me know when you plan on taking her home, and I'll send a driver for her."

"Fuck that," I answered. "I know the best way to keep our identities concealed from this invasion of my personal life. It turns out, my girl likes adrenaline and I think I have a better plan for our day now."

"Your girl?" Jim said with a smile in his voice.

"Whatever." I sighed.

"I just needed you to know that it's handled, but it's also still an issue."

"Got it."

WE HUNG UP AND I TAPPED MY FINGERS ON THE PHONE WHILE I looked out at Ashley, relaxing out on the patio.

"You want to get out of here and do something wild?"

"I'm not having sex on a sailboat." She laughed, sitting up.

"I just got off the phone with Jim," I said, eying her petite frame. "I need to run out for a second and pick you up some clothes for what I have planned. I need your sizes."

"Jesus Christ," she said with a laugh. "What is going on in that mind of yours?"

"Well, my personal life is fucked for a while, and I'm told it's going to fuck yours over too if these assholes get pics of us together. Jim's handling it, but for now, I'm not taking chances with people strangely wanting to know about my private life. So, sizes?"

"It depends on what I'm wearing."

"The place I'm going to could probably determine that from just your pant size. That's all I really need."

"Well, you're making this a bit exciting, but you don't need to go out and buy me an outfit."

I smiled. "Seeing your ass in black leather pants? Fuck yes, I do."

Her face wrinkled in humor. "We going to a nightclub at one in the afternoon?"

"Just answer me." I sighed with a smile.

"Size two pants," she eyed me, "that *stretch*. If it's *leather,* you might want your shop friends to know I'll probably run a bit bigger."

"Got it, be back in a few. Take a swim." I eyed the pool. "The place is fully private, so you can swim naked if you'd like." I pointed toward the video cameras. "I'll delete the footage if it bothers you that the cameras are constantly recording."

"You've got it all figured out, don't you?" She surprised me by walking up to me, standing on her toes, and kissing my chin.

"It appears I have to since I'll have cameras on my ass for a while."

I WAS BACK WITHIN THE HOUR AND WALKED OUT TO WHERE ASHLEY was lying on the lounge chair in a towel, and one of my white undershirts was drying in the wind behind it.

"I see you destroyed my shirt." I laughed at her peaceful expression.

"Good thing you have five hundred of them, or I would have had my naked body on display for your kinky pleasure after I left."

I pulled her up. "Well, since you took those perverted and creep show plans out of my life, I'll have to figure something else out now." I held the shopping bag with her leather pants and jacket in it toward her. "Go change into this. I have plans for lunch up the coast, but to keep you safe, you're wearing all leather, angel."

She took the bag. "Jesus Christ. Okay," she said with uncertainty.

When both of us were changed into my riding gear, I was grateful I remembered her needing boots too. I wasn't a jackass on my street bike, but I never took it for granted either. A rider could go down for the stupidest shit, and I never took chances, knowing there was riding gear out there that could save my life should something happen. Mainly, my fears were assholes changing lanes and not seeing me or wildlife coming into the road.

When Ashley walked out of the bathroom, I instantly grew hard, seeing her in all black leather gear. "Fuck, you look sexy."

"Fuck?" She walked over to me. "Is that your favorite word?"

"I guess so," I answered, running my hands over the silk top I bought her to wear beneath the jacket. "You're not wearing a bra. Are you trying to make it impossible for me to go without fucking you every second I'm with you?"

She laughed. "I figured with this combat wear you have me in, no one would know I wasn't wearing a bra."

I rubbed my thumb over her nipple. "Goddammit. I'm as hard as fuck."

"You're as sexy as fuck in your leather combat gear," she said, rubbing her hand over my cock. "Did you buy condoms while you were out?"

"Yes," I said breathlessly. "I'm about to use the entire box up on you before we even leave."

She giggled. "Fine by me."

I pulled myself together. I wanted her to see Highway One in all of its beauty farther up the coastline. I wanted her on the back of my bike. I would have her again, just not now.

"Stay with me again tonight," I practically begged.

"I'd love to," she said, soothing me to the core, knowing I'd get her for one more morning in my arms. "I have to be back at work on Monday, though."

"You and me both. So, let's make the best of the rest of our weekend."

. . .

WE WALKED OUT TO THE GARAGE AFTER I HELPED ASHLEY ZIP UP the complicated jacket, and she gasped, laughed, and sort of squealed when she saw me uncover the Ecosse motorcycle. The bike was tailored to my specs, but still known as one of the fastest bikes built.

"Are you sure this was made for two people?"

"Believe it or not, I'm quite grateful I allowed for the added room on the seat. Your tight little ass will fit perfectly. I didn't want it limited to just my riding alone." I ran my hand through my hair, eying the bike. "I've never taken anyone on a bike with me, so I don't know why I'd design it to work for two riders, but I'm glad as hell I did."

"Well, I love to ride," she said, shocking me. "My dad used to take me out on the Harley before he sold it when Mom got sick. It'll be fun to get back on the old Iron Horse."

I looked at her in disbelief. "I've seen women cringe at the mere sight of a street bike. I was certain you'd fight me on this."

"Well, I'm not like most women; you said it yourself."

"No," I answered, "you're not."

I think I was falling in love with this woman and it wasn't just about the bike, either. She was everything and more that I'd dreamt a perfect woman to be. Her free spirit, her daring side, and most of all, she was the first woman who didn't seem to do or say things to impress me. She was authentic, and somehow, she felt as though she was born to make me the happiest man on earth. I just hoped to hell I was making the same impression on her that she was making on me.

Chapter Fifteen

Ash

Exhilaration surged through my body, holding onto Jake tightly while he maneuvered the bike up the coastline. He was an excellent rider, and I could quickly tell that with how he rode at high speeds.

I'd ridden multiple times with my dad before, but that paled in comparison to molding my body tightly to the driver and becoming one with them and the bike while moving at speeds that sent adrenaline spiking in my system.

I screamed in the helmet more than once, enjoying this spark of energy that I can now say had been extinguished by despair for far too long. I had been suffocating for so many years, and now it felt like I was retaking my first breath.

We were on a long stretch of road that went on for a while, and I leaned my head against Jake, resting it on his upper back and enjoying the views of the ocean this part of the highway had to offer. The white foaming waves that crashed into the shoreline felt like they were rolling into the shore to greet my liberation and welcome me back home.

I sucked in a breath, letting tears slip out of the corner of my eyes in delight that this weight I'd been carrying around on my shoulders was suddenly lifted. Everything was remarkable, and to see the ocean sparkle beneath the sun was like staring into the brilliance of a diamond under magnification and bright lights to enhance it.

I was falling in love with life all over again after death had controlled me for too long. Getting back to work was the hardest first step to getting my life back, and it felt like Jake taking me out on this ride just catapulted me back to where I once was before tragedy broke me.

I owed this man in so many ways. Who would've thought a motorcycle ride could jolt my ass back to life? I smiled through my tears, letting each one that streamed down my cheeks continue to cleanse my soul and help me swiftly return to the Ash everyone remembered.

Jake brought the bike toward a parking area where people could walk out on the bluffs and sit under the large trees that were in a grove along this part of the coast.

He helped me off the bike, and in some crazy act of smooth speed, he had his helmet off and was helping me to ease mine off my head next.

His expression changed, and his hands came up and stopped mine from smearing the trace of tears from my cheeks. "I feel like a total asshole for not knowing I'd scared you to tears while on the ride." He framed my face with his hands, blue eyes raptly studying mine. "Why are you crying, Ash? Are you okay?"

I sniffed and smiled. "I'm just happy," was all I could say before I impulsively hugged him. "Thank you for doing this."

"Anytime," he said, his voice riddled with confusion. "Give me a second to walk over there." He pointed to a small restaurant nestled in the mountain ridge across the street. "I'll grab lunch, and we'll head out and have a picnic." He winked and smiled. "There are tables out there. Would you please try and grab us the best view?"

"And if I don't get the best view?" I challenged, loving to go back and forth with him.

"Well, then, it's going to suck for you." His lips pulled up on one side. "All I need to see is you, and my best view is handled."

He brushed his finger over my nose, a cute mannerism I adored in this side of him. It always seemed to come out when he was soft and sweet—dare I say, when he was possibly thinking about me on a higher level than just someone he'd had mind-blowing sex with?

I found the perfect table at the end of the ridge under the shade of some trees. Because of the few cars that were parked here, there were no people to compete with for picnic tables. It was complete solitude and the lovely sounds of the ocean below.

Jake joined me about fifteen minutes after I sat down, placing a large paper bag on the table with two bottles of water. "Are you cold?" he asked, eying the leather jacket I wore.

"Well, I know I'm not wearing a bra, and my nipples are hard." I glanced around. "With the way you sounded earlier, I didn't think sex in public would be a good look for the fancy doctor."

"Good look or not." He arched an eyebrow at me, pulling sandwiches and containers of fruits and raw vegetables out of the bag. "I wouldn't give a shit."

"Get your smart brain out of the ditch, Mitchell." I stood. "I'm stuck in this damn thing." I laughed, trying to fumble with the zipper that practically crisscrossed my body. "Hopefully, you didn't pay too much for this. It might be broken already."

He smiled and eased the zipper down. "It's tricky, but I paid for your protection, not the ease of taking it off."

I smirked at him. "Um, so if we did get my butt into a life-threatening situation, how would I get the thing off to save my life?"

"First of all." We sat together. "It would save your life, yes. Second of all, if you needed out of the jacket, I'd gladly rip it off of you if we had a zipper malfunction."

I rolled my eyes as I bit into the sandwich. "Wow." My eyebrows rose with surprise. "Chicken salad? It's delicious."

He swallowed the bite he took and popped a carrot into his mouth. "I noted your choice of sandwich for dinner one night after doing my rounds and checking on your dad. You had only taken a bite out of the hospital's chicken salad sandwich. So, in learning that was your favorite item on the menu for lunch, I easily could determine what to order from the menu for us today."

I swallowed the raw broccoli I'd just eaten. "What would make you think that chicken salad was my favorite sandwich after noticing I only took one bite of the disgusting one from the hospital?"

His face was alit in humor as he devoured his sandwich and moved on from the raw veggies to the fruit. "You'd already had me fascinated by everything you did by that point. I took note of the sandwich, and it concerned me that you weren't eating well, so I mentioned it to your dad, who was wide awake at the time. I questioned the dreadful situation of the abandoned sandwich."

He tipped his head back, gulping down some water, and I was the one becoming fascinated now—with him. "I could only imagine that and how many other conversations you and Dad had while I snored in the room."

He looked over at me through his dark, square aviator glasses and smirked. Damn, he was so sexy. I couldn't find a fault in the guy if I tried. "Well, that particular conversation alerted me to the fact that you hated the sandwich, so I had one of the nurses order your next favorite meal for when you woke up."

"Wait," I said, remembering that whole scene. "I woke up to a strawberry milkshake and an In-N-Out burger. Dad said he ordered it, but he did have a look on his face like he wanted to say more but couldn't."

"A cheeseburger, no tomatoes, if I remember correctly?" He arched his eyebrow over the silver rim of his sunglasses. "I might add that it was difficult for a heart surgeon such as myself to keep a vegetable off that burger, knowing tomatoes are good for your heart and blood pressure."

I rolled my eyes. "I can only imagine the horror of it all."

"It was a nightmare," he added, feigning drama. "The woman who I was fascinated by on all levels had found a way to let me down."

"All while she was asleep?" I played along with him, enjoying his handsome expression while we ate. "What a bitch. Surely she knew that you had her heart's best interest in mind."

"She obviously didn't have my heart's best interest in mind. She always found a way to be sound asleep when I visited her dad."

"Perhaps she didn't know your hours?"

"Seven in the morning and seven at night—every damn night." He popped a grape in his mouth and leaned over to kiss me. "Doesn't matter now. I ensured she had the best sandwich after having the best night of her life last night. I think she and I found a way to meet in the middle."

"Oh, listen to the confidence ooze out of your mouth," I said, unable to resist running my hands through his short, messy hair.

"I listened to your moans last evening. I remembered those well from San Francisco, and I also learned a few new ones after the sensational sounds of you screaming my name all night." He leaned on the table and took another drink of water, "I'll say, hearing *Jake* being called out all night while you rode me over the edge—all fucking night long again? Best damn sound in the world."

I felt my cheeks heat up. "Last night was wild."

"That is an understatement." He grinned. "And now I have to figure out where the closest restroom is so I can fuck you, or I have to deal with this hard-on for the rest of the day."

"There's no way I'm fucking in a roadside bathroom," I teased.

"Shit." He sighed. "She won't let me fuck her in a rowboat or a disgusting bathroom."

I laughed. "What made you what to become a heart surgeon?"

"Changing the subject." He pulled me in close to him, us both now straddling the bench and facing each other. "Good idea." He leaned forward and pressed his lips into my forehead.

"Answer the question, Dr. Mitchell."

"Now that you call me that, my sexual appetite has been destroyed." He laughed. He let out a breath and pulled his sunglasses off. "It's sort of a long story. I mean, since I was a child, I was fascinated with medicine. The science of it all, anyway." He pinched his lips together. "I'll never forget the look on the doctor's face when he walked into the waiting room where my brother and I waited with my uncle, who was alive at the time. We lost him and Dad both to a heart attack, but my dad's heart attack was different for me. The look on the doctor's face was distant, and there was no emotion. That played hard on me. He just came out and stated the fact that they did all they could do, and *Mr. Mitchell* didn't make it."

"God, I'm so sorry."

He smiled and ran his hands over my knees. "There's nothing to apologize for. It was that look, though. It urged me to want to be in his position to prevent a family from receiving such a devastating announcement from a doctor who couldn't do anything more." He pressed his lips together. "That's why I was driven toward being the doctor I am. Not only to save lives. I understand that I cannot save them all; however, it's my job to that family to make sure that good or bad the message may be, they receive it well. I won't separate that part in my life, and develop what some medical personal have—for good reason—which is more of a dark-humored way of coping with death. Everyone hands it differently. They have to, or we'd all go mad in this industry, but I know how I deal with it."

"And that's by being the most compassionate doctor I think I've ever been in the presence of. Trust me." I shook my head while his solemn expression looked over at me. "With my mom, the doctors were amazing, but I felt empty after she passed." I pulled my hair out of the ponytail that was suddenly too tight. And I'll "I didn't expect the doctors to show any form of sympathy. I knew that wasn't their job. Mom's case was obviously different since she went before we could even get her on hospice, but I didn't feel like it was the doctor's job to comfort us."

He shrugged. "As I said, I got into this line of work to save not only patients but also their families from grief. Becoming a heart surgeon was something I became passionate about after wishing I could have saved my dad on my own. Living in guilt as a freshman in college that I should have been able to do more, but knew I couldn't. Guilt plays with your mind—I know that now—but it drove me to learn more about the silent enemy that took my dad, then my uncle soon after. Heart disease runs in my family, and thankfully with my knowledge, my brother and I are doing well by taking precautions." He let out a breath. "Shit." He laughed. "I haven't thought this topic in a long time, and I think I'm making absolutely no sense."

"It makes sense. You became passionate to save others from what you went through. Now, look at you. You're the most amazing doctor in the world, I think. It's why you are a celebrity!" I laughed.

He rolled his eyes. "Yeah, *that* most definitely wasn't why I became a heart surgeon." He rubbed the outside of my legs. "I'm not the best. I've lost patients, and when I do, it's not easy for me to digest, but I do move forward in remembering why I became a heart surgeon."

"I don't know if I've ever really let you know, but I can't thank you enough for saving my dad and for calling me during his surgery when I was losing my mind out there."

He smiled. "You've thanked me in numerous ways. And yes, that's sort of a unique thing I do while in surgery. If I'm going over and I believe the family is concerned, I make sure I speak to them personally and assure them all is well."

"If it's not well?" I cringed at even asking that.

"I still believe it's my duty to call out to the waiting family. These families and my patient entrusted me with their lives for these surgeries. I feel I need to guarantee I am either having great progress or working with as much passion as I know they have to keep their member with us. I guess the best answer to *if it's not going well* is they need to know I'm in there fighting for their family member's life, and I won't stop. Anything to reassure them."

"How can you even think to do surgery and talk on the phone?" I laughed, grateful my lame question just now didn't affect him.

He shrugged. "Although everything down to the last stitch being made must be nothing less than perfect, I still have conversations with all the staff while working. It could be a long four to sometimes twelve or more hours standing there." He smirked at me.

"It's because you're a badass doctor, and you know it."

"As long as that's how you feel, then that's all I care about." He leaned forward and kissed my lips. "Let's get out of here and go for a hike. There is a perfect area out here that I believe you could capture beautifully in a painting for my home."

"You hiring me?" I chuckled, and he stood with me.

"Depends on how good you are." He draped an arm around me and brought his lips to my ear. "In bed tonight, that is," he said, and of course, I was the one who couldn't visualize anything else now.

One thing I knew I had to do was not get too close to this man, and what the hell did I just do? Ask the one thing about him that truly attracted me to him. His answers and being the most perfect and compassionate doctor who ever existed only made me more attracted to him beyond where I was, trying to guard my heart.

I wasn't stupid. An empty box of condoms in his house? Yeah, the guy could get any girl he wanted, and that was obvious. I didn't regret having unprotected sex, but don't think I didn't have concerns about whether or not he was truthful about me being the only one.

He could drop me tomorrow or next week from what I was learning about the rumors of him. It's why I had to be smart around him with my emotions and my own heart. So, when all was said and done, we wouldn't mess around without condoms again. With him buying condoms today, it only reassured me that he felt the same way as I did. No stable relationship should come out of this—or could come out of this.

Even if the man I learned about through hospital gossip was a player, then that let me know what I was doing with him. Playing. And dammit, I wasn't ready for a relationship. I just wanted to enjoy life again, and if having sex with the gorgeous doctor would be a part of me learning to live life again, then that's exactly what I was going to do.

Chapter Sixteen

Jake

After what seemed to be the best weekend I'd had in too long, dawn was here on Monday morning, and it was time to return to work. Never once had I dreaded a weekend ending and returning to work until now. I loved my job, there was no doubt about that, but I also loved every second of being with Ash.

She never fully opened up about herself, but instead, she did what she seemed to be a master of skill at: she turned all the questions on me, or she twisted the conversation into some bizarre way of looking at the world through a more creative mind.

Perhaps that's why I was drawn to her more than ever. She relaxed my stubborn, scientific mind and my black and white way of looking at the world. She might, in fact, be an art therapist. Who knew. I just felt more open and relaxed around her jovial spirit, which seemed to change after we rode up the coast and hiked around the area where we had lunch.

Her face seemed brighter, her voice was riddled with excitement, and she teased me constantly. After spending two sunsets and sunrises with her, I felt like the asshole player I was known to be was gone. Strange how a woman could change my way of thinking so much that I could hardly remember being the guy who slept with women for the hell of it.

I snapped out of my dreamy state—yeah, dreamy state—a whole new me that was going to be eaten alive by my brother and friends. All of my thoughts were recalling not just the fantastic sex with Ash, but the engaging conversations we shared when I was greeted by a mob of people outside my office parking structure.

Fucking hell! I thought as I found my parking spot, working up the courage to get out of my car. I shouldered my briefcase and worked vigorously to get through flashing camera lights, video cameras, and, God help me, a local news anchor with a microphone being shoved in my face. I smiled through my pissed-off feelings and worked to maneuver my way into the front door of the office.

Sandy was there, peeking around the glass entry doors and unlocking the sliding doors for me. "You okay, Dr. Mitchell?" she asked with a nervous laugh.

I eyed her, reining in my destroyed mood. I couldn't go off on her, my nurses, or any of my staff in the office. "Keep the doors locked until I can get security down there to get rid of those people."

"Jake." She laughed. "You're pretty much everyone's dream guy on social media, you know that?"

"What?" I forced out. "No, I didn't realize that."

"Right, you're not on social media." She winced. "Yeah, so you and some girl—"

"Me and some girl?" I felt my heart fall out of rhythm, and my partner in surgery, Dr. Chi, was going to have to save my ass if I didn't take a breath and get my blood pressure down.

"Some blonde. I guess you and James were at Gypsy's last weekend?"

"That's old news, why the hell is it just—" I stopped, half grateful Ash's face wasn't in this mess, and half outraged that this shit blew up almost overnight. "Don't worry about it. I just got back from my rounds. At least they don't know my schedule...yet." I rolled my eyes.

"Can you get the coffee on? I need to call security and get these people out of here."

"It's already done, and I'm going against everything you know I am when I say this," she smirked, "but I'll make you a cup. You deserve it."

"Thank you, Sandy. Are the rest in here?"

"Everyone is searching on Twitter—"

"Got it. I take my coffee black," I said. "I can't hear any more about this. Can you do me a favor and send Haley into my office?"

"Got it."

"She can carry my coffee." I softened up some at my receptionist. "It'll help to keep her off social media until I can talk to her."

"Good call."

AFTER A QUICK CALL, SECURITY DID A FANTASTIC JOB OF CLEARING out the media mob, and I had exactly fifteen minutes before my first patient was set to arrive. I needed to call Jim. This was a more significant issue than merely intruding into my personal life. This was a risk to my patients.

"Make it quick, I barely go into my office," Jim barked, answering my call.

"Good, so now you'll understand why you or Alex need to get someone down here to keep these mobs away from the hospital and my goddamn office."

"What?" he snapped.

"Yeah, from your shitty temper, I'm willing to bet you were met by a mob on your way into work this morning too. My situation calls for the security you have at HQ, so get them over here. We don't have the staff on security, and this sure as fuck is not their problem."

"Take a breath, Jake," he said. I could tell he was shuffling through the skyscraper to get up to his office on the top floor.

"I'm not taking a fucking breath until you tell me you have hired more security or sent your bodyguards over here to protect my patients from the impending heart attack I'm tasked to save them from."

"I've got it. Hold on." I heard him talking to Alex while I practically broke my pen in half, waiting for him to bark orders at the president of our family's company. "Okay, ten minutes?" he said to Alex. "Jake, you there?"

"Yes," I answered.

"Ten minutes, and you'll have men over there to prevent people from disrupting your patients."

"I want them off the hospital grounds completely!"

"We'll keep them a safe distance away from the hospital, that's all I can give you."

I couldn't believe this shit. My brother, who ran the goddamn world, was talking to me like his hands were tied. "If your bullshit resolution doesn't work," I seethed, "then they'll be reporting on cops arresting media and anyone with a cell phone on the hospital grounds."

"Jake, calm the fuck down," Jim ordered me. "That's not happening, and you know it. They'll be watched and removed from going near anyone who is visiting St. John's."

"Thank you. I'd hate to think we'd have women in premature labor, heart attacks—"

"Jesus, Jake," Jim snapped. "I get it!"

"You *get it*? If you *got it*, Jim, then it would've all been handled. We can't have the hospital in this state of chaos. Do you want to bring this place down? Fine, then just sit there and act like I'm dramatic or whatever you'd like."

"I'll talk to you later."

With that, both of us hung up. I could tell Jim was as frustrated as I was, and now the Mitchell building was probably being overrun with the press, wondering about God-knows-what in Jim's life and the company that our family started. This was a disaster.

"Haley," I hit the intercom that rang to her earpiece.

"Yes, Dr. Mitchell?"

"Everything cool out there?"

"None of us are on social media if that's what you're asking."

I pinched the bridge between my nose, and Haley walked into my office. The blonde nurse who was attractive as fuck waltzed in with her tits practically spilling out of the top of her dress.

"Why aren't you wearing a smock over that dress?" I asked, furious she was dressed so unprofessionally.

She gave me some look I was not expecting from her. I knew doctors fucked nurses—and all other manner of staff for that matter—but Haley worked as my closest RN for at least four years now, and there was never any shit like this between us. I felt a knot tighten in my stomach.

"Well," her voice was sultry and unexpected, "it appears that you, Dr. Jacob—"

I stood abruptly. "Is this a nightmare, and I'm just not waking up from it?" I questioned, turning my back to her and gazing at the cityscape view that I knew Ash loved. "Haley," my voice and blood pressure lowered, "you and I both have a job to do, and we both will do it well. You will do best to act like the registered nurse who works with me, or you *will* be working with another doctor. Whatever is on your mind due to this chaos, end it immediately, or we can no longer work together."

"I'm giving you a hard time, Jacob," she said with annoyance.

"I'm not in the mood. You know exactly how I feel about what *you* believe to be funny, and this dress that is highly inappropriate to wear in the office. Cover it with a smock, or get to the hospital, find your scrubs, and change."

"I get it." She sighed, cheeks bright red when I turned around. "Sorry. I really am."

"Thank you for understanding," I said. "I'll have Steph accompany me with all of my patients for this morning." She turned to leave. "Haley?"

"Yes, Doctor?"

"I want all phones off social media until all of this settles down. We have to run this office with *you* as the best example for all of our nursing staff. I expect everyone will honor that while we work to end the nonsense of the media taking an aggressive interest in this business."

"I'll talk to the ladies."

"I'm sure they've already seen you dressed like this?" I waved my hand over her dress.

"Yes," she answered.

"Talk with the girls, and make sure everyone is in scrubs."

"Yes, Doctor."

She walked out of the door, and I rubbed my forehead, trying to take a few breaths and remove every cluster fuck that had hit me sideways since stepping up to my office this morning. Shit, this wasn't going to get any better—I had to brace myself for the worst, and that was *not* in my personality. I went to my refrigerator, opened the glass door, and pulled out an ice-cold bottle of water, downing the thing instantly. I walked over and sat at my desk. Hopefully, going through Mr. Smith's charts, my first patient, would help clear my head and pull me into the zone of just doing my job—my job that was strangely ruining my life.

I should've never done that docuseries. In a million years, I would have *never* in my life had seen *this* coming.

Chapter Seventeen

Ash

It had been two weeks since I'd last seen Jake in person. I felt horrible for the guy. He and his brother seemed to adorn the cover of every magazine or celebrity news outlet since the morning after he dropped me off.

Both men were drop-dead gorgeous, to put it mildly, and I was pretty sure that was why Jake's passion for raising awareness for heart disease and the advances in science and transplants were being overshadowed. I ignored all of the stories about Jake and James being in this so-called *Billionaires' Club*. I tried to at least. This superficial title that was given to Jake, his brother, and their friends by women they had pissed off was the lamest thing I'd ever heard of. I was blown away to see these women stand in front of cameras—extra botox on full display—stating that the billionaire-club boys would only keep to the wealthy women and not entertain sleeping with gold-diggers. This had absolutely nothing to do with Jake's interview he was so passionate about. To see all these men have their personal lives dug into and put on display? I felt awful for all of them.

Having to working all week at the gallery, I wasn't able to go with Dad to his appointments to see Jake, but today, I called in sick. I had to see him at least. These vague texts from him had me worried about how he was doing since he was an overnight celebrity in all the worst ways. I wouldn't allow myself to believe I was falling for the man known in the headlines as *Saving Hearts and Breaking Them: The Dark Side of Dr. Jacob Mitchell's Fascination with Hearts*—and that was just one of the many different goofy titles Jake was given. All I was doing today was making sure the man I'd enjoyed being with—both sexually and in fun conversation—hadn't lost his mind.

I enjoyed learning more about the man I'd already deemed a player without all of these crazy headlines about him. He was one-hundred-percent dedicated to medical science and advancing it all. He enjoyed the ladies, yes, but he had tried to make it clear that time spent with me seemed to be changing that in him. I only smiled through his words. There was no way I was falling for that line. I was still convinced the man could drop me any second, but after watching some of these women talk—and wondering if they were right—I knew I would have been cast off either after our night in San Francisco or Malibu if they were right.

He was an extremely attractive man inside and out, and even if he wasn't a player, he had zero time for a relationship. Whoever the lucky woman was that would finally tame Jacob Mitchell would have to deal with being second best to what he made clear to me was his first love: his patients and his hospital.

"Jesus, I'm judging him as bad as the rest of the world," I muttered, smoothing the lip gloss over my lips.

"Are you ready, *mija?*" Carmen asked. "We need to go."

"On my way."

MY EYES WIDENED WHEN WE ROUNDED THE CORNER TO THE hospital. I saw groups standing at the edge of the parking lot to where

Jake's office was, and then another group by the front fountain in the garden by the side entrance of the main hospital building.

"This is crazy!" Carmen said with agitation. "Dr. Mitchell doesn't deserve this."

"He is a fine man," my dad said, smirking at me and knowing I'd spent that entire weekend with him, but Carmen and I were good about concealing *why* these people were out here and the stories making headlines on the media from him. If Dad saw that, Jake would be replaced with a new doctor, and I would be lectured for sleeping with a selfish man who would break his little girl's heart. "I just hope he doesn't drop me as a patient after people from around the world are lining up and sitting on waiting lists for him to be their doctor."

Carmen and I exchanged glances, knowing we kept dad to the docuseries and the media outlets that *did* talk about what Jake initially did that whole interview for. She smirked; the woman had some form of attraction toward Dad, and I loved it. Dad seemed to feel the same about her too. It was adorable watching the two interact as if they'd been married for years. The best part was when Carmen reached her limits with his stubborn personality and cussed him out in Spanish.

"Thank God those people are being held off," I said, glancing back at the jumpy crowd at the far end of the parking lot.

"That's because Jacob's brother has lawyers and security enforced for the protection of the patients at St. Johns," Carmen said in annoyance. "A shame it's come to this."

We sat in the waiting room watching some reality TV court show, and as I watched the famous, no-nonsense lady judge tear into the plaintiff for the fourth time, we were called back.

Why are my palms so freaking clammy? Am I that nervous to see him again?

The tall blonde nurse's striking blue eyes and facial features matched her perfect body, and all of them were complemented by the light blue scrubs she wore, which was saying a lot, considering scrubs were the least flattering things to wear. I'd met Haley on one previous visit, and didn't think much except that she was a crazy-hot nurse who worked for the man that I'd hoped had answers to helping dad.

Now, the stories haunted me, and I had to wonder if she was one of Jacob's many women. *Stop it! You're acting like a jealous weirdo!*

For someone vowing not to judge, I was doing a pretty shitty job of keeping it together. Dear God, I was as bad as the rest. The last thing I was here to do was get jealous over a nurse; hadn't Jake been dealing with enough shit?

She went through all of the necessary questions and protocols, entering Dad's info on her computer and chatting it up nicely with the three of us. Carmen and her giggles were contagious, and I couldn't help but join in on the high-spirited atmosphere of the room. Haley had an awesome personality. I wanted to hate her for seeing Jake every day, but I couldn't dislike the woman if I tried.

"So, with you both keeping Mr. Taylor in line," she swiveled around on her chair, "I'm pretty sure Dr. Mitchell will be pleased, and your visit should be relatively short today." She rose and smiled at us. "Everything looks great on my end. The doctor will be in shortly. You all have a wonderful day."

We kept our voices low for the few minutes before there were three quick knocks to the door, and Jake's voice accelerated my heart. Good thing Dad was the one hooked up to the heart and blood pressure screen because if it were me, I'd look like a total asshole.

I was sort of hidden, sitting in the chair by the curtain where Dad was front and center on the exam table. Carmen was at Dad's side, still watching all of the monitors when Jake came into the room.

"Mr. Taylor." He nodded, looking at the charts. "All looks well here." He flipped the clipboard closed and turned toward the monitor and started typing while going into the familiar banter I remembered him and Dad doing at the hospital.

I crossed my leg and relaxed into the chair, watching Jake in fascination. His white smock covered his pristine suit and complemented his perfectly messed hair and his sexy ass from me. God, I did miss this man. Running my fingers through his dark hair, his rich cologne, his brilliant knowledge of the woman's body, and how mine reacted to his every touch.

"And Ash," he said my name, and I snapped out of visions of this man, making me crawl out of my skin two weeks ago. "She's well, I'm sure?"

"Well, if it's not Carmen, it's Ash keeping my butt in line." Dad laughed, and his eyes moved over to mine. "Why don't you ask her yourself?"

Jake was typing stuff in at a computer at the desk that was along the wall across from me. His quick typing slowed, still not looking back. "Well, I would make time to say hi to her if I weren't behind in patients," he said as his typing picked up. "This circus outside has forced me to push out the times of my early patients. It's been quite crazy," he said. "All right, everything is great. What we'll do," he said, turning and clicking a pen closed and slipping it into his coat pocket, "is have the receptionist schedule you for four weeks from today." He rose and smiled at dad. "Congratulations, Mr. Taylor. You've made it to the milestone where you don't have to come in once a week anymore. In a month, I will reevaluate, and perhaps we continue moving forward with the device assisting your heart, and we won't have to bring up the transplant conversation again."

"I've been watching that documentary of you, Dr. Mitchell," Dad said, and I could see Jake's face grow solemn. "You're doing remarkable work. Between Carmen and my daughter pushing me, I might be giving in on this transplant idea."

Jake's face lit up, and his sapphire blue eyes were brilliant. "That is something I truly needed to hear," he said, almost breathless from shock. "Please think about this some more, and we'll continue this conversation next month when I see you again."

"You got it, Doc," Dad said, and I could see him smiling with delight that he just contributed to what we all witnessed, probably the best thing Jake needed to hear coming from the documentary.

After Jake helped Dad up and went to leave, that's when we made eye contact for the first time since he'd entered the room. He stopped, and his smile almost threw me off balance, making me sit back down in my chair.

"Haley," he called, door open and eyes never leaving mine. "I'll need a few minutes before I meet with my next patient," he said.

"Yes, Dr. Mitchell," her voice rang out.

"Ash." He smiled, and I swear it was that crazy feeling of having old souls reuniting again that was happening between us. "Mr. Taylor?" he questioned Dad.

Jake's smile was wide and I could tell that Dad understood why his doctor seemed to have a change in his mood suddenly.

"Yes." Dad said, now the one in control and not the doctor.

"Would you mind if I spoke with Ash while you were—"

"We'll be out in the car. Don't take too long, Ashley Jane."

My mouth dropped open at Dad for using this moment to drop my middle name on me and act like the crazy man I knew him all-too-well to be. He could be so embarrassing sometimes.

"Ash." Jake kept to the name I finally burned into his mind. "Can I speak with you in my office for a moment?"

"Yeah," I said, eying my dad's rascally grin and Carmen's knowing smile.

I followed Jake down the hall to the double doors of his office. I walked in, remembering the beautiful views of this room, and after the door clicked, I was abruptly pulled into Jake's arms.

"Holy shit," he whispered, cradling my face in his hands. "How could I forget how beautiful you are? This certainly is the best day since last seeing you, Ashley *Jane*," he said with playfulness.

"Glad my dad could give you something to tease me with."

He exhaled, and his eyes were transfixed on mine. His lips were closed but pulled up into a smile. His eyes dazzled as his thumbs brushed over my cheeks. "If I don't kiss you, I'm going to lose my mind."

That's when I pulled him into me. I imagined us reuniting in some aggressive kiss, his hands all over me as they'd been in the past, but this was different. He gently brought his lips to mine, and before I could open my lips to deepen our kiss, one of his hands cradled the back of my head while his other slid across my lower back. My body went limp against his strong body, and my head dropped back for his mouth to explore my neck. His soft groans were too much. I'd only wished he was not in this professional mindset. I wanted his hands moving up my dress.

"I've missed you too." I chuckled, trying to calm myself down.

His lips came back to mine, and we were in a crushing and tasteful kiss. The expensive fragrance of his cologne reminded me of our naked bodies, tangled up in so many crazy positions that worked to send me over the edge and into the best orgasms I'd ever experienced.

We both pulled away at the same time, and he stepped back and smiled at me. "Part of me wants to call out and have the rest of my patients canceled for the day." He arched his thick black eyebrow at me. "It's taking everything that I am not to fuck you right here and now."

"Easy, Dr. Mitchell," I teased, placing my hand in his extended ones. "Now's not the time."

"My office, my rules," he bantered back.

"Oh, really?"

He laughed. "I've contemplated this over and over because I need to see you, but I don't want to share you with all the assholes I have to join this weekend on the yacht."

My eyes widened. "What are you talking about?" I laughed as he walked me over to his desk, leaned against it and wrapped his arms around me.

He brought his lips back to my neck. "I have to be at some ridiculous party on the yacht this weekend. I was pissed that I forgot about it, but it's going to be filled with dumb-asses that my brother and friends invited along. It's probably another fundraiser, and I've tried multiple times to get out of this previous commitment I made over two months ago."

"You're willing to risk," I sucked in a breath as his lips explored my collar bone, and his hand rubbed over my breast, "me barfing on the boat, sick in some room?"

"I thought I could last the weekend not seeing you, but after seeing you today, it's confirmed that I can't. I need this weekend with you."

"Jake." I stepped back and laughed. "You already said in your little artsy vision that those two people couldn't enjoy," I mouthed the word *fucking*, "on a yacht."

"I believe I was wrong. They can." He smiled. "There is medication you can take to ease nausea if you experience it. The yacht will remain in the bay and not the open sea."

"Oh, God." I sighed, nervous about this idea. "I can't swim," I lied.

"You swam quite well in my pool after I chased your naked little ass down, and well, let's just say I haven't stopped thinking about our moment in the pool since impulsively taking your body then and there."

I glanced back at the door. "Shh." I giggled. "The last thing you need is office gossip, I'm sure."

"Don't destroy the moment I'm having." He smiled. "Come on the yacht with me. I'll ensure you don't get sick."

"What about all of those cameras and everything these people are doing to put you on blast daily?"

"We've already worked our way around that. No one will know where the two idiots they deem as celebrities are." He took my hand and kissed my palm. "Come with me?" he begged through his beautiful eyes.

"To save your next patient from waiting any longer, I'll go." He rose, but I pushed him back. "If I get sick on that damn boat and you ruin my love for the ocean..."

"I'll take you back to the beach house and will let you regain your love for the ocean through numerous ways you seemed to appreciate while we were there."

I walked forward and couldn't believe I felt the need to run my hand over his hard cock. His forehead dropped against my chest while he groaned. "Fuck," he said in a whisper. "I need you, Ash."

"You're working," I reminded him. "Can you even handle this?" I asked, rubbing along his long, hard shaft.

"You know the answer to that."

"Water?" I laughed unexpectedly at the fact he was so screwed.

I was dripping wet, but I was able to go home. He, on the other hand, couldn't, and I didn't think that water was going to do the trick.

"Jake," I said, bringing his eyes to meet mine. "You've got to pull it together."

He licked his lips, and the wild man from our weekend was in his face and eyes. *Shit, I'm going to ruin his life if I don't just leave.*

"Baby," he said, and my heart reacted to the one pet name I usually hated but loved when he used it.

"I'm taking off, or this will be the fourth time we've placed ourselves in a position of desperation to have sex without a condom. Unless, of course, you keep them in your desk." I arched my eyebrow at him.

That was a low blow, especially for all the shit that had been on television and social media about him lately; however, it seemed to work.

He grew serious and took both of my hands into his, standing up. "If there's one thing I can say is decent about myself with all the fuckery that's been all over about my personal life, it's that I have never had sex in my office or at that hospital," he confirmed as if he were defending himself.

I reached for his cock and smiled. "And there you go, all fixed. Your next patient can see the famous Dr. Jacob Mitchell now—without a massive erection, that is."

"You're good," he challenged me in response. "Allow me to make myself clear, though. You've just pulled in a fantasy that *will* happen between you and me."

"Sex in your office?" I chuckled.

He licked his lips. "But first, fucking on that boat," he said in a soft voice. "We're having drivers bring us there. Look for my text, and I'll be picking you up in some blacked-out SUV on Friday night around eight. I'll have everything ready to ensure you're not sick on the boat. Trust me, it's my yacht, and the thing is large enough to where you hardly even know you're on the water unless a typhoon comes in."

"Text me," I said, and turned to leave the room.

He pulled me back in. "No kiss goodbye?"

"I think we should stay away from that." I turned to leave. "See you Friday night, and you better not ruin my passion for the ocean for me."

"I'll bet you a weekend in Cabo of fucking on my yacht that you will have more passion and love for the ocean after this weekend."

I rolled my eyes. "A weekend in Cabo on a rowboat." I laughed.

"Yeah, I'm not asking for a death sentence." He smiled. "We are going if—for a split second—I hear you scream my name while forgetting you're even on the yacht with me."

"We'll see," I said. "Seriously, I have to go. I have to get out of here before my dad and Carmen jump both our asses for what they think we're doing in here."

"They wouldn't be wrong as this entire time, and even now, I'm finding it hard to resist your sexy little ass, baby."

"Quit using those names," I said, reaching for the door. "See you later."

I walked out, and this time, curious eyes from the supermodels who worked for Jake were all on me. I smiled, and they forced smiles back. Jake was going to have to deal with the fallout if he raised issues in his office. I would've fucked him in his office without hesitation, but I saw his professional and playful said battling each other, and there was no way I was going to add to stories that the press loved to write about the man.

Jake seemed like he controlled everything about that office, and when he pulled up the doctor side of him, I'd already seen him be a dick to people who were out of line. So, they could deal with that. I wasn't going to.

I needed to leave, and now I needed to dig up every excuse I could find to get out of this yacht party.

Chapter Eighteen

Ash

I sat in the den where we set up my room so Carmen could move in with us. All of her family lived in Northern California, her two sons grown and living near their wives' families. It was sort of meant to be for the three of us, I guess. Carmen quickly became part of our family, and oddly, I think a lot of it had to do with her and Dad's relationship. Those two thought they were sly, but it was just the other day when I spotted their conversation leading to Carmen kissing Dad on his lips before beating me to the kitchen to make dinner.

With those two in the living room, bickering about something on the news, I was left to paint the views from the bluffs where Jake had taken me. My eyes were crossing with this painting that I couldn't get right. All I could think about, if I was honest with myself, was Jake. Seeing him today ignited some fire of energy in me, and I just wanted to be with the man. I was going to get burned if I allowed myself to do this.

My phone chimed, alerting me to a text that just came through.

Jake: *Can I swing by for a few?*

Ash: *Sure.*

I chewed on the end of my paintbrush, shocked that I'd responded so quickly and that Jake asked to come over. Did he want a piece of ass? That wasn't going to happen in this make-shift room in a twelve-hundred-or-less square-foot home.

Jake: *Need your address*

I texted Jake the address while I walked out to where Dad and Carmen sat in the living room. "Your doctor is stopping by, Dad," I said with sarcasm.

He smirked at me. "I can guarantee it's because he was once again captivated by my daughter today. Do we have leftovers from dinner? He might be hungry."

"I have no idea why he's stopping by, but I might be taking off with him again this weekend." I chewed the tip of my nail, a horrible habit I needed to get rid of. "Wait, he might be coming over to cancel on that one. Never mind."

Carmen laughed. "*Mija*, that man is taking you away for the weekend and probably for the night too. Hope work wasn't too strenuous on you today."

She giggled over at Dad while Dad smiled.

"All right, you two." I stood and arched my brow at them. "You will not embarrass him or me when he gets here."

"Never!" my dad said.

"Right." I eyed my dad with a smile. "I'm sure Ashley *Jane* was just you being cute this afternoon in his office too."

Dad shrugged. "I love your name! I gave you the name. Am I not allowed to say the name I gave my precious child?"

"I'm going back to painting," I said with a roll of my eyes.

Two hours after Jake had texted me, there was a knock on the front door. I was dozing on the couch, Dad was in bed, and Carmen was in her room when Jake finally arrived.

I opened the door, and any exhaustion I had in my body dissipated. "You're late," I said.

"You live an hour from the hospital, and that's if there's no traffic." He arched that sexy eyebrow at me. "Although I have no idea how anyone ever knows how long the drive takes without traffic because there is *always* traffic, and tonight there was more than usual."

I looked out to see his sleek black car parked on the curb in the front of the house. "Um, that car might not fare well in this neighborhood."

"I have insurance." He smirked. "May I come in?"

I stepped out. "Everyone's sleeping," I said. "I mean, you can hang out if you want, but the place is kind of cramped."

He took my hand and pulled me into his chest, "I had to see you outside of that office. I almost texted you to meet me at the hotel or pack your bags to head back to my place tonight."

I smiled against his hug. "You're insane."

"I know." He pulled back and brushed his lips over mine. "This neighborhood seems safe, and I need to get some energy out of my system. Would you care to take a walk?"

I took his hand, and in my yoga pants, hoodie, and flip-flops, I joined the guy I was slowly deeming had lost his mind on a walk.

"So," I said as we turned down the sidewalk. "Shall we take walks like this every night?"

His face seemed concerned, and I had no idea what the hell was going on with him.

"Jake?" I asked, holding his hand and watching the many expressions play on his face as he took note of kids playing out in the street under the streetlights and smiled at them.

He stopped and turned to face me. "I have to know something before I ask anything of you. I believe I was abrupt and rude earlier by begging you to join me this weekend."

"Okay." I had no idea what the hell was going on with this guy.

"Ash," he sighed, "I'm fairly sure you've seen me and the history I've had with women all over the internet and whatever news that has strangely decided to peel my personal life open like a goddamn banana."

"Don't insult my second-favorite fruit," I teased.

It caught him off guard, and his lips pulled up on one side as he shook his head. "She hates tomatoes but loves bananas."

"And you insulted them. What an ass."

"That I am." He sighed and ran his hand through his coal-black hair. "I'm just going to come out and ask it." I watched him chew on the inside of his cheek. "Ash, I want more with you. I know you see a complete piece of shit all over the media outlets, and I was, in fact, that guy outside of my work. I swear to God, though, that something changed in me when I met you. I know it's fast and probably too soon, but I need you in my life. After the weekend we had—I hate going home and wishing you were there. Never before has my home felt empty until now."

I covered my smile. Poor guy was asking me to be his girlfriend but had no idea what the hell he was doing in just straight-out asking that of me.

"Say something," he said.

"Are you asking me to marry you?" I teased.

His face went ghost white, and I couldn't help but laugh. "Jesus Christ," he said, blue eyes wide and grabbing my hand. "No. Shit. I don't know what the fuck I'm saying."

"You need to relax." I hugged him and stood on my toes to kiss his chin. "Are you asking me on a date or for us to become an item?" I held up my hand. "Wait; are *you* asking me—the girl outside of the gold diggers' circle—to become the one lucky woman who Dr. Jacob Mitchell will—"

"Oh my God, stop." He laughed. "I'm just asking you to take a chance with me. You're unlike anyone I've ever met. I want you, and only you. Exclusively. I'm not the dick that they're talking about anymore. I want to ask if you're willing to trust me and give me a chance to date you. To have you stay at my place whenever you want. Shit, I don't fucking know. Maybe I am asking you to marry me."

"Let's keep it at asking me to take a chance with you." I smiled at him, totally shocked he was acting like he was proposing. "I've seen all the stories, and I've sorta come to terms with the fact that I'd had sex with a guy who could've gotten any girl he wanted."

"I hate that I was that guy."

"Jake," I started, "we can be more serious, yes. I'll just have to brace myself for an intrusion into my life now. Are you willing to deal with any demons they dig up on me?"

He let out a breath. "That's what I was getting at. I can't and won't let them come near you, but if you're with me, there'll be pictures, and more than likely, things will be said about you. I'm not sure I'm worth that at the moment. Any other time when I was unexpectedly falling for a woman, I would not have imagined it being like this."

"I can handle myself," I said. "I like you a lot, Jake, and it was quite shocking when I couldn't paint because you were on my mind the entire time. That's never happened before."

Before I could blink, I was in Jake's arms, him kissing me in a way that made me grateful that the teens playing in the street were now down by my house, checking out the million-dollar sports car.

I pulled away before we both forgot where we were. "So," I said with a smile.

"So," he repeated triumphantly, running his thumb along my bottom lip, "this weekend, we show everyone you're mine?"

"I think it's the other way around, but I guess so." I smiled at the man I'd promised myself I wouldn't fall for and knew already hours earlier I already had. There was no stopping this collision course I was on. "I swear to God, I will kick your ass if my heart is the one you, Dr. Mitchell, actually hurts."

He was somber for a moment, then smiled. "I can't lose you, Ash. I promise that I'm not going to hurt you."

"Then let's go public in this relationship we're trying to build."

"Stay with me tonight," he begged, putting his arm over my shoulder.

I wrapped my arm around his back. "Sorry, Doc," I teased. "Both of us have to be at work tomorrow, and thanks to the never-ending traffic you mentioned earlier, it's smarter if I stay home throughout the week."

"I hate that woman you work for," he said with annoyance. "It's like she's a splinter that I can't get out of my life. First, it's her and my brother, and now it's her fucking gallery that's too far from either one of my houses."

"Why do you hate my boss so much?" I laughed.

"You've heard the rumors about my brother and me, I'm sure. The fucking *Billionaires' Club* rumors?"

"Yes. That you four only screw rich bitches?"

He chuckled. "While that's somewhat true, she's the fucking idiot who spread the word about what one of the guys slipped and said while he was shit-faced drunk. Let's just say she needed the money. My brother was sympathetic in more ways than one, and because of him and his bullshit charity, she managed to get her gallery and continues to play my brother for cash with her lies. I hate you working there."

"Well, one day, I will have a gallery of my very own, and it'll be close to your houses, and I'll kick her ass in sales and steal all of her clients," I said, seeing him all worked up over something I didn't fully understand.

"I'll buy the damn showroom," he said with a smile. "We'll give these assholes something to report on. My brother's whore against my girl."

"Easy, bud." I squeezed his side I held. "Why don't you come inside? We have leftover fajitas, beans, rice, and I finally impressed Carmen with my homemade tortillas too."

"Impressive, and that sounds delicious. Maybe if I get some food in my system, my brain will function better." He smiled at me. "Carmen's cooking is out of this fucking world. She used to bring food for the doctors when she worked the night shifts with us."

"Then, you'll be fat, happy, and fully satiated after I heat up a plate for you."

He kissed my temple. "Let me get my bag out of the car, and I'll be up in a second."

. . .

I WENT THROUGH THE REST OF THE WEEK WITHOUT BRINGING UP the yacht party that I'd committed to attending. I would like to blame it all on being blindsided by Jake, but the truth was that I wanted this. I was doing a swan dive into life again, and I was fearlessly embracing everything I wanted. Being with Jake made me feel amazing inside and out. His expressions, the way we connected without even trying. I had no idea what I was getting myself into, and I think the daring part of all of this is what drove me toward being fearless and open to dating Jake.

I was dressed in one of the three silk cocktail dresses that Clay had picked out and had delivered with three sets of heels to match—all black. Each one had a deep V to accentuate my cleavage and a note saying, *"If you're going to do this, Hollywood, do it right, baby girl!"*

I'd already called and thanked Clay for everything. I hadn't seen my best guy since after Dad got home and then one time at the gallery when he and Joe showed up to become my first clients to buy a five-hundred-thousand-dollar portrait. I missed them and definitely couldn't get so lost in Jake that I left the best part of my life behind.

With Jake's text from earlier, I was instructed to bring along a swimsuit, sundresses, and whatever would keep me comfortable on the yacht until Sunday. I was packed and ready to go, and Jake must've rushed through his rounds tonight because he was already in the living room, chatting it up like old friends with Dad.

"You enjoy yourself," Carmen said as I brushed the last of my mascara along my lashes. "I still can't believe it, you and Jacob." She gripped my shoulders, and her bright red lips were on my cheek. "It's like my own kids are falling in sweet, sweet love."

"That's disgusting, Carm!" I said with a laugh. "You're too much, sometimes."

She raised an eyebrow at me. "I know this is true. Go. Enjoy."

After farewells to everyone, I was in the back seat of an SUV with Jake. He sat in the middle while I gazed out of the window, praying this wasn't a mistake.

He took my hand in his. "You are quiet tonight," he said.

I looked over at his gorgeous face, him still wearing his suit from work. "You're brave. I guess I lost my edge." I laughed.

"We could go sky diving?" He smirked. "It appears you enjoy adrenaline running through your system."

I let out a nervous exhale. "If I get sick, you know this weekend is over, right?"

He kissed my cheek. "You won't get sick. Quit putting that nonsense in your mind."

"How was work?"

Jake surprisingly laughed at that. "Who's the one acting like this was all a proposal of marriage now?"

"What the hell are you talking about?" I asked with a grin.

"Well, instead of being thrilled to spend the weekend with a bunch of obnoxious, drunk, and overly wealthy people, you're asking how my day was at work."

"Ugh." I leaned my head back against the headrest. "Maybe I just need to get on this boat and get it all started."

He twisted to face me. "Ash. The last thing I want in the world is you upset or nervous about this in any way. Can you trust me on this? If you get sick, I will hire someone to bring a rowboat out, and I'll row your cute little ass to shore."

"Very funny."

It was all small talk, and the closer we got to where his fancy yacht was, the more Jake seemed to be annoyed about this whole thing than I was.

"Yeah, we're right down this way," Jake ordered the driver as he pulled his phone out. "Jim, we're pulling in now. All asses on board within the hour. The captain already has orders to leave at ten..." he paused and then nodded. "Sir," he tapped the driver on the shoulder, "I'm going to need you to make a right here. Thanks. To that car," he pointed out toward some white sedan. "Are you serious, man? How did they find out about us leaving tonight? I'm about to cancel this shit. It's not worth it." He paused and exhaled while the driver stopped the SUV, and I stepped out.

God dang, we were surrounded by thousands of docked boats that screamed money, and I had a feeling the white car was taking us to the one boat that most likely was anchored out in a world of its own. What the hell was I getting myself into?

"What the hell are we getting into?" Jake snarled the exact words that ran through my mind. "Then use the boat to pick us up here. I'm not taking a fucking car over there if there's a goddamn press mob. This is a fucking mess." Jake exhaled, livid, "Bring the boat here, or I leave."

He ended the call and walked over to the man waiting in the white car. "Change of plans. We're going to get picked up here and brought out to the yacht," he said, slipping the guy some cash. "Thanks for understanding."

"Everything okay?" I asked.

"Welcome to my fucking life," he said, pissed.

"We can leave," I offered, chickening out.

Jake smiled. "Get over here." He brought me into his side. "Let me tell the driver who has our luggage that my idiot brother is bringing the smaller boat over here. You're not getting out of this."

"Are you dodging the cameras, Dr. Mitchell?"

"Hopefully," he answered, walking toward the car we rode in. "But if the driver of that boat picking us up doesn't floor it, trust me, they'll beat him here."

Within ten minutes, we were walking toward another loading dock, and then bright flashes of camera lights came from our left.

"Well, let's play, shall we?" Jake said in an annoyed voice.

We ran down the dock. The driver and another assistant—who'd come from out of nowhere—trailed us, and I started laughing at the entire scene. Poor Jake. He was being treated like some super celebrity, and I knew he'd been dealing with this every day since I'd last saw him. Crazy enough, even though he was pissed, he managed to smile and be courteous toward them. You would never think it was anything like this with the way he appeared on social media and television.

Once we were in the speed boat, and the luggage taken and thrown in by Jake, we were racing out on the dark sea toward a vessel that seemed too big for a guy like Jake to own. It was grand and beautiful. The lights coming from the yacht flicked and danced along the ocean.

The boat we rode on was pulling up, and men were working on lining us up to board Jake's yacht easily.

"This is yours?" I asked with a laugh.

"Yeah, ignore her name, though. I was drunk when I came up with the damn thing," he said, helping me up to the massive yacht.

"*Sex Sea?*" I laughed, holding his hand. "You named your beautiful yacht that? That's almost as good as my coffee-cup name."

"Any position?" He chuckled. "And you weren't even drunk."

"Shut up," I said as we walked through a side entrance and up an elegant staircase.

As soon as we walked through a back-lit glass entrance, we were greeted by a crowd of people.

"Happy Birthday, Dr. Sexy!" they screamed in unison, and then the music erupted to where I could only smile in response to Jake and I having drinks shoved into our hands.

"Happy Birthday, brother," the man I remembered as Jim said, greeting us in a sharp suit. "Ashley." He nodded toward me. "Nice to have you with us on Jake's big birthday. Goddamn, thirty-five years old."

Jake was somber, quiet, and more confused than I was. "I forgot about my own birthday party," he said, looking at Jim as if he should probably get checked into a mental hospital. He looked back at me. "Holy shit." He half-smiled and looked back as if he were ready to jump off the boat himself. "I'm so sorry. I completely forgot about this." He looked at Jim, "I'm not putting Ash through this. You guys do your thing and celebrate my life. We're out."

Jim grabbed Jake. "The fuck you are," Jim said. "What the hell is wrong with you?"

"Jake." I smiled. "You look like you might be going into cardiac arrest."

"I know you assholes, and this party is not going to happen with me present. Like I said, enjoy it."

"Oh, stop acting like a baby," Jim said with a sigh. "There's enough here, and we had a meeting earlier anyway. It's primarily agents and people we entertained for an acquisition of a company. You don't have to entertain anyone. That's what the staff is for, and we're heading to the privacy of the upper deck."

"Your tax write-offs are going to bite you in the ass one day. Fine. Ash and I need to drop our shit in our room, and I need a shot or two before I can entertain this idea—that I actually came up with and completely forgot about."

"Nice to see you, Ashley," Jim said after Jake chilled out. "We'll meet you guys on the upper deck. I need to finish up here anyway."

"I'm so sorry about this," Jake said to me.

"Hey." I took his hand and stopped him from walking. "Happy birthday." I ran my hand on his cheek, and he seemed to react as if he had a shot or two with just that.

"Thank you." He smiled.

"Good thing that I know what you like, and maybe I can loosen you up for the night once we get into the room?"

Jake smiled that greedy smile I loved about him. "It's the only thing I'd ask for—that and my boat off-loaded." He laughed. "Let's get out of the light, and I'll give you a short tour."

This night would be interesting, but at the moment, my concern was for Jake. He seemed certainly annoyed that he was on the boat with me—and this was going to be some crazy birthday *party*. I didn't feel like he was pissed I was there, but more that he was worried about how this might run me over with how my nerves were already acting in the car. We were sort of out at sea already, and I'd done the sea-sick research, and there were numerous remedies for it. I would be perfectly fine. Knowing it was Jake's birthday, I would do my best to make him feel relaxed.

Chapter Nineteen

Ash

I walked through the yacht with Jake and found myself in awe. The marble and slate were the leading décors, and the gold and silver accents that were sprinkled throughout the different rooms we walked through were more than the average person like myself could take in. This yacht was fashioned to exude wealth, and that's what was on display while Jake led us toward an elevator. An elevator. Inside a boat. I could hardly believe what I was seeing.

The crowds had parted for Jake, the women in high-end cocktail dresses while men were in button-down shirts and trousers. They fit the design of the interior of Jake's yacht as if they were made to live on it. We passed by two bars, and rooms with opulent lighting fixtures. The area we stood in now reminded me of those expensive hotel entry-ways with a slate waterfall, taking up the entire wall behind where we stood and waited for the elevator.

Jake politely greeted the guests on the boat, his hand clutching mine tightly. If he was worried about me getting lost in the crowd, he had no reason to be. I already knew I would stand out from these crowds. It was easy to put it together that Jake came from wealth, but to watch him engage with the company of this lifestyle was a different story. I had a feeling this was going to be a peculiar night for sure.

Once in the elevator, Jake remained silent with the attendant—yes, the small elevator was staffed like we were in a skyscraper. The man hit a button, and within seconds, we were on a quiet floor that seemed to be one of its own, another world of the boat, perhaps? No noise, no people, and I had no idea where we were.

"Well, that was exhilarating." He grinned back at me. "Fleeing the press mobs and my guests." He ran his other hand through his hair. "Exactly how I wanted to end our evening."

I laughed at him as he tried to process everything. "Um, I think the evening just started?"

"Nah, I'll lock this floor down, and they'll never find us where my room is."

"Funny," I said. "I have a feeling your brother isn't letting you off that easy."

He turned just before the hall we were in opened up into another seating area. Windows were on each side with cream leather furniture, and the bar I spotted was backlit with a beautiful cobalt blue, but there was no bartender or anyone out in that area.

"You still with me?" Jake asked, standing in front of the beautifully polished wooden door.

"Just trying to absorb this boat's beauty, that's all."

"Kind of sexy, isn't it?"

I smirked. "And now I understand the meaning behind the outlandish yacht's name."

He laughed. "Get your ass in here."

I followed Jake into the large living area of his room. "This is a bedroom?"

"It's living quarters or whatever you call them." He smiled at me. "See, I told you." He pulled me through the room to where a massive bed was set in front of a beautiful teak wood wall. "You wouldn't even know you were out on the ocean."

He pulled me close to him. "Our clothes will be here any second, or else I'd be fucking you right here and now," he said, towering over me with that damn smile.

"Are those windows?" I pointed to the coverings to each side of the bed.

"To the balcony," he said. "It runs both sides of the room. There's a hot tub out that direction." He pointed to where the cream window coverings were automatically pulling back to display the night lights over the ocean. "It's all private and quite enjoyable," he said, and for the first time, I saw his pride in his yacht. "I'd like to say you'd get lost on this boat, but after I win my bet from earlier, you'll have this all down like it's your own home while we're in Cabo."

I walked over to him after he took his suit jacket off and tossed it on the bed. I couldn't resist running my hands over his biceps in his blue button-down shirt. They always seemed to stretch against the fabric, and it wasn't helping me right now. Jake missed our sex, and I was feeling the same way. His texts throughout the week, teasing me with getting a hotel just to be together, were tempting, but I handled myself pretty good outside of his presence. Now, here he was with this navy shirt that set off the five o'clock shadow on his face, his piercing blue eyes, and his coal-black hair.

"You're as beautiful as this boat," I teased him, pulling me in close and kissing what seemed to be his favorite part of my body, my neck.

"Can't change the subject. Just admit you're coming to Cabo with me. Hell, I'll even allow you to pick out our room if you don't approve of this one. Boat's yours, sexy, do what you want with it."

"Oh, yeah?"

"Stay here," he said after the door chimed.

I walked over to the balcony where he said the hot tub was, and the door opened the minute I stepped in front of it. *Better fix that auto opener if the man holds to his usual way of throwing me up against a wall,* I thought with a laugh, stepping out on the balcony. If Jake did lose himself in a moment and this door opened like it just swiftly did, we'd both most likely fall overboard, and who knew what the press would have to say about Jake's sex life then?

I looked over, and in an alcove to keep with the sleek lines of Jake's dark gray yacht, a spa was shimmering in an array of different shifting colors.

Jake came up behind me and pressed his lips on my shoulder. "You smell delicious," he said, fingertips gliding over the outside of my legs, pulling my dress up. "I need you now," he said, his lips nipping at my ear.

"Jake," I said, and then my mouth was captured by his, and I knew our weekend on this yacht was going to have us acting as wildly as we did at his beach house.

I missed his aggressive and hungry kiss, his groans, and apparently, I'd missed them so much I didn't realize my guy was stripping me out of my expensive dress.

"Shit," I tried to cover up. "I hear people. Music." I was breathless, now feeling the perfect and smooth muscles of his chest. "We're so screwed."

Jake's flirty smile was a delicious sight to behold. "Hell yes, we're screwed, and I'm taking your ass right here. You're holding onto that rail while I fuck you into the orgasm that's going to make you scream my name louder than the music coming from the party floor of this boat. I'm taking you to Cabo, baby."

I turned around, teasing him with my ass and spreading my legs for him. He was just as flawless as I remembered as he gave me the best orgasm a woman could ask for. His enormous cock thrust deeply inside me after I cried out, riding the orgasm he quickly achieved with me in this state. I licked my lips, seeing and hearing the yacht cruising through the water as it gained speed.

His groans, his massive cock, all of it—he was about to win his little Cabo bet after another orgasm rolled through my entire body. I screamed out his name while running my fingers through his hair and gripping it. His hands clutched my waist as he thrust in deeper, his teeth softly caressing the skin over the side of my neck.

Jake braced an arm on the rail before us, and his hand brushed over my breast while we both fought to catch our breath with this impulsive decision to go for it right here and now. "I've missed you," he said, kissing my cheek as I tried to pull myself together. "Now I think I can deal with the rest of the night, especially seeing you in your swimsuit."

Jake and I pulled away from our sexual position and walked into the bedroom of his yacht. "This way," he said. "The shower is back here."

"What are you talking about? *Swimsuit?* For the rest of the night? Is there something about this little birthday party of yours that you forgot you planned that I should know about?"

He chuckled. "I'll be right there with you." He walked me into a bathroom fit for a king and turned on the water to the glass shower. "Come on, let me clean you up."

I stepped into the luxurious shower. "Why the bathing suits? I'm not cool partying with a bunch of people—"

His lips covered mine and silenced me while he grabbed the soap and proceeded to give me a massage with his strong hands like he always did when we hit the shower after our crazy sex interludes. "Relax, babe." He kissed my nose, running soap over my shoulders and down my arms. This guy should have been a masseuse. "Tradition of birthdays anywhere near a pool means the birthday boy and his girl go into the water. I've already texted Jim to leave you out of this, but my brother seems all-too-excited that his little brother is here with the first woman to settle his ass down, so I think you and I are going into a pool tonight for that reason alone." He laughed.

I kissed his perfect lips, grabbing the soap myself, and taking my turn with his body. "You seem a little too excited about this," I said as he dropped his forehead to mine. His muscles were tight with the tension brought on from dealing with this stupid celebrity crap that seemed to be a nightmare for him.

"Very," he said, his hands cupping my ass. "Though I knew something would happen like this tonight—birthday or not. The boys all know you're my girl, and so they're coming after us just for the hell of it tonight. I have a stunning cover-up for your swimsuit as well. Hopefully that will keep you comfortable."

"Comfortable?" I said as he began washing his hair. "Um, not being the victim of the crazy, frat-boy initiation that you're talking about will make me comfortable."

He looked at me with concern. "Babe, I'm not going to let anyone hurt—"

I placed a finger over his lips. "Stop. It's your birthday. Let's enjoy every minute of it. And yes, you win the Cabo bet."

He pressed his lips into my finger. "I already knew that."

This night was already kicking off in the wild and crazy way I sort of imagined it would. Now, here we were, cleaning up and heading out to Jake's birthday party with his close friends and the chicks from the Playboy Mansion on another private deck of this yacht. Jake opted for a beer, and I followed his pace in having one myself.

He interlaced his fingers with mine. "Time to meet the boys, Ash," he said, bringing me over to the far corner of the yacht.

I put on a brave face. I'd met his brother, but not his friends, and God only knew what The Billionaires' Club all thought of me. By the knowing grins on these three, drop-dead gorgeous male specimens, I had a feeling this was going to be one crazy night. I only hoped I could keep up with the company of these men, and the women who I didn't fail to notice were speculating about the woman who was walking with Jacob Mitchell.

I had to keep it chill. These were Jake's friends, and I was the outsider here. This was awkward, but I instinctively felt like I couldn't show weakness around the women who were looking at Jake and me like it was a shame we'd ruined their night.

If that wasn't enough, my boss, Lillian, was in the crowd of women. Fuck me. I'd barely tolerated the fake snob of a woman all day at work, and now she was here. *Calm down, Ash,* I thought, knowing Jake couldn't stand her, so who knew how she'd fare out here with him trying to celebrate his birthday.

Who the hell knew how any of this would work out. This was the party side of the man I'd fallen for, and it would be interesting to watch the night play out.

Chapter Twenty

Ash

After meeting Jake's best friend, Collin, I could see where the two had a connection in this crazy bubble of wealthy people we were surrounded by. I also noted their connection on the medical level, both exchanging stories about patients and their success—Jake's in heart disease and Collin's in neurosurgery. More than once, I found myself having to do a double-take on the young blond man with sky blue eyes and Jake. They were so gorgeous they could have made a fortune as models, but instead, their hearts and passion were in the medical science industry.

Collin was one whose eyes and smile could take any woman and bring her to her knees. I couldn't imagine the single life for these two, and I bet some women were praying that either one of them would look in their direction.

Then there was big brother, Jim, and his best friend, Alex, who was president of Mitchell Associates. Both men worked side-by-side to run the well-oiled machine of a company that owned everything under the sun, including some minor league sports team.

The men were good company to be in, and I found myself quieter than I'd anticipated as I listened to them talk and catch up after their long days from work. Maybe it was the beer I was nursing that was fizzling me out or just my interest and intrigue, watching the men talk.

"So, you're really going to let this nut date you, eh?" Collin asked while taking a sip of his gin and tonic. "He's a prick. You know that, right?"

I laughed. "You watch too much television," I said, Jake smiling down at me and joining in on the conversation. "Don't believe everything you hear."

"Ah," Alex said, joining in from across the bar where we all sat, "but he does have a complete douchebag for a brother," he said, sipping his bourbon. "One who, apparently, still hasn't figured his shit out yet." He looked over at Jim. "If you ran the company the way you ran your pathetic love life, we'd be fucked."

"God knows that." Jake raised his beer to Jim's smile.

"God may indeed know," Collin said, looking over his shoulder at the troop of girls sitting over in the lounge area of the upper deck. "But does Jake know how stupid you really can be?"

"What the hell am I missing?" Jake asked, glancing over his shoulder at the girls.

Shit! They're bringing up Lillian.

"What you don't see, you don't know, little brother." Jim winked, and then suddenly, this derail of conversation had me in Jim's arms as Jake fought off Collin and Alex as they dragged him away. Jake recovered from being flung out into the pool, and he turned what should have been an embarrassing moment into a swan dive into the pool.

"You'll have to forgive me, Ash." Jim smiled, and it was the first time I saw the man's face light and humorous. "But this might be the worst of your troubles due to Jake."

With that, Jim was more generous than the other two, and he softly nudged me into the deep end of the glowing pool. I was expecting to meet with ice-cold water, but this was lovely. Warmed to a perfect temperature, and now I was snatched up in Jake's arms.

His smile and laugh both were contagious. "You're all mine now, babe," he said, and our eyes locked knowingly. He watched as I smoothed my hair back, and he ran his knuckles along my jawline.

"You okay?" I asked, trying to remove the water from my face.

"Better than ever." He traced my bottom lip with his thumb. "I'm sorry that we got lost in decompression talk back there. It's sort of the thing we do when we catch up at the end of the day."

"I enjoyed it. Your little Billionaires' Club is quite the club," I mocked.

"Overrated," he said, eyes studying mine in a way they never had before. "Would I be insane if I said I was in love with you?"

I framed his soft, innocent face that was more sincere than I'd ever seen in him before. "I would say someone spiked your beer." I kissed his lips. "Don't go soft on me, Mitchell," I warned.

He held me close. "I know it's all sudden and fucking crazy." He laughed, nipping at my chin. "But I can't explain how you make me feel when I'm around you. How just having you here, I feel complete and actually pity the rest of these assholes who aren't as fortunate as I am."

"Someone must have spiked the beer," I said.

"No one spiked my beer," he teased back. "You don't have to recip-rocate my feelings or my words, but I'm telling you how I feel."

"You two going to stay in the pool all night, or can we cut this cake and move on with the night?" I heard Collin call out over the music.

"Cabo," he said. "You and me, the boat staff, and that's it." He pulled me in.

I kissed his lips. "Let's go eat cake, birthday boy."

This was moving at light speed between Jake and me, but I knew what Jake felt because I felt it too. I'd had boyfriends before—I thought I was in love my first year of college—but I'd never felt what I felt with Jake. The way it turned from the very first moment we met, started talking, the sex, and then these looks we both seemed to get lost in. It was intense and scared the shit out of me. Maybe Jake was braver than I, but to feel the way I was feeling about him lately was dangerous. Dangerous in the form of knowing if I lost him and he moved on, I'd be in trouble. I'd never met anyone so bold, so fun, and yet so passionate in his professional career.

No, we hadn't had a lot of time together, but there was a pull toward this man that I couldn't explain. I just wish I had the guts to tell him I loved him too. Because I did. He'd saved my dad's life and mine also. I may never know what the hell I did to draw his attention toward me like this, but I wasn't discrediting myself by saying I didn't deserve it. I deserved to feel the way only Jake would make me feel. I deserved to feel happy and alive again, and in all honesty, it was Jake that was bringing this out in me. That's what was the scariest part.

Soon after the cake was cut, that's when Jake's eyes fell on my boss. Surprisingly, Jake didn't throw a raging fit.

"Listen, Jim," Jake said, "if you want to bring her along, then fine. You know how I feel about her, and one day you'll understand it. Right now, I would rather go to the top deck and enjoy the rest of this birthday with the only person I'd wish to spend it with in the first place."

"Sorry, man. I'm not interested in the woman. She came along with the company executives Alex and I met with earlier. She followed me in tonight, and instead of mentioning it was a private party, I just allowed her in."

"She's here because she's stalking you, Jim. It's creepy, rude, and repulsive. She's a problem."

"Sorry about this, Ashley," Jim said.

"No need. I work with her every day." I laughed.

"I just feel bad for you, Jim. You have yourself in a tangled-up mess with that woman."

"Why don't I go introduce myself to the ladies who seem to be more curious about my being here than the cocktails they keep down-ing," I said, rubbing Jake's arm. "Besides, that's my boss, and I'll let you both know how much of an issue she really is."

Jake pulled me in. "You do not have to entertain them. I'm sure their slurred words are entertainment enough for each other, and Lillian is Jim's problem to deal with, not ours."

"Are you nervous they'll say something about you, lover man?" I arched an eyebrow at him.

He smiled. "You should be the nervous one; raising your eyebrow like that at me gets your sexy ass in trouble every time."

"I'll be back. You go enjoy the guys."

"I'll come to rescue you in about ten minutes. We're heading up to the upper deck. You'll enjoy the wind and the views as the boat cruises through the bay up there."

"And if I can gain my brother's forgiveness, we'll all be up there with you two," Jim teased. "I will handle your boss. Jake is correct, she's not your problem and most definitely an issue I need to sort out."

"I'll see you guys in a few." I smiled at the two handsome brothers then turned toward the ladies club that had a few men with them, but it was almost as if I'd jolted the boat and silenced the mob as soon as I moved their direction. Jesus Christ, the looks on their faces were not what I expected. Maybe they were way ahead of me in drinks, and I had only half a beer.

I could feel the judgmental vibes from across the pool, and I was bracing myself for what would most likely be said to me after they watched me with Jake tonight. I didn't know how this upper-class crowd rolled, but I did know Jake wouldn't send me into the lion's den if he didn't think I could handle it. However, he also had never shown himself to be controlling or overprotective.

Something told me this was a stupid, pointless exercise. Going to the upper deck to get away from the people who'd hitched a ride on Jake's beautiful yacht sounded like a better idea.

Ten minutes. I looked back to see Jake, watching me while talking with a group of men. He smiled and nodded as if he'd read my mind, and rescue would come for me earlier if ten minutes turned into an eternity.

Chapter Twenty-One

Ash

I felt like I was pulled back into middle school when I approached the beautiful women who surrounded another section of this boat's party deck. All conversations instantly ceased and forced smiles were put in place. Lillian walked out to the front, and for the first time, the woman hugged me and air-kissed each of my cheeks.

"Darling, what on earth are you doing here?" she asked with a strange giggle, the group behind her slowly surrounding me now.

"I came with Jake," I stated with a smile, trying to refrain from staring at the woman as if she'd transitioned into some other version of herself. "I'd ask the same question, but I'm guessing you're here with your friends."

"Oh, dear, you're too innocent." She cackled. "No, I'm here with James, his brother. I'm sure you might have met him."

"Unless you weren't present for the whole pool scene, I'm sure you'd know I've met Jim."

"Excuse me," a woman said. Instantly, I recognized her. She was with Jake at the coffee shop in San Francisco, and she was at my cousin's wedding. "What's your name again?" she asked, her eyes unreadable.

"Ashley," I answered. "I think we've met. In San Francisco. I spilled that drink on—"

"I know," she curtly cut me off. "I'm Vickie," she said, her voice dripping with venom. "Now that introductions are out of the way, I have to know something: how is it that you have turned up again?"

"Turned up again?" I asked the partially-drunk woman. "I came with Jake."

She smirked, and I'll be damned if I didn't see something wicked flash across her face. "I'm sure you did." She smiled back at the quiet girls that crowded around us. "However, if you knew him as I do, you'd understand what we all know—you're a party favor for his special birthday. A shame," she kept on, "I could have sworn everyone knew about how all four of those boys operate by now. Looks like someone is just another trophy in the Billionaires' Club for them to place on a shelf."

I pursed my lips after all the women laughed at the blonde who slurred her insult.

"You know, I'd think you were right about that, especially after following the news on the guy; however, I hate to let you all down by saying I'm not part of this Billionaires' Club bullshit."

"Easy on your language, Ashley," Lillian reprimanded with a laugh. "And if you're here with Jacob Mitchell, don't you dare think for a second that you're not a part of that club. These men want only one thing, and they're extremely particular about who they get that from."

"That's why I'm not part of this shit," I said, half defending myself and half defending Jake. "I'm not qualified."

"What makes you say that?" Vickie asked.

"Well, I don't know. For starters, I'm a college drop-out." Their faces grew serious, "Excuse me, sorry, a *junior-college drop-out*. I still live with my dad—Oh, Jake saved his life after a massive heart attack, so that's a fun fact."

"A charity case?" Vickie said with a laugh. "Jake is desperate these days."

"I found it odd, too." I smiled. "I mean, I get it. I was part of this bullshit of getting laid by a gorgeous guy and moving on the next day, but it turns out that fate brought us back together. I guess he's keeping me as a party favor for a while."

"Jake throws his girls away, and trust me when I tell you that you're not his type."

"I would imagine that decision is mine alone," Jake interrupted.

"Why is she here?" Vickie asked Jake, almost as if she and Jake had a history that'd just become that—history.

"Because over the past few weeks, I've learned there's a lot more to this man than any of you have the privilege to know," I stated.

"I guess that makes you the expert, then," Vickie responded to me, but her eyes never left Jake's. "So, when are you going to grow tired of playing with this toy?"

"You're drunk, Vick. Leave Ash out of our past."

She smiled and took a large gulp of her cocktail, rage igniting in her eyes. "When this whole game you're playing backfires in your face, don't expect me to be around for your fallout."

"Is that a threat?" Jake sneered. "Because trust me, any shit you have on me isn't something that hasn't already been smeared all over the fucking place." He took my hand in his, "And something tells me your ass is likely responsible for destroying my efforts to spread better news for the medical industry."

"Say what you want," she scolded. "We both know what you're most passionate about."

"Let's go, Ash. I won't listen to this shit anymore."

"Afraid she might know the person you *really* are, Jacob Mitchell?" Vickie said.

"As I said, if I were afraid," I interjected, "I wouldn't have shown up tonight."

"Let's go," Jake said, ending his stare-down with Vickie, the bitch.

We walked next to the pool toward Collin, Jim, and Alex. "Ash and I are heading to the upper deck. The blackout-drunk mean-girls are waiting for you all."

"We'll handle them," Jim said, then looked at me. "You look like you came out of that without a scratch."

"I think they were too drunk to tell me what they really thought of me." I smiled. "It was rather a dull moment. Oh," I said before leaving with Jake, "Lillian is sort of on one, so good luck with that." I winced at the intimidating businessman.

Jim's eyes roamed over to the women. "Alex," he said, "have someone babysit that group. I'd rather spend my brother's birthday with him instead of a drunk group of drama queens."

"Make that two of us," Collin added.

"And I get to corral them and let them know dancing on the yacht will be the only party they're partaking in for Jake tonight?" Alex answered and looked at Jake. "You invited them, dumbass." He laughed. "Get your asses up to the next deck. I'll handle the hospitality of the lonely-hearts club and be up in a few."

"That's why he's my right-hand guy." Jim smiled at Jake.

"Oh please," Collin and Jake looked at each other.

"Yeah, quit acting like you're God, Jimbo." He unexpectedly brought my hand up and kissed the back of it. "I'm getting Ash out of here. While you're in the act of apologizing to me for allowing Lillian on my boat." He looked at his brother. "You, *Jimmy*, can also arrange for drinks and food to be brought up there."

"Get out of here." Jim rolled his eyes and clapped his brother on the shoulder. "We'll ensure they're all taken care of by the staff so we can enjoy some privacy. We seriously need to warn Ashley about the man she's holding hands with." Jim winked at me, and then the three were walking off toward the party-goers as Jake led me toward a stair-case that spiraled up.

WE WERE OUT IN A PRIVATE LOUNGE AREA WHERE COMFORTABLE white canvas seating—something I imagined was much more boat-like—was set up. The couch-like accommodation was situated around a slate rock fire pit, shaped in a rectangle with glass to surround and protect the beautiful dancing flames that rose from the rock bed. The wind was muted by glass, but it didn't block the view as the yacht cruised along the coastline. I leaned against Jake's side, his arm up and around my shoulders while gazing out at the lights of the city, rolling through the dark water of the ocean.

"What are you thinking?"

I pulled my soft hoodie in tight. "How thankful I am that you thought to have comfortable clothing waiting for us in that pool locker area after we were thrown in tonight."

He laughed. "Well, I was thinking about how sexy you'd look in a beach poncho that should, of course, complement your yacht pants."

I ran my hands over the soft cotton fabric. "So, you've got my sizes memorized already?"

"No." He sighed. "Those lounge pants are shamefully too loose." He kissed my head as we heard the commotion of the guys coming up to the top deck.

"Here," Jim said, tossing a beer at Jake's bare chest, of which I was still grateful the man hadn't pulled on a shirt to conceal his perfect abs from me yet. "You both seem quite cozy," he winked and handed me a beer after twisting off the cap. "The guys are changing into their uniforms, and then they shall serve your royal highness the food you requested."

I sat up and curled my legs underneath me. "Is everything okay with us sort of ditching the party back there?"

Jim laughed. "Jake wouldn't care if they all fell overboard." He tipped his head back and took a drink of his beer. "Although I don't know how that would fare with their lawyers."

"You pity that group of desperate fools too much," Jake answered. "Besides, we're up here to avoid them." He looked at me and smiled. "They won't get their feelings hurt for our lack of being around them if that's what you're wondering."

"They're so wasted," I heard Collin's raspy, yet deep voice say from behind the door that opened to this private area. "Alex and I actually had to have security babysit the group."

"Nothing out of the norm," Alex said as the men sat down and joined the solitude of the environment.

"I saw one of the interns from my ward in that group." Jake shook his head. "That shit shouldn't be anywhere near me outside of work, especially with the media buzzing around me like hornets."

"What's that saying about the media, Alex?" Jim smirked over at the dark blond man. "If it doesn't bleed, it doesn't lead?"

Alex chuckled, his green eyes brilliant against the light of the flames from where he and Jim sat across from us. "Pretty much. And so long as they keep finding stories to dig up on you and poor Jakey here, they'll keep finding ways to make you bleed before this is over."

"When will that ever be?" Jake asked. "Good grief, at this point in my life, I'd like to think I knew I was a dumbass and reckless with my life outside of work. And now," he took another drink of beer, "I get to try and put that chapter in my life behind me while someone is begging to dig up yet another act of stupidity on my part."

"This isn't going to ruin your job," I spoke up. "My dad and I heard multiple patients in your office discussing how they're worried your talents are going to have them replaced."

Collin smiled. "It's a good day when your cardio doc replaces you with a new patient, and you're alive to move on from the man." He nodded at me. "Jake's not replacing anyone, trust me. Those patients—all of his patients—are his other family. Shit." He punched Jim, where he sat in a chair on Collin's right. "Even you ride second best to his family of patients."

Jim eyed me with a smile that reminded me of Jake's daring grins. "Make that third in Jakey's lineup." He leaned forward, resting both elbows on his knees. "I have to hand it to you, Jake. I swear you appear to be a changed man."

I felt my cheeks warm up, knowing this conversation could go a million different directions.

Jake's hand ran along my shoulders. "Quit getting sentimental, old man," Jake said, diffusing any stupid concerns I may have had.

"Speaking of old men," Collin said, "my dad told me you wouldn't be performing the surgery."

"I won't. I can't," Jake stated.

I listened in as I found comfort in the flames of the gas-lit fire. "What are the test results showing? He's not telling me shit," Collin asked.

Jake sat up. "I was hopeful." He ran the bottle of beer between his hands, looking at Collin. "But his kidneys are worse than ever. He and

I have been on this goddamn merry-go-round for over five years, and it's time he gets off the fucker and lets me take care of him. He needs the transplants, and he knows that. His diabetes put him in this position, and he's not even monitoring that well."

"It pisses me the fuck off," Collin said while Jim and Alex looked on with concern.

"He still won't consider the transplant?" Jim asked.

"Nope. He thinks Jake can turn water into wine." Collin smirked, but I could see the sadness in his face. "The son of a bitch is going to die because of his obstinacy, and I'm going to kick the goddamn casket over at his funeral when the day comes."

Jake smiled. "Aside from Ash's dad, your dad is the most stubborn man I've ever met. You don't run empires by being a pushover, I guess."

"Yeah, you run them by being smart and stubborn," Alex said, seemingly as disgusted as Collin was.

"No, shit." Jim chuckled. "That's old-man Brooks, though. We all know that Mitchell and Associates wouldn't be anywhere near where it is now if it weren't for his help after dad died."

"Why won't he do the transplant?" I asked, concerned that Collin was pretty much in my shoes—or where I was before Dad surprised us all by telling Jake that he was going through with the transplant.

Jake looked over at me. "Same reasons your father wouldn't do it at first, but we've been on this subject with Mr. Brooks for at least five years. It's being stubborn and believing they're too old to matter. Your father expressed it to me more than once, even when I asked him to consider it for you and not only for him. It's a difficult thing for one to accept," he said, eyes diverting to the dark ocean water. "I understand fully why anyone, regardless of their age, would find it difficult to accept a donor organ to save their lives. I've seen it first hand, and that's also why I've ensured I was with my clients when the donor family met with the recipient of a heart I transplanted. I've watched the donor family listen through a stethoscope, tears pouring out of their eyes. It's a very emotionally-charged moment, but I've seen when the donor family has found peace that their loved one has helped to save another."

"Wow," I said. "I'm so sorry." I looked at Collin. "Until recently, my dad has had me more than frustrated by not even considering the idea of a transplant." I looked at Jake. "I researched the hell out of success rates, and I didn't care if we had to sell the house. I didn't care about losing the material stuff. I saw where we could keep Dad around longer, and he shrugged it off like it was nothing. Thank you, though." I reached for his hand. "I had no idea you were in there advocating for my side this entire time." I glanced around the yacht. "However," I arched an eyebrow at his serious expression, "perhaps you only did all of that because you needed the money. You do seem quite broke."

Jake licked his lips as they turned up into a smile. "Goddammit, you busted me. I was selfishly pushing for that transplant for my own needs." He chuckled and brought his lips to mine. "Most definitely not yours. You've been the last person on my mind throughout this entire ordeal."

"We all know this is true." Alex chuckled. "The four of us can vouch for the fact that we haven't been badgered about you or even heard your name until tonight."

"Indeed." Jim sighed and smirked at Jake. "Whatever those women said down there about you and Jake, I'm probably going to have to agree with them."

I laughed. "That I was his flavor of the night or whatever?"

"Flavor of the night," Collin scoffed. "You did that shit to yourself, guy."

"We all did it to each other, dick," Jake said. "At least I shall be the first to find someone to change me from my wicked ways," he said dramatically. "All while you three watch it somehow bite me in the ass."

"I think Ash here is more confident in herself than to give your sorry ass that much credit, brother." Collin chuckled.

"This is true," Jim added. "If she's managed him, the bad press, the bad him in the press, and still managed to stay with this joker," he reached over and ruffled Jake's hair, "then I say all we can do is cheer to the best birthday present you've received in your life."

"To Ashley!" Alex raised his beer.

Jake rolled his eyes and smiled. "Cheer it up, boys, because I'm taking my birthday present to bed."

With that, the brothers and their friends made their silly toast, and Jake and I left for our room. We walked through yet another exit and ended up where the captain and a crew of two other men were in the wheelhouse of the boat. Jake introduced me, and we moved on, leaving the men to continue to relax after Jake asked them to set anchor and then worked with the men to pick out a new route for the next day. It seemed we were halfway up the coast, and Saturday and Sunday would bring us up toward Carmel-by-the-sea before slowly returning to Jake's marina.

Chapter Twenty-Two

Jake

My work schedule had trained my mind years ago that by five in the morning—no matter how late I stayed up—it was time to get up. For an hour, I enjoyed the peacefulness of Ash, sound asleep in my arms, her head resting on my bicep as it did the two nights she'd stayed over at the beach house.

Having her with me last night meant more than I thought it would. The guys sensed it, and I knew that with the way they behaved. Ash was a safeguard to the flack I would've gotten from the guys if she weren't there.

The guests at my nearly-forgotten birthday party were a reminder of the life I was gladly leaving behind, and the only thing that had me unsettled now was my dumbass proclamation of *love* to Ash in the pool. I had a feeling she was learning more about my impulsive self and crazy ways of doing things. From the first moment our eyes met in that coffee shop, she wrapped a spell around my soul with her eyes and flushed cheeks, and as fate would have it, it would all be confirmed that this woman was the one to change me forever by ensuring our paths crossed again. I enjoyed the breath of fresh air she offered me, and in my heart of hearts, I allowed myself to absorb whatever was happening with both of us without reservation.

She was still reserved, and I knew she was protecting herself from the monster that she'd been seeing on television or reading about. I had to hope that she'd eventually see me for who I'd become because of her. It would take time, but to keep her? I'd wait. Thank God for the career I'd chosen because patience was ingrained into my nature. If I could stand over a patient in my OR for fourteen hours performing tedious surgery, I think I could wait for as long as Ash needed to feel comfortable to have me as her own.

I'd been awake for an hour and a half, relishing in our fantastic sex throughout the night. I didn't want to leave this state, but I was getting restless, and though I'd love to wake her up to another glorious round of sex, her restful breathing prompted me to leave her to her peaceful state.

After speaking with my captain over a cup of coffee, I walked out of the wheelhouse to my favorite part of the yacht. I had the designers of the vessel create an area where I could recline in solitude on the bow. It overlooked another pool location where we had retreated to for the small party last evening. The area was beneath the wheelhouse's large windows, but it was set perfectly out of view from there or the lower deck on the bow.

Just as the stars were being erased from the black sky and replaced by the stunning magenta of the fresh summer morning sky, Ash walked out, looking like the angel I knew her to be since our first night together.

"So, this is where you hide on this boat, eh?" she asked, crawling up to where my open arms pulled her onto my lap.

I tugged on her topknot. "You look like some impressive man had his way with you last night."

She rested her head against my chest as she found comfort stretching out at my side. She ran her fingertips over the hooded sweatshirt I wore. "I don't know how he felt, but I sorta feel like I had my own way with him last night."

"Really?" I smiled. "I'm sure he enjoyed that."

"I have no idea. I woke up, and he was gone."

"What a douchebag," I said.

"Yeah, imagine the horror I suffered after having my way with him all night long, then he disappears on me."

"Sucks for him; sounds like you weren't finished with him."

She leaned up and kissed my lips. "I was only taking a nap, and when I woke up to give him the best blow job of his life." She ran her fingers over my hard cock that was threatening to bust through the Velcro of the board shorts I wore. "He was gone."

"What a fucking dumbass," I said, growing more uncomfortable with my hardened cock as I imagined her brown glazed eyes while she sucked my cock like it was hers and drank my cum with a hunger that always made me explode.

She giggled. "It's too bad you left the room."

"No, shit." I sucked in a ragged breath, wishing I knew for sure this area on my bow was concealed from any and everybody. "Fuck me." I blew out a sigh and ran my hand over her hair, seeing those same eyes from last night. "Goddamn, you're not lying, are you?"

"It's too bad you're sitting out here for some media chopper to break their morning news on you getting a blow job on your billion-dollar yacht." She laughed.

"You're a tease, and I'm going to fuck that little pussy so hard just to punish you for torturing me like this."

"Punish me? I'd enjoy that."

"All right, little miss artist," I said, forcing the subject change, "as badly as I want to clear the wheelhouse of the boat and fuck you while you hold on to the wheel of the ship, this part of the day I don't want you to miss."

"Oh my God," she said softly, sitting up with me. "I hate to admit this, but this is more beautiful out on the open sea than at your beach house."

I smiled at her as she marveled at the sun's rays shooting up from the other side of the horizon. "This is the bay, angel, but you will see a sunrise in the open sea when we bring this vessel to Cabo."

We sat quietly as I let Ashley absorb the beautiful sights of the shoreline to our right and the endless shoreline to our left as the captains engaged the yacht to follow the course that we agreed on last night, and I re-approved this morning. The wind picked up as the yacht smoothly proceeded in moving forward toward Carmel and the Monterey Peninsula.

"The weather says the marine layer will lift, and it will be a fantastic day to view the sea life in Monterey Bay this afternoon. One of the whale excursion boats noted the migrating blue whales were in the area last week. I'm hopeful we'll experience something majestic today."

She turned back to me, her eyes wide with excitement. "And the rest of the people on the boat?"

I smiled. "They'll all be hungover and mostly staying toward the back at the party decks. I've ordered the staff to have plenty of entertainment for them while I keep you to myself."

"I feel like they're already going to eat me alive—"

I held my finger up to her plump lips. "Those women are like hyenas and hunt in packs, but I watched you handle them when they were too drunk to think, and you did great. Furthermore, I couldn't possibly give a shit about what they think. They're on the boat so they can take their pictures and plaster them all over social media, pretending they're living the high life, I suppose. The only difference is, this time my ugly mug won't be in their pictures."

"So, they're not going to get all butt-hurt that you're not around?"

"God, no." He rolled his eyes. "So long as I keep the booze, food, and music going? They'll be the happiest party girls on the planet."

"Funny to imagine you hanging out with them." She bit her bottom lip. "Shit, that came out rudely. I'm sorry. I'm sure they're not horrible people. They're just not my crowd."

I pulled her back into my arms and brought my lips to hers. "You're damn right they're not your crowd, and after this boat gets back to port and they disembark, they'll realize it was their last voyage with the guy who was dumb enough to have wasted so many years around them."

"Do you feel like you're being a little abrupt with all of these life changes and saying you love me?"

"Is it frightening you?" I asked, wondering if I was coming on too strong and too fast.

"No," she said, seemingly shocked she'd said it. "I just worry about you. We are moving really fast, Jacob Mitchell."

I smiled. "When I want something, I go after it, and I won't let it go." Our eyes locked in the way that always reassured me that this woman was the other part of my soul. "Ash, I was not careless with my words when I told you I was in love with you. Those people you met? That's part of the life the media is using to attempt to destroy my career. I was uncontrolled and vain, but they were my only outlet. They are toxic people. I see that now."

"Well, let's enjoy our time alone then," she said. "Your friends and brother, they can—"

"They'll make sure they're hiding along with us. The only place they will not follow us is to our room."

"Have they had a sudden life change along with you, too?" She laughed.

"No," I answered her. "They're just highly intrigued by getting to know the woman who calmed my crazy ass down."

She arched her eyebrow, and damn it, she was going to get fucked before breakfast now. "I highly doubt I calmed you down."

I rose, helped her down, and rushed her through the wheelhouse, "As I have mentioned multiple times, when you raise your eyebrow at me like that, your ass is mine."

Our lips crashed into each other's as I carried her in my arms, rushing our asses to the closest empty cabin on the boat. "Where are we?" she giggled.

"In the room where I'm about to fuck you into a frenzy." I worked to strip her out of her clothes. "I let you have all the control last night; today, I get all of it." I reached down to find her as wet as my cock was hard. "Fuck me, we're making up new positions today, angel."

IT HAD BEEN TWO WEEKS SINCE THE WEEKEND ON THE YACHT WITH Ash. We vowed to stay away from the media after a helicopter decided to gain interest in the boat that I was either going to have to sell or paint a new color. This shit was driving me insane. Vick gave Ash more than enough bitch glances, and I had a feeling that the woman would become a problem if I didn't talk her down. Just to see her face on the boat and anywhere near Ash made me nauseous. I thought Lillian was a problem for my brother, but Vick was the head of the goddamn snake. She was pure venom, and if I didn't handle her in the best way I believed was possible the day I dropped Ash off, I knew she'd fuck my life over, but not before destroying or hurting Ashley.

The woman seemed to relax, stating she'd moved on from being the piece of ass she'd known she'd been to me. The worst part of it was, she fucking used my ass for sex too. She honestly had nothing on me, but I was the rich fucking dick, and the minute she found herself outside of these circles, she'd try to sink me. She would always be a problem until she truly did move the fuck on.

I used this weekend of being on call to go over the details for the trip to Cabo. Since our yacht trip and my declaration of love toward Ash, I'd spent my evening after work going to her place, or if she weren't tired, we'd meet in the middle and relive those first nights together in a hotel.

We spent the weekend at the beach house. Her love for the ocean was apparent, and that's mostly the reason she still hadn't been to my home in Hollywood Hills. That and I didn't want her in that bachelor pad, but I wasn't going bat-shit crazy just yet and selling the place.

While charting out the points of interest I wanted to bring Ash to on vacation, my OR paged me to a resuscitated cardiac arrest from the ER.

My heart sank when I called for the charts and saw the name. The RN handed the paperwork to me: John Brooks, male, age seventy-one. The words glared at me like I was looking into the sun.

I instantly disconnected from my best friend's dad, who was hanging on for his life in my OR. I scrubbed in, letting each brisk movement cleanse my mind and detach any personal feelings. There was a reason I wouldn't put this man under my steel. He wasn't a candidate for heart surgery, and now I was up against all the odds in saving his life.

. . .

"Jake." I barely heard my voice being called as I ignored all the machines around me, "Jacob," Dr. Samson called again. "Dr. Mitchell." I finally looked up at my attending physician.

"I need blood pressures," I said, knowing it was futile to continue.

"Jacob," the white-haired physician somberly called my name, "you need to call it. He's expired. There's nothing more we can do."

I glanced up at the heart monitor. All eyes had been on me for the last three hours before renal failure complicated the progress on John's strained heart. *No! No! No! Fuck.* I'd lost him. His labs had shown a stroke had triggered this bomb that was begging to go off for years, but my God, I had him. He was stable. Now, he was gone.

Stop it, Jacob! I ordered myself amongst the silence of the room. I was under the eye of my attending physician, my OR staff, and interns. I had to pull it together. I looked up at the clock, "Calling time of death, two thirty-three a.m.," I said. "Nurse Andrews."

"Yes, Doctor."

"Work with the staff to prepare the body for the family."

"Yes, Doctor. The family is in the ICU waiting room."

"I'll need you, Dr. Samson, and two nurses with me," I said, turning to have an OR staff member remove my headgear while I worked to dump my bloodied protective gear in the trash.

I maintained supreme focus as I walked toward the waiting room to give the news to my best friend and Marilyn, John's wife, who I knew were waiting for those doors of horror to open and deliver a verdict.

I couldn't.

When I walked in, Collin was still in his scrubs, which was not like him. I instantly went to Marilyn after Collin nodded in understanding that I wasn't here to bring the news they'd hoped for.

I took Marilyn's hand and sat down. "John's stroke forced him into renal failure. His heart could not be revived, and despite my greatest efforts to keep him with us, he wasn't able to pull through." This was not how we talked to families, mostly, but this was mine and Jim's other family, and as I spoke to Marilyn, Collin called Jim to give him the news.

Marilyn crumbled in my arms, and I held her as close as I could while keeping my strong front. "Thank you, Jacob," she sobbed while Collin pulled her into his arms.

"I'll bring you all back to him when you're ready."

"Hey, man," Collin said, his voice cracking and eyes filling with tears. "You did everything you could do."

I nodded in understanding as Collin looked at me somberly. My best friend knew me well enough to understand this was going to spin me out the moment I allowed that part of me take over.

Fuck me to hell. I lost John despite everything I could do.

"Jim's on his way down," Collin said, bringing me back to the present.

"Dr. Mitchell to OR four," I heard my name called out. "Dr. Jacob Mitchell to OR four."

What the hell, was it a full moon? I'd lost my other fucking dad, and now I had to perform another emergency surgery?

I needed to pull my shit together and now. What I'd learned in losing John on my table less than an hour ago might serve to save my next patient's life. I heard my name called again and looked to Collin. "A nurse will be out to escort you to John," I said.

"Go," Collin said, knowing another patient's life depended on me getting my shit together. "We'll talk to you later."

I cleared my throat and my mind. While it wasn't uncommon to have busy nights like this, it wasn't typical either, but I was grateful I managed to muscle through it and join Dr. Samson as his attending. We saved a thirty-five-year-old woman's life by clearing a blockage with a stint.

Walking out to the ICU waiting room to find her husband and parents helped ease the pain of losing the man I had no choice but to grieve for later.

Chapter Twenty-Three

Jake

I stood on the perfectly manicured lawns of the cemetery, staring at the polished mahogany casket. I held Ash's hand as she stood quietly to my right while Jim stood stiffly at my left. We listened to Collin eulogize his father before the minister stepped in and finalized the burial service.

I managed to push everything down since losing John on my table and was able to force conversation and smiles that would show everyone around me that I was doing fine with it all. I was grateful Ash was with me, more shocked than anything she took me up on my request to join me for this farewell to the man who'd taken the place of my father after Dad succumbed to a heart attack as well.

I went into this line of work to prevent my standing here with this grieving family, and yet, here I was, staring at the casket of a man who fell to the silent killer anyway.

I pulled my eyes from the casket and slid them over to the beautiful woman standing soberly at my side. I needed the distraction of the one thing in my life that was good. The one person who seemed to bring out this new side of me to which I would forever be grateful for.

Sadly, even having her here wasn't helping the grief, guilt, and despair I was currently experiencing. Fuck me to hell if I couldn't just cope with John's death and move the hell on already.

After the burial, I went through the motions of celebrating John's life with immediate family and close friends at John and Marilyn's house. The mansion suddenly felt claustrophobic as people came to thank the doctor who tried to keep John with them. I had to get the fuck out of this place.

Ash and I left when I noticed the drinking had commenced. It was the perfect out, and I didn't hesitate to take it.

"We're almost at my place," Ash said, breaking through my auto-pilot driving and gripping the steering wheel harder than necessary. "Are you sure you're okay, Jake?"

I forced the smile I'd been using since John passed. "Fine, Ash. Thanks again for coming with me today. I hope it wasn't too much."

She reached over and placed her hand over mine on the stick shift. "It wasn't too much. In fact, it's got me thinking."

"Oh, yeah?" I absently answered her.

"Dad and I have been sort of stuck in some bizarre state in the idea that keeping Mom's urn with us would help to keep her with us." She softly chuckled. "We need to put her to rest in Santa Clarita. We need to move forward with the acknowledgment that we've been blessed to have her and learn from her, and now it's time to do what she'd requested before she passed."

"What was her request?" I answered, not necessarily listening, but trying to hang onto something I knew was monumental for the woman I loved.

"She said to live for her." Ashley choked out the words, causing me to turn my hand from gripping the gearshift and to intertwining our fingers together. "Not to die with her." Her fingers gripped my hand. "All these years, and I never realized it until today—listening to Collin talk. It's our duty to live for our lost loved ones. How in the hell could I have imagined my mom being at peace when Dad and I weren't?"

"You've been doing an amazing job accepting that loss." I smiled over at her. "Both you and your dad are proving to move forward and live your lives to their fullest."

I pulled my hand from hers as I shifted gears and steered us down the road toward her house.

"Do you want to come in?" she asked.

"I think I'm just going to head home." I placed my hand around her neck, helping to bring her face close as I leaned over to press my lips to hers. "Not trying to be a dick, but this week has kicked my ass."

"I get it." She smiled. "Tomorrow is Saturday, so if you want to do something this weekend, you know where to find me."

"Fuck," I said, knowing I'd barely survived the fucking week. "I've lost track of time."

"It's understandable." She ran her hands along my cheek. "I'm here for you, Jake. Take all the time you need."

"Thanks," I said.

I would have never believed this whole thing would bring me not to see Ash for the next three weeks, but it did. And three weeks later, I found myself going to do the only thing I believed that could wake me from the fucked-up state of mind I was in—surfing.

"Bruh," the group of surfers I'd spent the morning trading waves with approached. These guys were hardcore surfers, and this was their territory. "If it isn't the media-famed playboy," the young man said, paddling over.

"Good to see you too, Flex," I said, acknowledging this surf group's leader.

"What brings you out to Trustles today?"

"Waves were more aggressive. I needed to get some fucked-up energy out of my system."

"Lose one, man?" he asked, these guys knowing more about me than myself when I came out to surf their waters.

I nodded at the man I'd become friends with years ago after he saved mine and Collin's life when we thought we were badass enough to surf this location on new boards we weren't familiar with. Truth be told, I never understood why the man didn't kick both our asses for almost killing ourselves and him and his buddies rescuing us in the process.

"You know me too well," I answered, straddling the board and watching the best sets of waves line up, but not in the mood to ride into the perfect curl they were creating.

"You only bring that board out when you've got shit you need out of your system." He nodded toward my shortboard. "Though you've only ridden through a few good pipes, and I have to question why you're watching the last of the best waves we'll get today head to shore."

I smirked at him. "I have to ask why you suddenly give more of a damn about my state of mind than those waves."

"Smartass," he answered. "Who'd you lose, a young one?"

My lips tightened. "Nah, Collin's dad."

"Shit," Flex said. "Collin okay?"

"Collin's managed through it all pretty well. He's got a ton of bullshit with the company, though."

"You know," Flex started, "when the ocean brings life—"

"Flex," I interrupted, "I swear I don't want to sound like an asshole, but I'm not out here to listen to metaphors about the fucking ocean. I just had to get away from the noise."

"I get it," he said, straddling his board, now floating in the water next to me. He reached over and chuckle. "Looks like Collin might be taking my place in the words of encouragement department."

I squinted out and watched the surfer who duck-dived a breaking wave and popped up from the other side reveal himself as my best friend.

"Yeah, I'm sorta fucked now. Probably best to take the next set."

"Your dumbass isn't going anywhere," Collin said as he paddled over to where Flex and I sat on our boards. "What the hell? If this were the morning we were going to surf, I'd think your stupid ass would have invited me. What's up, Flex?"

"Just sitting here catching a board-tan with your boy." Flex laughed.

"And we all know how much you love watching sets roll past you." He pinched his nose clear of the water that splashed up in his face.

"'Sup, fucker?" Collin asked, sitting on his board facing both Flex and me.

"Just trying to get it all out of my system," I answered, looking at the shoreline filling with people—and fucking media as usual. "Those assholes follow you here?" I nodded toward the crew coming down with tripods, gear, and of course, the mighty camera lenses.

Collin looked back. "Well, you are the doctor who did everything right to try and save one of the world's greatest billionaires." He chuckled.

"I seriously can't believe that shit didn't backfire in my face."

"Yeah, Dad's laughing at your sorry butt from the great beyond."

"Why?" I smirked. "Because he knew my personal life being blasted all over the place wasn't enough, so he thought he'd die to make these people travel from around the globe to follow me now?"

"Hey." Collin laughed. "He was definitely the type of man who would have known how to get you good publicity and not just local —global."

"That was his style." I exhaled. "Always about building global platforms."

"Unfortunately, I have a feeling," Flex added, "that those mother fuckers might have a new way of twisting shit up for you now that you're out on the board."

"Yeah." Collin chuckled. "And all the hot chicks in the bikinis will serve to kick a can of gas on that fire of bullshit they'll come up with."

"What?" I snapped. "I can't have a fucking sport I enjoy? These assholes think I sit in a basement all day or some shit like that, researching medical science like a mad man?"

"Hell," Collin said, "I thought that's where you wound up after I called Ash looking for you."

"Ash," I said her name as if I was shocked she was still in my life. "Fuck, I haven't seen her in weeks."

"Good thing she's not giving in to the BS stories about her being the latest victim of the Billionaires' Club."

My stare darkened. "What?"

"You knew that shit would be plastered all over the place," Collin said. "As soon as you and Ash stepped out together, all they've done is watch you two and wait for Ash to become absent from their photos."

I scooped up water and ran it over my legs. "Fuck me, man."

"Who's Ash?" Flex asked, studying his guys as they rode the last of the good waves.

"A woman who we all actually believed changed Jakey here from the asshole we all know and love."

"You son of a bitch," Flex splashed me with water. "I'm losing money on your stupid ass."

I smiled at him, the thought of Ash making me relax some, but I was also tense in the fact that I'd been blowing her off with lame-ass texts. God only knew what she thought of me. These stories exposing my life never really had an effect on her, but now I was stupidly living up to the love 'em and lose 'em headlines.

"Losing money?" I shook my head at my Tahitian surfer buddy. "How many of you dipshits have bets going on my life?"

"The whole world at this point, brah," Flex said while he and Collin laughed in unison. "Well, you two enjoy these ankle-biters. I'm closing up shop for the day."

"See ya."

"You've got this, Jake. You looked good out there this morning," Flex said. "I almost thought you knew what you were doing."

Collin grinned as Flex popped on his board a road a small wave into shore.

He looked over at me. "You need to move past this. You know it's exactly what Dad wanted."

I looked down the coastline. "I know I couldn't save him on that table. I know that. I've come to grips with that."

"Then why are we into this for at least two weeks now?"

I pinched my lips together. "I can't get it out of my mind. What if I used different words when trying to persuade him? What if there was a better way to talk to him? I should've been able to prevent this."

"And there we have it. Dr. Mitchell is playing God with lives."

I moved the water through my hands. "Not playing God at all, Coll," I said. "Just thinking about what I could have done differently in convincing him."

"You couldn't have done anything differently," Collin answered. "Dad was a stubborn ass, and we all knew that. Why carry the burden of his hard-headed personality that put him in the grave?"

"As a doctor of medical science, it's my job to fix and find answers to each patient I have. I use my experience with patients I've saved and lost to move on and learn what I can do differently with future patients," I said.

"And so you're going to ride the board until the answers come?"

"I'm out here to get a little fucking peace, and you're not allowing that."

"That's what best friends are for." Collin smirked. "Let's get out of here and go grab a beer. It's fucking five o'clock somewhere."

"Very original," I said, conceding.

"Jake." Collin reached out and snatched my board. "Let it the fuck go. This goes beyond your research bullshit you just fed me. I'm a doctor too; I've lost patients too. We both grieve their losses differently, yes. My dad hits close to home for you, yes. But you've got to get your ass back in the game."

"I've operated on two hearts this week, both patients successfully recovered and home now. I'm in the game."

"You're hiding behind patients," Collin said. "Listen, I'm your best friend, and I know you better than anyone, even Jim. You're vacant, man. You're going to lose Ash, and you know it. But do you even give a shit?"

"Of course, I do."

"See," he said, scowling at me. "Your face always had this sappy, giddy, and breezy as fuck look whenever her name was spoken, but now." He blew out a breath. "Hopefully, she'll still be around when you come out of this."

"How do you expect me to switch gears?"

"Stop going over the bullshit of an idea that you could have found the words to save Dad. Knock that shit off. You know better, and you knew him better than that. My dad would kick your ass from the grave if he knew his stubborn bullshit was the reason you're falling the fuck apart. You're not saving anyone by using John Brooks as your example of what you should have done differently."

"You're right. Well said," I answered. "Let's paddle these boards in. I'm in the mood for some fish."

"Fish tacos are calling my name," Collin said. "How about we bring Ash out tomorrow and teach her the one thing her man is most enthusiastic about when it comes to sports."

"Ash loves the ocean. She already threatened to kick my ass if I ruined that love she had if she got seasick on the yacht. There's no way in hell I'm destroying that while sharks are migrating through the pacific."

"For fuck's sake, Jacob," he said. "You need to pull your shit together. Why don't we let Ash decide if she's going to fear marine life killing her and not the fearless chump who went softer than a wet turd on me?"

"You're such an idiot sometimes," I answered, bringing my body to lie on the board. "You're right, I'd much rather see Ash's expression when I ask her to join me surfing instead of assuming that I was trying to kill her off."

"That's a great story for these Billionaires' Club headlines." Collin laughed. "The Billionaires' Club moves to the next level in ditching their so-called lovers—"

I popped on the board after paddling forward with the momentum of a small wave rolling in. The four-foot wave was perfect enough for me to cut back and forth before allowing a final ride into shore.

Chapter Twenty-Four

Ash

I was in the process of putting the final touches on the portrait of
the sunrise I'd experienced on Jake's yacht when I heard a knock at
the door. I brushed my hands over the smock I wore, smearing any wet
pet I might have had on them away.

It has to be Jake, I thought, looking at the clock. It was ten-thirty at
night, but it was also Saturday, so what the hell was happening?

I crossed the living room and peeped through the hole to see Jim
standing out front. I quickly unlocked the deadbolt, keeping it quiet
because everyone but I was sound asleep.

"Jim?" I questioned.

His lips rose on one side. "Sorry, I'm not the brother you—"

"Were hoping to see for the first time in three weeks?" I chuckled
and stepped back. "Come inside."

We sat on the couch, and the expression on Jim's face made me
more concerned about Jake than the random texts he'd been
sending me.

"What's wrong with Jake?" I went straight to the point.

Jim ran his hand through his onyx hair. "I think it would help if you visited him. He's functioning fine, but I can tell John's death is hanging over his head."

I bit the tip of my fingernail. "I don't want to be a nuisance to him if he needs his space."

Jim leaned forward, his elbows on his knees. "You'd be far from that." He smiled over at me. "Jake's not used to being in a relationship, and the fact that the woman he's fallen for would help him, he—" Jim looked at me, his stark blue eyes seemingly begging me to catch on to what he was saying.

"He doesn't realize I might be able to help him through this?" I suggested.

"Exactly," Jim said with a sigh. "We've all tried to get him to shake this out of his system. He blames himself for not having the right words as John's cardiologist to help the man prevent his death."

"From what you all have said about Mr. Brooks, I would assume that Jake would understand there was no getting through to him."

"Yes, but Jake losing him on that table to multiple complications— not just the lack of a heart or kidney transplant—he's shouldering all of it. Perhaps being with you may help him. I've never seen my brother harness this much guilt over losing someone."

"He mentioned that he became a heart surgeon after losing your dad. Maybe grieving that loss and the fact that he feels defeated is what's holding him down."

"Yes." Jim nodded, and he reached for my hand. "Ash," he said in some pleading tone, "I know it's a lot to ask of you, and I'll understand if you can't, but Jake needs you more than he needs us or using work as a distraction."

"You don't have to ask. I'll leave tonight, but if he's at his house in the Hills, I have no idea how to get there."

"He's at the beach house. I'll have my driver take you there."

"You think he's still up?"

Jim laughed. "I would be shocked if the man had fallen asleep in the last three weeks."

"Got it," I said, getting up. "Let me pack a bag, and I'll be out in a sec."

THIS ENTIRE TIME, I'D FORCED INSECURITIES ABOUT JAKE MOVING on from me out of my head. I pointedly ignored all stories from the media, knowing I might see Jake and someone else. He did text me, but it was mainly vague texts about how busy he was. I'd believed they were all excuses to move on, and he was trying to break it to me gently after all the excitement we'd shared on the yacht.

Now, I knew the man was in trouble. He was mentally struggling, and if his brother was showing up, I could accept it wasn't him just going over the edge in lust with some chick he had fun sex with. I hated that I couldn't easily accept that he was in love with me, but Jesus, we were moving fast, and I had been fighting my feelings.

Now that I knew the extent of his distress, I felt horrible. My heart was shattered that I didn't put my selfish thoughts aside and see through the texts. I was more worried about keeping up my guard than I was about letting the man in and helping him when he needed it most. As I sat in the back of this Bentley with Jim, I knew that I was in love with Jake and would do everything I could to help him.

"God," I said as the freeway exit came into view, and Jim ended the conversation he'd been having on the phone since we left my house.

"Sorry about that," Jim said, resting his head against the headrest. "I swear my job has me by the throat at times." He laughed. "And in the act of looking like a complete douchebag while riding with my driver, it's these damn phone calls that keep me from actually enjoying driving myself around."

"You don't have to explain all of that to me." I laughed. "But do you ever get a break from it all?"

"Never," he said with a laugh. "Well, sometimes I'll push the work down to Alex, but he's occupied with some other nonsense at the moment. It can be annoying when we're in a position with a client that can't be avoided."

"So, your love life is well, then?"

He smiled at me. "It's a dreamy one." He held up his phone. "This baby and I never leave each other's sides."

I rolled my eyes. "God forbid."

"I can see how my brother has taken to you as he has. I'm sure you give him snarky responses even worse than this."

"We play around some," I answered, enjoying this side of Jim. The arrogant businessman I'd seen in him before was exhausted and stressed, which was easy to understand, but I could also sense his concern for his brother had grown, and now here he was with *me* of all people.

"It's good for his crazy ass," he said. "You're good for him."

"Thanks for telling me that. I try not to let all the shit that's going around about him being the world's sexiest player get to me, but I'll be honest, I have. I just don't want to put myself out there and get smacked in the face for it."

Jim nodded. "Completely understandable. Jake was the wildest of us all, and yet," he grinned at me, "he met a lovely young woman who he was smart enough to appreciate when she came into his life. I doubt we'll ever encounter the Jake you read about or see on television again. I'm glad for that."

I pursed my lips as we turned into Jake's driveway. "I'm sorta nervous."

Jim opened the door. "Don't be. I'll let you in. Have a nice evening, and I'll be praying you can get through to him." Jim helped me out of the car. "Don't let him close off to you or play you like a fool." His eyes locked onto mine. "I've heard you both in conversation. You are wise to him, so stay that way."

"Got it."

AFTER JIM WALKED ME THROUGH ALL THE SECURITY OF THE HOUSE, he practically growled when another call came in. "Fuck, it's Saturday night, and my phone is blowing up with business calls like it's Monday morning!" He looked at me. "Sorry about the language." He sighed. "I have to go. You comfortable hunting him down?"

"I love this house. I can find my way around it. If he's asleep, I'll wake him up with a kiss." I laughed.

"A sleeping beauty recreation." He winked. "I'll give Jake a ring in the morning. He can thank me then."

"Hey, Jim," I said, stopping him. "Thanks for this. I would've never known he was in trouble if you didn't show up."

He arched his eyebrow and nodded in response, looking just like Jake with the gesture. "Talk to you later, Ash."

I walked through the house, and as I glanced out at the back patio, I saw Jake hunched over in swim trunks, intently studying the water.

"Hey," I said, startling him. "Someone told me the sexiest bachelor lived here."

Jake leapt from his lounge chair, and the next thing I knew, I was in his arms. "How in the hell did you find your way into this place?" I felt his lips press against my hair. "God, I've missed you." His hands roamed over my face. "I'm sorry I blew you off. I just didn't want you around me while I was in this state."

I took his face in mine, and at that moment, our lips found each other in desperation. I reluctantly pulled away. "Jim sent out the SOS for you and brought me here."

"Looks like I owe my brother more than a beer." He smiled, but I could see the pain in his eyes.

"You do," I said, taking his hand in mine. "Mind if I join you out here?"

"I would like that a lot."

We sat together, and he instantly stood again. "Let me get us some wine or food or something."

"Relax." I laughed. "I'll take a beer." I peered around him. "Looks like you have a cooler?"

Jake chuckled. "Yeah, pretty fucking stupid since my outdoor kitchen is right over there and stocked with these things."

"But you're drinking water?" I eyed the glass bottle on the table.

He shrugged. "I won't go anywhere near liquor when I'm feeling like this."

"How *are* you feeling, Jake?" I asked, taking the beer he'd handed me after he popped off the top.

"Like hell, if I'm honest." His eyes pooled. "I should be moved on by now, but the guilt won't leave me."

"Guilt of not keeping Mr. Brooks alive?"

"It's everything really, I guess. The media that backfired on us isn't helping either. I've watched my interview and sort of wondered who the hell that man was that was speaking. The shit that seemed to be so important for people like John—to help people like John—it's all a waste with my personal life taking precedence over everything. The media's obsession with that is beyond me."

I took a sip of my beer. "My dad has watched the documentary. You convinced that stubborn man to go through with the transplant. I know it's me just speaking about him, but trust me, Carmen was ready to throw a pot of albondigas soup at him one night, she was that frustrated with him."

Jake smiled. "I could only imagine how those two are getting along."

"I think they're kind of a secret item. I've caught them more than once."

Jake's eyes widened. "Doing?"

"Whatever it is that couples do when they sneak into each other's rooms like teenagers hiding from parents." I laughed.

"Oh, shit," Jake said, picking up a beer and taking a sip of it. "That has to suck."

"Thank God I was in the process of sneaking off to hotels with you during their little rendezvous."

"Damn." He curled his lips after another sip of beer. His eyes sparkled under the enchanting lighting of his island-getaway backyard. "I would give anything to go back to those days."

"Go back?" I questioned with a laugh. "Did we break up, and I'm just now finding out about it?"

Jake's face was humored, and I could see him softening up the longer we talked. "Break up?" He scoffed. "After seeing you tonight, and how being in your presence is making me feel, I'd marry you now and never let you leave."

"Marriage talk again?" I arched an eyebrow while tipping my head back and taking a gulp of beer. "You are all over the place, Jacob Mitchell."

"I'm solid," he said, his face serious. "Come here."

We both stood, and he pulled me in close. He had music playing in the background, or I'd have thought he'd gone off the rails when he pulled my body close to his and began to sway to the softly playing music. His lips were on my neck, but it was nothing like before. Everything Jake was doing was making me coming undone. We slowly fell into a dancing rhythm while we held each other silently, and I absorbed this closeness that I'd needed longer than I realized.

Jake kissed my cheek and twirled me away from him and then back into his arms. "You're a fantastic dancer," I said as he dipped me backward and kissed me.

He let me up and pulled me close. "And so are you. I recall a night where I danced with a beautiful woman, believing I would marry her one day. Never once did I believe those thoughts would be more profound than they are now."

"Getting soft again?" I nervously asked.

"Never," he said, pulling me back, his knuckles brushing across my jawline. "I'll wait until it seems rational, of course. Until I know you are comfortable with me. I'll wait." His eyes raptly studied mine. "But I promise you this: you *will* be my wife one day."

Something happened at that exact moment. Both of us switched some gear in our heads, and instead of moving into the crazed and wild sex we loved having, we slowed down in a way I didn't think was possible.

"I love you, Jacob," I said after we walked into my favorite room of his house, the master suite with views that went on forever. "God." I shook my head and felt my eyes sting with tears. "I really do love you."

He smiled and ran his hands over my shoulders. "I truly hope you mean that because I'm about to show you how I treasure you in ways I haven't before." He touched his lips to my bare shoulders. "You are the other part of my soul, Ash."

I would have naturally fought those words off, but I understood exactly what he was talking about. I felt the same, though I had no idea he experienced it too.

I was helplessly in love with this man, who was successfully undressing me and laying me back on his bed. His lips drifted up my knees, to my thighs, hips, my stomach, and my lips. Jake and I had never had sex like this. This was a different Jake, and the look in his hungry eyes made me fall deep into this moment with him.

Chapter Twenty-Five

Ash

Having our bodies reunited like this was something I never expected would happen during all the sexual moments we'd shared since our initial one-night-stand. It was more pure, sincere, and it felt like some poetic thing was happening. I'd never fallen for the idea of the conception of souls uniting as one until this moment. Jake's eyes were filled with devotion, his kisses soft yet lingering against my skin as he intertwined our fingers together into the pillows above my head.

I felt my orgasm building without him working my G-spot with either his fingers or his cock. My clit wasn't used to this rolling and feverish response my body was having to him, gently guiding himself in and out of me.

I was in a state of total bliss. Having him fill me up deeply while his lips caressed my neck and over my breasts sent me into a state of pleasure I'd never experienced before, and that was saying a lot. Jake was a sexual genius who could keep my body rolling with orgasms all night long.

His groans were muffled against my lips as I tried to hold back, but I lost that battle after trying to prevent the inevitable for too long. I bucked into him, and Jake's hands went immediately to my face after my eyes rolled back, clinging to his back as this powerful orgasm pulsated through my entire body.

"Look at me, baby," he said, his teeth gently nipping at my bottom lip while he thrust in and out in perfect rhythm.

I moaned in utter satisfaction, almost purring like a freaking cat while this deep sensation continued. I opened my eyes to see his vivid blue ones studying mine. "Jake," I whispered breathlessly, my legs falling slack, giving him all the access that he needed to bring himself over the edge.

"That's right, angel." He smiled and captured my lips, his kiss rougher and more devoted than ever before.

I ran my hands over his lower back and tight ass. He was the epitome of sexiness. "Oh, my fucking God," I said, feeling like that was a tremor compared to what was bubbling up inside me.

I reached up into his hair, wondering how I was coming entirely apart under him, and he kept himself in unyielding control as our bodies moved together in perfect harmony. I rocked my head back into the pillows, so fucking sensitive, and my body was quivering in response to the hard cock stretching me at every angle now.

"You are so wet and tight," he said, and I finally heard the strain in his voice. The low voice of Jake when he was riding the edge and right before he came inside me. "You feel so good, Ash."

His lips captured my hard nipple, his tongue swirling around it and flicking at it with soft moans. My hands went to his biceps—he was fully flexed and holding back. "Come inside me, Jake," I said, feeling like I was about to reach yet another climax. Shit like this just didn't happen to me. I had to have something working my pleasure points to come, and especially if I was going to have multiple orgasms while having sex.

I fully understood that my body must have been responding to Jake on another level than I imagined possible. Jake's smooth rhythm, his eyes, smiles, the looks of ecstasy all over his face. It was everything. The smell of the salty air blowing into his room while his rich cologne filled my senses. This was paradise somehow, and I'd only hoped that I could pull this magic off with Jake time and time again.

"I've missed this. You're coming on your own, aren't you?" he said, eyes wild now.

I licked my dry lips after watching him bite down on his lower lip, "Yes, fuck, this is amazing." I squirmed beneath him. "Deeper," I insisted.

"Holy fuck, baby, that's it. Squeeze my cock, Ash." Jake fisted my hair, tilting my head back, and giving him access to running his lips and tongue over my neck while he drove his cock in harder and deeper.

I didn't have to try to squeeze anything. I called out louder while my pussy throbbed in acceptance to him. I had to admit I loved it when we had sex without a condom, which was the entire time on his yacht. He had them, but we were so impulsive, we never used them. It was birth control that was in full effect now.

Jake was so different when he was inside me without a condom to mute all of the sensations that he'd mentioned sent him over the top—skin on skin—like this. His expressions were different, and it was crazy how much closer we both were when we threw the added protection and caution to the wind.

I felt Jake's entire body tense as it always did when he was one hard thrust away from coming inside me. An array of Jake's usual cursing filled the room as he rode his orgasm out hard into me. His lips were usually all over my body after he came inside me, but this time, his lips were so soft and tinder against my own. Our tongues beautifully captured each other to complete our sincerity of this moment.

His hands caught my face while we continued to kiss, Jake's cock slowly moving in and out of me. "I love you so much. That was intense. It was beyond that." He nipped my chin—a new thing I noted on our nonstop sex-filled weekends together.

"You reached a new level with me, Jakey-boy," I teased as I squeezed his cock inside of me for the hell of it.

"Shit." Jake flexed, his forehead hitting my chest. "I forgot that's your favorite thing to do." He chuckled and kissed my collar bone. "Always catching me at my most sensitive points."

I ran my hand through his messy hair when he laid his cheek on my chest. "Just making sure you know that may have been all you and the best sex of my life, but you're always at my mercy."

He softly laughed as I ran my fingertips over the tense muscles of his back. "I've been at your mercy since the first time in San Francisco."

"I think tonight beats all of it," I said, turning my head toward the moonlight peering down on the ocean.

"You're correct on that." He sighed. "Your hands feel so good on my back."

I could tell that beyond this passionate sex we had, Jake was exhausted, but it seemed like he may have found peace for the time being. We'd never had sex this intimately and with a true meaning of devotion behind it before.

Jake kissed my forehead and gently pulled himself away and brought me into his arms. I loved falling asleep in his arms like this. This time, he held me tightly as if I were a security blanket. His chin rested on my head while he molded his body into me, and before I could tease him, his breathing was deep and sound.

I ran my hand over the arm he had resting along my abdomen. I hated myself for being so insecure that I wouldn't at least check on him in the last few weeks. In everything that he'd said to me before, I never believed it to be wholly sincere until tonight. I was learning that Jacob Mitchell was quite impulsive and also wasn't afraid to go after what he wanted. I think anyone in my position with a ridiculously gorgeous man—smart, known for being a player, and full of ambition— would have to have felt the way I did in our relationship.

You don't just snag the gorgeous man you had a one-night-stand with a year later, then find out that he was a renowned heart surgeon who saved your dad, who also happened to be extremely wealthy. I wanted to be confused, slow it down some, and question it all more, but where did that leave me over the last three weeks? Selfishly wondering if he'd moved on while the man was stuck in a state of guilt over things I'd never imagined could have sat with this man.

I didn't imagine that he would be this shaken or hurt over Mr. Brooks' loss, though, because I was as bad as the rest. I judged the former Jacob Mitchell just as everyone in the press had.

I took his hand and brought it to my lips before gently intertwining my fingers into his still ones and allowing myself to absorb our closeness. I knew he most likely had more to work out with his grief and anger with the media for destroying his image and his docuseries, but I think we had the good doctor back and on the mend. That would be all that mattered, especially if his mind had been in this guilt-ridden state since he lost Collin's dad that night.

I was grateful to be back in his arms, and I would fall asleep tonight in peace after weeks of believing Jake was trying to get rid of me. What an idiot I'd been. At least Jim had intervened for both of us. We owed big brother a world of gratitude for stepping in as the businessman he was and handling things without reservation.

Chapter Twenty-Six

Ash

When I woke up, I thought Jake had left the room already. Instead, he was lying flat on his back, one arm over his head and a hand covering his abs. It was silly thoughts like this, the body that would make a Greek god jealous, that would run through my mind when I was able to take in the perfection of the man.

His chest rose and fell in perfect rhythm, showing Jake was fully resting and proving he'd gone too long without. With the sun rising and the rays of it waking me up, I knew Jake was sleeping well past the time he naturally got up. Mister Four-in-the-Morning was sleeping-in past six.

I smiled at the thought that this man was mine—he loved *me*? It was a hard thing to grip for a simple person like myself. I wasn't that girl who all the guys in school wanted. Not even close. Then I magically land Jacob Mitchell? It was beyond flattering, and more than that, I was in love with everything about him.

I softly traced the lines of his hard stomach, the V-line muscle tempting me to pull the sheets completely down to appreciate the man. He was perfect in every way. Smart, talented, fun, witty, and well, just perfect.

I slipped out of bed and moved toward the shower, giving Jake his needed rest. The warm and inviting shower was refreshing and a perfect start to whatever this day would bring.

I SHUFFLED THROUGH THE FRIDGE, LOOKING FOR BREAKFAST FOOD. The guy was a health nut. There were fresh fruits, vegetables, free-range eggs, almond milk—all of the stuff I only wished I could afford to buy when I went grocery shopping.

I opted to cut up some fruit, found some whole grain bread in the cabinet, and began the process of making breakfast. The fragrance made my stomach leap with excitement, and I was starving. I wasn't as talented as Jake in the presentation department, but hell, it tasted delicious.

I spent the morning watching surfers ride the waves into shore, families setting up their spots on the beach for the day, and smiling at the sailboats as they came through. I pinched my lips, wondering if I should take Jake up on the offer of going out on the sailboat. As impressive as the yacht was, it was like a floating five-diamond hotel. Don't get me wrong, I loved it and would love to one day go to Cabo with him, but I felt that a sailboat would be more fun and more intimate.

After cleaning up my cooking mess and returning Jake's kitchen to the squeaky-clean way it was before I came in like a tornado, I walked past the pool and leaned against the iron rail, watching the sailboats intently.

It was relaxing, watching them glide and the sails moving in different directions to catch the wind, allowing the boat to be pulled through the water.

"I wonder if Jake knows how to navigate one of those things," I said to myself softly, seeing all of the work the boater was doing with the ropes and the sails.

"Why wouldn't I?" Jake asked, startling me.

Before I could turn around, his arms were around my stomach, holding me and bringing me close into his bare chest.

"Well, if I recall your artistic portrait of the sea, you couldn't be doing what the person is doing with those ropes," I said, leaning my head back into his chest.

Jake kissed my cheek. "Little do you know, I am quite savvy in the ways of boating, especially a sailboat. I grew up on those things."

"I'm talking about your vision of the two people on the bow."

He chuckled. "Yes, I would handle the boat." He kissed the back of my head. "Prepare the sails, lock them in, and then take your sexy ass to the bow to have the portrait masterpiece of what I see out in that ocean."

"A masterpiece, is it?"

"What other words could be used for such an amazing work of art?"

I turned back to see his face bright and youthful again. "You look like you slept well."

"I did." He dipped his lips and pressed them against mine. "The woman I had over actually allowed me to sleep the entire night."

"How nice of her. You might want to keep that one around for a while."

"She's going to stay." He pressed his hands into my lower back, bringing me tightly against him. "Forever."

I smirked. "How does she feel about that?"

"I don't necessarily know. I mean," he smiled and brushed my hair from my face, "she did just show up randomly last night." He leaned forward and brought his lips to my ear. "I think she thinks my place is hers."

I laughed at his whisper. "Well, that could be a problem since there are so many women after you these days."

"Yeah, but the sex is good."

"Good enough to have some random chick move in and stake claim on your place?"

He rose and stared at the ocean. "Good enough that she already staked her claim on my heart, but the sex last night?" His eyes met mine again. "Best of my life." He cupped my ass with his hand.

"You hungry?" I asked, knowing things could go from zero to ninety out here in less than a second. The energy between us was palpable.

"Already ate the plate you left for me."

"What? When?"

"While I was watching you stare out at the ocean." He grinned. "What were you thinking besides the fact that you fear I can't navigate a sailboat?"

"Just how beautiful it all is," I simply stated. "You look a lot better. Why wouldn't you come by and hang with me these last weeks? We could have talked, at least."

He took my hand and walked me over to a beautiful, custom teak wood swing. "As I said, I couldn't have you see me in that state. I was an inconsolable mess. I believe my brother was the last to hang on with dealing with my depression or self-pity—whatever you might call it."

We sat on the twin-sized bed mattress of the swing, and I leaned against his side. "Jake, all of it was understandable. I mean, I'm not one to talk since I had some serious issues in letting Mom go. Still, from dealing with that, I do know you can't blame yourself for any of it."

"I understand. I battled with right and wrong emotions, and it all just frustrated me further. I was finding no resolution. I believe I was angry with myself, John, John's other doctors, the media chasing my ass down everywhere I go...it was everything. I had no way of finding peace nor any way of figuring my way out of the rabbit hole I fell into."

"How do you feel about it now?" I shifted to lay my head on his lap and stretch out like we'd done before on this bed-like swing. He began running his fingers through my hair. "I can see that look on your face. If you say I showed up and solved it all, I'll punch you."

He laughed. "How would you discern the look on my face as you see it from an awkward angle."

"You have that distant look, the tightened lips, and those wild eyes of wanting to have sex here and now. I'm not that naïve."

"Fine, then. I'll admit that at the time I saw you, I felt like my thoughts had somehow manifested you. I had been adding the stress of losing you for being a dumbass in hiding and trying to figure out the words I'd say to get you back. I couldn't believe I'd let myself spin-out that hard and for that long. Then all I wanted was you, and suddenly, you show up?" He looked down at me, his foot gently pushing the swing back and forth. "It was the one thing I needed at the end of all of this, and the one thing I certainly didn't deserve."

"I believed you'd be harder to pull out of everything than you were."

"You told me you'd punch me if I said it was you showing up. I guess I'll take the punch for that because you were the light in this dark hole I was stuck in. Sounds lame," he continued to play with my hair, "but it's the truth."

"So, you've come to terms with it?"

"I believe I'm in my right mind again. I'm no longer feeling like a piece-of-shit victim to everything as I have been. I'll miss John, but I need to focus on pushing out the word better in saving lives. I'll use John and the other million different ways I know I could have talked to him now and keep them in mind when I consult with patients in his situation. Instead of being upset with the other doctors for not working with patients in John's condition with other underlying health issues, I will work with them too. Perhaps a united team of healthcare workers can help a patient more effectively." He shrugged. "We'll see."

"I think that's an amazing plan," I said, sitting up. "You come up with that while you slept?"

He brushed his finger over my nose, "I haven't slept that hard and so long in...well, never. The craziest part was waking up and not being panicked or pissed off I'd slept in." He brought me to lie on my back and lay next to me. "I am just thinking more clearly and with a more rational mind."

"Uh, oh," I teased him as he planted tender kisses on my shoulder. "He's thinking with a more rational mind? Does that mean the wedding is off?"

He traced my closed-lip smile. "You're not getting off that easy." He smiled, and then I saw the devilish and daring man I'd fallen in love with return to me. "In fact, you actually will be getting off that easy and all day long."

"Oh, is the big bad and newly renewed doctor going to take me right here and now?"

He licked his lips. "I'm going to take you back into that house and fuck you in every room."

I laughed out loud. "Good lord, man. Are you trying to kill me off?"

"Now that you bring that up, Collin mentioned something that I believe might make you think I am."

"You both trying to kill me off?"

"I went surfing, and—" He laughed. "I want to take you with me tomorrow."

"Tomorrow?"

"Yes, it's a holiday. Believe it or not, I only remembered because Chi is on for me, checking in with my patients at the hospital because I worked for him last Memorial Day weekend. I know that bitch isn't working the gallery because this is the weekend where women like her go on the prowl."

"No, I'm not working tomorrow."

"Then, we're up at the ass-crack of dawn and surfing."

"Hell no," I answered. "If you want to surf, fine. I'll watch, but I'm not killing myself out in the water."

"I imagined your expression in saying no so differently." He laughed. "You afraid of the sharks?"

"I'm afraid of drowning in some crazy wave or riptide, dumbass," I teased back.

"She's not afraid of sharks?"

"She's not afraid of sharks," I repeated.

"Then, you're out on the board tomorrow. We'll stay in the shallow ankle biters, and I want to see your sexy ass on the board."

"You give me way too much credit."

"You enjoy a good adrenaline rush, correct?"

"Yes." I sighed in disbelief that he was roping me into this.

"Then it's time I introduce you to a sport that is one of the most invigorating treats for the human mind and soul."

"I swear, Jake," I said.

"We'll go easy, I promise."

"Why, though?"

"Collin's idea." He shrugged.

"Blaming it on him?"

"Always." He smirked. "Now, I'm going to take your sweet ass back into the house, fuck you wild, and then we're shopping for a board and a wet suit. Tomorrow we go a little crazy."

"I think you've already gone crazy."

"I love you, Ashley Taylor," he said with his eyes glittery and riddled with excitement.

He's damn lucky I'd missed the hell out of him, found the old daring Ashley because of him, and was edgy with some excitement to give this a try. Time to do something I swore I'd never do—challenge the ocean instead of just paint it.

Chapter Twenty-Seven

Jake

Ash and I pulled the Jeep next to Collin's truck, and I shook my head at my best friend, who was here before us, proving to me that he was excited to see my girl try out this sport. Truth was, I wasn't going to force her into this. We had a nice long and wide board that would serve to help her pop on it and ride the waves easily, but I could already sense her nervousness about the impulsive decision to do this.

"Collin's already here," I said, pulling the keys out of my open-top Jeep.

"Thank God." She laughed, pulling her hair out of the ponytail she had it in. "Now, you have a buddy to surf with, and I can relax on the beach."

I smirked. "It's all up to you."

She eyed me. "Don't think I can handle it?" she asked with that damn sexy arch of her eyebrow.

"You can handle anything. If you managed to handle me so far, you could handle trying this out." I looked out at the aggressive swells that

I knew would die down after reading the surf reports for Trustles this morning. "You're not taking those waves. You can watch them beat mine and Collin's ass up this morning instead."

I reached back and grabbed the bags and supplies we packed for food and Ash's comfort while laying out under the warm morning sun. Once out of the Jeep, Ash took them from my hands and laughed when I went back to lock the steering wheel with the club.

"After all I've seen you own, I can't believe that you have an older model Jeep Wrangler." She chuckled. "And to see the club's power back in action—now that's a blast from the past."

"No one is stealing this baby from me. They can take all my other shit, but not my first vehicle." I smiled over at her. "I learned to drive in this thing," I said as I started unlocking and unstrapping the boards that I had secured over my roll bar. "My dad mandated that I take my driver's test in it, thinking I'd fail as I tried to maneuver the short wheelbase and stick shift."

"Did you fail?"

"Nope," I said with a smile, remembering Dad losing that bet. "And it only made him smile with pride. I miss that old man sometimes." I cleared my thoughts and redirected them. "All right, let's do this."

AFTER SPENDING THE MORNING TRADING WAVES WITH COLLIN, Flex, and his gang, we sat out and took a break out in the open water between the sets rolling in. "What's up, brother?" Flex asked as we finally grouped in, his gang bringing it into shore as they always did when the waves became milder. "By the way, you're carving through these waves and fuck," he laughed, looking over at Collin and me, "you're even jumping the white. I'd think you'd become Dr. Death at this point."

Collin laughed. "Far from that, my man," he said, steadying his board as the currents moved us inland.

"What the hell, then? Is he suddenly trading the medical field for the freedom of the ride?"

"See that chick laying out?" Collin pointed toward Ash where the waves were starting their break to my right. "That's the reason for him showing his ass off."

"No shit?" Flex shielded the sun reflecting off the water, glaring into his eyes. "The brunette next to that nine-foot rhino chaser?"

"Gotta start her out on a longboard. If I put her on a blade like this and she survives, she'll kill me herself," I said, admiring Ash's beauty, hiding under the beach hat she wore. Her body was calling to me from out here.

"I got the kid coming out tomorrow."

I looked over at Flex. "He's barely learned out to walk. What the fuck?"

Flex laughed. "I was the same age. Three years old and Pop had me gearing up to ride barrels like he did." He leaned over and smacked my arm, pulling my eyes away from the beauty on the beach. "Day-dreaming out here like that will get you killed, man."

"If not by the ocean, then by Flex and his boys," Collin chimed in. "You think she'll do it?"

"I have no fucking idea." I cupped the water, pulling the board and me back. "The waves are probably perfect for her to try it out, at least."

"Why are you sitting on your ass, then?" Flex laid on his board and started to paddle in. "Let's go get this girl and see if she really does want to be with a crazy fuck like yourself."

Once we were all in, Ash popped up, and I could see the nervous smile on her face, either because of the three men approaching her or knowing it was time for her to give this a try.

"Ash, is it?" Flex asked before I could even pull the top portion of my wetsuit down.

"Yes." she pulled off her sunglasses and shook his extended hand.

"I'm Flex." He popped me in the chest. "The reason this dipshit is still alive."

She laughed. "I can only imagine the stories," she smoothly played along. "Let me guess, he was out here with a board that didn't work, and you could instantly tell he wasn't part of the surf community?"

Flex grinned. "Pretty much. So," he said as Collin and I stood by, "he's got you on the perfect-sized board. Do you know how to pop up on it?"

Ash's eyes darted toward mine. "Um, I've got no idea what you're talking about. Which must mean that I'm safer on shore."

"Fuck that, gorgeous," Flex answered, no filter as usual. "You're riding today, and Jakey here will work with you on some shore techniques. Collin and I will watch the water. It's breaking nicely, and they're long breaks." He looked over at me as if he'd just controlled the Surf Instructor scene. "She'll enjoy a smooth ride on those if you can get her moving quickly."

"Thanks, surf god," I answered.

"Surf buddha," Flex corrected me with a cocky grin and a laugh.

"Ash, you sure you're still comfortable with this?" I asked.

"It seems like I have a master of the skill that washed up on shore to ensure I'm not getting my ass handed to me out there." She smiled at Flex. "Let's see if all these years of yoga help me learn quickly."

"You'll definitely appreciate that, Ash," Collin added. "We need to get you out there before the tide shifts, though, and," he looked at me, "we don't want her on this board with ankle snappers for waves." He turned with Flex. "Get her comfortable with the board. Flex and I will go out and keep an eye out for surfers who might want to drop in on her."

Ash and I worked for close to fifteen minutes, and I watched in awe at how much of a natural she was. "You sure you haven't surfed before? You've got this down so well, I'm starting to wonder if I'm going to have to kick some surfer's ass that you might have dated before me," I teased.

"Oh, good God." She laughed, pulling her hair out of her face. "Is he suddenly jealous of my ex-boyfriends?"

"Not until now," I answered, picking my board up and watching her zip up her wetsuit like she was some badass surfer chick from Northshore Hawaii. "Shit, babe." I laughed. "If some asshole had the privilege of watching you ride a board before me, I will kick his ass."

"Oh, whatever. I'm just determined. I've never done this before in my life. Quit acting like some territorial surfer, Dr. Mitchell," she said, putting me in my place. "You looked sexy out there, by the way. Maybe

I should ask the jealous Jacob if it was a previous girlfriend who taught him all those moves?"

"Touché," I acknowledged. "Flex saved mine and Collin's lives when we were out here in his waters, acting like a couple of dumbasses. We were both fresh into med school when we went on a suicide mission, and thank God we said or did something right because he took us in and taught us how to respect the sport."

"Got it." She seemed nervous now as we stood in the ankle-deep water, holding our boards.

I pointed to where the waves were breaking to the left. "That spot out there, the waves seem large from here, but it's an illusion." I smiled at her. "You'll see when we're out there. They're not as large as they appear. As I said last night, this board is perfect for you when the water begins to break, and you paddle into the wave. There's more board for the water to move. Remember, your right foot is your strongest one. That's going to help you keep the nose up and steer the board. Once you're up, let the water push you in. It's all smooth, babe," I said, reaching my arm around her and kissing her temple. We were waist deep and letting the boards float now, "As smooth as the way my cock glides through—"

"Jake," she snapped with a sigh, "don't put thoughts like that in my mind. Jesus, I'm trying to focus, not think about sex with you."

She lay on the board and began to paddle out. It took me duck-diving a wave and her going up and over it for me to confirm that the girl was a quick learner, and I was thrilled for her. She'd most likely have this down after a couple of falls, and I might be pushing her onto a shorter board in less than a few trips out.

"So," Flex said after we all situated ourselves to sit on the boards, me continually looking back at the water and how it was breaking and moving toward the shoreline. "If you get dumped, shake that shit off. Just watching you from out here, Collin and I are impressed. You and Jake must have spent the entire night going over techniques."

She pinched her lips, looking at me, and knowing exactly what we spent the entire night doing. Talking about how to surf was not part of that. "Yeah, we—"

"Let's just say we didn't do shit with surfing last night. Instead, my girl is making me think I should have her on a shorter board."

"You've never surfed?" Collin asked with a laugh. "Cause you sure as hell looked like you were humoring Jake from where we watched."

"Maybe I'm just a natural," she said with a shrug.

"It's happened before," Flex said with a sincerity that I was used to, but the smile on Ash's face told me she was trying to follow his genuineness. "God bless it when it does too. The ocean's called you, and you've answered that call."

"Flex's love for the ocean has me wondering if he's a mermaid at times," I said. "His love is profound, and while you love the mass body of water in your artistic mind, his love runs through his veins."

"It's true," Flex said. He was a pure badass on the board; his heart and soul were in the water, and he took it to a level of reverence that anyone who knew him well easily understood. "You love painting the water. Now, it's time to *feel* the reasons for that."

"No disrespect here," Ash said. "If I don't catch on, and I can't click in like you might think I can, you're not going to ban me from the beach, are you? Break my board and kick me out?"

Collin and I laughed in unison while Flex shook his head with a big grin. "Girl, you watch too much television." He smiled. "Now, clear your mind of these thoughts. Move them away and let the ocean roll them into the shore. You're going into this with the thought of being one with the ocean. Feel the power of the water behind that board, pushing you into shore."

She exhaled while Flex laid his Tahitian surfing ways on her pretty hard, but her eyes changed into that look I always saw when she became fascinated with something. I felt like I could see right through her kind and daring soul. She was alive, happy, and determined. It was all there in the expression I studied on her face. She was in the water, seeing it differently now, having been in it and vulnerable to it.

Flex was practically chanting to sanctify her spirit in becoming one with the water. His reaction to Ash was not because she was my girl. He saw more in people than a mind reader would. It's like he picked up on their vibes and read them. Ash had truly impressed him in a way that I felt he was beseeching the water gods to bring her into his brotherhood of surfers.

"Let's snag her a wave," I said, interrupting Flex's fascination with Ash's soul and the unity it found being in the water. "We'll go deep into the victory chants after she's taken a turn on the board."

ASH BLEW THE HELL OUT OF ALL OF OUR MINDS, AND PART OF ME WAS wondering if her and Flex's free spirits about the ocean were going to collide into one strong force, and I'd lose my girl forever. She only lost it once. After that, her brain must have rewired in a way to move with the next waves she caught. It was insanity, but so were the reasons I was in love with the woman. She surprised me at every angle. She unimaginably captured me by doing nothing but being a woman that was different than any other I'd met.

The day ended with stories of Flex's life before moving to the U.S., and Ash's smile plastered right where it had been since she glided through the waves like she was built to ride them.

I dropped her by her house, the evening breeze blowing through the Jeep and keeping both our spirits high and still roused from the day together.

I took her hand in mine, kissed it, then pulled her over to where I sat. I kissed her deeply, burning this feeling and sensation into my mind to get me through the week of work, during the day when I wouldn't see her.

"I wish you'd just stay at my house in the Hills," I said after withdrawing my kiss, "After watching you today, how in the hell am I supposed to get through the next twenty-four hours of not fucking your sexy ass?"

She licked her lips. "Tomorrow night, as we planned," she reminded me.

"I'm booking that suite for the entire week," I said. "That or I'm buying us a home closer for both of us."

"Asking me to move in after buying us a house now? Damn, I must've been exceptional today."

I laughed. "You were beyond that."

"I think it was the chanting prayer your friend Flex sent out, blessing the surfing experience for me." She chuckled.

"Flex is passionate. That's for damn sure."

"I like him," she said. "He's probably the most authentic human I've ever met."

"Damn it!" I feigned being pissed. "I knew your souls were aligning out there."

"The only aligning I'm doing is by jumping in the shower and getting this salt and sand off my body."

"It's nine," I said. "You think they're awake—or sharing a room?"

"We're not having sex in my dad's house."

"We could, but your moans are insanely too loud, and you screaming out my name might shake the entire place to its core."

"Stop it." She smacked my arm. "You're getting me all worked up."

"That's the whole point, babe," I urged with the best smile I could. "At least allow me to do my part in ensuring the sand is removed from every part of your body?"

"Tempting," she said. "Go get cleaned up. I love you."

The way she said that meant more than I think she knew. "I love you," I answered. "Tomorrow night, your ass is entirely mine."

Chapter Twenty-Eight

Jake

I walked into my OR to find the surgical team streamlining their work to perfection as usual. Dr. Chi was my attending, and today we had a scheduled bypass that shouldn't keep me, the patient, or his family, waiting for long. The patient was healthy and had followed all my diet and pre-op plans perfectly. All of the monitors were displaying precisely what I wanted to see, and after going over Mr. Knox's charts, I couldn't find an issue with anything. All the x-rays, exams, and blood-work came out nicely, and now it was time to clear up these arteries and get this man safely into recovery.

"I see Jen has you hooked up to the good stuff, Rick." I smiled over at his nervous expression. "Thank God you showed up, or you'd be missing out on it."

He smiled as most of my patients did once I worked to loosen them up in such an awkward environment. "Good to see you again, Doc," he said in a slur.

"Dr. Mitchell, Mr. Knox," the anesthesiologist acknowledged us both. "We're on the countdown."

"Best part," I assured him. "Get some rest, and I'll get to work. We'll see you in a bit, Mr. Knox."

While the anesthesiologist team worked to assure Mr. Knox was under, I walked over to my team. "Doctor, the patient is ready, and all vitals are looking great," my charge nurse, Patty, informed me.

"Great job, team. Now for the most challenging part of the operation," I started while going over the surgical tools I'd be using, ensuring everything was placed in the order I preferred. "Who's picking the music? It's my turn, isn't it?"

Everyone in the room chuckled, especially the interns who were learning that I ran a clean surgical room, but also had peculiar rules I enforced.

"I believe it finally is your turn, Jake," my attending said, feigning annoyance.

"Better than your—" I paused, "What the hell is it you listen to?"

Dr. Chi was working on his side of the patient's prep. "If you don't appreciate my jams, Jake, then you don't deserve to know what it is."

I rolled my eyes. "All right, my phone is hooked up to the room. We're letting James Hetfield sing us through this surgery."

"Metallica?" I heard a male voice ask from behind me.

"The new intern has yet to learn what keeps me motivated while I stand over a patient for four hours," I said, placing my scalpel and nodding toward Dr. Chi for confirmation of beginning the operation.

"I love the band, Doctor," he added, to which I smiled while going to work. "I was just curious as to why a metal band while performing surgery."

"Chi, care to inform the new intern how my OR works?"

"I think he'll catch on."

The music started, and my mind focused solely on the heart that needed repairs. Chi and I worked flawlessly as a team. Truth be told, I was shocked when he bowed out of being Chief of Cardiology. The man was the best, and he was the only man I'd trust to cut me open and take care of business if I were ever in a situation to require it.

"I need procedure time in, please?" I asked for the time, knowing I was prepping to closed up, and Mr. Knox would be in recovery in less than an hour.

"Three hours, Dr. Mitchell," one of the interns informed me.

"No calls out to the waiting room today, folks. Mr. Knox is almost buttoned up and good to go."

TWO HOURS AFTER SURGERY, I GLANCED UP AT THE CLOCK FROM MY office desk. I had to text Ash before I completely forgot to inform her about my prior engagements.

> **Jake: Hey angel, I have to meet up with the guys tonight. Going over business shit with Jim. You want to meet up at the hotel, or will you finally let me fuck you in that house?**

I SMILED AT THE ONE DUMB FANTASY I HAD BECAUSE I KNEW IT WAS off-limits. It'd only been a few days since Ash blew my mind surfing, and I couldn't get enough of her. Every night, we'd met at the hotel, and I wasn't playing the boyfriend's hanging out at my house shit this week. I was in a constant state of craving more than just sitting next to my girl on the couch. I longed for her closeness and was seriously considering fixing these living arrangements. Damn hotel and the elevators were getting old.

> **Ash: I'm still at work with a last-minute client. You can head over to the house, and no, we're not having sex in the bedroom or the backyard.**
>
> **Jake: What happened to my daring girl?**
>
> **Ash: She has brains and knows her dad. Text or call when you're done. I'll be home late anyway.**

Jake: *One day, I'm getting my way with this.*

ASH DIDN'T RESPOND, BUT IT WAS FINE. I KNEW WHAT EXPRESSION she wore, and I was hornier than hell for her now. When she was all business and shit with me, was a total turn on—that combined with her sexy eyebrow arch, and it was over. I had to pull it together and get over to Kinder's to meet up with the guys. I needed a scotch anyway. It was the perfect way to loosen me up so I didn't attack Ash when I walked into her house tonight.

A knock at my door pulled me out of my thoughts about tonight. "Come in," I said, finishing up packing my bag.

"Doctor, do you have a minute?" one of the interns who was placed on my surgical team last week asked.

"Elizabeth?" I said, glancing at her scrubs for her name. "What brings you to my office?" I asked, concerned by her expression.

The petite blonde's face was dangerously familiar to me. *Shit, she was at the party on the yacht. What the hell is she in my office for?*

She ran her hand over her swollen abdomen, her small frame revealing she was pregnant. "We need to talk. I didn't know how and when to approach you with this, but after being transferred onto your team, and you obviously not remembering me, I knew this all would be difficult."

"*What* would be difficult?" My heart was beating wildly out of control as the beautiful woman who approached my desk sat down as if she'd already had me by the balls. "I'm not sure I'm following. I'm a direct person, Elizabeth; please just tell me why you are here."

"You might remember me from the club close to five months ago?" She continued to massage her stomach, and I was now going to lose everything in my stomach. "Liz? Don't you remember that night?"

I felt the blood leave my face. I wasn't a fucking idiot. She was here to tell me she was pregnant with *my child*. What the fuck was happening?

"You told me to call you Mitch—"

I held my hand up. "Stop," I said in a low whisper. "Why. Are. You.

Here?" I questioned curtly and wanting her just to come out and make her claim and completely fuck up my life.

"Well, if it helps, I first met you when you spoke in San Francisco as our keynote speaker." She smiled while I remained paralyzed, my memories returning to the night I fucked this chick after I saw Ash again for the first time since San Francisco. This person was just another woman I'd fucked to get Ash out of my head, and now, she was most likely here to pull Ash out of my life. "I've followed the news," she shyly spoke. "I was more than a little shocked when I saw that one of my childhood best friends, Ashley, was—well, as the media is stating, *the woman*—"

"Ashley and I are in a serious relationship," I said, my voice lethal as I listened to this woman relate herself to Ash. "If you have a point, I need you to get to it immediately."

"The night after we went back to your place, do you remember any of it?"

"It's all slowly coming back to me," I spoke through gritted teeth. "I'm sorry if I treated you insensitively; I'm no longer that man. I also can assure you that if I knew you were anything closely related to working with me, I would not—even in a drunken state—have taken you home and had a relationship of any kind with you."

"I'm pregnant with your baby," she said, tears spilling down her cheeks.

My lips were parched, and my tie was suddenly a noose around my neck. I gathered myself to speak. "I'm going to be as polite as I possibly can, given it's been five months since I made the mistake of taking anyone back to my place. Five damn months since I learned quickly that I needed to end that ridiculous life, and you want to come in here out of the blue and say that I'm the father of the child you are carrying?"

"Your decision to change your lifestyle doesn't change *this*. I didn't know how to tell you. It's why I requested to be on your surgical team. I felt if you and I got to work together and know each other, you'd accept the news better."

What kind of demented human being thinks like this? And she wants to be a heart surgeon? My career, her career, my fucking life—everything hung onto the way I responded to this woman alone and in my office.

"I can assure you that was not the best way to go about informing me of this." I stood and motioned for her to as well. I needed her out of my office, and Jim's little meeting was about to become an entirely different discussion tonight. "We were together *once*, and *we used protection*. I just—I can't do this right now. I must request that you are moved off my surgical team and over to another hospital for your internship. I do hope you also understand that lawyers will be involved, and I cannot discuss anything further with you regarding this matter. I —yeah. I can't do this."

"You don't remember that night or me," she seethed. "If you did, you would know that you didn't use protection. I don't blame you for that because I was a willing party. Safe sex or not, I wanted it too, but because of that, I'm pregnant. This is your baby, and all I have to say is that you *are* such an asshole."

"Call me what you want. Believe what you want. I remember that night. I have never had unprotected sex with anyone. You might want to go through your memories to ensure it wasn't someone else. I will need paternity tests run, and I will also put your reasons for transferring onto my surgical team on record. Right now, I must ask you to leave my office. My lawyers will be in touch with you to discuss this matter further."

She stood, gave me the darkest look she could muster, and then I watched as she stormed out of my office like a spoiled child—not a broken woman who should have reacted so much differently if the man she believed was the father of her child spoke to her like this.

I leaned against my desk, gripping it tightly and breathing long slow breaths, trying to calm everything in my body down. What the fuck did I do now? Was she really Ash's friend? What could be the fucking chances?

I calmly and lethally stared at my phone. "Call Jim," I ordered the phone.

"What's up, Jakey?" he asked.

"My life is fucked," I answered. "We need to talk serious shit tonight. Find a different place, a quiet place. I'll go to your fucking house. I'm in no condition to be in public."

"Jake," Jim's voice was riddled with concern. "Slow down. What the hell happened? Is it Ash?"

"It's worse than that," I said with some whine in my voice I never knew I had.

"Okay. What happened?" Jim maintained his calm authority. "It's Jake. We're heading to my house. Close the tab, Collin," I heard him say, the men already at the club.

"Some chick I took back to my place before Ash and I got together..." I was being brought to my knees in fear as I was saying it all out loud. "Fuck, Jim, it's one of Ash's friends. The crazy bitch transferred to my surgical team last week to *get to know me better*. She was on my goddamn yacht—"

"We're on the way to my place, get your ass over there," Jim said.

"She's claiming I'm the father of her kid," I finally said, wanting to collapse at the sound of my words.

"All right, then," Jim said, always fucking chill even if a bomb blew up in his face. "We'll talk about this at my place. Calm the fuck down, or I'm sending you a driver." He paused. "Jake, can you drive?"

"I can drive," I answered.

"Okay, traffic is a bitch, so take side streets, and I'll see you in thirty. Are you going to talk to Ash about this?"

"Not until I know it's fucking true."

"Good point. Get to the house. I sort of wondered if this shit would pop up with all the media. It may be a false claim."

"It is a goddamn false claim," I snapped.

"All right. Get your ass out of there, and we'll talk about it when you get to the house."

Chapter Twenty-Nine

Jake

I hadn't heard anything more from that woman since being slammed down on my ass by her accusation of my being her unborn child's father. It had been two days since she walked into my office and turned my world inside out—two days since Jim, Collin, and Alex had talked me down—and if I didn't tell Ash about this, I was going to implode with feelings of fear, guilt, and remorse.

"Jake," Jim said, sitting across from me in the booth, "did you hear what I said?"

"I heard," I answered, and I rubbed my forehead. "I'm sorry I wasted your time and asked you to meet me here. I just think I need to get out of here and talk to Ash. There's no way I'm going to go down this road without having told her before the media or that woman—who claims to be her best friend—tells her."

"Did Ash bring it up last night when you were with her?"

"No," I answered. "Which tells me that the bitch hasn't gotten to her yet. She can't find out about this through anyone other than me." I wrapped my hands around my coffee mug. "What kind of *best friend* wouldn't have told Ash first? Maybe that's all a lie to get me to freak out and buy her off."

"You heard the lawyers today," he said. "Don't give this Elizabeth woman anything to hang you with."

"I understand that perfectly well," I said, almost crushing the coffee cup I held in the diner.

"You're not *acting* as though you understood them," he said in his big brother, CEO-dick tone.

"Seriously?" I snapped at him, my nerves shot to hell. "I understood every word they said. Don't engage the fucking media if they approach me about it. Ensure the hospital staff is not bringing up my personal life. I already know that, and I've *been* handling my goddamn personal life being exploited."

"Jacob," Jim said with some sorrow in his voice, "I'm only making sure that you're locked in with everything. The woman will be doing a paternity test, and the lawyers are overseeing it. Don't go losing your shit."

"I get it, Jimmy." I calmed some. "By the way, thank you for making that transfer from Saint John's more appealing for that woman to leave and join the staff at Mount Silas. You do handle shit and handle it fast."

"She was guaranteed a healthier wage, and I don't think she wants to lose her position over any accusations toward the Chief of Cardiology at Saint John's. I think she'll appreciate the transfer, and if this *is* your child, *you will* own up to it, or she'll have no reason to appreciate that promotion as intern—"

"I know," I seethed, my temper flaring. "She's pretty much got me where she wants me if that test comes back that it's my kid."

"Not necessarily. You already admitted you have multiple witnesses and staff that understand you don't bring relationships into the work-place. She'll just take your ass for everything she can." He leaned back in the booth. "That's if she doesn't trap you in worse ways than—"

"I'm done talking about this. There are a million different ways this woman can fuck me over, and the only one I give a shit about is waiting for me to show up at her house." I sighed. "I can't keep Ash in the dark a second longer."

I stood and threw cash down on the table while Jim looked at me as if I had lost my mind—which I had, two days ago.

He pushed the money back toward me. "This isn't a saloon, you idiot," he said. "I'll handle the bill. Pull yourself together. Do you have any surgeries tomorrow?"

"I finished the last of the surgeries scheduled for the week this afternoon. Chi has been working my rounds on recovery patients since my bedside manner sucks. I think once I talk to Ash, I won't be sitting around wondering how bad shit will be. I'll at least get this first part out of the way."

"You're right. I'm glad we met up, it was worth the drive to make sure you're still functioning." He smiled and stood. "Get out of here and tell Ashley about the woman's claim." He gripped my shoulder. "It's going to be fine, Jacob."

"What if I lose her over this?" I finally admitted my greatest fear.

"You know, I don't believe you will. From what I've come to see, Ashley's a reasonable person. I'm sure the gravity of it all will sting, but you two seem to have a connection. Just brace yourself for it hurting her because that's a natural response. Don't forget that Ashley has also witnessed what this media shit has been doing to you as well. In the end, I feel that she'll probably think what we all think."

"This Elizabeth bitch is after money."

"Yes." He slipped his hands into his suit pockets. "Get this part over with. It's something you should have done last night after you cooled off some, but now is a good time as well. I'm glad you're willing to tell her, she deserves that much."

"Right. See you later," I said and turned to leave.

ASH'S HOUSE WAS ONLY TEN MINUTES DOWN THE ROAD FROM HERE, and it was why I made Jim meet me at the diner. In this frame of mind, I shouldn't be in her presence, but I didn't want to be anywhere else either. I wanted to be with her in the comfort of her home. The idea of meeting at the hotel didn't appeal to me since this happened, and I could see where that was confusing to Ash. She had to know what was going on with the disaster in my life. I couldn't keep her in the dark.

I'd managed to pull off one night with her, no questions asked about my despondent mood. She also fell for my lame excuse the night before last when that woman walked into my office, and I wound up staying at Jim's place. It wasn't a lie when I told her I'd had a long day after surgery and needed to crash.

Now, here I sat, parked next to the curb out front of her house, trying to gather myself. Even though we'd just had the time of our lives surfing together four days ago, this bullshit I'd been hit with made it seem as though it had been months since I had peace.

I rested my head against the seat rest, inhaling and exhaling in silence, knowing very well that admitting everything to Ashley could be the break in this relationship we'd jumped into without caution. I should have known that my fucked-up history would come to destroy my most meaningful relationship in one way or the other.

I couldn't blame her if she couldn't take this—there was no way I'd blame her. I would walk away but walk away knowing I'd hurt the only woman I'd ever fallen in love with.

Without another thought, I unclicked my seatbelt, opened the door, and headed toward the front door of Ash's house.

"You're late," she teased after opening the door. Her eyes were brilliant, and her expression flawless—I loved this woman more than I knew.

"You're beautiful," I said, and that's when I couldn't restrain myself from reaching for her and pulling her tight into my embrace. I heard her muffled laugh against my chest while her hands rubbed softly along my back.

"Hey, are you okay?" she questioned.

I brought my lips to her delicious neck, smelling the floral and vanilla fragrance of her enticing skin. I finally withdrew, making sure I took every sensation I knew I was about to lose with me.

When our eyes met, her eyebrows pulled together with concern as she reached for my face. "Baby," she said. "What's wrong?"

"We need to talk," I solemnly said, not knowing how to start.

She stepped back. "Come in."

I noticed two men in the backyard that her dad and Carmen had successfully turned into a beautiful, quaint party pad. Party lights, a swing, outdoor kitchen—all of it was quite impressive, and I still hadn't made good on my promise to barbeque carne asada out there yet either.

"Am I interrupting you having friends over?"

"Jake." Ash laughed. "You texted four hours ago that we were hanging here tonight after I asked about the hotel. It's just Clay and Joe. They stopped by for dinner, and I asked them to hang back to meet you finally. Here, sit down for a sec," she said with concern. We sat next to each other on the sofa. "Dad and Carmen already headed to bed, but I was looking forward to introducing you to two of my best friends."

"Best friends?" I mused, and it reminded me of her other *supposed* best friend, Elizabeth. "Well, I believe I may have met another one of your best friends..." I trailed off watching her intently, her eyes now humored.

"Unless it was Clay or Joe, I guarantee you haven't met any other close friends of mine that I'm aware of," she said.

"What about Elizabeth?" I questioned. I knew I was screwing up this way of breaking the news to her, but I didn't know where else to start.

"Elizabeth?" she said, confused. "Are you drunk or something?"

"I'm far from that. Does the name *Liz* ring a bell?" I stated. "She said she's one of your best friends."

"Liz?" Ash looked at me in disgust while two well-dressed men walked into the house.

I immediately recognized the one with long black braids from being at the hospital with Ash. The taller, copper-haired man, however, I'd never met before.

Both their eyes widened when they walked toward where I stood and extended my hand out to meet them. "Hey. I'm Jake," I introduced myself.

"Nice to finally meet you. I'm Joe," the copper-haired man took my hand first, "and this is my boyfriend, Clay."

"Clay." I nodded, shaking his hand. "I believe we crossed paths while you visited Mr. Taylor in the hospital."

"We did." Clay smiled.

"Well, it's nice to meet you, Joe, and it's good to see you again, Clay," I said. "Sorry that I've kept your friend occupied these past few days."

Shit. I couldn't even hold down a goddamn normal conversation at the moment.

"There's nothing to apologize for. Ash has never been brighter or happier, and we now know why. You've helped bring our girl out of the funk that's been driving us insane," Clay said with a boldness that could only make me smile and forget why I was here.

"Sorry if this comes off wrong, but you don't look like you're feeling too well," Joe added.

"I feel like hell," I answered.

We all sat in the small living room. I really didn't want an audience for when I told Ash this shit, but hell, if that bitch, Liz, got to the media and her before I did, these two guys would be nothing compared to the spectators I'd have. I debated withholding the information, but these two seemed to be excellent friends, so much so, that if I crushed Ashley, they'd be here for her.

"Oh, God," I started as I ran my hand through my hair. "Part of me needs to have this time alone with Ash, but I can see where you two are close friends with her." I started inquiring in my usual office voice.

Clay smirked. "If you're here to break up with Ashley, then you're about to get your ass kicked, Doc."

"I have a feeling it might be the other way around," I said.

Ash reached for my hand. "What the hell is going on? Why are you bringing up Liz? I went to high school with someone named Liz, but we aren't anywhere close to bordering on best friends."

I rolled my lips and pinched them together.

"Wait. Liz, Liz?" Clay questioned with an arch of his eyebrow. "The trick who invited you to that party and ditched your ass?"

Joe looked at Ash. "If that girl has anything—"

"Guys," Ash silenced her friends, "let Jake finish." She looked at me. "What's up?"

"She transferred onto my ward last week as one of the interns—"

Ash shot up and covered her chest, leaving my ass glued to the couch in fear. She spun back to me, "Please, God, tell me you didn't sleep with her, and now you're here to confess."

All eyes were on me—naturally. The media had painted this scenario a billion times over with all their fucked-up reports on my personal life. Ash made the front pages with me a month ago, and from there on, it was this picture of my eventually cheating on her they put on display for everyone watching this fake soap opera to follow.

I stood. "Ash, I haven't been with anyone since you and I became an item. You already know I admitted to trying to curb my liking you through being other women before we got together. That none could help me move past you and what we shared over a year ago."

"Then why are you bringing up that woman?" She finally spun back around. Her eyes were like fire at first, and I accepted our fate with the look of disgust alone. "She's not even my friend, let alone my *best friend*. She was a friend from high school. After the night she got wasted drunk and slept with some random dude..." she trailed off, and her face went white. "Wait. Are you the one she slept with in Frisco? She woke up flipping out and texting me about getting so wasted that she went to a hotel with a random guy," she said in a quiet yet lethal tone.

"I assure you that was not me. I only slept with you that weekend. I did not sleep with that woman or any other woman my entire trip." I gripped my waist, sensing Ash was completely untouchable with her arms crossed. "I did not recall her being your friend until she came into my office after surgery on Tuesday wishing to speak with me. I was highly confused and didn't know her name, but instantly remembered her being on my yacht because I was pissed that someone from work anywhere near my personal life."

"Liz was on the yacht?" she asked while the men remained as silent bodyguards, waiting for me to drop the punchline to this horror story and kick my ass. "How the hell did she manage that?"

Fuck, Jake, it's obvious Ash can't stand this bitch, I thought. "I have no fucking idea," I managed to keep my voice down. "I only recalled her from seeing a familiar face from *work* on my boat—I have rules against that. However, before she transferred to Saint John's—and before you and me—after first *seeing you* again, I was with her, thinking she was just a woman to remove you from my thoughts. Jesus Christ, I didn't know who the hell she was."

Ash was quiet, and it scared the fuck out of me.

"She walked into my office after having transferred to my ward, which I still have no fucking clue how she managed since there's a five-year waiting list to intern for me after the media storm fucked my life over."

"Spit it out, Jake!" she said.

"She came into my office and claimed that I'm the father of the child she's carrying." *Fuck!* I finally said it.

I couldn't believe my nerves didn't make me throw up, finally accepting I had a nightmare on my hands that wasn't even getting started yet.

"What?" she said in a near growl.

"She claims I'm the father—"

"I heard you." She shook her head and looked over at the grave expressions on her friends' faces.

"Do you believe you're the father?" Joe asked carefully.

"Fuck no," I said. "Jesus. I don't know what to believe." I ran my hands through my hair and gripped the side of my head. "She was a one-night stand, who has seemed to ruin my entire fucking life with her accusation." I looked at Ash. "I'm so fucking sorry, Ashley."

Without notice or warning, the one thing I never expected to happen, happened. I was in Ash's arms, and she was holding me tightly. "Okay. Let's take a breath," she said, stepping back, her serious eyes focused on mine. "You're a fucking idiot for sleeping around so casually, period, but I slept with you because you were like this too. So, while I can't hate you for this, part of me wishes I could. I know you're not that man anymore, though, and thank God for it. I'm in love with you, and I'm not letting your history fuck up that or *our relationship*." She rubbed her forehead. "Liz. What a fucking bitch. Why would she say she was my best friend?"

"She made that claim after she saw that we were together through media outlets."

"Of course she did. And you're sure the baby is not yours? How far along is she?"

I could hear the shock, disgust, and nerves in Ash's voice. "She believes five months, and she also claims I don't remember that I didn't use protection."

"Did you?" she snapped.

"Unequivocally, yes." I looked at her, forgetting the men were in the room. "Ash, you're the only woman I've ever had sex with unprotected. I've never been that fucking drunk to forget protection. With you, it was different, though. Everything was different. It's the only reason I was okay with it. I was in love with you even then. Either way, I'm demanding a paternity test."

"Good. Yes." She took my hand in hers. "It seems like we have a lot to talk about. One thing is certain, though. She seems to be more of the blackout drunk than you."

"Honey, don't forget what's really going on here. Your boy also has money and fame," Clay chimed in.

"That's true." Ash looked back at me. "Liz may stop at nothing, so if we want our relationship to survive this craziness, both of us need to accept that the baby is yours," Ash told me.

"I can't ask you to pick up the burden of what I'll be going through while determining if the child is or isn't mine. The press's part in all of it. It's all going to come out with me as the asshole who knocked her up."

"You know what? I love you, Jake. If I didn't, I'd definitely not have the stomach to listen to this. Does it all piss me off? Yes. Is it this baby's fault? No." She rubbed my arm and smiled. "I'm here for you. I'm not letting the media, this girl, or anything else destroy the love I've found. The past may come back to haunt you, but I knew who you were before I settled in with the idea that I loved you. I'm not leaving your side."

"I don't deserve this or you." I pulled her into me. "You are, in fact, my angel."

"She's the world's angel, brother," Clay said as he and Joe both seemed to sigh in relief that Ash and I were in this shit show together. "We're both here too. Let's go out to the patio. Jake looks like he could use a beer or seven."

Ash smiled at me. "Are you in a safe frame of mind to drink, or do you want water?"

I brushed my knuckles along her cheek. "I love you."

"Let's go hang in the back. We'll get through this. If you're too tired to drive, you can stay here."

"What if I wanted to take you to the hotel?"

"I'd say you should make that decision after relaxing for a while with a beer or two." She kissed my lips. "Actually, I'll make that decision after I see my Jake is back. Trust me," she pulled me toward the patio, "you're going to love Joe and Clay. It's therapeutic to be around them."

I had no idea if Ash was on something or if she truly was the sincere woman I came to know and love. It was beyond me that she was sticking by my side through this. I owed her so much more than the future I might have in helping raise a child that I still couldn't accept was mine. That fight was not over yet.

Chapter Thirty

Jake

It had been a week since I broke the news to Ash. Yesterday, with the media following me in full attack mode, I went to the diagnostic center to have the DNA tests conducted. The idea of these test results coming back anywhere from two to four weeks was enough to drive me insane, but I wasn't going to do the test anywhere else, and definitely not where she wanted them done. This place was known for its accuracy, so I'd wait for their usual time.

The woman hadn't contacted Ashley since she bailed out at that party in San Francisco, yet she had no issue walking into my office and lying to my face, stating they were childhood best friends. And she waited five goddamn months to tell me? Transferring onto my surgical team because she believed that fucking insane idea would make it easier to break the news to me? Who does any of those things?

I was a male-whore prick when I had sex with the woman, that I already knew, but I wasn't a goddamn idiot. This whole thing would make me look like the biggest dick in the history of asshole baby daddies because I wasn't accepting this as one would imagine.

Along with questioning this woman's claim, I had to face her again after ensuring she'd be at the diagnostic center when we both were tested. I was certifying there would be no confusion as to who the father of this child was. I was not letting the pregnant woman out of my sight for something crucial to my life—the results of this test. I didn't trust her, and the media—

who'd taken more of an interest in this shit than anything else in my life—was a reminder as to why.

Outside of the media storm, I was grateful that the hospital hadn't exploded with rumors regarding what was going on. I believe I owed that shit to Jim and the lawyers. I had enough distractions in my life, and Saint John's didn't need to be turned into some hospital where the staff fed off of bullshit gossip about the Chief of Cardiology's life. These men and women were professionals, though, and I saw that more now than ever. I appreciated their care of maintaining a professional environment at the hospital more than I could express.

To add another conspiracy layer to all of this shit, after Ash tried calling Liz's number, the person on the other end of the line had no idea who Ash was. Ash had to triple-check to make sure she was calling the correct number to the high school friend she'd met up with in San Francisco, and the texts were there and associated with the number. However, the old man on the other end of the line had no idea who Ash was.

I had to get this shit out of my system. It was finally Friday, and I'd accepted Ash's offer to get the fuck out of town and away from the chaos that followed me everywhere. Ash was right; I needed a break from it all, and I wouldn't find that reprieve anywhere except for out of town with the woman I loved.

We were heading up to Santa Clarita with her dad, Carmen, Clay, and Joe to allow this family their final farewells to Ash's mom. Watching Ash in her moment of healing and moving forward would serve to get my mind off of this shit and only on her.

I rolled up to the house at ten in the evening. Ash had the door open and rushed me quietly in. "I have a surprise for you," she said with the smile that always eased my nerves. "You have to be quiet, though."

I dropped my overnight bag and work bag over by the sofa and let her drag me through the house and out to the backyard. I glanced around the pitch-black area and pulled her into my side, waiting for the lights to flash on and everyone scream surprise or something.

"What am I looking at?" I asked.

"Look up," she said softly.

I did and was shocked to see brilliant stars sprinkled throughout the black sky. "What the hell did you do, call the city and have them turn off the street lights?" I asked, kissing her temple, shocked I was in a residential backyard and seeing stars as if we were in the mountains.

"No," she laughed. "They are changing them out, so tonight they killed the power."

"How'd I miss that?" I asked. "I swear to God I'm walking like a zombie through life these days."

"Well, you do have a car that stays lit up until five minutes after you hit the lock button." She laughed. "That must've been the light that kept your mind off of seeing the dark streets tonight. Come here," she said, my eyes adjusting some to the dark backyard. "I laid out a blanket for us to get lost in the beauty of the starry sky."

We both laid down on our backs, Ash softly squealing when she saw a shooting star stream its light across the bluish-black sky. "It's almost as beautiful as being out on the open sea," I said as she rested her head on my chest and curled up around me.

"Almost," she said. "I have food if you're hungry. I forgot to heat-up a plate. I was too excited to show you this anomaly."

"I ate lunch late today, so I'm good," I said.

Unexpectedly, she ran her hand over my cock. "Are you good, Dr. Mitchell?" she questioned.

Aside from the fact that Ash had better not be playing with me or my sanity, she and I hadn't had sex since before this shit went down. Oddly enough, it was the farthest thing from my mind. Ash had been working late all week, and even when we were alone, my mind was a cluster fuck of bullshit concern and worry.

My dick instantly hardened and ached for her the moment she ran her hands over it. "Ash, unless you want me all over you, it's probably not the best idea to torment me like this."

"On the contrary," she said, straddling my legs and unzipping my pants. "I'm going to be all over you."

I softly moaned, and any care I held moments ago was gone.

"It's been too long," she whispered. "No one can see us." She freed my hard dick and began smoothing her hands up and down my shaft. "Lose yourself in the beauty of the sky while I take care of the rest."

Goddamn, how was I supposed to look at the stars? Every time she eased her hands up and down my cock, my eyes rolled back with the sensations that I hadn't felt in far too long. My balls tightened, my cock already dripping, and her tongue indulged in the precum that was seeping from it.

As much as I loved her lips around my cock, I wanted to be inside her. I reached down to where she sat, massaging my cock, and ran my hands up the skirt she wore. "You're not wearing—" I groaned when I felt her warm and wet pussy.

"No, I'm not wearing anything. I want you, Jake. I miss you."

I swallowed hard, my heart racing with transformed energy of needing this as bad as the need I heard in her voice. She moved back, my hands losing her warm pussy, but the entire situation replaced with her lips and tongue working my cock over. I always teased her for being the loud one, but tonight, I was the one trying to stifle my groans of ecstasy. My cock was throbbing and aching for more, prompting me to grip her hair, rolling onto my side.

"Fuck," I said in a restrained voice. "I need more, baby."

Her lips released my cock and found my parched lips. Her hand continued to stroke me fast while my urgency in her tasteful kiss was hard and aggressive. I relished in her soft moans against my tongue and lips, my hands slipping under her dress again.

I slid my fingers into her pussy. "Fucking hell, you are so tight," I whispered against her throat.

"Fuck me, baby," she said, her voice catching when my fingers found her G-spot.

"Come first, angel," I nipped at her neck. "I won't last a second inside you."

I massaged my fingers over her spot and used my thumb to work her clit in circles. My cock was slick with the precum that was dripping out as she pumped it fast to match her breathing and soft moans. We were acting like sex-crazed teens, needing to fuck in her dad's backyard, and I didn't give a shit.

Her hands left my cock as she whimpered and dug her fingernails into my back. Her hips jolted into my hand, and I could have sworn I was about to come right then and there. Her lips were at my ear, her hands gripping my head now.

"I'm coming, baby," she said.

I felt her pussy pulsating and clenching hard on my fingers. We both needed this release desperately. She brought her leg up over my side as I intently focused on my fingers, ensuring she followed through with this intense orgasm. She was beyond sexy in this state.

"That's it, angel. Ride my hand, baby," I encouraged her.

"I can't stop coming..." she trailed off. "I need to feel you inside me, Jake." Her voice cracked with need that I wouldn't dare turn away.

I rolled her onto her back and thrust my hard cock deep inside her. As soon as she went to call out, I instinctively covered her mouth with my hand. I brought my lips to her ears. "As bad as I need to hear you scream my name, you gotta keep it down, baby."

Both of us chuckled at the close call, but I found my rhythm in her tight pussy, using her juices to help me smoothly guide myself in and out of her. I pulled the top of her low-cut dress down and found her hard nipple with my mouth. This was paradise. I pumped in and out while massaging her nipples and breasts with my tongue and mouth. I wanted to taste her pussy, but we were pushing it already.

Her tight pussy clenched hard down on my cock while she whined softly. "I'm close, Jake."

"I'm coming with you," I stated, then I licked the nipple of her other breast, and that sent us over the edge together.

I buried my cock deep into her, covering her mouth again, knowing she loved being fucked deeply, but also knowing how she audibly reacted to it. My entire body was covered with goosebumps while I shivered through this jolt of electricity, sending my cum deep inside her. As our actions led us both over the edge into ecstasy together, we both slowed in lucid motions, coming off the strongest orgasm I'd felt in far too long. I gently pumped my softening cock in and out of her tight pussy, relishing in the part when my cock was most sensitive.

"God, you're so perfect," I said, kissing her lips, her neck, and her breasts again.

Ash was breathing heavily, her legs slack like they always were when she took me deep, and her hands massaged over my ass. "I've missed this more than you, I think," she teased as we became more coherent and pulled out of our craving state of mind that took over both of us like a violent storm.

I thrust myself deep and took her face into my hands. "I can never lose you," I said, our eyes meeting.

She crossed her legs around my lower back. "You won't," she promised. "Now, you've had it all." She pressed her lips to mine. "You've won the battle and have fucked me in my backyard."

"Now, to fuck you in my car."

"You're too much. Did you enjoy your partial blow job while seeing the stars?" she asked.

I rolled off of her, pulling up and zipping my suit pants. "I saw stars, but not the ones in the sky."

"I wanted you to experience that."

"Well, so long as we get to sleep before midnight, Cinderella, perhaps that wish will come true."

"You're sleeping on the couch, by the way." She softly giggled.

"The couch?" I questioned.

"Yeah, Dad's rules about your sleeping over."

I pulled her in close. "Your laugh, your body, all of you," I ran my hands over her hair, "You're perfect, Ash. I love you so much. I don't deserve any of this."

She sat up, leaving me to lie on my back. She placed her finger over my lips. "We already discussed you not talking like this anymore. I already had my breakdown over all of this for you and for me. I'm not letting it ruin us."

"And if she ruins me?" I questioned her.

"How? Losing your job? Losing the media following your ass around everywhere?"

"She can take a lot of my shit if she finds avenues to."

"Then let her," Ash responded. "Let her take everything." She kissed my lips. "You'll be the one who will have to accept whether or not you want to drive an off-colored Honda Accord or not."

I laughed. "I'd give it all away. The only thing I can't lose is you."

"Well, it's settled then. Let's stop talking about it. It works you up, and I'm not going anywhere. If this kid is yours and you're still willing to keep me in your life while helping to raise that woman's kid, then I guess the child will be blessed with an amazing dad and two moms— who hate each other, of course," she finished with a laugh.

"You are truly the best woman alive," I said with sincerity in my voice. "I would have probably found a monster wave to go surf and die in the waters by now."

"Nice, drama-king," she said, kissing my chin.

"Hey, about that car of yours."

"What about it?" she asked.

"What do you think about pulling mine into the garage for the weekend and taking your car?"

"That's actually a good idea. I've noticed the media is in a frenzy lately."

"That bitch went to them a few days ago. I'm shocked she hasn't shown up here yet."

"Yeah, Dad and I were talking about that too."

"I can't believe he's letting me off the hook with this."

"You heard my dad earlier," she said, lying on her back as we both looked up at the stars. "He gets it. I guess it's dude talk for guys just being horny dumbasses before finding the right one."

"Your dad kills me sometimes." I started playing with her hair. "And Carmen."

Ash laughed. "Carmen thinks Liz is a piece of trash who belongs on one of those court shows we watched in your waiting room."

I laughed. "I hate those damn shows. I don't know why Sandy puts that shit on for my heart patients."

"She's smart. It keeps your mind off the clock while you wait."

"True. I'd request to change the channel if it were me."

"But it's not you, and unless you get complaints, it's better to have that on instead of the news these days."

"That's for damn sure." I propped myself up on my elbow and ran my fingertips over her collar bones. "Are you sure you're ready to do this tomorrow? Do you have a minister or anything planned for the internment?"

"No." She smiled. "We're all just going to say something special."

"I'm honored you have me along for this."

She intertwined her fingers with mine. "You helped me reach this stage in my life. It was you who helped me see it all and start living again. I couldn't imagine doing this without you there."

I kissed the back of the hand I held and lost myself in the stars above us. This would be a good weekend with my Ash, and in the process of not being stuck in grief, I was already feeling the liberation from the nightmare that struck last week. I couldn't get caught up in it all. Like the angel that I knew her to be, Ash had already helped to resuscitate the Jake I was before this crisis entered my life.

Chapter Thirty-One

Jake

I woke up on Saturday, feeling as refreshed as I had since the day that I took Ash out surfing. The energy was charged with excitement as Ash and Carmen battled over who cooked what for breakfast, and I headed to the shower to get ready for the day.

Two hours after eating and getting ready, we followed Ash's dad and Carmen's minivan toward the freeway, and that was honestly the last we saw of them. God in heaven, the Ash that I'd come to know sure as hell wasn't the woman behind the wheel of her car. Part of me wondered if I should've fought her harder to drive or even took the risk of the media chasing our asses up to Santa Clarita in my car. This was not the ideal situation I expected us to be in while driving, and it wasn't because I drove like a damn race car driver in my car at times, either.

A blaring horn from the car passing us once the freeway opened up made me jump, yet Ash was steadfast, driving worse than a granny who couldn't see over the steering wheel.

"Is this a joke?" I asked, glancing over my shoulder to see an eighteen-wheeler, riding up on our ass.

"Is what a joke?" she asked, hands at ten and two, sitting a little too upright in her seat. "My driving?" She looked over her shoulder and flipped off a car that had honked at her.

"You might as well flip me off also," I said with a smile. "You're driving too damn slow for comfort. I'd say get in the slow lane, but you might cause those poor truckers to lose their momentum."

"I'm doing the speed limit, Jake," she said, not taking her eyes off the road.

"Well, the speed limit is sixty-five, babe, and the big-rig on our ass is going to roll over the top of us if you don't speed up some."

"Stop telling me how to drive," she said with a nervous laugh.

"She surfs, she says she'll go sky diving with me, scuba, all this shit that puts her life at a greater risk than a goddamn drive on the freeway." I readjusted my sunglasses. "Is the car gutless, or are you?"

"Don't make fun of the car. It drives fine."

"Then drive it, sweetheart," I encouraged her. "Seriously, that or pull over and let me drive."

"I hate freeways. They make me nervous," she stated. "But I am driving."

"You're *not* driving. You're going to get us killed by driving too slow."

"I'm doing sixty-five now, happy?"

"Your knuckles are white. So now you're nervously driving." I shook my head. "Your dad lost us as soon as we hit the freeway. That's saying a lot."

"My dad drives like a maniac."

"And I don't?" I asked. "I've had you in my car going over a hundred miles per hour and on the bike opened wide up, and so I'm wondering if between then and now you were somehow possessed and you're not the same person I remember?"

"Close your eyes if you're that worried about it. I'm in the middle lane and out of everyone's way now."

I reclined my seat some. As frustrating as Ash's cautious driving was, it was also comedy. I had no idea she feared driving out on the open highway and would make a note to myself to insist—in front of her dad—that I get the keys and drive us home...after we showed up an hour after them to the cemetery, of course.

I opted to scroll through my emails instead of watching the catastrophe that was Ash's driving. The woman was going to force me into high blood pressure if I wasn't careful.

"What are you looking up?" she asked after fifteen minutes of me finally shutting up about her driving.

"Side-by-side plots," I said while reading through an article from a London-based hospital.

"Side by, what?" She laughed.

"Burial plots," I answered, still reading.

"Ah," she said, smoothly changing lanes back to the slower lane.

I kept my mouth shut.

"So, where are you looking to purchase graves for us to be buried after we both pass on?"

"Well, I believe it would be easier if I just purchased the plots for us up at the place we're interning your mom. You know, we're already halfway there and more than likely halfway into the grave ourselves."

"Oh, God," she said as she shook her head. "Seriously. Talk to me. I'm getting bored."

"Well," I said, wanting to finish this article on a new treatment, "I figure I'd like us to have side-by-side plots under a tree."

"Because we're going to get too much sun from our caskets being six feet under the ground?"

"Perhaps. I want it to be a comfortable final resting place since the way we're most likely going out is not going to be comfortable at all."

She smacked me in my arm, pulling me out of the article. "You're such an idiot. My driving is fine, and we're making good time."

"Say what you want about that."

"Fine, you can drive us home," she conceded.

"Thank God," I answered. "I was planning to pry the keys out of your hand while you said your final goodbyes to your mother."

"That would've been a dick move." She smiled.

"It would've, but at least it would save me a shit-ton of money in arranging our funerals on the drive up to spare everyone else the trouble."

She sighed. "The exit is right up here."

"And so she amazes me once again," I said, sitting up and praying that she was cool with exiting the damn freeway because God knows she barely managed the on-ramp.

"See, we're safe, and it's because I don't drive like a bat out of hell like you."

"You know those cars that drive themselves?" I said, gripping the armrest with her jerky breaking, feeling like I was with a student driver on their first time out.

"What about them?"

"As soon as we get back, I'm buying you one. Jesus Christ almighty, I'm never letting you drive like this again. At least I know the car will take over and keep you safer than you driving like this."

"Breaks are just touchy. I don't need a new car, Jake."

"You're getting one anyway. Consider it a gift for being the best girl in my life."

"Nice try. Get me some daisies then, not a damn car."

I smiled over at her. How many women had I been around who were all about my money? Too many to count. Then there was Ash, the woman who was with me even when my mistakes of the past came to haunt me. I'd already sensed her not being about the money when I saw her passion directed toward other things instead—like nature, life, helping others—and it attracted me to her like none other.

"I'm getting you the car so you can remain alive and the best girl in my life." I ran my hand over her tense arm, "Next time, let me drive, Supergirl. You're as tense as fuck."

"I should have," she said. "I just wanted you to relax after everything. Driving up here was a favor you were doing for me."

"It's a part of your life I'm proud to be a part of. I love you, and I can easily see that this is a big day for you. I wouldn't miss it for anything." I glanced over my shoulder as she merged onto the street that led to the cemetery. "Although we both almost completely missed it. That or I would have gotten to meet your mother personally with the way those rigs were riding up on our ass this entire trip."

"Well, we survived it. You can meet Mom another time," she said, pulling into the cemetery and parking next to where her dad and Carmen stood next to their car, talking to Joe and Clay.

"I wonder how long they've been out here waiting?" I questioned with a smile.

"Shut up," she said. "I'm already going to hear shit from Clay and Joe for not letting you drive."

I looked at her over the silver rim of my sunglasses. "You're kidding me, right?"

"No." She giggled. "They hate the way I drive."

"You're too much." I brought my hand to her neck. "Get over here, gorgeous," I said, kissing her, and, in the process, taking the keys out of the ignition and putting them in my pocket. I opened the door. "Let's not keep your mother or anyone else waiting any longer than we already have," I said, seeing more than a few others who were attending this internment.

"Why did Dad have to invite them?" she asked.

"Who?" I asked, seeing two families with young women Ash's age.

"Just family. I have no idea who they are."

"Do it for him too, Ash. I know it sucks, but this is about you and your dad. The rest of us are here to support you."

She linked our hands together and smiled up at me. "I love you."

I kissed her temple. "You put my very own thoughts about you into words. You ready for this?"

"More than ever." Her eyes were hidden behind sunglasses, but I could see the smile in them. "If it weren't for you, I know Dad and I wouldn't be here right now. Thank you for this."

I held onto that with everything that I was. I hoped that no matter how dirty shit might get with lawyers and this scandal I was trying to manage, Ash would remember how she was feeling about me right now. Would I take credit for this? No. Ash did this herself. I was just a means to help her back into living a full and happy life that she deserved.

Chapter Thirty-Two

Jake

To say my life had spun out of control in the two weeks since I took the paternity test would be an understatement. It had been utter chaos, and the media was feeding off of it like frenzied sharks in bloodied water.

The only good to come out of anything this week was my appointment with Mark, setting him up with a strict diet plan, and preparing him for a heart transplant. We weren't rushed at the moment, his heart being assisted well by the machine, but still, once the donor heart was available, we would go through the process of assuring it was a perfect match and then do the surgery. I wanted to be excited about this, but I'd had zero reprieves to be able to.

I was in my office after my evening rounds, looking at the envelope I came to pick up. The results were in, and with the hectic day I'd already had, I wasn't sure how I'd respond to either being a father or not. If the latter were the case, then that proved what we all knew— the woman had been lying about everything.

With my nerves trying to settle after being called to the ICU for an emergency crash of one of Dr. Anderson's patients, I knew I needed to take a breath before I opened the envelope. I'd tried everything to save the man to no avail, and my frustration grew even more when I went through his charts and saw that Anderson should've never done the surgery in the first place. The deceased man we couldn't revive despite everyone's most considerable efforts was not a candidate for open-heart surgery, and I was reasonably sure, knowing Anderson, he told the patient and the family so, but they opted in anyway. When I walked out to inform the family, they seemed to be more under-standing than surprised this happened to their family member.

With all of that having happened, fighting media mobs over the past two weeks, seeing where I was now the asshole doctor living a happy life, and leaving the mother of my child to raise my child alone, I was reaching a breaking point. How the hell could they say this shit about me without knowing whether or not I was the father? The lawyers' advice was to keep my mouth shut while this Liz bitch cried daily in front of the cameras and reporters. Why the fuck did anyone give a shit about my personal life anyway?

I rubbed my forehead, my thumb absently running over the embossed seal of the results I *needed* to know. Shitty day or not, I couldn't go another night without having some answers.

I felt emotionless as I opened the folder and read the results. I shouldn't have been surprised, pissed, or in the red-zoned state that I'd just hit after learning the child was, in fact, mine. I shoved the paper-work in my work case and shouldered the bag, leaving my office and needing to be alone to process things.

"Jacob," I heard a woman's breathless voice call out after I pulled my keys out from locking the back door of my office. "Jacob, wait."

I turned to see the very last person that wanted to be in my pres-ence. "Liz," I said, glancing around to find us alone and pissed this woman practically came out of the trees to talk to me. "Now's not the time. What are you doing out here by yourself this late?"

"I've been waiting to talk to you," she said. "I'm sorry about what happened with the patient you—"

"Hold up," I looked at her in disbelief. "This is bordering on psychotic stalker behavior. How do you know what I've been doing, and why are you waiting for me in the dark?"

"I tried to talk to you earlier when I got my results—our results—but you were called to the hospital in an emergency. So I waited."

"You're positively insane," I snapped, my sense and voice of reason fleeing from me rapidly. "We can talk when we're in front of lawyers," I said, turning to leave.

"We need to talk now," she said, trailing me. "We need to talk about the future of us and our baby."

I stopped, closed my eyes, and tried to breathe out the fury I felt as I heard those words come out of her mouth. I wasn't in the right frame of mind for this. Not even close.

"There is no future between *us*, and I can assure you that. We'll talk about the baby in front of lawyers."

"I'm scared to do this alone," she whimpered, and I glared in response.

"Scared?" I scoffed. "If you were so *scared*, then why did you come to my house that night? If you were so goddamn scared, why did you wait five fucking months of knowing you were pregnant to tell me about it?"

"Because of this reaction."

I ran my hand through my hair and closed my eyes. The woman's tone was grating on my nerves, and her lies about being Ash's friend led me to believe the woman had far more significant issues than carrying my child.

"Listen," I said. "You and I need to find a way to deal with the outcome of a condom failing because I was a dick who wanted a piece of ass. I know this."

"The condom?" She laughed. "You didn't use a condom, Jacob. That's how I knew the baby was yours."

"Believe what you want," I said. "The bottom line is that I'm the father, and trust me when I say that I still question that. I'll have another test done once the baby is born as well."

"Why are you questioning it?"

"Because you walked into my office after having covertly joined my intern team, all with the most ridiculous excuse I've heard in my life. If that wasn't enough, you fucking stalker, you lied about being Ash's best friend. What do you want out of this—out of me? Money? Name the price, and I'll pay your ass off right now."

"Any price?" she looked at me with confusion or excitement—hell if I knew. The woman was a lunatic, and she was taking the bait.

"Any price."

"You're disgusting," she said. "I will get child support, but our baby needs its father in its life."

Is she fucking serious? I thought, nauseated and furious to hear the words *our baby* come out of her mouth. "You'll get your child support," I said almost in a growl, "but don't expect me to be the father you might want. I don't even have the time for a bullshit relationship much less deal with raising someone's kid."

I didn't mean any of that. I'd just fed this woman what was far from the truth, but I was incensed. My fucking day had been hell, and now I was spouting off because I was pissed at the world.

"Wow," she said, "does Ashley know this is how you feel about her?"

"You have no idea what you're talking about," I said, pissed at myself more than anything. "As I said, the lawyers will be involved from here on out. Do *not* come to my office ever again. If you need to meet, I'll arrange the time and place. And after the child is born, another DNA test will be run to have foolproof accuracy of the child being mine. I have nothing else to say to you."

With every step I took toward the parking structure, looking over my shoulder to see if the parasite was following me, I'd realized I said shit that wasn't anywhere near the man I was. Psycho mother or not, I *would* be there for my child—no hesitation, no doubt in my mind. I couldn't believe the rage that woman managed to pull out of me to make me respond in such a manner.

The woman was seemingly not right in the head, and I was definitely calling for a psychological exam to warrant her fitness as a mother *and* a medical professional. Shit, I'd screwed some crazy chicks in my life, but it just so happened that the craziest one of them all was carrying my kid.

I got into my car and immediately called Jim while pulling out of the parking lot.

"Eleven o'clock on a Friday night tells me you had a shitty day," he answered from the speakerphone in his office.

"Pull me off speakerphone," I said.

"It's just me. I'm settling out the last of the paperwork," he said, "What's going on?"

"I fucked up," I said. "The kid is mine. The results came in. That bitch—"

"Jake," Jim cut me off. "Slow the hell down. How *exactly* did you fuck up?"

"Liz was hiding out in the trees like a psychopath, and I confronted her."

"Regardless of how crazy the woman is or not, you understood very well that you're to keep your damn mouth shut around the media, the office, and, more importantly, *her*," he said in frustration. "Damn it, why in the hell did you open your mouth?"

"Bad fucking day, to say the least."

"I heard about Anderson's loss. You tried, man," he said. "Collin said you seemed to be faring well after it all, though."

"Well, that shit stays with me sometimes."

"Fine. What did you say to her?"

"It started by me setting her up to take the money. I tried to bait the woman in and pay her off, but she wasn't biting."

"Fuck, Jake!" he growled. "That is *not* your job! We have the best team of lawyers in all of Southern California, yet here you are trying to negotiate while fucking yourself in the process. Why would you do that?"

"That's not the worst part. I lost my shit and said I had no time to raise a child since I was barely handling a relationship or some crazy shit like that. If that woman hates Ash, I just gave her—"

"The lawyers already told you not to talk to her—especially alone—because of her mannerisms already. Her feeding everything to the press these days is the reason the lawyers told you to keep your mouth shut. Now to hear you *baited* her? Do you know how shitty that's going to come across to the fucking morons who are obsessed with this personal-life circus of yours?"

"I don't give a shit what the morons think. I just don't want this broad giving Ash some distorted version of the truth."

"Thanks to this stunt, this is probably going to blow up in your face, and you need to brace yourself for that."

"I can't lose Ash."

"Should've thought about that before you let your temper take over," he said with no sympathy. "Where are you headed now? Are you going to talk to her? Perhaps you should."

"I think I'm just going to text her and head home for the night. I can't trust myself talking to her in this state of mind."

"Good call. Make sure you get up to see her tomorrow, at least. If you think it could be an issue, you should to get to Ash before this woman does."

"I know. I'll talk to you later."

"Hey, Jake," he said before I ended the call.

"What," I responded flatly.

"Take this any way you want, but I'm going big brother on your ass. You need to shut the fuck up from here on out, you got that? I'll watch the press, and I'm getting a team of lawyers on them as well. It's gotten out of hand, and I'm worried about you not being able to perform your job well with all of this harassment."

"It's taking you *just now* to see how those dicks are fucking with my life?"

"You're pissed. Go home. I'll handle my part, and you handle yours."

I hung up with Jim, and who knows what possessed me, but I took the freeway to head to Ash's house to let her know what'd happened, and get that out of the way. By the time I'd pulled up to her house—after two major traffic jams—I looked at the time and was annoyed more than before. There was no way I was going to wake her up just to lay this shit on her and ruin her sleep, not to mention waking up her dad and Carmen. I decided to text her instead and head home to where I should've gone directly in the first place.

Jake: *Hey, it's been a pretty shitty day. Found out I'm the father. It's past midnight, or else I'd have stopped by to tell you myself. I'm just heading home for the night. I'll talk to you tomorrow.*

AFTER I HIT SEND, I STARED AT THE TEXT, WISHING I'D NEVER SENT it. It was something I definitely should have told her face-to-face. I was in a fucking downward spiral tonight and needed to go home.

Chapter Thirty-Three

Ash

I woke up to thoughts of the text Jake had sent me the previous night. He should have just called, and I would have let him stay over, but I understood why he didn't. This wasn't something we could cuddle up to and go to sleep. It'd been a rough couple of weeks for both of us since getting back from Santa Clarita. I missed the hell out of the guy and still couldn't believe the swarming of the press that happened after we came back home. It was a beautiful day, letting Mom go, but it was destroyed by the media after Liz went to them in tears.

Jake was solemn when his brother gave him the news and told him to prepare for this turn of events with the media probing into his personal life. I felt horrible for him. Good grief, who cared about this shit? Apparently, it was making these outlets good money because everyone seemed to talk about the billionaire doctor who cared more about his girlfriend than his own child.

I couldn't resist checking to see where the gossip was after Jim mentioned Liz was a frantic idiot in front of the camera. My headlines were no better than Jim's as of last night: the woman who the doctor is using to avoid his baby. It was all so lame. I couldn't believe anyone would give these stories credit.

I stared at the text Jake had sent me last night. It was finally done, and the results had come back with Jake being the father to Liz's baby. I loved him even past all of my selfish desires of wanting him to myself, but it sucked to know I would have to share him with this chick he got pregnant after a one-night stand. I needed to see him, but had a feeling he needed some space.

"*Mija!*" Carmen called from the kitchen. "Someone's at the door, and your dad is in the backyard. Can you get it?"

"Yep," I said, jumping up from where I was stretched out and trying to sleep through the day. I walked past the kitchen and smiled at Carmen. "You're just—"

"Yes, ma'am," she said, stirring some sauce. "You're not sleeping all day. There are bigger problems in the world than this." She winked and pursed her lips while dancing to her music and cooking.

"What the hell are you doing here?" I said, my smile instantly fading when I saw Liz and her tear-streaked cheeks.

"We need to talk," she said.

"I see you brought your friends with you." I stared out at the media. "Why are you here, and how did you get my new address?"

"I followed Jake last night. I needed to—"

"Get in here," I pulled her in, seeing the reporters creeping up the walkway. "You *have* lost it," I snapped. "Following my boyfriend now?"

She collapsed on my couch, leaving me standing there and glaring at her. "I couldn't help it. I needed to talk to him."

"He texted me. I know the baby is his. I have no idea why you're here, but from mentioning you're stalking Jake, I'll keep it simple. We have talked about this and have determined to—"

"He tried to pay me off," she stated, interrupting me.

"I'm sorry, what?"

"Last night, Jake and I talked after work. He stayed late, and we discussed our baby." She stopped, and it must've been because of my expression, knowing she was alone with him after hours.

"Go on. You discussed the results," I said flatly.

"Yes. It got out of hand, and he said horrible things."

"Jake's been under a lot of pressure with the shit show of the media since *you* decided to cry to them about your unfortunate situation."

"That was stupid. I know that now." She sniffed. "Ashley, I'm here because of what he said about you. I recorded our conversation after he got violent."

"Jake got *violent* with you?" I asked darkly. "Did you tell those assholes that?" I nodded toward the front window. "Are you recording *this* conversation? What kind of person are you, Liz? I mean, what the fuck happened to you? I can't believe half the shit you're pulling."

"I just want you to know that I feel like you're with a man who won't appreciate you or doesn't appreciate you—"

"We're *not* friends, Liz. I don't need you filling me in on things you honestly don't know about between my boyfriend and me."

"Really?" she snapped, running her hand over her stomach while pulling out her phone. "This is the father of my poor baby and *your disgusting boyfriend*," she sneered, and then the next thing I knew, I was listening to Jake's voice.

I stood first in agreement with him being pissed off, then stunned and silenced when the last words I ever believed could come out of his mouth did.

"I don't even have the time for a bullshit relationship much less deal with raising someone's kid." His statement on top of him offering to pay the girl off was *not* the man I'd fallen in love with.

"Get out," I snapped. "And delete that goddamn recording."

"I'm using this if it goes to a custody battle between us," she snarled.

"Does it *sound to you* like he wants the kid?" I asked, thoroughly disgusted with her and Jake. "Sounds to me like he's willing to pay you to get you and the baby out of his life."

"What a stand-up guy you've got, Ash," she said smugly. "You heard what he said about having a relationship, right? I'm sorry, a *bullshit* relationship."

"Yes, so delete it all," I said. "His point of view of not having time for that or a child should tell you that custody battles won't be a problem between you and him."

She sighed. "I'm going to my lawyers with this."

I stepped in front of her as she headed toward the front door. "You're not going anywhere with that but to those assholes out front. You play that for those idiots, and you'll ruin him."

"Isn't that the point? He ruined my life by fucking me and calling a cab to get me out of his house that night. Karma is a bitch."

"Shut your mouth," I snapped, looking for my dad and Carmen and hoping they didn't have to listen to this trash. "You getting screwed over by some dude for sex is between you and him. You realize that if you go for his throat like this, the man I just heard on that recording sounds like he'll bury your pathetic ass."

"The media sees me as a victim."

"Is this a game to you?" I said in disbelief. "Some crazy soap opera that led you to the girlfriend's house, knowing what you caught on tape would end the relationship? You are a delusional snake, Liz. The man is a billionaire. He has an army of attorneys, and if you're dumb enough to try and end his career after having given the media that tape, there's no telling what he'll do."

"So you get it, then. He's out of his mind."

"What he said to you was wrong, and I'm disgusted those words came out of his mouth. Does he deserve to be smeared all over the media for it? No." I stood firm. "Delete it, Liz," I said. "The man saves more lives than you know. Don't cost people their lives by giving them a soap opera opinion of him and making them not trust him as their doctor. He's the best heart surgeon in the fucking world. I won't let you cost him that. You've done enough already. Delete the recording."

I reached for the phone she held, snatched it from her hand, and stared at it with contemplation. She was stunned by my childish gesture, but I instantly deleted the recording that was already seared into my mind.

"There," I handed her the phone. "I might have saved your ass from him, slapping you with a lawsuit if you were stupid enough to cost him his job."

"He was bribing me!" she seethed.

"And you were recording Jake without his knowledge. I'm pretty sure his lawyers would find a way to bury you with that one. If you want to keep your medical license, then I suggest you slow the hell down on all this crap. Let him cool off. I'm sure you'll have the support you'll need when the baby is here."

"You're a coldhearted bitch and an absolute fool."

"Say what you want, Liz. It doesn't affect me in the slightest." I opened the door. "Go cry on their shoulder."

"You think I'm going to tell them about this?"

"I *know* you're going to tell them about this. Get the fuck out of my house. Good luck with the baby."

I watched Liz storm out of the house and erupt into tears out on my lawn. "I can't fucking believe him!" I shouted.

"Ash," I heard my dad.

"Not now, Dad. Please, I can't."

"*Mija*," Carmen said. "You and me, now."

I looked at both Dad and Carmen, standing side by side in the doorway. "There's nothing to talk about. You heard Jake. He tried to pay the woman off. That's his damn kid too. Who does that? How could anyone's first reaction be to do that?"

"That boy has been through hell and back, and you know it," my dad tried to scold me.

"So, you think that gives him the right to use his wealth to get rid of the burden of a child? That's heartless, Dad, and a whole other level of wrong. You know that." I sighed. "I'm taking off and heading up to Joe and Clay's. I have a lot to think about. I can't be with a man who's made it clear he can barely handle a *bullshit* relationship, much less a kid. I love him, and this hurts, but I can't waste my life on a man who sees things like that. I have no business in a billionaire's world when his first reaction is to bust out his checkbook to make his problems go away. That is how he views being a father? Hell no. That's never going to be me. He may be under pressure, but he wouldn't have said that if he didn't truly feel that way."

"I'm so sick of the media doing this to both of you," Carmen grumbled.

"It made the inevitable happen, but the media didn't make Jake say what he said, that was all him. If Jake feels this way, it's better to end it now than later. He will have more than enough on his hands, especially with the crazy bitch he decided to take home that night. She's insane, and I wish him all the best. Perhaps with me out of his life, he can deal with all the trouble she's going to throw his way."

"Will you be back for dinner?" Carmen asked.

"I may stay with Clay and Joe for a while. They've wanted me to come up and see their new pad." I smiled, feeling tears in my eyes. "I need to get out, and it's closer to work."

"Honey, we're here for you. Take some time; Clay and Joe are good friends. Maybe they'll help you feel a little better."

I smiled at my dad through my tears and walked over and hugged him. "I love you so much, Dad." I kissed his cheek. "You heard what I told that woman, right?"

"I'm not leaving my doctor if that's what you're worried about."

"You're still getting the transplant when the call comes in," I said, wiping the tears from my face. "Promise me that."

"*Mija*," Carmen chimed in, "you've got nothing to worry about. We don't pay attention to the trash that follows Dr. Mitchell around. Your dad will be a new man after that call comes in, and the transplant is done." She held her arms out. "Come here," she said, and I hugged her slender frame. "Go breathe. This was all too much. Men are selfish assholes sometimes. We know this, though." She pulled back, her ruby red lips parting into a sly smile. "Don't we?"

I grinned. "We do."

"Don't you girls dare bring me into the middle of this," Dad said.

I ruffled his gray, curly hair. "You're the best of them all."

I PACKED A BAG AND FILLED A GARMENT BAG OF WORK CLOTHES after checking in with Joe and Clay. Both of my guys insisted I come up and stay with them. They'd mentioned they had a room set up already to surprise me with in hopes of getting me to visit often. I loved these two more than anything. I could only hope that they'd help ease the pain of hearing how Jake truly felt about us.

I had just walked in from the patio after saying goodbye to Dad and Carmen when I heard the doorbell. I was indifferent when I walked toward the door, knowing in my heart it was the last person—aside from Liz—I wanted to see, but I was going to face this head-on and end mine and Jake's relationship now rather than later.

I opened the door and ignored every handsome feature of the man I'd come to love and trust. "Come in," I said, avoiding eye contact.

"You got my text, I see," he said, standing next to the couch.

"I did," I answered. "I got a lot more than that, too."

"What are you talking about?" he questioned.

"I'm talking about Liz. She paid me a visit."

"Are you *fucking*—" he paused, and his low growl matched the voice I heard on the tape. "Please, tell me she did *not* come in and talk to you."

"I'm not telling you that because it would be a lie," I said. "Kind of like our *bullshit relationship* is a lie, I suppose. You know the one that you made me believe was something real?"

"I—I'm sorry. I *did* say that, but that's not—Ash, I was out of my mind last night when she appeared out of nowhere to talk to me and—"

"I'm glad you can be honest about saying that, I guess. Now, when were you planning on telling me that you were going to pay her off?"

His eyes were dark with anger. "She certainly had a mouthful to say to you, didn't she?"

"She recorded everything, Jake. I heard all of it. I can't be with someone who feels like a relationship with me is *bullshit*. I *won't* be with a rich asshole who believes he can buy his way out of his problems, either."

"Fuck, Ash," he said, running his hand through his hair. "Nothing I can say will fix me going off on that lunatic last night. I'd had a shitty day, and I just lost it."

"Yeah, well, shitty day or not, at least I know how you feel."

"I can't lose you, Ash," he said, and I swallowed hard when I saw tears fill his eyes. He bit his bottom lip, his glassy blue eyes practically pleading with my soul.

DR. MITCHELL

"You have bigger problems to deal with than me. You need to accept this like I thought we'd both agreed. You need to go live your life and do the right thing for your child."

We both stood there, staring at each other. My heartbreak was there, but I couldn't feel it. I was numb, seeing Jake broken in front of me, but my guard was pulled up to protect myself.

"You're the best thing that's happened to me. I'm sorry I hurt you."

"Yep," I said, holding back all emotion.

"The media will have her recording, I'm sure. I'll be sure it doesn't portray you in a bad light."

"I handled her recording. The media won't be getting this part of the story," I said. "You don't have to worry about them."

"I don't give a shit what happens out there anymore. The one thing I cared about—"

"Stop, Jake!" I snapped. "It's done, over. I get it. You are not the man I thought you were. I want you out of my life. Do what you must so you can sleep at night. Actions speak a lot louder than words. Do the right thing with that woman," I advised through tears.

"I'm sorry I hurt you. I swear I'll never forgive myself for this."

"Forgive yourself, Jake. Don't worry about me. I should've known better. I'll be fine. I'll move on. Thanks for helping me through the struggles I was lost in. If anything, you saved me from that."

"Would there ever be a chance that—"

"No," I said. "When I heard you offer to pay that woman off, that's when I realized I was with a man that I could never be aligned with. We are from different worlds. You come from money, and it shows. I don't fix my problems by paying them off—you obviously do. You sank to the lowest of lows by not taking responsibility for your actions and making your child suffer for that. You disgust me," I said, my emotions firing in every direction. "Get out of my house. Do the right thing with Liz, and do it for your child."

I didn't have to say another word. Jake pinched his lips together and nodded.

"Hey," I said while he was halfway down the walkway, "what happened between you and me today will not affect my dad being your patient. You're an amazing doctor, and I don't trust anyone else with his transplant."

"Thank you for that."

I nodded, and he turned and got into the car, leaving my emotions for him dry and callous. He could take that hundred-thousand-dollar car and his Billionaires' Club attitude and get the hell out of my life.

Chapter Thirty-Four

Jake

I was in the lunchroom at the hospital, sitting amongst nurses and doctors, absently eating the fresh strawberries I'd picked up at the farmer's market over the weekend. I was doing everything in my power to keep my mind off the one thing in my life that was good before it all went away, but here I was, eating her favorite fruit and bringing Ash's beautiful smile back to my mind.

"Jake," Missy, the RN, called my name with a laugh. "Did you hear that?"

I lifted my chin and smiled. "Yeah, Tanner is all comedy today." I smiled over at my usual attending physician.

"Somebody has to be. All you've done is read articles from the journal of medicine for the past two weeks," he teased. "Man, where's the Jake that keeps us all entertained?"

"Prepping for a child," I said with a smile. "God knows this poor baby is in trouble with *me* as its father."

"God help us all," Jenny, another physician, teased.

"The question is," I said as I rose, "can the world handle another Jake?"

"Shut up," Lisa said, one of my favorite RNs. "Has she found out what the baby is?"

"Yep. Apparently, she live-streamed it all on social media," I said with a shrug. "It's a bouncing baby boy."

"She did tell you first, though, right?" Lisa asked. She was the only one who knew the challenge on my hands with Liz.

"I joined her on this particular visit after she asked me to." I smiled at the group, who was doing their best to stay away from the bullshit of my personal life. "See, I'm not that big of a jerk that's being plastered all over the internet these days, am I?"

"You can say whatever you want." Chi laughed. "You'll always be a jerk, Jake."

"You of all people know that first hand, Tan." I glanced at the group. "Enjoy the rest of the day."

With lunch out of my way, I walked out toward my office. The media was still swarming like bees outside, and I honestly had no idea why it would interest them when I walked from the hospital building to my office. What the hell kind of story was that going to give them? These people were insane. Almost as insane as the woman carrying my child. I was doing my best with her, though. Once I'd accepted the entire thing, I found peace with it. Soon after I'd lost Ash, of course. Either way, the child was mine, and the little guy deserved to have a good father in his life. That's what I intended to be.

"Dr. Mitchell," Sandy said after I walked in and turned toward my office, "you have a call from the Heart Institute."

My eyes widened. "I'll take it in my office," I said, knowing this may be the donor heart I'd been waiting for. I walked in and hit the speakerphone button before I could sit in my chair. "Give me good news," I said, having worked with this heart care unit multiple times.

"We have a heart, Dr. Mitchell. We need to go over the final details, and the helicopter will be on its way. Is your patient prepared?"

"I'll call him as soon as we finish, yes," I said.

"We'll keep you updated. It should be there in an hour or so for cross-matching."

"I'll have the transplant team called in and prepared to receive it. Thanks, Allison," I said to the woman who'd always brought good news from this institute.

I hung up and hit the intercom to the reception desk, "Sandy."

"Yes, Doctor."

"I'll be a few more minutes. I was just informed that we have a heart for Mr. Taylor. Can you please call out to the transplant team? The helicopter will be arriving with it in an hour or so. Please put the staff on alert and prepped for the heart and Mr. Taylor's arrival."

"Absolutely. This is wonderful news," she cheered.

"Thanks, Sandy."

Next came my call to Mark.

"Mr. Taylor?" I said when he answered the phone. I missed his tone, his relaxed mood, and just being around the man. I lost a whole lot more than Ash in saying the hateful words I did to Liz that night.

"*Mr. Taylor* again now, Doc?" he asked in his humored tone. "To you, it's always Mark."

"Very well, then, Mark..." I smiled through the phone, not under-standing how this man didn't hate me more than Ash did after learning the truth about what I'd done. "We have a heart. Can you be down here within the next couple of hours?"

"No kidding?" I heard his laugh, but it was hoarse as if he were crying.

"Yes, sir. And if I find everything is matching up, we're going to be transplanting tonight."

"Carmen!" he yelled, not listening to me but making me smile. "It's Jacob."

"Go on," I heard Carmen's voice, wondering if Ash was getting this news as well. "What's he got to say, *mi amor*?"

"We have a heart! Can you believe it?"

Carmen squealed an array of words in Spanish as Mark laughed, and I couldn't believe that I, myself, had tears of joy for all of them too. I hadn't realized how much I missed this family. I cleared my throat, pulling myself together.

"Can you be down at Saint John's within the next two hours?" I asked. "I'll be heading over to you once the heart arrives and we start running tests against your antibodies," I said, trying to regain control of the call.

"Yes," Mark said, and I could hear the smacking of Carmen's lips meeting his. I could visualize the woman, climbing all over Ash's dad in her contagious excitement of this news that Mark would most likely be well on his way to a new heart and new life. "Thank you, Doc."

"You can thank me when we're confirmed the surgery is happening," I said. "You do remember our discussion about this, correct? Don't get me wrong, I'm as excited as you all, but if the antibodies don't take, we have to wait for another."

"I know," Mark said, his voice riddled with excitement. "We'll be on our way. Carmen, call Ash. She's going to flip."

With that, we hung up. My lips and throat were suddenly dry with remorse that I couldn't be with Ash to see the look on her face when she learned her dad was most likely getting his heart transplant. I couldn't be a part of this at all, except to be the doctor who successfully helped this family get a great man back and healthy again.

I walked over to my office fridge, pulled out a water bottle, and almost downed all of the contents. Over the last week or more, I'd finally pulled it together, and now I was collapsing again. I leaned back against the wall, letting the cold surface calm me down. I wasn't going down this road again. I knew it was best for Ash to move on as she had. I knew I was a dumbass male-slut for putting myself in this position. I'd accepted the consequences of my actions for how I reacted—pissed or not—to Liz that night. Thank God Ash erased that recording; the last thing I needed was that shit in the media's hands. I had to forgive the malice of Liz, setting me up like that. Hell, I'd tried to bait her in with money myself, so I wasn't getting on my high horse about who was more despicable.

Focus, Jake. I snapped out of this frame of mind. This wasn't about me. It was about Mark and his family. I also had patients to treat and a heart being flown in. This was a big night, and it was barely getting started.

. . .

HOLY SHIT, IT'S GOING TO HAPPEN. I SMILED AT ALL OF THE bloodwork, the screenings, and the fact that after every little intricate piece that had to come together in this complicated puzzle; it was a perfect match.

"The patient has been informed?" I asked the nurse while heading to change into my scrubs.

"Yes, Doctor. Most of the transplant staff has met with him. He's waiting on your final word," my charge, Becky, said. "Dr. Chi is scrubbing in."

"Excellent." My mood was encouraged that it all came together and so quickly. There were too many times that the antibodies of the patient would not allow the heart to be a match. It was my worst enemy sometimes, and until we had Mark on that table, I had to be sure this heart was ready to go. Time was of the essence now.

"Someone in here shopping this place for a heart?" I asked, walking into Mark's room, seeing Carmen, Joe, Clay, and then my eyes fell on Ash.

Her eyes were filled with tears. Those same tears I saw in her eyes that day I took her up the coast on the bike. She was so beautiful it was painful to stand here as Dr. Mitchell and force myself to ignore the woman I'd forever love and focus on my patient. I smiled at everyone in the room but returned my focus to the critical matter at hand.

I walked toward the computers that were monitoring Mark. I quietly studied them, bringing the room that was once filled with nervous, excited chatters to silence.

"Well, do we still have a date tonight, Doc, or are you going to leave me hanging here?" Mark said in that tone I loved about the man.

I turned to him, standing at his side. "I'm not standing you up tonight, Mark. The date's still on." I smiled at him and Carmen, who was at the other side of the bed. "You think your heart is up for a date with me?"

Goddammit, lame choice of words.

"I know the ladies can't handle you, but I think I can."

I chuckled, signing off on one last lab, and glancing back at the monitors. "The question is, can I handle you?"

Carmen laughed. "Bring him back to us, Jacob," she said sincerely, her eyes darting over to my right where I knew Ash sat.

I turned back to see her smiling and the look in her eye that made me come undone at times. "I'll bring him back." I looked back at Carmen. "Though I'm only hoping you're all ready for this guy once he has a new heart."

I used that to make my exit, and I glanced back at Mark. "One last hurdle awaits. We're moving you in and quick. We can't keep your new heart waiting all night."

ONCE EVERYTHING WAS SET IN PLACE WITH THE TRANSPLANT TEAM, that's when the final assessment of Mark's new heart would be done. "Mark, you're getting the good stuff, my friend, we are definitely a go. You ready for this?" I asked, nodding toward the team with the waiting donor heart and walking back over to Mark.

"You're a good man, Jacob," he said, and it was too sentimental for me.

"You're already getting high on the good stuff," I said.

I watched tears stream out of the corner of his eyes. "I can't thank you enough for this. For everything."

I nodded toward the anesthesiologist, maintaining supreme professionalism. Mark was sending out words that would naturally affect me in ways I truly needed to hear from him after losing his daughter, but now was not the time for that. I had to compartmentalize this and focus. It would be a long night, and by morning, we'd be finished. Taking out the heart assist and bringing in the new organ was easily an eight to ten-hour surgery, and it was close to ten. These were the nights that I learned to function without sleep a long time ago. My mind or body wouldn't go near exhaustion. This is what I lived for.

"Lights out for you, Mark. I'll see you in the morning," I said, and then soon after, Mark was out, and we were ready to go to work.

"I believe it's my turn for music," Bethany, part of my transplant team and my right-hand surgical nurse stated while I went through my medical tools.

I looked at her through my headgear and magnifying glass loupes. "God help me, Beth. The last time you were up, we were stuck with that love-channel station. I'm not doing that again."

The room softly laughed while I returned my attention to Dr. Chi. "Can't it be your turn?"

He smirked. "Love is in the air, Dr. Mitchell. New heart—new life."

"What if we all took a vote?" I suggested, making the cut and beginning the surgery. "Perhaps anything *but* Diana Ross all night long? Doctor's orders," I tried with a smile while making a smooth cut to begin the process of opening Mark's chest.

"We voted for love songs." Chi chuckled. "Sorry, Mitchell."

"Then love songs it is," I said, following Chi in preparing the opening and getting this intricate surgery underway. "That heart waiting for a new body better approve," I teased as I heard Lionel Richie's and Diana Ross's duo of "Endless Love" come over the speakers to the OR. Just my damn luck. I could only be humored as to what Ash would have thought of this entire situation. Good God, "Endless Love"? I knew the woman I loved would have given that smile I longed to see again in response.

"Time in?" I asked.

"Eight hours in surgery, doctor," an intern answered.

The heart was in, and we were at a critical point. "Bypass machines off," I said. Chi nodding and glancing toward the technicians. "Let's get our beat."

As many open-heart surgeries as I'd done and attended, this part was the part that astounded me the most. It would never cease to give me a feeling of utter excitement, watching a transplanted heart, not beating, and then—as we waited—it began to beat on its own. It was a miracle, and a miracle I would never take for granted.

Slowly the left and then right, the heart started beating and quickly got up to a rhythm that matched what the body desired in feeding blood to all organs of the body.

"We have a heartbeat, and it's happy that it's found a new home," I announced. "Can we please flip it to Iron Maiden or something else? Celine Dion isn't adding to my happiness."

"The heart *will* go on," Chi said.

We both went back to work. "Yeah, funny, but unfortunately, that song of hers isn't playing. Nice try, though."

"We can turn it to it," Beth said at my side.

"You can turn it, period," I winked at her. "Grab my cell, please?"

She did and helped me unlock it. "Call Carmen," I ordered the phone.

"Jacob!" she answered on the first ring. "Please tell me it's all good, baby boy."

"We have a heartbeat, and all of the monitors look great, Carm," I said.

I heard the room erupt into cheers and smiled at Carmen's knack for always throwing people on speakerphone without telling them.

"What's this baby boy nonsense?" I questioned, everyone on my side hearing it too and laughing.

"I'm proud of you, is all." She sniffed. "Is that Celine Dion in the background?" She chuckled, and I eyed Bethany while taking the scalpel from her.

"Beth got to pick the music for the surgery," I said.

"Beth, *mija*, how are you?"

"Great, Carmen. We're taking care of your man in here," she said.

"Ladies," I interrupted, "can we play catch-up when my patient is in recovery?"

"He's just upset because we've had it on love songs all night."

Carmen's cackle was enough to make me laugh. "Laugh it up, Carm, and I'll slow down."

"Get to work, Jacob. Thank you for updating us; we've been restless with worry," she said. "Oh, you're on speakerphone too."

"I gathered that. You guys get comfortable and rest. We're doing the easy stuff now."

"Yeah, you call it easy, we know it's highly—"

"Carmen," I lowered my voice, "no need to concern those waiting around you."

"True," she said. "He's in good hands. I know this."

"Thanks; we're moving forward with the process now."

That's when we hung up, and I ensured everything was functioning properly. Mark was well on his way with a functioning new heart, and another beautiful miracle had taken place for Saint John's. It was the kind of success story I wished the media would focus on. These were the stories I would give anything for people to hear about. Not the stories that played a role in ruining my personal life.

Chapter Thirty-Five

Ash

We celebrated Dad reaching the eight-week milestone after his heart transplant surgery. Everything had gone perfectly smooth, but I'd never had the opportunity to thank Jake like I'd wanted to, even after the surgery.

Saint John's was terrific. Instead of seeing Jake as I thought I would, Dad had an entire team working with him during his hospital recovery. I was never around when Jake had slipped in to check on Dad's progress and speak to the transplant team about how Dad was progressing.

It was probably for the best. Seeing Jake walk through those doors before and after surgery made my heart race with admiration of the doctor in him, and that's what started me getting twisted up in this mess in the first place. Gawking at the gorgeous doctor who saved Dad's life, and then I fell for the man's charms soon after.

I wanted to hate him like any hurt ex-girlfriend would, but I couldn't. He'd brought me back to life in more ways than one. He was fun, witty, and an all-around great guy. Catching wind of him being fully supportive of his son was sickening to hear at first, and it wasn't lost on me how contradictory of me that was. It was my jealousy flaring up—jealousy that this happened when I wasn't there for it. Because in reality, the kind of man I wanted him to be was a man who would step up in the first place, and that's what he was doing now.

As fate would have it, I walked by the nurses' station while they were talking about how excited they were when Jake told him he was expecting a son. There was no malice or gossip in their words. They were genuinely happy for him, given his own excitement about it.

Knowing that Carmen and Dad were still hopeful Jake and I would end up together, Carmen probed her nurse friends who worked around Jake for information. She loved to bring up how well he was doing in his support of—in Carmen's words—the crazy woman carrying his baby.

"You know," a woman's voice said from behind where I stood in the gallery, staring at the portrait I wished I could afford. "I've seen a different version of this portrait."

I looked to my side, and my eyes narrowed when I saw the woman I'd first met after I spilled my drink on Jake in the coffee shop. What was her name, and why was she in here?

"This is the second edition, painted to become a set with the first," I said, stepping back from the portrait that was the missing piece to the one in Jake's master bedroom.

"Yes," she said, her eyes leveling me with a death stare. Then her smile appeared in some creepy, snake-like way. "The first edition is at Jacob's house. I believe you've seen it?"

"I'm sorry, are you interested in buying this one? Perhaps for him?" I said, trying to keep this business and not allowing the woman to take this conversation where I knew she wanted it to go.

"Jacob can buy it if he wants. I prefer the one he has already. It's stunning in my favorite room of his home in Malibu," she said.

"Good. I liked it there too."

"I'm sorry you two didn't work out," she said condescendingly. "At least you understand why he doesn't keep women around for long."

"Are you here to bring up my ex, or are you here to purchase a painting?"

"I'm only talking to you," she lowered her voice and stared darkly at me, "to let you know it was never going to work between you two. I hope you aren't too crushed." She chuckled. "I've known him for far too long, and if only I could've warned you."

"What makes you think I'm crushed or that I needed you to warn me about him?" I asked. "Jake's a great guy. I'm pretty sure you're just here to let it be known that you have him back, and your super clever way of telling me he's sleeping with you again is by mentioning you've seen the first-edition portrait to this one? Well, I'm not interested. If that's what you want, then, by all means, go get it. I've moved on. Now, can I guide you to a portrait you might be here to buy, or are we going to talk about how great the sex is between you and Jake?"

"How dare you speak to me that way!" she scoffed. "Why would you assume any of that?"

"Why are you talking to me if you're not interested in buying anything? I remember the way you acted on the yacht. It was obvious you weren't happy that I was there with him. And now, here we are, suggestively talking about the portrait that matches the one above Jake's bed? I'm not an idiot."

"Could've fooled me. You're the one who thought you were in a relationship with a man who is incapable of holding one down, much less raise a child." She smirked. "Coincidence that your little friend gets pregnant by your boyfriend, right? And, true to form, the relationship is over because Jacob can't handle it."

"Are we done here?" I asked, pissed off that this woman was digging up the past, and for what fucking reason? Jake and I hadn't been in touch for almost three months.

"Yes, I believe we are."

I watched in disbelief as Lillian practically ran out to the woman, screaming the name I'd forgotten.

"Vickie, darling! Oh, my heart is full," she declared as if the Queen of England had walked into her gallery. "Ashley, dear, your shift is over. I'm closing up. Would you mind locking the front, and I'll go out the back? My keys are over in Brea Hall on the desk."

"Got it. See you on Monday," I said.

"Bye, dear."

The woman was three years older than me and treated me like I was five years old whenever people of importance showed up here. I hadn't seen Jim since being on the yacht, so I'd assumed he kicked her crazy ass to the curb, but if he hadn't, maybe after seeing Jake's situation with Lunatic-Liz, Jim would think twice before staying with this nut job of a boss of mine.

Shit! Goddammit! My mind had been pulled back to the past after Vickie-the-bitch had shown up and tried to stab a knife through my heart. I hated these arrogant, rich assholes. They were the absolute worst. My confrontation with Vickie made me so rattled that I'd locked up the gallery and left without my car keys. I did not want to see either woman right now, but I also didn't want to ride the bus home. *What the fuck ever.*

Walking in and hearing the shrill laughs coming from Lillian's office, where she left her door cracked open, made my skin crawl. I rolled my eyes and walked toward my desk but froze when I heard Vickie say my name.

I walked toward the door, wondering what the hell these bitches could be saying about *me* when I was sure they had other fake shit to talk about.

"I can't believe you managed any of this. I thought you were drunk and totally joking when you said you would ruin their relationship. I didn't really think you'd be able to do it," Lillian said.

"Jacob was mine. That girl had no idea she was in dangerous territory, coming into my world with my Jacob."

"Hold onto that, let me pour us a drink. I want all the details. I love this." Lillian giggled.

The tone in the woman's voice made me instinctively text Jim. I don't know why, but while they laughed, I had a strange feeling the shit these women were discussing was something he might want Jake's lawyers to know about. The man could kill me later for wasting his time if this was nothing.

Ash: *Hey, it's Ash. Can you get to the gallery? Something's up between Jake's friend Vickie and Lillian. Not sure, but I have a weird feeling.*

Jim: *I'll have my driver turn the car around. I'm about thirty out.*

Ash: *I'm going to record this.*

Jim: *Go for it.*

A FEW MOMENTS LATER, AFTER SILENTLY TEXTING JIM, THE THINGS that came out of Vickie's mouth had me sick to my stomach and utterly in shock. And my phone was recording all of it.

"SERIOUSLY, THOUGH. I DON'T EVEN UNDERSTAND HOW YOU managed it. Girl, this goes beyond stalking." Lillian laughed. "How did you know the pregnant one was connected to my Ashley and then make it all out to be Jake's baby? That is serious masterminding."

"You have no idea. I actually saw Liz—she's the pregnant one—she was with Ashley in San Francisco about a year and a half ago. They were at a rooftop reception that Saint John's had put on after a medical conference, which is why I assume Liz was there because I came to find out later that she's in the medical field."

"This was all that long ago? I thought Ashley and Jake were more recent than that. I didn't realize it was going on for so long. Was he with both of them the whole time? I'm so confused."

"No, he wasn't. It's a pretty convoluted story. He met Ashley that weekend, and I was pissed because Jake wanted nothing to do with me after that stupid girl spilled her drink on him. That's Jacob for you, though. When he sees something that he wants, he doesn't stop until he gets it.

"Anyway, I think Liz is a total fluke in all of this. I only remembered she was Ashley's friend because I was so furious that Jake was talking to Ashley that night that I couldn't stop sizing up her and her group of friends. So, when Liz happened to be at a club in LA, I recognized her immediately, and in predictable Jake fashion, I saw him take her home. This was—I don't know, it was about seven months ago or something like that. It was before Jake and Ashley got together officially."

"Then, how did you get to the pregnant girl—Liz?"

"Obviously, I didn't know she was pregnant when I went digging, but once Jake started blowing me off when Ashley came into the picture, I made it a point to find her friend."

Lillian's laughter sounded like a witch cackle, and this entire exchange was reminding me of Cinderella's evil stepmother talking to her stepsisters. These women were wicked and enjoying every second of this. "Oh, you're so bad! I love it. How did you find Liz?"

"It wasn't hard. I knew she'd gone to that medical conference, so I started asking people from Saint John's who went if they knew who she was. It wasn't long before a resident told me Liz's name and that she was always hanging around one of the lab technicians. And," she said the word as if she were a game show host, getting ready to tell Lillian that what came next was a new car, "it turns out, that guy is the father of her kid. Agh! Can you believe it?"

"Wait!" Lillian screeched, nearly choking on whatever they were drinking. "That baby isn't Jacob's?"

"Oh, hell no. Jake would never sleep with anyone without a condom. Trust me, I've tried to lock him down that way more than once, but that's one thing he never lets slide." She giggled. "But, since the universe loves me, by the time I found Liz, I knew that she was pregnant, and I couldn't help but go in for the kill. Condoms break all the time, right?" She feigned innocence, and I had no idea how I was able to keep listening over the ringing in my ears.

"But what about the paternity test?" Lillian's voice seemed shocked as my heart was falling out of rhythm.

"I'm the president of the lab that did the DNA test, for Christ's sake. I can manage whatever I want."

"Does this girl believe Jacob is the father? I'm so spun out about this. You know you can't tell anyone else this. This borders on you seeming quite obsessed, you know."

"I *am* obsessed. Jacob is mine! I've watched him change since Ashley came around, and it drives me absolutely fucking crazy. I'm the *only* girl Jake's never abandoned. Then to see him so fascinated with her? I had to end it all. I *don't* lose. Ever," she said like she was normal. "Liz knows that isn't Jake's son, but she's desperate for money, so I paid her a shitload and arranged the transfer onto Jake's team after seeing her pregnant. I also made sure she was on the yacht that night too. I needed Jake to put together the pieces of meeting her before. I had to have him think the girl was stalking him. A million dollars and a perfectly-timed pregnant woman he'd previously slept with? It was all primed for me to use to ruin Jacob and that lowlife employee of yours."

"Wow." Lillian softly laughed. "Remind me never to piss you off."

"You have no idea of the connections I have," Vickie said.

"I thought he was going to have more than one paternity test. What if they have it done somewhere else, and you can't access it?"

"That test won't be tampered with anyway. Once he finds out the kid isn't his, the only person he'll take it out on is Liz. What's done is done with Ashley. There's no coming back from that. After all of that is said and done, I'll be innocently waiting for my man, as always."

My body was paralyzed with the information download that I was previously moments away from never overhearing. Nothing in my life could've ever prepared me for being the target of such a sinister plot. I thought people as purely evil as Vickie were made up for television shows. Never in my wildest imagination did I think someone as vile as her could be real.

I couldn't hold myself back anymore. I threw the office door open so violently that it crashed against the wall and dropped one of Lillian's paintings. Lillian shot up from her chair as if she'd been caught by the FBI while Vickie stayed seated, staring at me wide-eyed but restraining herself.

"Thanks for that confession. Everything you said just went on the record for Jake's lawyers," I said as calmly as I could. "You're an evil, psychotic bitch. What are you going to do next, boil a fucking rabbit in his kitchen, you sick fuck?"

"Give me the phone, Ashley," Lillian said in a panic as if her life depended on no one knowing what'd transpired.

"I hope his lawyers bury your crazy ass. You need a psych eval—something's not fucking right in your head. No one pulls *that* kind of crazy shit off." Vickie sat there, still and unflinching. "And you can sit there and laugh like you love this?" I said to Lillian, who was eighty shades of red.

"Give up the phone!" Lillian shouted. "You're not going anywhere with this."

"Fuck both of you," I said, and then the next thing I knew, the claws came out—literally. I was being clobbered by these wicked bitches—scratched, hair-pulled, and mauled.

I found a way out of the attack and ran right into the chest of a tall man who rushed into Lillian's office.

"Come any closer, and the cops will be dealing with both of you," Jim said.

"James," Lillian cried out. "I had nothing to do with this!"

James held me protectively at his side. "Don't come another step closer to Ashley, now or ever again. We're leaving, and I suggest you take this time to find some good attorneys. Don't bother calling anyone I know, either, so good luck with that," Jim said in that commanding, CEO-tone that Jake always talked about.

"Oh, please, James," Vickie said. "That trash clinging to you needed to be pushed out of the circle. She was there for Jake's money—your *family's* hard-earned money."

"Save it, Vickie. We're leaving." Jim looked at me as I pulled away and steadied myself.

I handed him the phone. "Take this. It has everything she's admitted. She's all over the place, but it's enough of a confession."

Lillian collapsed theatrically, crying in her chair as if she'd been convicted at a murder trial, but Vickie held her stiff upper lip, almost unaffected by getting caught. She must've been entirely out of her gourd not to be freaking out about being caught on tape, confessing to committing multiple felonies.

Jim put his arm around my shoulders and ushered me out of the room and out the front door. "Where am I directing the driver?"

"I'll drive," I said through tears. "My car's parked in the back."

"Are you worried about it? I can have it brought to your place. You're not driving in this state."

"Jim." I tried to dam up these tears of betrayal. "I can drive."

"Sorry, Ash," he said, walking me to his car. "You don't have that option. I don't trust those women enough to let you out of my sight, and I need to hear that recording anyway. We need to get it to my attorneys. I can handle all of this while we drive you home."

"Clay and Joe's place is closer."

"Where are you most comfortable?" he asked as he guided me to sit in his car.

"I'd rather head home," I honestly responded.

"Then that's where we're going," he said, taking my phone and working it to airdrop the recording to his. "I'll tell Jake about this later. He's not going to take this well at all, and I need to be with him when he hears the news."

"Were he and Vickie that close?" I asked, pulling it together.

Jim remained focused on his phone. "Perhaps once, but not for a long time. Vickie was a woman who filled his—" he paused and sighed. "She was part of the life he left behind after he met you. I'm concerned about his reaction to her vicious attack on his personal life, and the attachment he's taken to this child. I think he'll be relieved of the news, but after having accepted the child—he's looking forward to meeting his son. A son he will soon learn was all a lie and not his to begin with. Are you going to be okay?" Jim asked.

"I'll get through it," I said. "I feel horrible about Jake. My God..."

"Don't," Jim said. "Jake will be fine." He smiled at me, but I saw the concern in his eyes. "If I may say this...Jake does miss you."

"How has he been?" I asked, curious as to if he'd moved on.

"He's Jacob," Jim laughed. "He lives in the water on weekends, and we get him out to the club now and then." He looked over at me, and his smile was Jake's. "He misses you."

"I miss what we had," I said.

"Maybe one day, fate would see to it that you both will get that back." Jim winked and then went back to work on his phone once he was finished with mine.

Chapter Thirty-Six

Jake
Two months later

I walked into the county jail to see Vickie, not because I wanted to, but because I needed to close the chapter of my life with her in it forever.

When they escorted her to the holding unit, I instantly saw that she looked like hell, hair pulled back in a bun and no makeup. It did not look like her stint in the clink had done her any kindnesses.

"Jacob." Tears filled her eyes. "I thought I'd never see you again. I'm sorry."

"Yeah, you look sorry," I answered. "You couldn't post bail and couldn't find anyone to help you out with that either, it seems. Was it all worth it?"

"Was it worth it..." She repeated my words retrospectively, looking at her handcuffs. "Thanks to no one helping me with bail, I could be in here for years before my trial even starts, you know. All I wanted was to have you to myself again."

"You never had me to yourself in the first place. You realize that not only did you destroy my happiness and fuck with my mind by lying about that kid being mine, but you also fucked over a lot of other people with your sick-ass, demented plans. And for what, to take Ash away from me? That's why you did all of this?"

"I was foolish."

"That would be the understatement of the century," I said. "Dumping all of your stocks to the company you worked for the night that Ash caught you wasn't exactly the brightest move either, wouldn't you agree? Did you *actually* believe you'd get away with any of this? What the fuck, Vickie?"

"I lost everything, and that was before I lost you."

"So, it all comes full circle? You used me for my fucking money?" I couldn't help but half-smile. "Did you come out here with the hopes I was posting bail for you?"

"I may still get out," she whimpered.

"More lies?" I shook my head. "They're probably going to do a psych eval on your ass and slap you into a mental institution. Jesus, Vickie, I'd think you'd be smart enough to have stayed the hell away from a guy whose entire life was being recorded live for the fucking nation to follow. Even if you do get out of here, with what they know about you, you're going to have to move to a deserted island." I shook my head at this psychotic bitch who'd fucked my life worse than the media could have tried to. "It's over, Vickie. I came here to tell you that I don't want to see your pathetic face again, but I'll be sure to show up at any court dates to continue to testify against the evil, vindictive woman you truly are. People don't like assholes like you."

"Go to hell."

"I've already been there," I said with a smile. "It seems like it's your turn now. Enjoy your five-diamond facilities. I'm sure life behind bars is quite enjoyable for a parasite such as yourself."

She called for the guard, and I watched the broken woman walk back toward the door, a correctional officer following her like the brazen and heartless criminal she was.

Thank God Ash had caught her. I owed her everything. I was a fucked-up mess after Jim sat with me and explained everything. Trying to detach from a child that I'd finally accepted only to learn it wasn't mine wasn't easy, but I'm glad it didn't happen after the baby was born, and I was able to bond with it.

I wanted to strike Vickie with all the hatred I held for her and what she did with my life, but it was pointless. She wasn't worth it. Hell, she wasn't even worth my showing up today, but it was something I had to do for myself.

Now, I had to see Ash. I had to hope I had a second chance with her, at least. An excuse to check on her dad and personally thank her since not seeing her since her dad's surgery should help.

I left the detention facility and drove to Ash's place, bracing myself for where this might take me. I was slowly taking back my life since the media had shifted their attention more to the doctor who'd muscled through the gossip and managed to celebrate breaking ground on Saint John's new heart facility.

That was one of the happiest days of my life. Saint John's Heart Institute was finally being erected, and a dream of mine since medical school was happening. I would head the entire unit once the building was up, the staff was hired, and patients were transferred over. We would specialize in everything I pressed in that docuseries, which by the way, was the new greatest docuseries out there. It was about damn time.

Once I got to Ash's house, I knocked on the door, nervous as hell. Carmen answered, chilling me out some.

"Jake!" She braced my face, kissing each cheek and most likely smearing red lipstick all over it. "Get in here. Watch the boxes, sweetie," she said.

"Boxes?" I questioned.

"Moving time, *mijo*. Mark's heart is doing so well, you know." She looked back and smiled. "Don't worry, he'll always be your patient. Although, we might need you to recommend a good doctor up by Santa Clarita soon."

"Well, the closest doctor I know of is me," I smirked, glancing around, my heart sinking they were moving. "Is Ash around?" I asked.

"She's visiting the art institute up north. Baby girl is thinking about getting back into college." She smiled back at me. "I'm happy it's all worked out for you, Jake Mitchell. You're a terrific doctor, and you do remarkable things. We watched the dedication of the heart hospital. It must be a dream come true for you."

"You know me well enough, Carm," I said with a smile. "Smells delicious in here."

"Why don't you stay and eat with Mark and me? We could use the company."

"I have to meet up with the guys later," I said. "Actually, I left some stuff here. Maybe I'll grab my toiletry bag unless Ash burned that," I teased.

"Ash wouldn't burn a thing of yours. She's not psycho like those others." Carmen hit me with that motherly eyebrow arch.

"It's all in the backroom. Be careful, though. Her paintings are all over the place too."

"I'll only be a minute," I said.

I walked into the room where Ash had a small bed in the corner and what seemed like a gallery full of artwork. My eyes were drawn to the one with the sparkling ocean. It was the view from my beach house. I walked toward it and ran my fingers over the brilliant specs of light, wondering how the hell she'd managed to make it look like diamonds were shimmering on the canvas. My eyes drifted up toward the sailboat, gliding through the water that looked like glass around it. The sun's rays pointed down on the couple on the bow, and I smiled at the way their clothed bodies were tangled up together. She recreated my dumbass statement of what I saw on the water, and it was a master-piece because I saw the beauty of the portrait through her eyes.

I thumbed through the canvases and noticed that when the light of the room hit the painting, it came alive in a 3D effect, almost like a black light was shining on it. It was mesmerizing. How did this woman not have a multi-million-dollar gallery running?

"Her work takes your breath away, doesn't it?" Mark said, standing behind me.

"How does she manage this?" I questioned. "The way it lights up as if it were backlit." I pointed to a butterfly she'd painted, the colors shimmering.

"It's interesting," he said, walking up next to me. "She paints the white canvas black, and then she slowly brings her acrylic paint to life as she works magic with her brushes." I looked at his smile. "Funny how darkness can be used to find light in fascinating ways, isn't it?"

"It's how she sees it all, isn't it?"

"What?" He smirked. "Taking a white canvas, blacking it all out, and then bringing it back to life more beautiful than ever?"

"Yes," I answered, somehow relating this to our pure and happy relationship being blacked out and hoping life as beautiful as this could be pulled out of that darkness and made to be more beautiful than the white canvas of our lives that we'd started with.

"It's who my daughter has always been. She stopped painting when her mother passed. Her final piece after her mom died was painting a canvas black. She left it at that, and then Ash went through her life for too long in that dark stage. Then you came into her life, and I've never seen her paint more beautifully." He walked over toward a portrait, and my heart nearly stopped when I saw it. "This was her first portrait after spending that first weekend with you."

"Oh, my God," I said, walking toward it. "I took a picture of her, walking toward the edge of my patio to the rail when she saw the ocean." I ran my hand over the brush strokes of the woman's hair being tossed in the wind. "It was the most beautiful moment. She was so beautiful that it captured my breath, and I took the photo, texted it to her, and told her this is what I wanted over that million-dollar painting in my house."

"Then it's yours," he said.

"No," I answered. "If it were, she'd have given it to me already. It looks more real than the day I snapped the photo."

"She's an amazing young woman," Mark said.

I looked at him and smiled. "The best woman I've ever known. I'd give anything to reverse the hurtful things I said. The life I had—"

"Easy, now," he said with a smile. "I believe the strongest relationships are the ones that go through hell and back. If it's all roses, then what's there to challenge the love two people have. You both have gone through hell and back, so will you come out stronger? Will you let the fire have burned you both and purified a love to what others could only dream they had?"

"Getting sentimental on me, boss?" I teased.

"I think I am. Don't let this beat you. You both love each other, but you got beat down. Fight for her. I think she deserves that, don't you?"

"She deserves more than that," I said. "But will she have me again?"

Mark smirked. "That's the best part of fighting for a woman you love. Having faith that it's meant to be."

"Look at you, giving me all the advice now."

"It's the new heart." He smiled. "After meeting the donor family, that day taught me to live for the one who passed and gave me life."

"I wished I could've been there for that."

"Ash was there, and she came out of it a different person too." He shoved his hands in his pockets. "I believe Clay and Joe are bringing her to a place called Kinder's tomorrow night." He smirked. "They're doing everything they can to convince her to stay. Clay even offered her work as a real estate agent for his firm. Maybe you can convince her to stay too."

"Perhaps I might try to show up."

"You do that. Now, let's grab a beer and show Carmen we can make better corn tortillas than she does."

"I believe I owe you both carne asada on the grill as well?"

"My doctor is allowing me to cheat on my diet?"

"For one night only," I said.

Chapter Thirty-Seven

Ash

I couldn't have been more relieved that psycho Vickie was behind bars, and from the list of her charges, she wasn't going to see the outside of a prison cell in a very long time. The empathetic part of me wanted to feel sorry for her, but she was a wicked woman, and her bad karma caught up to her with a vengeance. If only I hadn't been a part of the fallout.

Despite everything, my life was undoubtedly adding up nicely. I still painted, but I couldn't afford to attend the College of the Arts in Valencia, so I'd signed up for online college courses for the fall semester. I could get my general education out of the way, at least, and then working at a ritzy restaurant as a waitress was giving me enough tips to hold down the rent for my new studio apartment. All of the money I'd saved, living at home with Dad, was enough to go to college, but I had two choices: stay and live with Carmen and dad *forever* to pay for school, or move out, give them their privacy, and figure the rest out later.

I wasn't going to bury myself in student loans, and the financial aid wasn't enough to pull it off at the college of my dreams. Instead, I used the funding to go through city college, finish my Associate's Degree, and move onto the Bachelor's.

I'd been watching television with Carmen and Dad, but tomorrow I planned to head to Beverly Hills to stay with Clay and Joe for a week.

"I think I'm going to head out," I said. "Thanks for having me over, guys."

"Wait," Carmen pointed to the television, looking at Dad. "Turn it up. Ash." She looked at me. "Oh my goodness, they actually ran a segment on this."

"What are you talking about?" I asked, sitting down again and looking in shock at Jake's boat. "What the hell is this?"

"Shh," Carmen said, sitting erect, crossing her legs, and winking at my dad.

"For all of you who've followed the story we broke over the weekend, here's a tiny look into the *Floating Gallery* auction that took place," the reporter said. "Joe Ruiz has your inside look at the event that took place on billionaire heart surgeon, Dr. Mitchell's yacht."

My body froze as I watched the television in silence.

"Yes," Joe said. "I'm standing on the deck of the yacht named *Sea Angel,* where Dr. Jacob Mitchell held a floating art auction with magnificent pieces from a completely anonymous artist. Why Dr. Mitchell went to such great lengths to put something so unique together, and something so shrouded in mystery, is the burning question on all of our minds. The boat set sail on Friday night with astounding events and a lot of interested buyers on board. The yacht remained in the bay over the weekend, but when it returned to shore, it appeared everyone who'd joined in on this unique journey came back with a treasure of their own."

The camera rolled footage of all the paintings I'd ever painted. They were placed on Jacob's yacht with iridescent light shining down on each piece. My eyes filled with tears, just seeing it on display like this. It was more beautiful than I'd imagined when I'd fantasized working for Lillian, having my artwork for sale in her gallery. The cameraman toured the boat, which was transformed into a breathtaking gallery with people everywhere. I listened to the guests speaking about my artwork with such passion and desire to own a piece that I was nothing but speechless at this point.

"Dr. Mitchell declined an interview except to state that all proceeds will go to an undisclosed recipient to help achieve their dreams."

"It appears the doctor is as secretive as he can be these days since that horrible scandal that happened to him, yes?" the anchor asked.

"No one can blame him. When asked who the artist was, he only smiled and referenced the individual's signature with a brushstroke of the letter *A*," the reporter said.

"Well, rumors are swirling that this may be the artwork of Miss Ashley Taylor?" the anchor pried.

"That could very well be."

"Oh my God," I said, looking over at Carmen and dad. "You both knew about this?"

"Yes." Dad smiled. "We were given an exclusive tour of your beautiful work on Jacob's boat before the event."

I ignored the anchor and reporter, still going on about Jacob's floating gallery and auction. "Why didn't you tell me?"

"Because you wouldn't have gone," Dad said. "You may have pushed Jacob out of your life, but we didn't."

"Dad," I scowled at him, "you know that's not how it all went down."

"I know my daughter forgives people who've made mistakes, yet she won't forgive the man who took all of the paintings she left behind."

"He's the one who took them?"

"Yes," Carmen said. "The second I heard you were getting rid of them..." She rolled her eyes and shook her head. "To the dump, *mija*? Really?"

"I had no room to haul all that shit around," I said.

"Well, that *shit*, young lady, sold for over six million on that floating auction of Jacob's."

All the blood left my face. "What!"

"I told Jacob it was all priceless art, and I was insulted for you," Carmen teased. "Jacob agreed with me."

"How the hell did he make this happen?" I wondered out loud. "Where's he donating the money, his heart clinic?"

Carmen chuckled. "Did you think the man ran out of money, Ash?"

Dad laughed. "We have no idea where the money went. All we know is that your work was put on a beautiful display, and a lot of people are still interested in more from the artist that Jacob is staying tight-lipped about."

"Oh, my God," I said. "I can't believe any of this."

"You still heading down to Clay and Joe's tomorrow?"

"Yeah," I said, stunned. "I have the next week off before I start prepping for school."

"Well, maybe you can make time to see Jake and ask him all these questions yourself."

"I might have to do that," I answered, unable to conceal my smile.

I GOT TO MY HOUSE AND CALLED CLAY AS I THREW THE MAIL ON the table with my keys.

"Hey girl," Clay said with a laugh. "You're on speaker with Joe and me. Did you see the news tonight?"

"Yeah," I ran my fingers through the mail, seeing an envelope addressed from a Mr. James Mitchell. "Did you guys know anything about this?"

"Of course we did. We bought one of the pieces when we were on the yacht," Joe said.

"How am I just now hearing about this?" I asked.

"You moved on from him, and he didn't want to piss you off. I can't believe you were going to have those paintings hauled off to the dump, Ash."

"Well, I had no room for them, and unlike what I just saw unfolding, I never believed they were that big of a deal."

"You could have at least let us be the judge of that," Clay said. "Thank God your dad thought to call Jake and ask if he was interested in them."

"Dad and Carmen need to slow down with all this Jake relationship stuff. They probably begged him to take it all."

Joe sighed. "No, try the other way around. Jake had already been by your place when you were checking out that college. He saw it all and told your dad before he left that if you didn't take it with you, he wanted it."

"I didn't get that memo. They only told me that he'd stopped by and was thankful I'd helped guide him in the right direction or something like that," I said, chewing on my nail. "He was supposed to meet up with me at Kinder's the next night when I went there with you two, but I never saw him."

"You're a damn liar, Ashley Taylor," Clay said. "He was there, and you weren't interested in even looking in his direction. It seems you tamed that boy. He didn't even so much as disturb you."

"Though he was enjoying the sight," Joe added.

"Well, I wish I was paying more attention," I said.

"You were too busy fighting us when we were begging you to move in and work for Clay," Joe said.

"I'm not a real estate agent, you goof."

I opened the envelope from Jim and nearly choked when I saw the letter, asking me to accept my funds donated by Jacob Mitchell. "Holy shit," I said. "You're not going to believe this."

"What, the fact that we're dragging your ass to the celebration of your proceeds tomorrow?" Clay chuckled.

"No." I ignored their implications of what that meant. "Jim is handling the proceeds from that auction. I have to show up at his place for the bank transfer. I can't accept this, guys."

"Is there a note or anything?" Joe asked.

"Hang on," I said, pulling out a white envelope that was hidden inside the bigger one. Scribbled in all caps and true-to-form Jacob *doctor* script was my name: Ash. "There's a letter from Jake," I softly said, unfolding the paper inside it.

"What's it say?" Clay pressed.

"Jesus, Jake's handwriting sucks." I laughed at the short note. "It's like reading a goddamn prescription."

"Take a picture. I'm sure we'll get it."

"No, no," I smiled. "Here we go."

Ash,

A wise young woman once told me that she earned her money and didn't come from it. Although I've never been one to use my money to further myself, I'd sadly made that impression on her.

You may find the proceeds from your spellbinding art a bit overwhelming, but I believe it is priceless work from an angel who I was fortunate to know and love, and I happily shared the world through her eyes to many.

Forgive me if this is not what you desired, but I believe you may find a great place to apply these proceeds in furthering your talent.

Congratulations,

Jake.

I WHISPERED THE WORDS AS I READ THEM, TEARS STREAMING FROM my eyes, feeling the sincerity of the man I'd fallen in love with. I couldn't get mad at this if I wanted to. I had no idea what the hell to do with that kind of money, though. All I knew was my heart had never let Jake go, and now I felt the pain of needing him again.

"Hey," Clay said. "That's beautiful, honey. I'm getting another call that I have to take. We'll see you tomorrow. And bring a decent dress because we're getting your ass out to celebrate."

I hung up with the guys, blown away by all of this. Hell yes, we were celebrating tomorrow, and if I couldn't celebrate with Jake, at least I had Clay and Joe.

WE ROLLED UP TO AN EXQUISITE BUILDING WITH MUSIC FILLING the street and people standing in line to get in. We were close to Clay and Joe's place. I was wearing the cocktail dress Jake had peeled off of me in San Francisco our first night together. It was the only nice dress I had and especially on short notice. I had donated the rest, but I'd held onto this one because Clay would kick my ass after the money he'd spent on it for me to wear to the wedding.

Clay was less than impressed that I hadn't gone out and bought a new dress for this, but Joe did my hair and makeup, and I could easily say that I looked pretty goddamn hot. If their object was to get me on the arm of a guy tonight, I'm sure any dude would fall for this trans-formed woman, caked with makeup to remove any flaws. Only my Joe could pull this kind of shit off.

"Over here," Clay said, bringing us to a table of friends they had introduced me to last time we had gone out. "You guys all remember Ash, right?"

"Hey." The two couples smiled. "How's Santa Clarita?"

"Same as it was when I grew up there." I smiled.

The lights were low, and the dance floor was filled with people. I hadn't been out clubbing in forever, and this definitely wasn't my style, but we were here to celebrate the proceeds of my artwork.

"I'm heading to the bar. I want a strawberry martini," I said.

"Make that a double, girl." Joe laughed. "You're way too sober."

"Love you." I smiled at him as he danced in place. "Get your ass on the dance floor. I'll catch up and be out once I loosen up more," I smiled through my lie.

"Hey," I said, sitting at the bar.

The bartender walked over. "What can I get for you?" he asked over the music.

"A strawberry martini, please," I requested.

"Right on," he said and danced over to where he started making the drink.

"I knew a woman who was passionate about the taste of strawber-ries," the familiar voice of Jake said to my left.

He stepped in and motioned to the bartender, who instantly acknowledged him. "Two more, thanks."

"Really?" I said, my body doing an internal shiver for being this close to him and being reminded at how gorgeous he was. His blue eyes, black hair, and five o'clock shadow. Damn, I missed him. "Pas-sionate about strawberries, eh?" I answered to which he smiled, and somehow the packed club disappeared, and it was just him and me again. I wanted to be nervous, but all of that faded. The connection I always had with Jake surfaced, and I absorbed being in his presence and feeling like we were oddly picking up where we left off.

"Yep. In fact, because of her, I grew to find the same passion in the fruit."

"Interesting." I smiled and sipped my martini. "How did you find yourself passionate about fruit because of some girl?"

"Well, I think it was the flavor after having her bite into one, run it down the center of her chest, and..." He smirked, and his eyes dazzled. "Well, you know."

"I do?" I feigned surprise.

"After tasting the flavor of it from her delicate skin, there's no other fruit that comes close anymore."

"Wow, kinky," I said while he took a sip of his scotch.

"It was heavenly." He smiled. "The woman was an angel in every sense of the word."

"Sounds like she was a fallen angel, given the way she introduced you to such an innocent fruit."

"On the contrary," he said, licking his lips. "I'd never found a strawberry to be so good. The best part was her love for them and me at the time."

"Is she here with you tonight? Perhaps seeing you share her intimate stories with me?"

His eyes held mine. "She is here tonight, and part of me believes she might enjoy that I'm sharing these stories with you."

I took another sip of my martini, my lips suddenly dry. "You're quite confident in yourself, sir."

"A trait I carry that almost ruined my life." He pursed his lips. "Although, hopefully, it will help me regain it again."

I nodded. "So, you're the man," I whispered.

"The man?" he asked in question.

"The one who stole her heart and made her regret every day since letting you go without giving you a chance with all the bullshit you and her went through."

He licked his lips, and both of us became more serious. "She had no other option. I never gave her a chance to know me well enough to understand the man who'd hurt her with words was an asshole throwing a fit."

"Perhaps she was an asshole too."

"Never," he said.

"You have a high regard for this woman."

"I would hope she knows that I will forever love her."

"Jesus Christ, Jake." I smiled after taking a sip of my martini. "Kiss me or something."

I barely got that out before his hand was behind my neck, and he smoothly covered my lips with his own. His rich fragrance, his strong arms, and his lack of giving a damn for what people would think of this gesture brought me back to Jake stronger than ever before.

He pulled away and ran his finger over my bottom lip. "I've missed the hell out of you."

"Jake, I'm sorry about everything," I said.

"Baby," he said, "*I'm* sorry for everything. I lost you, and I can't lose you again. Please tell me you'll give me another chance."

"I lost you once," I smiled. "And after that ridiculous pick-up line, I'm never letting you go."

Jake pulled me off the stool and held me tightly against his strong body. "You'll have to forgive that. I've been off my game for quite some time."

I felt his hard cock press against my stomach, and I discreetly ran my hand over it. "Please tell me this part of your game still works." I arched a flirty eyebrow at him.

"That part of my game," he said, "is ready to get your ass the hell out of here and back to my place. I believe it's been too long since my neglected cock had any attention."

I laughed. "I'd hate to keep it waiting any longer."

"Where are your friends? I'm taking your ass home."

"Being rude?" I teased.

"Nope," he said, walking into the mob on the dance floor. "Taking care of the only thing I care about."

Chapter Thirty-Eight

Ash

As we left the club, I saw Clay and Joe giving us devious smiles, and it told me that my guys had set this whole thing up. I held on tightly to Jake's hand as he pulled me out to where his car was covertly parked.

I was a giggling schoolgirl, and I didn't care. The man sporting his jeans and a button-down shirt was unraveling me inside. How was it that he and I were meant to be like this? We had been completely done. Over. And like that significant moment of seeing him after a year with dad's heart attack, we were thrust back together again. Just when all of my fears came true, and I witnessed firsthand that he and I were from two separate worlds and wouldn't work out, here I was, running toward Jake's car with him.

We were two souls that were born to be together. Two souls that had found each other on a higher wavelength than I think either one of us truly understood.

Jake pulled me around, my back leaning against the car he'd just unlocked. He captured my face with both of my hands. "I love you, Ashley Taylor," he said sincerely.

Before I could respond, his lips captured mine, and we resumed our consuming kiss. I loved hearing his groans when his kiss was aggressive like this. I was out of breath, and my head was spinning when his lips went to my neck and lingered there before massaging down my cleavage. As he worked his way back up the center of my chest, his lips grazing my collar bones, his hands slipped under my dress.

"Jake," I said, running my hands through his messy hair. "You're killing me."

He chuckled and intertwined our hands together. "I'm not sure you're going to be able to handle me tonight."

"I think that might be the other way around."

WE TOOK OFF IN HIS CAR MOMENTS LATER, HIM NOT LETTING MY hand go even while shifting gears. I laughed as I looked at his somber expression. "You can let go of my hand. Please, don't get us killed."

He smirked and kissed the back of it. "I'm never letting you go again, angel," he said. "And besides, I drive a million times better than you so I can work with distractions and still get us to my place in record time."

"Really?" I said, reaching my hand over his hard cock. "Can you drive with this distraction?"

"I'm managing just fine," he said, sighing and gripping the steering wheel tighter.

I teased him by fighting with his zipper. "And this?"

"You bring my dick into this situation, and I'll definitely concede," he said with a ragged breath. "I want you so bad."

"I want this," I said, as he turned into a gated community of mansions.

It was the only thing that stopped me from progressing farther. I'd seen the beach house and the unbelievable homes that neighbored his Malibu house, but this? Holy hell, this was where they all hid.

Jake's car snaked through the neighborhood of multi-million-dollar homes, each one gated inside the gated community. Jake's house sat at the end of this particular street, his gate opening as soon as it recognized his car.

"Damn," I said in awe, his driveway looking like it was a street of its own. Beautiful lamps lined the road that cut through manicured lawns, leading to a mansion that sprawled across the top of the hill his home sat on. "So, this is your house in the Hills, huh?"

"I almost sold the place," he said and looked over at me as he parked the car on the curved driveway in front of his home. "Clay talked me out of it." He smiled at me and then stepped out of the car.

I was out soon after him and taking his hand. "Why would you sell this place? It's private—Good Lord, it's beautiful here."

"I associated it with my past shitty life. I always insisted on being a reckless dumb-fuck, but then I lost you, and I hated coming back to this place. It was the one home you'd never been to and I lost all attachments to it."

"You're insane." I laughed as we walked into what I'd like to call the freaking governor's mansion.

"Maybe." He smiled, watching me take this place in. "Per Clay's advice, and the reason you're the *only* woman to see this house now, I had all the furniture replaced and walls repainted. The place was due for a small renovation too. The kitchen counters and sink were remodeled to match the beach house. I've always loved cooking at the other place, but never enjoyed it here."

"Is that my..." I saw the picture I'd painted for him but never gave it to him because I hated the way it turned out. "Jacob Mitchell," I scolded him when we walked into a formal living room that was filled with mahogany leather sofas, chairs, and portraits, all situated in front of a large fireplace that was carved with a stunning wood mantel to set it off. Above it was that portrait I'd tried to recreate for him. This time, I saw it under a beautiful light that shined down on it from the ceiling. It looked so different—and real.

"You can almost see the water shimmering under the sun you painted," he said, putting an arm around me. "When I saw you captivated by the ocean, it was angelic. It's why I took the picture and challenged you to paint it for me," he said.

"The way I used the brush strokes to spread her hair out, it's practically an illusion, and it's screwing with my eyes under this light." I looked over at his proud grin. "It looks like the wind is slightly blowing her hair."

"Your hair," he said. "I can finally say that now without seemingly sounding like a creepy ex-boyfriend." He laughed. "And yes, your strokes in that portrait," he pulled me into his chest, "and in other ways, are well worth more than a million dollars, I might add."

"Oh, yeah?" I teased.

"Come on. Let's go to my room—unless you'd care for a tour of the house?"

"What if I wanted a tour of this house?"

He chuckled. "Easily done. I'll fuck you in each room, the sauna, the pool, the spa, and the wine cellar. I'll never sell the place after that."

"Slow down, cowboy," I teased.

"I've prayed this moment would happen." He brushed his lips over my nose. "Never once did I believe I would get a *third* chance at getting you back into my life."

Our eyes went into that trance of hunger, and I smiled when he audibly called for music and the lights to dim, and then classical music played in the background.

"What is this, a movie?" I laughed.

"It's me and you, angel," he said, not playing along with my jokes anymore. "That's what this is."

Without another word, Jake had me cradled in his arms, and I buried my face in his neck, kissing him and tasting his rich cologne. I craved this man.

He set me down in a massive room filled with masculine touches that matched Jake's personality. I went directly to slowly unbuttoning his shirt. "Slow," I said, looking into his dark eyes. "I want to relish all of this."

"You and me both," he said as I pulled down his shirt, and he instantly took off his undershirt.

I ran my hands over his muscular chest. "You're so beautiful." I leaned in, and it was my turn to worship his body instead of him always taking the lead.

He stood still, his breathing showing me what I was doing to him while undressing him. Once Jake stood there like a perfectly carved statue, I stepped back, not taking my eyes off him. His eyes left mine when I slowly undressed in front of him. He made me feel so beautiful and so secure about everything as his eyes lovingly stared at my body.

He licked his lips and shook his head. "Now what?" He smiled. "We're going slow, and as I imagined it, we'd been done with round one by now."

I silenced him when my hand went down and started stroking him slowly, his precum already dripping as I resisted tasting his delicious body. I stood on my toes, Jake's hand slipping behind my back and over my ass while I nipped at his bottom lip. He fell entirely under my control, standing there with his soft groans sending electric sparks between my legs. His mouth slowly captured mine as I ran my lips over his.

I was coming undone with the gentle way he kissed me, his eyes locked onto mine, and the moans when I squeezed my hand over his large tip. "I need you inside me," I said, kissing his chest and directing him toward the bed.

Jake and I crawled onto the bed, lost in a desperate kiss again—Jake was holding back for sure. He let me stroke him while he stood there patiently as opposed to an aggressive, unleashed kiss and strong hands all over my back and my ass. The guy would tear me apart right now if I let him.

I rolled him onto his back, and he instantly fixed his eyes on mine, running a hand over my breast while his eyes followed it. "You're so beautiful," he said as I worked to line his hard cock up to my opening.

I watched as Jake closed his mouth, rolling his bottom lip between his teeth as I slowly used his massive cock to stretch my entrance, feeling more than just ecstasy as I buried his cock deep inside me.

I started to slide up and down, feeling his cock rubbing against my spot, but staying focused on Jake, who reached over his head into the pillows, thrusting himself up into me.

"Fuck!" he barked. "Goddammit. Baby, you feel so fucking good," he said through gritted teeth.

"I've missed this," I said as I started moving my hips faster, feeling him deeper. I might just come all over his cock if I wasn't careful. "Feeling you inside me again."

Jake's hands gripped my waist, slowing me down. His eyes met mine while he licked his lips, "I'm going to come inside you, angel. You have to go—"

I took his hands from my waist and intertwined our fingers. He gripped them, closed his eyes and moaned when I started moving my hips in circles. "Look at me, baby," I said through uneven breaths. He did, and I smiled, "*You're* first this time, not me."

"Fuck you're so amaz—" Jake's groan sent shivers through my pussy and throughout my body as he jerked his cock up into me. "I'm coming," he moaned in utter ecstasy. "Fuck me," he panted, following multiple cuss words and groaning.

He flipped me over and ran his tongue under my neck and chin until his lips met mine. "I'm still hard. I'm riding your pussy over the edge."

I reached for my clit, and this time, Jake let me. "Fuck, you are hard."

"I have a feeling I'm not done for a while," he smiled. "Come on, angel. Squeeze my cock with that pussy. You're so fucking tight and wet. You feel so goddamn amazing," he said, pumping into me.

"Right there," I breathed out. "God, yes."

I removed my hand from playing with myself after Jake used his magic touch, and his cock found my G-spot. "Fuck yeah, baby. Move that hand. I'm on it, aren't I?"

"Yes." I was practically hyperventilating when Jake's lips sucked on my hard nipples, and he kept rubbing his softening cock on the most sensitive spot in my body. "It's been too long," I admitted.

"Way too goddamn long," Jake said, bringing his face to mine while holding my leg up so his cock could work my spot. His eyes were so hypnotic and beautiful. "Let it go, angel," he whispered.

When I came, it was so intense that I saw stars. Jake moaned and froze as my sex clamped down while I came with intense pleasure and satisfaction. This was so long overdue. I couldn't help but smile at his dazed eyes once I regained my focus.

"Holy fuck, you're so beautiful when you come. I love you, angel."

"I love you, Jake."

Slowly and gently, Jake and I reunited our body and souls where they had been torn apart for far too long. The way his strong body moved over mine, his expression when he gripped my waist as I rode him hard, him always finding the spot inside me that sent me over the edge every single time—all of it. It was us, moving in harmony and relishing in what we loved about being together, and finally, I had peace for the first time in what felt like forever.

It was three in the morning, and we both were still wide awake but curled into each other and staring like a couple of happy fools. "Stay with me," he finally said. "Don't leave me and go back home or wherever the fuck you were before I saw you tonight."

"I have the week off of work."

His eyes roamed away from mine. "And then?" he asked, looking toward the corner of the room.

"And then maybe we see if we can survive a long-distance relationship?"

"Ash," he said, brushing my hair from my face. "I can't do long distance, not with you."

"You work long hours. I think we can pull it off. I'll come down on the weekends, or you can come up."

"I'm not fucking losing you again," he said, more serious.

"I just moved into an apartment." I laughed. "I finally achieved something on my own."

"Um, I believe your artwork proves you did that a long time ago," he said. "If you don't want to stay with me, then use the money to stay closer—down here."

"Jake," I tried to be reasonable. "Let's start like this."

"What do you think about taking the boards out today?"

"Surfing?" I laughed at the kid I found in Jake when it came to his crazy impulsiveness.

"Why not?" he said, sitting up. "I still have your wet suit. It's all at the other house."

"Jesus, you're not going to stop, are you?"

He leaned over and kissed me. "I could fuck you for the entire week you have off and demand you stay with me, yes. But to take you out this morning—early like this—I think you'll enjoy experiencing the water while the sun comes up.

"Let's do it," I said, feeling just as excited as I was when I got my man back.

Chapter Thirty-Nine

Ash

"Where's your surfer buddy?" I asked while I sat on my board, watching the waves roll into shore.

"Flex?" He looked down the coastline. "The waves sort of suck today, so he's likely not in this spot."

"Hmm," I said, looking at the shoreline. "Well, they're perfect for me."

"That's why we're here. Are you enjoying yourself?" he asked.

"I really am. I still got it." I splashed him with water. "You don't look too bad yourself. Though, that wipe out was pretty *gnarly bro*," I teased him.

As the sky turned a lighter hue of magenta, I smiled, looking up. "You're right. It's amazing being out here. It's like we're the only people in the world."

Jake unzipped the side of his wetsuit, popped off his board, and swam to the front of mine, gripping the tip.

I instinctively gripped the board. "What are you doing? Dumping me?"

"Do you trust me?" he asked with a smile.

"Depends?" I said, brushing my hair out of my face.

"I have to know."

"I wouldn't be here with you and wouldn't have left that club with you if I didn't trust you, Jake. Now, what the hell are you going to do, dump me off the board?"

I covered my chest when a soaked, bright blue velvet box was opened in his hand, his other still holding the board. "Marry me," he said, his eyes so brilliant in their blue hue reflecting off the ocean. "I know this isn't the ideal way of proposing. Trust me, I went over a million different scenarios in my mind after Jim and I shopped for this ring together. It all went to hell soon after I bought it, but this morning before asking you out here, I could think of nothing more than needing you in my life and knowing I could never let you leave me again, Ash."

"Jacob." I chuckled at this moment with him. He looked so vulnerable, adorable—almost like a young boy in the water waiting for the answer he was pleading for. This was the man I had fallen in love with.

"Ash." He spit out the water and shook his head from a wave that had slapped him in the face. "I'm as close to a submissive position as one can be while getting down on a knee and asking the woman he loves to marry him."

"You are the biggest nut I've ever met in my life."

"Let me make you the happiest woman in the world. You've already made me the happiest man. I love you more..." another wave smacked him again with the chop of the water. "Jesus, I'm going to drown out here. Throw me a bone or something."

"Yes, Jacob." I slid off my board and over into his arms. "I love you. I can't imagine leaving you either."

"You're the love of my life—you are my life." He pulled the ring onto the tip of his finger. "Here, this will seal the deal," he said. "Put it on quick before I have to dive and pick it up from the bottom of the ocean."

"My God," I said as he slipped the ring over my finger. "This is gorgeous," I said, staring at the platinum band that revealed a massive square-cut diamond.

He held onto the board with me in his other arm, "Hell. I should have thought before I put that thing on you. Your tiny little ass is going to sink straight to the bottom now." He kissed me. "I love you, Ash."

"Love doesn't even begin to describe how I feel about you. Shall we go celebrate?"

He nipped at my chin. "I have just the place in mind," he said.

"Oh, yeah?"

"It's a gift, and it better be done by now, or I'm going to look like an asshole."

"What are you talking about?"

"Let's just say Clay and Joe had a superb idea to get you back into the city. It's why they invited you down. Me showing up last night was just wishful thinking that we'd get back together. Those guys are the craziest nut jobs I've ever met." He laughed.

"They're a lot of fun. I've missed them."

"Well, let's get into shore, and I'll give them a ring. A couple more phone calls, and we might pull off one of the best days of my life."

"What are you up to?" I laughed.

"Get on your board; you'll see."

BY TWO O'CLOCK IN THE AFTERNOON, WATCHING JAKE MORE nervous than I'd ever seen him, we were back in his Jeep and driving down the coastline.

"Well," I said, trying to keep a straight face to his concerned one, "one might think that you had pulled another rabbit out of your hat, and we're heading to our wedding."

"What makes you say that?"

I laughed. "You're acting like the end of the world is waiting at our final destination."

"I'm sorry. Just go with me on this. The brunch was good, though, wasn't it?"

"It was delicious. That restaurant was adorable," I said about the beachside cafe he'd brought us to.

"It was," he said, changing lanes, and then we were turning toward the ocean where beachside businesses were. "Okay," he sighed, and for the first time since his ocean proposal, he smiled.

He pulled the car into a parking lot. "Here goes."

I stepped out of his car and looked at the storefront that was completely blacked out. "Are we going shopping?"

He took my hand. "Already done," he said as he entered a security code and unlocked the glass doors, pulling them open. "I bought this after the floating gallery was a hit," he said, turning around to face me. "I had staff hired, and after I got your written permission, I wanted to gift this form of revenue to you. Little did I know I'd be standing here with you as my *fiancé*," he smiled as he hung onto that word, "and showing it all to you myself."

"A gallery in Malibu?" I said, seeing what was hidden behind the glass.

"Yes." He smiled. "Jim and I discussed it after Lillian's business tanked, and we wanted to see you take the woman's place. At the time, we didn't think you'd leave Southern California, but we also didn't think that we'd have numerous requests for more of your work, either. Jim was going to talk to you personally about working and running the business for *Mitchell and Associates*, but I told him to hold off. I guess I had hope that somehow this moment would happen. Babe." His kiss was soft, and he pulled back his thumb rubbing over mine. "This gallery is yours. We haven't named the business yet or given it an opening date, but it's close to the beach house—*your home*—and an easy commute." He nodded to the ocean behind me. "The ocean is right out your front windows. You also have a client list that's pretty large after the auction."

"This is the most tremendously generous and thoughtful thing anyone has ever done for me," I said, wiping the tears of joy from my eyes. "But I can't paint fast enough to keep up with a client base." I sniffed and smiled at his light expression.

"After selling your originals on the yacht," he answered with a joyous smile, "we had prints curated to replicate the originals and bring them into editions for the time being. Those are already hung in the gallery. It's why I had to call Clay and Joe. This was partly their doing as well," he said. "Go inside and tell me what you think."

I walked in alone, and the soft sounds of soothing harmony played softly in the entryway. It was heavenly in here. The pictures were hung to be displayed under that same lighting Jake had in his living room on that one portrait he kept. The entire room's ambiance was serene, and even though these were mine, it didn't feel real. Nothing felt like it was mine in this place—there was no way in the world that these gorgeous prints came from me.

Glass cases held sea art and crystal-like creations that complemented the theme of the rooms I quietly walked through. This was beyond any gift or anything I could have ever accepted. This was too beautiful to be mine.

"Clay was the brains behind all of this," Jake's voice slid into my thoughts, and oddly enough, the way he spoke blended well with the space. "The guy is a wizard when it comes to getting stuff done. He redecorated my place, and he also designed this in a day. He also hired people to get the job done, and voila, you're looking at your masterpieces all together. What do you say?"

"I don't know what to say," I answered. "I have the best guy," I leaned into where he held me from behind, "and the best friends I could ever ask for."

"Will you take this on? Is it something you'd like?"

"I couldn't say no to any of this if I wanted to."

He kissed my cheek. "You'll have to schedule it outside of when you'll paint, of course. Perhaps our vacations of all the oceans we'll be traveling to. That is why it will be staffed well enough." He pulled me around to face him. "And of course, we'll plan your grand opening after we get back from our trip to Cabo. You still owe me that, remember?"

I laughed. "Yes."

"Perhaps we honeymoon in Cabo?"

"Dr. Mitchell, do you rush your heart surgeries like this?" I teased.

"I run my heart surgeries with precision and to perfection. I will settle for nothing less when it comes to ensuring my angel is the happiest woman alive."

"So, when do you plan on the grand opening?" I asked, seeing that dark and sexy look of want in his eyes now.

"After we're married, two to three weeks of a honeymoon on your yacht..." He smirked.

"Sea Angel?" I ran my fingers on his cheek. "How drunk were you when you came up with *that* name."

"You'd rather have the other name back? I mean, I had to go through a shitload of maritime superstition laws of renaming a vessel that size and rededicating the damn thing." He laughed. "I'll say if you don't like it, you're renaming it and going through the rituals with Flex performing the ceremonies." He laughed.

"I love it, and I love you. I'm speechless."

"Tonight, we announce our engagement. I'll put in for my vacation with Saint John's after you agree to marry me at our beach house or on the yacht—I don't care where, but I know you love the ocean and you're going to be Ashley Mitchell before the week is over."

"Holy hell, Jake."

"I'm more than ready to spend the rest of my life with you. I'd marry your gorgeous ass right here and now if I could."

"Clay's a legal minister." I bit my lip and laughed at his expression.

"Do you think this is too much too fast? I mean, do you want to plan a wedding that some little girls dream of having? Perhaps something to—"

I silenced him with my finger. "I just want you. I'd be proud to have your name too. I love you, and I love us. Yes, we're moving too fast, but we're moving fast in the right direction. Let's do this."

"We'll plan the details tonight. The guys and your friends will be there. For now," his eyebrow arched, "the doors are locked, and I'm the only one with the key. I believe you and I are going to have to christen this gallery ourselves."

I laughed, and within seconds, Jake and I were back in each other's arms, naked and molding our bodies and souls together. I loved this man, and I couldn't believe I'd almost lost him forever.

We lay on a sofa that was situated in an alcove, both of us catching our breath after another satisfying round of fantastic sex.

"Well, there goes this couch." I laughed, his lips still caressing my neck.

"I didn't like the color anyway." He chuckled.

"So, what happened to the portrait like the one you have at your house in the Hills? Or what about the sailboat one I recreated as a joke for you?"

"Those were priceless, but only on display and never for sale. They're mine with no prints available to the public. Sorry, but I wasn't sharing those two prints."

"I'm so amazed that you've done all of this. I mean, I expected you to hate me after I was so harsh to you."

"I could never hate you." He kissed my cheek. "I understood everything. I hurt you, and I only hoped you didn't hate me for this. It also took a lot of convincing from Carm, your dad, and your friends for me to do any of this. How in the world could you ever dump those portraits?"

I pinched my lips together. "I guess I just didn't see them like this."

"Who's the crazy one now?" He winked. "Let's get back to the house. We'll enjoy a nice hot shower, and we can go out tonight, or I'll have a small party catered at the beach house for you. There's time to invite your dad and Carm down too?"

"That sounds good," I said. "Let me call them."

"Shit," he said. "I forgot to ask him..."

I elbowed him as we got dressed. "My dad loves you more than he loves me, I think. Let's just get them down here. I think they'll love your place."

"The house is large enough to keep them with us for the week."

"You honestly plan on marrying me before the week is out?"

"Don't push it. I might pull Clay in and have an impromptu ceremony tonight."

"Carmen and Dad would love the beach house," I said. Then the excitement of everything truly set in. I reached over and pulled Jake into my arms as he was bent over, putting on his shoes. "We're really doing this."

He chuckled. "Thank God that your mood finally shifted into this.

I was seriously beginning to worry that I was going too hard and too fast for you."

"When have I ever complained about you going too hard or too fast? In fact, I love it."

Jake studied me. "I swear I'm fucking you all over at that house before tonight. Hard and fast." He winked and then offered a hand to pull me up. "Let's go share the fantastic news with everyone, shall we?"

"Already calling Dad," I said, overjoyed to inform him about what took place in less than twenty-four hours since I'd left them and come home to Jake.

Chapter Forty

Ash

It took me getting a massive sinus infection and feeling like death itself had come for me to slow down our wedding plans and make us decide to have a small wedding, three months after he proposed. I had loose ends to tie up in Santa Clarita, and he needed time to properly reschedule patients for us to take off for three weeks at sea while we took the yacht for his winning bet to Cabo.

Now, it was the day of the big event. I hadn't seen Jake in over a week since he'd stayed close to Saint John's with three new patients in recovery, and he finalized everything with his staff for him to be gone. I could have easily driven there, but we both felt this time apart would make for a neat reunion when Clay married us. I still couldn't believe I'd jumped headfirst into this.

Some people—like me—could live with their soul mate without a piece of paper to validate their union, but Jake wasn't having that. Thank God I was a fool in love because I enjoyed this playful, overly romantic side of him.

"*Mija*, you look so beautiful," Carmen said after Joe finished with my hair and makeup. "Jacob is one lucky man, baby girl." She kissed me while Joe nearly collapsed at the bright red lip stain on my cheek.

After Joe fixed the issue, I walked over to the mirror and smiled at my simple, silk dress. It was a cream-colored strapless dress that had no embellishments, but I thought it looked more exquisite than a full-blown wedding gown. It flowed from my waist and stopped just before my ankles. It was undoubtedly a perfect pick for the beachfront wedding on the shoreline in front of the beach house. I was under strict orders to stay in the rooms at the back of the house all day, which was fine. Jake had a painting room set up back here, and since we'd finalized everything with the gallery, I had been addicted to painting these days anyway. He's lucky I was leaving with him instead of staying here to finish the canvas I'd been working on.

"And here comes the bride," Dad said from behind me. "You look gorgeous, Ash," he said, tears filling his eyes. "A woman in love is the most beautiful sight for any man to behold."

I hugged him. "Are you and Carmen ready to enjoy your three weeks here, having the house to yourselves?" I smiled at him, trying to remove the emotions, or I'd be balling my eyes out. I couldn't even think about Mom right now, or I'd be walking down to Jake balling like a baby—ugly cry.

"Well, if it isn't the woman who tamed the wild beast in my brother," Jim said with a smile. "Let's go seal the deal, shall we?"

"Always business, eh?" I teased.

He smiled and walked over to me, and for the first time, the stiff and commanding man brought me in for a hug. "Always," he said, stepping back. "My brother is likely to cry like a baby when he sees his beautiful bride walk down the aisle." He looked at Carmen. "All right, Joe sent me up to bring you down. If Jacob has to wait another second, I think he's going to lose his mind out there."

"See you both in a few," Carmen winked at Dad and me. "Love is in the air."

"I love that woman," Dad said.

I laughed. "You should be considering a little wedding yourself," I said with a smile. "But your stubborn butt is too chicken."

"Steal the show from my stunning daughter?" Dad held harm out for me to take. "Never in a million years."

WE WALKED DOWN THE STAIRS, THE IRON STAIR RAILS COVERED IN ivy and lilies. The floral fragrance of the abundance of white flowers combined with the soft, salty breeze was an aroma that should be bottled up and sold as perfume. We walked through an archway covered with more white lilies, and the cellist began to play a beautiful tune.

I was doing great, walking barefoot in the white sand and through the three rows of chairs, seeing Jake standing there with a vibrant smile. His brilliant blue eyes shone as sapphires, and my heart was overwhelmed with the love I saw in them. I completely lost it when I looked to my left, and an empty chair was situated. *Mom. Oh my God, he placed a chair for Mom!* I thought, crumbling into my dad's side.

"She's here too. She's always watching over you, honey," he said.

"Dad...wow..." I couldn't speak, and Dad only smiled and nodded toward Jake.

I felt Jake's hand rub along my arm. "Come here," Jake said, ignoring my near breakdown. He hugged me and tilted my chin up to lock eyes with him. "She's with us, and I think she approves." He arched his eyebrow, helping to bring some humor to his future wife losing it.

"She does. I'm sorry," I mouthed.

Jake brought his lips to my ear. "Never be sorry, angel. I know how much you loved her and miss her. I only wanted to show she's with here if not physically, then in spirit."

"Thank you for honoring and remembering her, Jacob." I sniffed.

"I wouldn't have married you any other way." He winked. "Is the wedding still on, by chance?"

"Yes." I inhaled and pulled it together. "Clay's been dying to marry me off since he got this license. Let's do it."

· · ·

AFTER JAKE AND I EXCHANGED SIMPLE VOWS, THE SUN WAS SHIFTING in the sky, heading toward the horizon. His lips had been one with my cheek since we made it all legal and stood in a small reception on the beach with cake and delicious food that Jake had catered. Instead of doing the tradition of throwing a bouquet, I simply offered the arranged lilies I carried to Carmen and told her she was next.

"Thank you all for being present for the happiest day in my life," Jake said, raising a glass. "To my beautiful bride, the enchanting Mrs. Ashley Mitchell." He looked at me "May she live happily ever after with me."

Jake's brother and friends burst out into laughter, along with me and everyone else. "I love you, silly guy," I said, reaching for his face and kissing his lips.

"You'd better." He sighed. "This next part—our exit? Well, let's just say, you're legally mine, no matter if I screw this up or not."

"What are you talking about?"

I heard a loud horn as if a cruise ship were out in the ocean. I turned to see Jake's yacht lit up brightly and magnificently.

"Let's get out of here," he said, his white muslin shirt blowing in the wind against his khaki shorts. "Thank you all again. Camera crew? My brother has your check, and you can leave now."

Jake turned and pulled me toward the shore. "What the hell? Are we swimming out to the boat?"

The guests and wedding photographers were following us like a mob, and until we passed the wedding podium, I hadn't a clue as to what the hell we were doing.

I stopped on the wet sand and covered my smile. "Jacob Mitchell." I started laughing when I saw a white rowboat parked in the sand. "What are you doing?"

He kissed my lips and pulled on his aviator sunglasses. "I'm about to live out one of my many masterpieces with my bride."

"Jake." Jim laughed. "Have you ever rowed a boat before?"

"Jesus Christ," Collin said. "This one takes the cake with you. I've seen you do some crazy stuff, but this?"

"This is going in the cloud, never to be erased," Alex said. "You sure you don't want an annulment?" He winked at me.

"You're all overreacting," Jake said, whisking me up and into his arms. "Let us fulfill my dream of rowing you in a boat."

I laughed and kissed his cheek. "Let's do it."

Jake set me in the flower-adorned, white rowboat, and until we were both in it and he was gripping the oars, I seriously thought this was just for a photo op. No. Jake was seriously letting us get shoved offshore and pushed out to the waves—small and rolling ones, thankfully.

He had a look of determination on his face that I could only admire, yet still find this as one of the craziest things I think Jake could do. "You look handsome," I offered while he concentrated on getting the rowboat out to the softly rolling sea.

"You impressed?" He smirked at me, now past the breaks, rowing us smoothly toward his yacht.

"Highly," I teased. "Most people have a getaway car like a limo—perhaps a horse-drawn carriage."

Jake smiled, looking over his shoulder. "And you have a rowboat."

"You're the best man ever," I said, enjoying this unique ride through the sea and toward the extravagant yacht that looked like it was lit for a huge party. "How the heck did you—I mean, what made you think of this?"

"Well, our first conversation, of course," he said, working the oars like an Olympic medalist, still profoundly funny to me. "But I knew I had a time limit. Bringing the yacht in?" He smiled at me. "Permits and working with the coast guard was a bitch. You were right, babe." He smiled. "The rowboat is much easier, and the couple could enjoy amazing sex in it."

"Well, since I can still hear them laughing from shore? I think we should opt-out of my idea." I rubbed his leg, and he stopped rowing, locked the oars, and framed my face with his hands.

"I couldn't give a shit what they'd all think." He brought his lips to mine while sliding one hand under my dress, feeling me instantly getting hot and wet with this kiss alone. "You're wet for me already, angel," he said, pulling away. "When we get to our yacht, your ass is mine."

"Better row your little boat faster, buddy," I said, trying to calm myself down.

It might have been a simple and fast wedding, but it was memorable and beautiful. And to have Jake row me in a boat out to the yacht? This one could never be outdone. How is it that you could love someone more than you believed your heart could take? I was learning very quickly that there were no limits in love—especially loving my Jake.

Chapter Forty-One

Jake

I had just gotten out of the shower. The past week on the yacht was the best time I'd ever spent on the thing I deemed as worthless and merely a party vessel. It was now mine and Ash's, and I swear I could keep this damn thing in the ocean and never go back to our homes in California again.

Ash and I had watched every sunrise and sunset and found ourselves living in our own world as husband and wife. Did the idea of me ever getting married cross my mind during my entire adult life? No. Not even while I first realized I loved Ash would I consider it. Then it just hit me one day, and I wouldn't stop until Jim had helped me find the perfect diamond that could hold up to the beauty of the woman I loved. I promised her a car and wound up shopping for a ring. With the rowboat experience, I think Ash was learning quickly that I was a man who switched gears and would do anything to keep that beautiful smile on her face.

This morning, Ash had slept in after we anchored late last night and went on shore to stay in a gorgeous suite, giving us a sprawling view of Cabo from this height. Jim and Alex had worked hard to acquire this hotel and multiple chains of this particular resort, and their wedding gift to us was as many nights onshore in this luxury suite as we wanted.

I glanced down at my phone, standing with a towel wrapped around my waist after my shower, looking at my missed calls from Jim. I sighed but figured that while Ash slept, I'd figure out whatever in the hell it was my brother was blowing up my phone for.

Before I could call out, Jim was ringing back in.

"The suite is amazing. I'll send you flowers," I said, answering.

"You're on speaker. It's me, Alex, and Collin," he said. "How are the lovebirds?"

"Doing fine," I answered, staring out at the ocean view, seeing my yacht just off the coast. "Is there a reason for..." I paused when my towel was pulled from my waist, and Ashley was kneeling in front of me.

"Go on," I heard Collin chuckle.

"Fuck," I exhaled, gripping Ashley's hair, hunching over as she took me as deep as she could in her mouth. "What?" I said, my eyes closing while sparks of energy surged from my cock to my balls and up my spine. "Fifteen..." I exhaled, unable to pull Ash off me. Goddamn, did she research a new blow job method? "Fifteen missed calls, Jim. Did my house burn down?" I managed.

My eyes closed as Ash licked under my shaft, gripped my tight balls, and massaged them. Her lips sucked while her tongue pressed hard against the most sensitive spot underneath the tip of my cock.

"You there, Jakey?" I heard Alex say in a humored tone.

"I would be," I said, my voice soft in the sensation of Ash working me like she was a master of the art in blow jobs. "If your dumbasses weren't on the other line."

"Hey," Jim said, "we're heading to London for a conference and staying for a couple of weeks after that. You need to be there. We're going over the details of Saint John's new heart facility."

I gulped, having been staring at Ash's sparkling eyes while she continued to worship my cock. "We're not going to make that, sorry."

"Ash would love it there. And why the hell not? Her gallery doesn't open for three more months," Collin added.

"I'm going to come, baby," I mouthed, and she pumped, licked, and sucked my cock harder as I fought off the cum that was aching to shoot into her hungry mouth.

"We're not coming. We'll talk about it when we get back," I said.

"The room nice?" Alex chuckled.

"It's great, talk later."

I hung up and practically howled in my release, watching Ash take me deeply as I came in her mouth. "Fuck. Fuck. Fuck," I said, coming in her mouth as if we hadn't had sex from the moment we got on the yacht until now. "Holy shit, Ash," I said as she licked and worked the last of the cum out of my cock.

"You like that?" she purred, standing up, my cock still throbbing from the unexpected and beyond sensational blow job.

"I'm sure the guys could tell what was going on," I said with a laugh.

She kissed my lips. "Let them guess. Here," she handed me a pair of shorts, "put these on. I need you to sit down."

I did as she asked and pulled her slender frame to stand in front of me. "What's up?"

"I still have no idea how this happened, and I hope that it comes out well given all the crap we've been through—"

She started fidgeting, and I took her hands in mine, "What happened?" I asked, seeing tears in her eyes. "Ash, talk to me."

She ran her hands through each side of my hair. "I'm pregnant," she said with a happy yet concerned look on her face.

I instantly stood and pulled her into me. "You're sure?" I asked. I pulled her back to see her nod.

"It's what the tests are showing."

"How long have you known? I mean, holy shit." I smiled, feeling tears brim my eyes. "You're pregnant," I stated.

"For about a month. I missed my period last month and was pissed we'd planned our honeymoon while I'd be on it this month. Carmen told me to take the test. I did, and just to be sure, I took another on the day of our wedding."

"To have the most beautiful woman in the world carrying my child, my Ash—pregnant with our baby?" I laughed. "Hell, I don't even know what to say."

"I was so scared that what happened with Vickie and Liz, it would've ruined all of this."

"No." I shook my head. "This is a dream for me, Ash. Don't bring them into this moment. Damn." I laughed and held her tightly. "I guess the birth control pill let a little soldier through, eh?" I teased, hearing her crying. "Are you okay with this, Ashley?"

"I am," she said. "I really am. I just don't understand how it happened. I haven't missed a day on the pill, and we've been having unprotected sex for quite some time on it."

I pulled back and chuckled.

"What?" She smiled. "What's that look?"

"Your sinus infection. It's the antibiotics." I laughed and kissed her lips. "They have a way of fucking up the pill."

Her eyes widened in humor. "I was on two rounds of them, the second more powerful."

I nodded and bit my bottom lip. "We're going to have a baby. Holy shit. The most beautiful soul in the entire world is going to continue making me the happiest man alive." I wiped the tears from her cheeks. "Thank God I made an honest woman out of you."

We both laughed and held each other tightly. My God, how fate had weaved its way into my life and ensured this woman would cross paths with me. God only knew the path that I'd been on, always wanting something, and never happy and never understanding why. That's the wild man I was before this woman. A man in need of something—I just didn't realize it was this free-spirited woman who would be what I'd been yearning for, for years.

Now, she was pregnant with our child. Complete, whole, and happy were simple words for how I felt to my core. And this was just the beginning of the eternity I planned to share with the woman who'd captured me the moment that damn iced drink spilled on my shirt and with such a silly alias of *Annie Position*.

Hell yes, this was my happily ever after. I'd gladly slap a fairytale title on my life without reservation.

Ready for Jim's story? Click here to learn more about Jim in Book 2 of the Billionaires' Club:
Mr. Mitchell

Chapter 1 of Mr. Mitchell, Billionaires' Club Book 2

Avery

I was going to miss my flight if this stupid Uber driver didn't step on it. *What the fuck, man.* I looked over at him, driving with great concentration. "Hey, buddy," I started as nicely as I could, "I am going to miss my flight. Can we go a little faster?"

"I'm going as fast as Chester can take us," he answered while petting his dash.

"Chester?" I questioned as he continued down side streets that I only prayed he was being directed through because his GPS had a quicker way to get us to LAX.

"The name of this little guy," he exclaimed about his tiny little microcar.

"Ah," I answered. "Well, is *Chester* by chance small enough to fit down the back alleys of this neighborhood we're in?"

"Chester doesn't do illegal." The middle-aged man smiled.

Of all the Ubers I could've gotten—in this horrible time in my life —it's a guy who named his car Chester that will prevent me from my much-needed week-long escape to London with my foster sister.

"Here," he said softly, turning to the right, "we...are," he stated nicely and calmly. "You enjoy the flight, Avery. Keep the tip. Chester could've done better and gotten you here earlier. He doesn't deserve the good gas."

I looked at the man and forced a smile. *You're a whacko!* "I've got your tip—"

He stopped me from reaching into my purse. "No." He frowned. "You were too stressed. Chester and I will rather have a good review."

"Got it," I said, grabbing my carry on and taking off, never looking back at that crazy scene again.

I never thought I'd be sitting here, air blowing on my face and engines running on the plane. I closed my eyes, sitting in serenity only to have my neighbor—a two-year-old kid—poke my nose. I was never going to survive this ten-hour, non-stop flight to Europe.

Ignore him, and he'll stop, I thought, knowing this was not the solution. Trust me, I knew my three-year-old daughter would only take it as a greater challenge.

"Excuse me, ma'am?" My eyes snapped open to see a flight attendant on my left. "We have an opportunity for you to upgrade to first-class if you'd like to take it."

"Oh?" I said, knowing my wealthy sister had booked the flight on her mileage rewards and I just hit the damn lottery. "I'd love to."

She escorted me up to where passengers were seated with more room and luxury.

"Right here," she directed me to the seat where a businessman sat, staring at his phone.

He glanced up, and his brilliant emerald eyes framed by dark lashes met mine, throwing me completely off. Goddamn, I'd never seen a man this handsome before in my life. Guys who looked like this modeled Gucci suits and lived on the covers of magazines for women to drool over. They never fell off the pages a joined me on a non-stop flight from L.A. to London. Maybe I died from carbon monoxide poisoning when I was riding in Chester?

He smiled, stood, and allowed me into my seat next to the window. So this was awesome; now I was afraid I'd have to go to the bathroom the entire flight, constantly disturbing *Mr. Sexy in a suit* because he was too damn tall to shift his legs for me to get through.

"We'll serve drinks once we're in the air," the flight attendant said. "Anything you need, we'll ensure you're taken care of. Enjoy your flight, Miss Gilbert."

"Thanks," I said. My phone rang, and it was my sister—God love her. "What, do they instantly send you notification that I accepted the first-class seating on your behalf?" I snickered.

"Hey," Britney said, "your dick-bag ex is giving mom shit right now."

"What?" I asked. "I don't have time for his bullshit. Period."

"You need to call him. I just left the house. I'll be landing after you, but the hotel suite is ready for us in London."

"Fine." I sighed and hung up.

"Please turn off all electronic devices..."

"Fuck," I whispered. Okay. *Breathe.* I dialed out anyway.

"'Sup?" Derek answered.

"Listen, asshole," I growled into the phone. "Your parents aren't getting Addison until *after* I get home."

"You should've thought this through," he growled.

"I thought it *all* through, dick." I tried to keep my voice down. This drug addict brought out the worst in me, and now I was going to get kicked out of first class by Mr. Sexy himself. "My mom is staying at my place with her. You need to figure out your new drug charges before I let you anywhere around her again."

"Avery..." he said in his manipulative voice.

"Don't *Avery* me, Derek. Your kid or not, Addison stays with Jill, got me? I don't trust your enabling parents, and I don't trust you. Please don't do this to me."

"I'll do whatever I fucking want."

"I'm getting a lawyer—"

"You can't afford a lawyer," he sneered. "So, what's next, Avery?"

A tapping to my right arm brought my angered expression to the man sitting at my right with a smirk, he rose his eyebrows and mouthed, "I can handle this if you'd like?"

I looked at him in confusion. I couldn't take off and leave Addison, my foster mom, Jill, or my mind in this state. Derek could screw me over hard in the week I was gone. I had no other option—either trust the man dressed like a lawyer sitting next to me to bail me out, or get off the plane. My life only led to option two, so I decided to go for it with this guy.

I handed him my phone—his hands were even beautiful.

"Excuse me, Derek?" he said in a commanding, confident, and supreme voice. "Yes," he paused, people staring at us while the plane started backing out. "I understand how you'd feel that way, yes." I looked at the man as he frowned. "Are you done? Good. Now, all of this has been recorded for my team and me. We will keep this while we continue to look into the custody and your sanity as the father of Addison. Now, I'll advise you to heed—" he looked at me and mouthed *your name* in question.

"Avery," I said with a smile, knowing Derek—the low life drug addict—was shitting his pants on the other end of the phone.

"You will regard Avery's request in Jill watching over the child. If I learn that this has turned out to be more upon mine and Avery's return from London," he gave me a thumbs-up as if asking, *you are going there, right?* and I nodded. "Then you and I will be in court." He paused while I heard Derek kissing his ass. "That's fine. I would assume you would believe that. So, we're clear? If there is so much as one phone call toward Addison...er, excuse me, Avery, while she is away, then under-stand this will get extremely ugly." The gorgeous man who bullshitted my psycho ex handed me my phone. "Your friend hung up on me." He smirked. "I believe he got the message, though."

"I can't thank you enough for that," I said, my eyes captured by his, and his smile instantly made me grin like a girl, crushing on a Holly-wood star.

"Not a problem. I couldn't help but overhear you talking to him—a drug addict?"

"Yeah, long story." I sighed. "And now I'm stuck with him because I was stupid enough to get knocked up by him."

"I believe it takes two to make that decision. I wouldn't carry the blame alone if I were you." He smiled. "You appear to be a good mom.

I'm sorry if I was overstepping boundaries—being a stranger and all, but I do hope it helped."

"I'm Avery," I said with a smile.

"I'm Jim," he extended his hand out toward me. "I guess we're no longer strangers, then."

"Easy as that."

I wanted to join the mile-high club with this guy, but we just became friends over me telling him that I made the mistake of screwing a drug addict and got pregnant with his kid. I mean, that was three years ago, but still. I highly doubted *this guy* would stoop to anyone less than a socialite, much less some random chick who got upgraded to first-class that was drooling over him. Who knew, free drinks were in first class, and he just ordered two for us.

Please, God, don't let me start my trip off to London by screwing some guy while I was drunk on an airplane. I've done crazier shit, yes, but this trip was meant to be fun, but I suppose a girl could have fun, especially with a man like this dreamboat sitting next to her.

Click here to grab your copy of Jim's story in Mr. Mitchell: Billionaires' Club Book 2

About the Author

Raylin Marks is the author of steamy contemporary romance novels. She absolutely loves her readers and enjoys bringing them on adventures with sexy alpha males and strong, witty heroines.

Email Raylin at raylinmarks99@gmail.com

Look for Raylin on Facebook

Check out all the books in the Billionaires' Club series on sale or for preorder here